The Angel of Barton Townes

by Craig W Thomas

Part One – The Ballad of Giles and Leah

1

The Thing

Sunday April 30th 2006

When he woke that morning he was still being Giles McAndrew and The Thing was already crawling over into its second day. The Thing was the problem and the problem was another row with Leah.

But it wasn't in his mind yet. Cool spring air had only just flowed over his bare skin in enough quantities to open his eyes. It was three-minutes past eight. He heard a blackbird warbling away madly, and for a while, he just lay still and listened. I suppose birds don't have Sunday, he thought. Then a sharp breeze blew through the wind chimes that hung outside the kitchen door below, sending a rippling jangle of sound up into the room. A wire tripped in his brain and The Thing dropped into his mind like a stone falling into a box. That was it. Time to get moving.

In one swift twist of his slim body he left the duvet behind and sprang into a standing position. His head ached from last night's alcohol and his eyes were blurry. He bent and touched his toes one, two, three times, noticing beams of sunlight come and go on the carpet in front of him. Yawning he looked up at the skylight window, saw racing white streaks of cloud stream past, then a square of bright blue. Maybe it'll go away, this Thing. Maybe she'll just wake up and it'll be forgotten. He wanted to glance behind him but didn't dare in case he woke her.

He trod lightly to the bathroom to urinate and wash.

With a little optimism now, he said to himself, you should relax on a Sunday morning; maybe that's part of the problem. But Giles could never relax on a Sunday morning. It was a matter of job-lifestyle. Monday to Friday he began work before dawn; on Saturday's only a little later. But the Giles McAndrew that did his job so well more than coped with the early starts: he thrived on them. And he was a doing-man not a thinking-man; so anyone expecting him to relax on a Sunday was kidding themselves.

When Giles came back, Leah was still facing away from him on her side of the bed. He looked at the long shape her body made under the bedclothes; loved the bit in the middle where the curve of her hip rose and made a nice round hillock. And her hair looked good even mussed-

5

up and spread across the pillow. He waited a moment to see if she was going to turn over to him but she didn't move a muscle.

Being careful not to make a noise, he went to a chest of drawers and took out a clean t-shirt. It was the blue one from last summer's holiday in the south of France; the one with *Club de Voile Antibes'* on the front and the white sailing boats. He pulled it over his head, inhaled the perfume from the conditioner and thought, I love that smell. He went back for a pair of thick socks then sat on the floor where he pulled them over his long bony feet. He listened again for a waking Leah, but still she dozed, her breathing slow and almost perfectly rhythmic.

Giles tip-toed out on to the landing and moved lightly down two flights of stairs to the kitchen to make coffee. When he got there, the sun was streaming in through the windows. The beautiful morning pushed him forward. He went to the back door to let the cat in. I might go biking in a bit, he thought, if Leah doesn't mind. He started to behave as if The Thing didn't exist anymore.

He made his automatic, everyday kitchen moves: to the fridge to get the water jug, the coffee canister, the milk bottle and the cat food, picking up speed as he shifted things around. He thought about the spring and its weather. April showers: is that a myth? He mentally tucked away the task of finding out. Skydays circled around his ankles, desperate for food, meowing at him. Giles put a bowl full of ugly meat down by the back door and went back to the coffee.

The kettle began to softly roar. Giles had a sudden thought and switched on the radio that sat neatly by the toaster. Two men were talking about the weather and what the effects of a late frost would mean for the local bulb growers. He listened on for a while, quite intently, but when the kettle switch went *'Clack!'* he flicked the switch to CD with a speed that said,

'That's enough of that.'

While he waited for the coffee to brew he took a warm coat from the hall and pushed his feet into some trainers. He didn't bother with the laces. Back in the kitchen he milked and sugared his favourite mug, tossed in a teaspoon, then took down a mug for Leah. He poured her coffee out, splashed in some milk, and carried it on the small tray back upstairs. The bedroom door creaked faintly as he pushed it aside with his foot but now it didn't matter. He walked right round to her side of the bed and put the bright yellow mug down on the bedside table.

'Coffee, Leah,' he said. He glanced at her as re-traced his steps out of the room but she didn't move.

On his way back to the kitchen he stopped in the hall to grab a beanie hat off a hook and put it on. I'm not missing this sunshine, he'd already decided. He poured his drink, grabbed a pack of biscuits from the tin on the counter, and went outside.

There was a bench out in the back garden under a tree but the one right outside the kitchen was good too. He sat down, took a quick sip from the mug and tried to decide how to play the situation but he was quickly distracted. It wasn't the view - there wasn't a view. The line of trees beyond his hedge and the track to the farm screened that out. It was just being outside in the spring sunshine, with the crisp air and the warm sun. It was being in his own garden with the brightly coloured tulips that Sid the gardener had put in and the feeling of being miles from anywhere. If Giles had possessed a poetic mind, he might have felt that the cool northern air had come to pause a while at his garden gate, before pushing on westwards to keep the people of the two counties honest on this last day of April. But he just sat and drank his early morning coffee, chewing on a piece of shortbread, thinking how nice it was to have a secluded place that was all your own. It was a boring thought, but, as Giles reminded himself, he was nearly forty. So.

A tractor started up with a roar somewhere in the distance then and began to move off. Giles closed his eyes to the sun and began to feel good.

Then he heard movement from the bedroom above his head and looked up instinctively even though there was nothing to see. His peace dissolved into The Thing. A strong breath of wind made the wind chimes collide again, sending a chord of uncertainty out into the Corumby air. The man who was still being Giles McAndrew frowned, and went on sipping, down to the bottom of the mug.

The Thing had almost certainly crawled over into a second day. The Thing was the problem and the problem was another row with Leah.

2

A Domestic

It was time to get busy and to hope that her temper had cooled down overnight. Giles went inside, dumped the coffee things in the sink and went up to get dressed. As he pushed the bedroom door open Leah was just sweeping across the carpet to the bathroom in her birthday suit, ignoring him. Even half-asleep it was a sight that still widened his eyeballs. Stripped naked she looked like a Goddess. He prayed she hadn't noticed him looking; this was not a day for being caught with a stare of absolute longing on his face. A blink later the bathroom was closed to him and three further on the shower was hissing like frying bacon.

It was hard not to picture her under the shower. In his weaker moments she became a trophy companion who threatened his self-confidence but this morning he wasn't having that. He made himself mechanically go about the process of properly dressing himself: bed pants in the wash basket; underpants on; blue jeans fetched and climbed into; clean blue sweat shirt from the chest of drawers pulled over the *Antibes* t-shirt. As he was about to go into the bathroom to check his hair, the door fully opened from the inside and Leah swept past him again, her eyes deliberately glazed over, her body swathed in a light blue towel from chest to calf. This was much easier to deal with.

'I'll get breakfast ready in a minute,' he called from in front of the bathroom mirror trying to sound not too flat but not too hopeful. As he left the bedroom on his way downstairs once again, Leah sat on the bed facing the window, brushing her hair.

Giles had laid out plates, mugs, cutlery, fruit, cereal and yoghurt on the breakfast bar and filled the cafétiere again to the two-thirds mark by the time Leah and her sandals clacked their way into the kitchen. Giles could feel the atmosphere she brought in with her: one of silence that still managed to shout at him as he moved around the wide, bright room. He felt an uncomfortable pressure under his diaphragm; felt it push all the way down to his feet. He had to get this thing dealt with. He needed to see her smiling at him again before this thing became serious.

'What's the matter?' he said, cutting some bread for toast, trying to keep it light.

'Nothing's the matter – just because I don't want to have sex with you on a Saturday night doesn't mean there's anything the matter.'

Giles felt his face grimace. Then he was puzzled. Did the fact that she was reducing this to sex mean that this wasn't going to be too bad? He poured her raspberry tea from a bright yellow china pot and spooned her muesli onto a smooth slick of natural yoghurt – laid out slices of apple on a side plate.

'And why do you have to organise me all the time? Why do you always assume I want the same breakfast every Sunday morning?'

'I thought you liked me getting you breakfast.'

She said nothing. Giles expected to hear her voice grating his skin, saying, 'I don't want you anticipating my needs all the time; I don't want you forever making decisions for me' but he got the silent treatment which was even worse. Then she suddenly and unpredictably changed tack.

'And don't not say anything because you think I'll accuse you of being right all the time. You think you know everything…'

He wanted to give her an answer but held back: it would only ratchet up the tension another notch.

He was starting to get anxious. He didn't think he'd ever heard her go at him verbally with such a biting, self-assured edge. It was as though she'd lain there in bed half the night writing herself a script for the morning battle.

Giles exhaled a couple of lungfuls of warm air and started to count to twenty. And she would have to look more beautiful than ever, wouldn't she, the bitch - my breathtaking, sexy, beautiful bitch of a Leah. Even now, given the smallest positive signal, he would rush over to her, strip her in four seconds and have her right there on the kitchen floor.

The sigh was too much for her.

'Alright, Giles! Sod you, I'm going out!'

Leah got down from her stool and with a face already set like concrete made for the door. Giles gathered himself. Pleading with a woman went completely against all his instincts but something new happening here. His head dizzied with the idea that the new day contained a Leah he couldn't control. Before he realised what he was doing his mouth opened and he started to beg.

'No, don't! Please don't. Stay and talk. Let's deal with this and sort this out now. Please!'

She'd reached the door and begun to open it but she stopped and turned round. He never begged. She had him.

'Why, Giles? You always twist everything around to make yourself the innocent party. I'm sick of it.'

Her hand left the door and dropped to her side. She looked out of the tiny hall window at the sunny morning. She knew how big this victory was for her, but tried with all her might not to show it to Giles.

'I won't, I won't! I promise,' said Giles, panic setting in and meaning every word.

'And you can stop whining…'

Whining? I'm not whining, am I, he thought? But he knew she was right. He, Giles McAndrew, was whining like a four year-old child.

'And don't sulk, either – just because you couldn't get your end away…and don't give me one of your "she's pre-menstrual" looks either because if you do, I'm out of here.'

She was back but he still felt he was dangling from a high ledge and only just holding on with one hand. It was the coldness in her voice. If only she was pre-menstrual – that I can understand and deal with. But this: this was way beyond hormones. He saw Leah's breasts shaped against her top as she pushed two loose strands of hair back behind her ears and the nipples pushing out at the material. She would have done this on purpose, left her bra off, knowing the sight of them might easily drive him crazy.

Christ, help me to deal with this monster she's turned into, he thought. Giles wanted half to soothe her, half to hit her. Hit her? God, what am I thinking? He would never, ever do that. But he did want to hurt her - with words - but he couldn't think of any to aim at her.

I should tell her I love her, he thought. But in two years he'd never told her. It wasn't what he did, the way he operated. It was an unspoken thing between them. She was supposed to be smart enough to know how he felt about her. Or to guess and be right. Maybe just saying 'I love you' was the daft, simple answer to a fight about nothing much or the clever key to unlock a devilish riddle. But Giles looked down at his feet and knew he couldn't do it.

Leah came back into the kitchen slowly, edging past him as he stood in the doorway trying to avoid trailing along behind her like a dog. She took two slices of apple off the plate on the table and walked out of the back door to the garden. She went to Giles's bench seat and sat down. The sun was already moving round to the south-west but this side of the house was still catching its warmth and light. Leah chewed without much interest and avoided looking at Giles as he padded outside in her wake, affecting patience, feeling that to pass this test he had to walk on eggshells without breaking a single one. He sat down beside her. She gave him a look of feigned boredom, but she was still fuming with anger inside. Then she turned to look at a tractor that came bumping and roaring along the lane. Seemingly annoyed at this she got up and went back to the kitchen.

She poured away her tea and emptied the pot; re-filled the kettle, plugged it in and switched it on. She got a mango tea bag from the cupboard and put it in the cup and leaned back on the counter with her arms folded waiting for the water to boil. She checked to see if Giles was about to follow her in then looked hungrily at the muesli and yoghurt mixture. She suddenly really fancied it but she was damned if she was going to give Giles the relief of seeing her acting normally. Not when he was in control freak mode. Not when he'd hurt her. She listened to the kettle moving steadily to boiling point and felt something inside let go. It released a small torrent of thought: O my maddening, gorgeous, Giles, my trophy Giles: I love you so much, why do you do this to me?

She wasn't going to cry and give him the upper hand; she was going to make him grovel his way out of this on his hands and knees. Then she would deal with the thing that scared her out of her wits. The kettle came to the boil behind her. She poured some water into her cup and went outside. Her use of body language was not all that subtle for a 29 year-old, only Giles missed her display of reluctance and her pouting lips because he was looking at the apple tree in the middle of the back garden, hearing his heart thumping and thinking that maybe he could get out of this yet. He coughed softly, then turned himself around so he could see her and spoke:

'Okay, Leah, look, listen to me: I'm *really* sorry.' He watched her cross her legs and turn away. Christ, he said to himself; she knows damned well how hard it is for me to apologize to people, but still she wants to rub my nose in it, an 'It' that was *nothing*. If this was just about Lucie, then she'd got it all wrong, completely wrong. If she was scared of losing him or something, she was scared of something that didn't even exist. And she should come out and tell him how she felt instead of turning Sunday into a war zone.

'I said, "I'm sorry." I'm really sorry, Leah.'

She nearly fell off the bench in surprise. Giles never used her name when addressing her, even though he'd always said he really liked it.

'What for, Giles? Being a bloody know-all, for fancying Lucie or for being too old for me?' She almost winced at herself. She was playing her biggest card but this time she felt she needed to hurt him really badly – to break him if she could. Things were reaching some sort of peak. She was sure this was true, even though she didn't know what it actually meant.

Giles looked down at the ground and spoke:

'Look – I know what I called you last night - but they're only words – they can't do you any real harm. They're not...' He looked her in the eye. '...bullets or something. And I'd unsay them if I could, but I can't.'

'Are you talking to me?' said Leah looking straight ahead. 'Sounds like you're talking to yourself: I've never heard such rubbish in all my life.' She'd raised her voice to a shout. Giles hated it in case someone might hear. 'And you who talks for a living! You've got no idea, have you? Or you're just too bloody big-headed - you think you can just undo the damage you and your big mouth does with more words...' She placed a look of disgust in the pause. '...slimy words the next day.' She didn't have to feign it – she was burning inside with fury again. It was true as far as she was concerned; all of it.

Giles got up and went inside. The edge of his contrition was beginning to harden. I just can't play this role, he said to himself. I need to but I just can't.

Shit, thought Leah, he's stealing my role. I have to beat him this time. But Giles came back almost instantly with a slice of toast in his hand. No jam or marmalade. He was going to ignore most of the shit he'd just taken and come back fighting.

Suddenly Giles found what he thought he needed.

'And I'm sorry I laughed at you,' he said, and sounded almost smug. Leah's face fell. He'd got her. He'd turned this around and actually found the words to beat her with. He looked at her face and knew it. Still, she wasn't going to give in that easily.

'Yeah, well, you bloody should be…even though Lucie no more fancies you than bloody Dave Plymouth.'

'Well, make up your mind: last night she apparently hangs on my every word and can't keep her eyes off my groin and now she's not interested.'

That was clever, he thought. That came out much better than I thought it would. His smug expression became a big, fat self-satisfied grin.

'You bastard.'

Oh, no. 'You laughing at me again, you BASTARD?'

'I'm not lau – agh!'

Half a pint of the hot mango tea landed on his sweatshirt, a large splash wet his crotch and the rest just missed his face by a fraction of an inch.

Giles jumped up twice as fast as Leah as she made off for the inside of the house again. He pushed past her in the doorway, Leah squeaking, 'Ouch!' and stood in the centre of the kitchen ripping open his jeans and pulling off his top at the same time.

'You satisfied now you've ruined my clothes?'

In a moment, Giles was standing in his socks, t-shirt and Calvin Kleins staring hard at his girlfriend waiting to take what she had left. Leah leaned against the sink looking desperate, her hair falling into her face. His heart started to reach out for her.

The real shouting started.

'Frankly, no - if you don't want me and you want her, tell me now and I'll go!'

'I don't want-'

'I'll leave and get a fucking attachment somewhere!' She was still shouting.

'You're out of your mind. I'm not interested in Lucie, I keep telling you!'

'If you want me to go, it's that easy – just tell me you want her.'

'No, Leah, you're being silly.'

Giles ducked a fork that flew out of Leah's hand across the room at him with startling speed and accuracy to boot.

'I'm NOT FUCKING being SILLY! And I'm NOT TEN YEARS OLD!' Leah screamed.

This time a plate missed him by three feet but smashed into the window frame behind him, chipping off some paint. Leah ran out of the room beginning to make sobbing noises but still saying, 'you fucking patronizing bastard' as she left.

Giles went after her. She was making the stairs at an alarming rate of knots. Giles was desperate - she was leaving. He saw her in his mind's eye already: getting her bag, her spare clothes, the lot. He chased after her.

'What are you doing? Come here! Don't be so...'

'FUCK OFF, GILES!' said Leah pushing away his hands as he reached up the stairs to physically stop her. Giles closed up to her and tried to pinion her flailing arms. He leaned most of his weight on her so there was no chance of them both crashing down the stairs and ending up with broken necks. But realizing this wasn't going to achieve anything more, he rushed up the stairs ahead of her and sat down so she couldn't get past.

Leah, panting and looking awful, turned and went back down. Giles looked at her feet: she had shoes on. He let her go. She ran down the stairs and across the hall and slammed the door behind her. He could see himself chasing her down the lane watched by Mrs. Freeman and her dog or the lad on the tractor and before you knew it, it would be all over not just Barton Townes but the whole of Bartonshire and Bilt. He couldn't risk making a complete fool of himself and, who knew, hurting his career even.

Giles remained where he was on the stairs. He was panting and the hurt was beginning to appear inside. He felt it spreading out like a blood stain. Is this what he was? Was his ego bigger than his desire to hold on to his girl? So did that mean then that he didn't really love her? God, he didn't need an extra layer of complication on top of everything: the whole situation was one colossal mess already.

He put his head in his hands and tried to work things out. She wouldn't get far; she didn't have her car keys. She would be angry for a while and then she would calm down a bit, come back, and they would make it up somehow. Maybe even end up in bed. It would be tough, but in the end it would be okay like every other time. And somehow they would work out a way to stop this happening: this mad, bad arguing every time a problem blew up between them.

Then the door opened again. Giles took his hands away from his face. Leah. What? - she wanted to make up already? Apparently not. With windswept hair she moved left to a row of coat hooks, stood looking at what was on offer for a short second and grabbed Giles' favourite navy bomber jacket and turned to leave. Maybe she won't slam the door this time, which will show me that she's already calming down, he thought.

Crash! it went a second time.

At least she's wearing my jacket out there, thought Giles – it shows she still loves me and wants to make up eventually. Okay, he would wait. He would calm himself down. And when she came back he would apologize again from the start and this time he would actually tell her he loved her. He promised himself again – I will, I'll definitely tell her.

He went downstairs and turned right into the kitchen, switched on the radio and began to pick up the pieces.

3

Why Do I Always Have To Win?

Giles opened a kitchen cupboard to get something to clean things up with and followed the trail of the disaster back to the night before. Maybe if he could remember in precise detail how this had been triggered it would help him put it right. He took it back to his bedroom at around eleven pm when Leah had provoked an argument out of nothing about him and Lucie, a girl they both worked with. It had started with a remark about her being good at her job.

'You're always talking about her.'

'No, I'm not.'

'Yes, you are – and you see, that's what makes me worried. You're being defensive, which shows you're covering something up.'

'No, I'm not.'

'Don't lie to me.'

'It's not a lie!'

'Yes it is - you can't just oil your way out of this one.'

'Oh, yes I can, because there's nothing to oil out of. You're crazy – she's only 23 – she might as well only be 14.'

'If I'm crazy, you're a pervert.'

'Oh, ha-ha. I mean, can you imagine me going out with a 14 year-old? I'm nearly bloody 40!'

'It's also in the way you look at her!'

'I like her – so I must have been smiling at her, so what? Can't I smile at another woman?'

'And you should see the way she looks at you. She adores you. It makes me sick.'

'You're crazy. If it's anything, it's that she looks up to me as a presenter – that's all.'

Giles almost said, 'and you can't blame her for that,' but managed to stop himself.

'Fine, I'm crazy, I'm imagining it.'

'Yes, you are…'

'Am I? Well you ask anyone at the station about it, Giles, and they'll agree with me.'

'Don't be silly, of course they w-'

'…they think there's something going on between you…and I'm not going to be bloody humiliated.'

She was exaggerating wildly, he was sure of it. And she was beginning to run out of steam. Now was the moment to really begin mending fences. He went over to her and kissed her bare shoulder.

'You're mad. There's only one woman for me and it's you.' He tried to say it softly, tenderly, but it came out sounding to him like bad television. There was a pause as Leah chewed the matter over.

'If you're lying to me, Giles…'

Leah wasn't good at sustaining rows – she much preferred ending them somewhere in the middle – if it got that far – and leaving: shutting herself down and shutting her opponent out, then running away somewhere, preferably home. She wasn't one for slugging it out.

Then Giles watched a tear fall down her face and was amazed. Her words throughout the exchange had sounded so hard she was like some kind of female Hitler: she had the knack of looking hurt and wanting to kill you at one and the same time.

Giles thought that was it; that the storm had passed, and went to kiss her on the neck again but she brushed him away and went back onto the attack.

'Look, you can have her, you know, if that's what you really want! If it is, I'll be better off without you! And you *can* have her! Everyone seems to fall at your feet - so go on, have her!'

'Don't be so ridiculous,' he said, still trying to soothe her. The tear didn't make him happy.

'Ridiculous? Look who's talking! Who's the man who's so insecure he used to use his position to get weak, stupid girls into bed?'

Giles listened to her dragging up the distant past now to try to hurt him. It wasn't going to work for her.

'You know, Giles, without that skill you wouldn't have had them, and frankly, without it you wouldn't have had me!'

Giles winced inside now at the memory of her words, but at the time he'd decided it wasn't worth rising to the bait. He knew she was only trying to find anything she could now to try to wind him up and reel him in. She'd stepped back from the verge of storming out. He knew what she was up to; just as he knew her storm was now on the point of blowing itself out. All I have to do is let her go on for a little bit longer, he thought, and it'll all be over.

But as Leah began to cool down, Giles felt a resentment rise inside him: Why was she always trying to bruise their relationship? She did it all the time – or at least, every so often. It was like an obsessive form of game playing. Every time, she took what they had to the edge of a cliff and left it hanging over the drop. Didn't love mean you wanted to protect a relationship? Nurture it? And she couldn't seriously believe he

16

had a thing for Lucie – even though the girl was lovely - when Leah herself had been given so many natural physical advantages in life? It was selfish of her to indulge in jealousy as far as Giles could see – ungrateful even.

And surely, if she loved him, she'd believe him when he protested his innocence. Maybe she didn't really love him. Maybe this was all just manipulation. Giles remembered his thinking this all too clearly now and how it went on: what if this was her way of slowly moving the relationship to an ending? Because she lacked the courage to come out and cut clean.

Then came the fateful moment: when he his hurt and resentment distilled into a drop of pure hatred. Needing to hurt her back, he'd laughed at her. It took everything that he had as an actor to make the thing stick, but as a pillow hit him in the face he thought, 'yep – I've done it' and was pleased.

Leah threw herself down on the bed to start a bout of sobbing that went on for twenty minutes. Giles watched her kicking her leg up and down on the bed like a child that didn't get its own way and felt pleased to have won the argument. He was pleased too that he seemed to be wrong about her feelings for him. So maybe this was, after all, about her insecurity; but it was still a hard conclusion to swallow.

He went downstairs to make some tea and leave her to it. He'd come back up in a while to see if she'd calmed down. He would try to make it up to her again.

He thought about these women who were ready, supposedly, to fall at his feet. He had to admit, it was nice to think he wasn't past it yet. He let his mind think about Lucie Bastable wearing out her carpet, pining for him, but hardly thought it likely. In all probability she was out on the town dancing and drinking herself into a frenzy like all the other girls her age. I wonder if little Lucie does have a thing for me, though, he said to himself? He didn't like idle daydreams but he let the thought dangle there in front of him for a few seconds until the interest in it wore out. He and Lucie: she's far too young for me, but I'd bet my mortgage on the fact that she'd be a bloody sight less trouble than Trophy Leah.

When it really came down to it, though – *really* came down to it, Giles knew that for all the trials of strength and the expended energy, Leah was worth it. One happy trip to the coast or a night in bed with her was worth every single minute of trouble and strife. The thought was not a happy one, but there it was. It was true.

Giles went back up to his bedroom that ran along the whole length of The Barn House to see how Leah was doing. He sat on the bed where she lay quietly and stroked her arm.

'Hey, come on. Are you okay? Are you going to forgive me?'

She didn't move. He kissed her again on the neck, then on the cheek, and laid his palm on her stomach and began to caress it gently. The rapid movement under his hand was explosive. He had to rear backwards as she sat up sharply.

'You don't get it, do you? Saturday is over. I know it's your house but you can fuck off!'

She practically threw herself across to the other side of his big double bed, as far away from his as she could get. He got the message and went downstairs again comforted by the thought that at least she wasn't running out on him.

As he replayed his performance and his tactics, Giles moved calmly about the kitchen with the dustpan and brush sweeping up crockery fragments. Why did you laugh at her? Why did you do it? Why do you always have to win all the time? He was just about to step open the pedal bin to dump some pieces of broken plate when the front door opened again in a hurry. He looked to the kitchen door instinctively, waiting for Leah to come through it and sure enough she did.

She crossed the kitchen threshold and came towards him at breakneck speed. Face ablaze, eyes wild and demented, she threw herself at him with talons for fingers. He tried to dodge the fingernails of her right hand but was too slow. Three of them took flesh from his left cheek where his bone was prominent but this knowledge was momentary as Leah's knee cost him a glancing blow in the testicles. He would have dropped to the ground to bend himself double but his weight was still falling backwards. They hit the breakfast counter, which took their combined weight while Leah's claws tried to take more pieces of his face. She was too close-in though. Giles tried to neutralise her by hugging her tight but she was wild, he couldn't hold her. He was suddenly aware of an immense pain in his under groin when Leah began shouting.

'You fucking, fucking arsehole!' she screamed. 'Fucking, fucking bastard! Bastard! Bastard! Bast-'

She was stopped by Giles's feet slipping under him causing them both to go flying. He hit his head on the floor with a bang that would have shocked him were adrenalin not spurting into his brain and from there all over his body. Leah came off better, landing on Giles to start with, but sliding on until her head collided with the metal breakfast bar support. It was round but still hurt when she hit it.

'Agh!' she went, her voice rising to a high-pitched scream at the end of the ejaculation before she flailed again at Giles with her right arm. She was almost running on empty though, shocked by her fall. Her words were now replaced by grunts but she still threw all she had left into getting out of the bear grip Giles had regained upon her. She spat in his face, once, then twice, Giles being unable to sway out of the way. Then she lowered her head and bit his chest.

'Owww!' It was Giles's turn to scream. It hurt. 'Get off! Get *off!*' Giles managed to get a hand on her hair and to pull hard enough for Leah to let go her teeth. Giles held on and pushed with as much forearm strength as he had to get her right away from him. She was still so out of control he didn't trust her not to bite right through to the breast bone if he allowed her a second chance. It worked, except Leah pulled for all she was worth at the neck of his sweat shirt. She tried to rip it but it was too well made. Still, the neck was going to be ruined, thought Giles.

'Owww! You're hurting!' squealed Leah.

'Good!' said Giles, struggling for breath and a grasp of what was happening. He got out from under his girlfriend without letting go of her head and brought his right hand into play to grab the neck of her top, and thus had her at last at arm's length. He got to his knees, then stood up: Leah had no choice but to do the same.

'Have you calmed down?'

'No! You fucker!'

'Calm down! Calm down.'

Leah's eyes still exhibited signs of her wanting to inflict pain on him, but showed enough self-control to show resentment, pain and hostility too. Her mouth hung open, bleeding and a strand of saliva was trailing down her chin. Giles still had to use body strength to hold her but less and less with each passing second.

'Can I let go?' She didn't answer – just carried on staring at Giles, panting and hating. 'Can I let go yet? Can I?'

'Yes.'

''Cause I'm not letting go of you until you stop. 'Til you calm down.'

'I'm calm, I'm calm,' she said, still breathing like a fighter. Giles was not out of breath, but his blood was dripping steadily onto his socks and the floor, the back of his head hurt, and so did the bridge of his nose. He felt spittle dribbling down his cheek too, but wasn't ready to let go of either hand from Leah. His gorgeous, precious, trophy Leah.

'I'm calm, I'm calm. Let go.' Her head dipped then jerked up with having to take in another huge breath and Giles felt her body relax

19

enough for him to think about letting go. What the hell was this? What had he done?

'Okay – if I let go will you tell me what this is about - what I've done?' Nothing – I've done nothing, he thought. He really didn't know where this attack had come from.

'Fuck off, Giles.' But the anger in her eyes was subsiding. Tears were coming. She began to collapse on him, until the only thing holding her up was his hand and arm strength. He let go and felt the warmth of her body against him and her still heavy breathing. She didn't have the jacket on. Where is my jacket, he thought? It was expensive. She better not have thrown it into a stream or a hedge. Not just because I laughed at her when I was playing stupid because I'd lost my temper. But Giles knew – he knew something else had gone wrong when he hadn't even been there.

'What is it, Leah? What on earth…'

Leah moved away from him and walked out of the kitchen. Oh, no, thought Giles, not again. But she came right back, with the jacket. She stood, mouth set in concrete now, and reached into the padded jacket to produce something from the inside pocket.

'This,' she said, holding a folded page of what looked like a letter out towards him. 'I found this. Talk your way out of this, Giles. Talk your bloody fucking way out of this.'

No tears, now, just glistening eyes as far as Giles could see, and he was close enough. What was it? Oh, the letter. But…

'I'm leaving you, Giles, we're finished. Don't try to come after me. It's over.'

Giles started to say, 'but Leah…' then decided that in the circumstances, it wasn't going to get him anywhere. For the second time that morning, he let her go. She went upstairs, to get some or all of her stuff, he assumed, while he considered the possibility of trying to talk his way out of it. But too soon Leah was back with coat on and bag in hand and was out of the door before he could make a decision. He stood in the doorway to the kitchen and watched her go.

Giles lifted the front of his sweatshirt to wipe off at least some of the blood, the saliva and the humiliating taste of defeat in battle.

4

The Letter in the Pocket

Page 1 of 2

----- Original Message -----
  From: Catherine Garner
To: Giles McAndrew
Sent: Friday, April 28, 2006 10:49 AM
Subject: Re: That Thing We Talked About

Hey Gilles! How are you? I'm sorry our phones keep missing each other.

Thanks for the note. The need for secrecy is well understood, don't worry! I got it safely. I can do what you want, no problem. It's only a matter of how much you like what I have! I'm really pleased you called me – it'll be a good thing for both of us! Hope we can meet real soon to fix everything.

It'll be lovely to see you again of course. It's been such a long time, hasn't it. An amazingly long time. I've been doing a lot of thinking about the past. You know I haven't laughed as much as we used to do for a long, long time. You always made me laugh. Those summer holidays in Gadham - they seemed to go on and on, the summers of your youth. And was the weather as good as I remember it? It always seemed to be roasting hot.

I blush now when I think about the things we got away with and the things we did back then. Do you remember? Swimming in Lees Brook like that – God, I couldn't do that now, though everyone tells me I've worn well. Why were we never embarrassed? (Hope I'm not embarrassing you now bringing it up, but for some reason it's what I seem to remember most!)

Have had some very difficult times over the past few years, if I'm honest. Split up with husband Jack, two years ago. We didn't have kids though we tried for a long time. This was one reason for the split, but there was a lot more to it. I can tell you more about it if you can bear to hear it when I see you.

As I was saying last time, I listen to you as often as I can. It's amazing what computers can do. I meant to listen to you in Canada but never got around to it. But being over here and not so many miles away, it's easier. And it's a good show! Really, it is! I think you have a wonderful voice - very warm and welcoming and very sexy! I bet that the women are literally falling and swooning at your feet these days

5

Pieces of The Thing

The Thing was in pieces now scattered all over The Barn House, its shell blown to fragments by the explosive material inside. Had the detonation been inevitable? It didn't much matter. He sat in shock on the kitchen sofa unable to move except to get a wad of kitchen towel and press it against his cheek. He no longer heard wind chimes or blackbirds. After a while he got up to pour himself a tall drink of water. He threw some ice into the tumbler and swirled it around, then took a couple of big gulps. He pressed the cold surface of the glass down onto the cut. The ice wasn't cooling the glass quickly enough. He went to the freezer compartment of his fridge, took out a pack of peas and held that to his cheek.

Giles sat down again. He looked up at the clock to try to get a sense of how long she'd been gone. Five minutes? Then he stretched forward to look out into the hall as if that might bring her back, but there was nothing to be heard. He tried to take a drink without moving the pack of peas and just about succeeded. Then he rested his head back on the sofa and thought about the fight again. He was angry at Leah for misinterpreting him, angry at himself for leaving the letter from his cousin in his jacket pocket, angry at Leah for jumping to the wrong conclusion and angry with Fate for the whole bastarding thing. The result was one unholy mess.

He became angry with himself again. Why did I provoke her? Why did I need to laugh at her to deliberately hurt her? Why on earth am I trying to score points off this woman? She's Leah. If every man who knew her had seen me trying to upset her like that, they would condemn me as insane. To risk losing Leah *Caighton*? A woman like her comes round once in a lifetime for only one man in a hundred.

Giles understood that, but they didn't know what it was like to be in a close relationship with her. Yes, the highs were incredible, but there were lows too and they were hard to deal with. But even so, when he ran the events of the night and morning through his mind again and found her wanting on several counts, he still found himself guilty. He should have known better: he was stupid, stupid, stupid.

Giles didn't like to think for long about anything, but his mind was stuck on constant repeat. He kept shaking his head. Why did she attack me? What was I thinking of? Why did she have to choose that jacket to

23

wear? Then, if the clouds weren't heavy-laden enough with rain, a monster storm cloud moved towards him accompanied by a vast low rumble of thunder. As it arrived it carried dreadful questions: what if this really was the end? What if the split was a natural result of their differences? What if, by the natural laws of relationships, the fight just proved that their coupling had just run its course?

Cold with terror, Giles got up, thinking, this is no good, I can't sit around thinking like this, I've got to do something. He went to the downstairs toilet mirror and took a closer look at his real wounds. The cuts looked more like holes and when he looked down at the wad of paper he was shocked to see that the patch of red there was huge.

Giles patched his face up with two plasters, put on some fresh clothes and went out for a long ride on his bike. The cool air of early morning was now warm but Giles didn't notice it. He pedalled determinedly down the lanes of the Bartonshire flat lands working up a sweat and trying now just to empty his head of all thought. He had all day to think out a strategy to get Leah back but before he could do that he knew he had to calm down - to put his mind into the recovery position, so to speak. When he found a long, straight road ahead of him, he really turned on the speed, figuring it would help to use up some of the adrenalin. He pushed himself as hard as he could for another hour. He let the thought that Leah could easily be there when he returned come in to spur him on.

When he got home the house was empty. When he looked in the mirror the Band Aid was so soaked in blood he knew he'd have to go to the A & E at the Royal Bartonshire – he had no choice. He didn't shower; he drank another glass of water – a huge one - and leant on the sink trying to compose himself for the drive into town. He found another warm coat, came back for his car keys, locked the door carefully and drove off down the empty, sunny lane.

His turmoil continued. He had to rebut the ideas those questions had thrown up. He had always had bust-ups with girlfriends, so there was no need to seriously consider the idea that this relationship was fundamentally flawed. No, he said to himself: I have to win her back and that's that. This is nothing we can't solve together, especially when the last part of the fight was a ridiculous misunderstanding. Catherine was no threat: she was just the cousin he hadn't seen for over twenty-five years! He thought about the email Leah had screwed up into a ball and thrown at him. He couldn't remember where it was. He'd have to find it and read it again: see the thing through her eyes. That was the first positive thing he would do when he got home. He would do others too. That was it: he had to be positive.

Of course, the nurse who looked him over in A & E would have to know his name.

'Are you *the* Giles McAndrew from the radio station?'

''fraid so.'

'I listen to you every morning – well, when I'm on a late shift.'

'Thanks. That's really nice to hear.'

Now spotted, Giles had to hold his end up: try to use some of the charm that had always served him so well – that had won him the job at BRBC Two Counties radio five years earlier and that had taken him forward since then.

'I won't ask you how you did this.' His nurse was motherly and sweet and Scottish.

'I fell off my bike.'

She began to deal with the plaster that was now almost completely soaked through with blood.

'Is that right? You want to be more careful, Giles.'

Giles didn't think he could fool Nurse Hood for one second. Her accent and the tone of it reminded him of his grandma. As a child he would tell her wild made-up stories. 'Is that right?' he could still here her saying in reply, indulging him.

'Y'know, You've got a lovely voice for radio.'

'Thank you. You're too kind.' He heard the words, 'Do you want to marry me?' die away in the back of his head. He couldn't manage that much flannel.

'And it is really true you've a tabby cat called Skydays?'

'It is true, yes,' said Giles.

'And that the name came to you in a dream?' She began dabbing and wiping.

'Ouch!'

'Sorry. It's going to sting a wee bit.'

'That's okay. It's true, yes.'

She smiled, pleased to be so close to even a minor celebrity, and one she liked, to boot.

'I heard you talking about that - when was it? - I can't remember.' Neither could Giles: he'd done so many shows, they all tended to blend into one.

'But that fair made me smile. I thought that was lovely.'

People could be so nice. Why can't you be like this, Leah? he thought, and in the circumstances it felt like a reasonable question.

'And I like what you did for the hedgehog sanctuary the other week.'

'Oh, that.'

'I sent them a fiver!' she chuckled.

'That's great,' said Giles. But he hardly heard her; he was wincing with pain as she tended his wounds further.

'And with a name like McAndrew you must be from Scotland...'

Giles had been to Scotland a number of times as a tourist, but was about as Scottish as the Duke of Edinburgh.

'Well, yes and no, actually...' - he had his stock answer ready – 'my mum was from Canada and my dad only had a Scottish father. And he died before I was born. So...'

Giles' father, a Simon Wilkinson of Enfield, now retired, tending his garden at that moment, would have been surprised at the very least to know he'd had a Scottish father.

'Oh, I see...This is very nasty, Giles.'

He was always telling Leah about those nails of hers though they joked about them too sometimes, usually in bed.

'I'm going to have to get the doctor to put in some stitches for you,' said Maggie Hood.

Fortunately, few injuries being suffered by the good people of Barton Townes and outlying rural districts this Sunday morning, Giles did not have to wait long to be seen. He spent twenty minutes on a hard plastic chair building up his hopes of Leah being there when he got home before a sudden swish of cubicle curtains revealed a duty doctor in green scrubs. He was short, heavy and balding, but also brisk and professional. He also thought he was a comedian.

'So, Mr McAndrew, did you get into a fight with your pet eagle, ha-ha?'

The stare Giles gave him was so toxic the man backed off in a hurry. He offered little more conversation other than to remark on the lovely weekend weather they were all enjoying. Giles grunted a response. The doctor concentrated on his stitching: three for one hole; four for the other. It was agony, but at least it short-circuited the thought that this might be the day when he lost Leah for a while.

Driving home, Giles focused on what he should do to straighten things out instead of wallowing in self-pity. At the best of times self-pity was a waste of time. There was no point in his falling into that trap yet while there was a chance that Leah would be waiting for him when he got back. But if she wasn't, he would work out a plan to get her back. It might be a little like climbing a mountain or hacking his way through a forest but he would do it. And he would do it successfully for no other reason than he had to.

He knew he could figure something out. He might not have a degree like almost all of the reporters at TCR but he prided himself on being a smart thinker. At review meetings he was surrounded by graduates: his producer, Leon; news editor Sarah and assistant-boss Greg – they'd all done their years on easy street picking up their pieces of paper – but Giles could more than hold his own with them. His thinking had a practical bent theirs lacked. He would push out ideas for solving problems and getting things done while they were still getting out their pens. He had no axe to grind with the university brigade, but they used up too much time talking around an issue for ages and ages; he liked to cut through the rubbish and make a decision quickly, no mucking around. In fact, he felt a little superior to them, which might explain why they were a little cool with him. Except Leah, of course. She had a degree but of course, he'd never held that against her. When you see someone like her you put all reservations aside. At least, to start with. She was a decent reporter too. More than decent. That was worthy of a lot of respect.

A solution, then. A minute or so ticked by but nothing came to him. He stayed positive: he thought about his good points to give himself strength and energy. He was good at staying detached from the emotional side of the news; that had helped to make him what he was. He knew some people thought Giles McAndrew to be a cold hearted bastard at times, but he knew that that was only him on the surface – he really felt for people who found themselves in difficulty and distress; he just didn't go 'aah' and 'bless' and mollycoddle people. Look at the campaigns he'd done for charity: that proved he cared. Plus there was his love of a challenge: he wasn't frightened of anything or anyone: he could interview a prize leek grower one minute and the Prime Minister the next and be just the same: unfazed and professional all the way. He didn't panic when thing went wrong – like when some idiot set the station on fire. He carried on broadcasting as smoothly and calmly as anything; he even made jokes about it while wisps of smoke crept towards his studio door.

Okay, so Leah's walking out had left him with a real challenge on his hands. Fine: to work. He parked his Range Rover in the drive and strode into the house with a real sense of purpose. And if she's already back, he thought, walking round the to the back door, better that she sees me looking confident than as if I couldn't cope without her.

She wasn't there.

Giles refused to let this knock him back again. He made himself some coffee and a sandwich, and almost ran upstairs to get some plain paper from the printer tray in the office. He almost rushed back down into the kitchen. He perched himself on the edge of the sofa, opened the French windows just behind it to let some air in to keep him fresh and put the paper in front of him on the coffee table. He didn't have time to relax, eat and then set to the task. He munched while he got ready to scribble some notes as he went along.

Reason told him that he was like a general in command of a war that was fast being lost. Okay, so he had to come up with a good plan for the campaign. He thought about his options. He could get hold of Leah on the phone and tell her again he was sorry. Very sorry. He would plead for her to come back. He frowned. He didn't like pleading. Then he would text her another 'sorry' and just say 'I want u back.' No: too feminine. He needed something else. He got up and paced the kitchen floor. Nothing came into his mind, apart from going to her flat - waiting for her if she was out – and pleading his case there. But what if she wouldn't listen to him? She could be hard, could Leah. He began to lose faith in the persuasion solution. He had no experience of having done this before. He saw Leah with her hard face on, looking up at him with contempt at his pleading. He heard her saying, 'Is this the best you can do? I'm not interested.'

For a long time, maybe ten minutes, perhaps twenty, this went on, this fruitless thinking. He was going round in circles. It was no good he'd have to start thinking more widely. What did they call it? They'd done something on this a while ago on the programme. Thinking outside the box. Right. He would do that. How would I normally do things? I need to do the opposite.

His natural inclination was to sort out his problems alone. He always had. He winced at the thought of getting in help from outside, but five minutes later he still hadn't come up with a better idea. He began to give way, then, as the afternoon began to spread out across the canvas backdrop of his mind unseen, almost unfelt, he succumbed. He would find a second-in-command to help him through this. He wrote the words 'Get someone to help you' on the pad and put an extravagant full stop at the end which saw the pen almost bounce right back out of his hand. 'Right – we're moving,' he said aloud.

The problem was, who? It was a fact that he didn't really have anyone to confide in. A presenter's job could far too easily be a lonely one. He was a freelancer, which was more prestigious than being a staffer, and he got paid a lot more money. But it meant that he didn't muck in with the newsroom crew of producers, reporters and staff presenters so much; he didn't do their compulsory eight-hour shift. The fact that he was Two Counties' most important and most popular presenter also caused him difficulty: they were jealous of him. He had no doubts about that.

'I'm not that egotistical,' he would often protest to Leah, who would almost invariably laugh in response.

'Giles,' she'd said more than once, 'what makes you a great presenter also makes you a bit of a shit bag.'

'Is that what they think of me in the newsroom?'

'No comment.' She would laugh a little to spare his feelings; as if she might really be joking just to keep him on his toes.

No one could argue with his ratings though.

'What about my ratings, though, ay? No one can argue with my ratings, you know.'

'This is why you're not popular in the newsroom, honey.'

'I'd rather be popular with the people of Bart and Bilt than with those...' - he nearly said 'losers' – '...people in there. Marcus and Dave and that crowd.'

Giles could see all too easily why the newsroom crowd never included him in a Friday night down the pub or a trip to one of the local curry houses. But he would turn them down anyway if they suddenly asked him: he preferred doing his own thing, or doing it with Leah.

He had a sudden realisation of just how little he knew the people at TCR, and how little they knew him. He began to feel a pang of discomfort about it and that surprised him – he never had before. Not only was he set apart as a presenter and set apart again as a freelancer, in the BRBC - the British Radio Broadcasting Corporation - people moved around so much it was hard to make close work friends. Hard for Giles, anyway. But all of it, in the end, didn't matter. If this was the cost of being a successful hired gun at the microphone, so be it.

So it looked like he could get no help at work. He reviewed the situation anyway, briefly. He got on well with Leon but he couldn't let him right into his private life like this. It would be too embarrassing. He thought of Lucie but even if it worked out, Leah would kill him if she ever found out, so that was a non-starter. There was Simone, the station boss: he'd always got on well with her; she was the only one who really understood him, knew what made him tick. But I can't, he thought, I can't show her this much weakness.

He put the search for a helper on the back burner for a minute. This was much better – his mind was moving now. He put a hand to his wound and felt it throbbing underneath the bandage. He liked it. He felt stronger still when a couple of huge positives suddenly occurred to him: One. He knew he could sort the letter problem out because Leah had got the wrong end of the stick completely. Two. Leah was wrong about Lucie – he was completely innocent and she had nothing to fear.

But then he frowned when the two problems that still remained bounced back at him off the ropes and swung punches at him. Firstly, when Leah Caighton made up her mind about something, shifting her was like trying to push open a locked door. Secondly, if he could make Leah listen to him and neutralize the acid in the letter, then talk some sense into her with regard to Lucie, there was still the unhealthy state of their relationship underneath that still needed curing. He was reminded of why he liked to avoid bouts of intense thinking: it just brought too much discomfort to the surface. It was better left where it was while they tried to skate on over the top of it.

Suddenly, Giles, despite his determination to remain strong, began to fight back the tears. Yes, they were a volatile, unstable mixture, he and Leah, but it had to be this fact that had led them to some amazingly intense times too and incredible sex.

He dried his eyes and gave up the struggle for the time being. He wasn't admitting defeat, he was just pausing to re-gather himself. He suddenly felt a wave of tiredness overcoming him. He needed to get himself upstairs for a sleep. After a nap he would be re-charged and be able to think more clearly.

He had no problem in falling asleep, even while he wondered how demeaning it was to be crying about your girlfriend when she was ten years younger than you.

Later, as the last winds of April blew the day from early afternoon into evening, Giles sat in his big lounge on his huge, L-shaped sofa with Skydays on his knee trying to watch the TV, still wrestling the monsters. The antiques show turned into a wildlife programme, then melted into a cosy domestic drama but if his helper was out there somewhere, he hadn't grasped the fact. Then it hit him: a real brainwave. Naturally, once the synapse was made, he kicked himself; it was obvious and should have struck him hours ago. But he was excited, both by the fact that he'd made the breakthrough and by the idea itself. He sprang into motion, sending the cat jumping and mewling, and almost ran to the kitchen. He picked up the biro and printed a name on the page in big letters. He underlined it, added an exclamation mark, then threw both pad and pen onto the floor in defiant triumph. The pen skidded to a stop at the cooker while the pad hit the floor with a splat! and stopped dead. Giles had already left the kitchen but the page he had written on remained, its single word in black ink bothering no one yet.

'Catherine!'

said the pad.

6

A Piece of Paper on the Floor

Giles McAndrew went to his office and wrote an email to Catherine, flagging it up and typing 'URGENT' into the subject box after 'A Bit of Trouble – Help!' He didn't tell her what was wrong, he just said,

'Get in touch with me Catherine, as quickly as you can! Help needed.'

He signed himself 'Gilles' for the first time in a long time. 'Yes, why not "Gilles",' he said aloud? That's how she always knew me, after all. It was eight o'clock just gone.

He walked along the long landing and up the short flight of steps to the attic bedroom to finally get showered, feeling as though he was now emerging from his darkness. May 6th: that was the key, and Catherine was the key to that key, even though she wouldn't know it yet. Hang on, thought Giles, is that right? My thinking is disintegrating - Jesus. He knew what he meant. He tried again. Catherine had got him into this mess - in a way - so it was appropriate to involve her in trying to get him out of it. It might not work, of course - they hadn't seen each other for a very long time – but she was the best idea he'd had by far, so he was going to go with it.

The story was this: ten days or so earlier, Giles had learned from his mother that Catherine had been back in England for two months already – 'didn't you know?' – news that came to him completely out of the blue. It turned out that she'd made something of a name for herself in Canada as an artist, and wanted to come to England for a year or so to paint and see if she couldn't sell her work over here. She was recently divorced.

Giles had thought straight away that there was an idea for a future Christmas or birthday present for Leah. She loved art. So now what he'd do was bring the present forward. Leah had been going on for about a month about the second anniversary of their going out in early May. May 6th – Leah had circled the date on his kitchen calendar and work diary and written 'Ann.'. She'd done it with a smile on her face both times so he hadn't given it much thought. If he had, it was only to consider where they might go for a nice meal that evening. Nothing more.

But now, what about giving Leah one of Catherine's paintings as an anniversary present? His original idea had been to commission an original piece from her if that was possible, but something she'd already done would still really knock her out and make up for today's catastrophe. The more he'd thought about it, the more the idea appeared to have sprung right off the genius tree. He was terrible when it came to remembering birthdays and the like, and wasn't one for splashing out on presents for no obvious reason either. An amazing gift, so perfectly matched to Leah's interests would be the last thing she'd expect. She wouldn't expect anything on that day, in fact, that was the thing; so the impact would be huge. He was sure of it. It would also make her realise how much she meant to him. He'd find a way of subtly making sure she knew it cost him a lot of money; that would help too. And with a bit of luck she would love the painting itself of course, which would just top the thing off.

So, Giles had quickly got himself organised and emailed Cath the next day, and within twenty-four hours she'd emailed him back. It was this letter that Leah had found in his jacket. He cursed his luck: he hadn't worn it since he put it there, probably the day it came; or if he had, he'd stupidly failed to remove it. But what he couldn't work out was why it had sent Leah completely off the deep end. He could remember that it was a warm and quite affectionate note, but he was sure that Catherine had made it quite clear somewhere in its contents that she was only his cousin. Yes, Leah could be jealous and insecure, but jealous of a cousin? Even if you factored in the current Lucie issue, it still didn't make sense that she should read it and attack him like a mad woman. It just didn't add up. This gave him hope again. The cause of this was a simple misunderstanding, that was all.

At last, he brought his aching naked body to the shower to get rid of the sweat and dried blood, really feeling an improvement now he had found his big idea.

But what a day, he thought. What a bloody God-awful day. It's a crisis day; I'm like a government having a crisis. He pulled the shower attachment down to his chest level to keep the scalding water off his cheek and the bruised bridge of his nose. Then, sod it, he said to himself and put his whole face under. The physical pain wasn't so terrible after a few seconds, and it shut off the Leah pain for a while.

Then the argument and fight re-played in his mind and took him down again. 'I don't blame you, Leah,' he muttered to himself whilst turning off the shower, 'I made a bloody mess of things again.' He stared down at the white tiles and felt like he was looking at his own mind: something blank and empty. The sense of hope he'd just spent hours manufacturing had seemed to evaporate in seconds. The pain of reliving her anger spiked him painfully. He thought of Leah's naked body and groaned so loudly inside he thought the sound was really there in the bathroom. The thought of masturbating flashed into his mind and out again. It was replaced by the return of tension and angst: thoughts milling around his head where he realised how difficult Leah was, or worse, how difficult he made her. Then he realised suddenly that he loved Leah so much he had to try – he had to give getting her back everything he'd got.   The emotional bumping up and down went on. Towelling off, he found himself thinking about Catherine and his good idea and that sparked off hope out of the gloom once again. He thought about their phone call after he got the email. It was strange to hear her voice for the first time in twenty-five years; strange to hear a Canadian woman's voice in place of that of the little girl he'd once known.

He immediately Googled her name and found her website. He wasn't what you'd call an art lover but he thought he knew quality when he saw it. More to the point, some of the reviews she had up there were incredibly impressive. He texted her straight away to tell her what a massive favour she was doing him, allowing him to buy one of the few paintings she'd brought over with her. She rang an hour later.

'Thanks for the message, Gilles. It's no problem, don't worry. I'd love you to have one,' she said.

'Really?'

'Sure!'

'That's great. How many did you bring with you?' he said.

'Twelve.'

'Are you sure you can spare one?'

'Sure. I wouldn't want to lose two, but I can lose one. For you Gilles, It'd be a pleasure.'

He heard her pronouncing his real name correctly, with the 'G' softened in the French manner. It made him smile.

'Why don't you come up and see me at Corumby and bring a selection? Is that possible?'

Catherine thought about it, and how much she wanted to see him again.

'Sure,' she said, 'I can do that. I've got a car. I don't even need the train. When?'

'How about this Tuesday?'

'Hang on – what date is that? Hang on, I'm taking my diary out here...'

Giles had the calendar on the wall by the kitchen phone. He lifted up the April page to see May.

'May 2nd is Tuesday.'

'I've nothing after midday.'

'You sure?'

'Yeah! I'd love to see where you work.'

It had been as easy as that.

As bad as things were, the fact kept coming back to console him: yes, Leah had got this all wrong. Catherine Garner was his cousin and was about as harmful to Leah in reality as fresh air. Cousin Cath was a good memory from childhood that was all. Admittedly she was the first woman to see the Gilles Wilkinson penis but as he was nine at the time and she eight, he didn't think it mattered very much here in the present. A lot of old memories now came flowing back. He'd seen Catherine's very nude private area too, something he hadn't thought about for a long time and he could have laughed about it had he not been so down, about how he'd thought for a long time that the event was an important rite of passage. This idea was dispelled when he went out with teenage girls; now Catherine's naughty parts became innocent skin as hairless as the moment she'd been born. But at the time it hadn't stopped Cath getting really mad when he said he wanted to touch it. Gilles had never forgotten though how he had distinctly heard her giggling as she ran away home. He thought about that getting dressed. That's girls for you. Cath, Leah, others he'd known. They were a dangerous, unpredictable breed alike.

More memories came back to him thick, fast and chronologically uncertain. They used to meet at Christmas at family gatherings and in the summer her parents and his would holiday together up in Scotland on a big loch or on the west coast near the place where the ferry left for Skye. Having just each other to play with, they spent most of whole weeks together, so she'd been a big part of his small, young life. Neither of them having brothers or sisters, they hadn't had much choice but to become inseparable for the short time the families were together. Gilles had a vague memory that they'd decided when they were seven and six that they were going to get married when they grew up – definitely. Later, slightly older - Gilles thought cousin Cath was pretty. And fun. She liked swimming, making sandcastles and playing ball games. She even played rugby with him until one year he dislocated her finger. One year he'd made it a priority to find out whether cousins could marry or not, but a week into the new school year he'd forgotten all about it. What had I been, then, twelve, he thought?

Later on, she liked listening to pop music on his transistor radio. When alone they would talk about all kinds of things, private and personal, that began to get – hang on – hadn't they talked about sex for the first time the summer before she went away? Yes, they had, but he didn't remember what exactly they'd said to each other. When she left for Canada they were thirteen and twelve, too young even then to have done anything but play games. At that age, the rules of attraction were blurry, but even so, Gilles, who naturally felt stirrings of childhood love, knew deep down that his attraction to Catherine was just an annual thing, that it was false and most importantly, wrong. But really, knowing what he knew now, how innocent they were. He almost wanted them back, those days. It was good, really good to remember them.

After Catherine went to Quebec, in '77, she had written one letter to him, but had faded away from his life quickly and inevitably. Soon enough there were real girls to get to know and proper games of rugby at school to play in, where Gilles, now preferring 'Giles', could be as rough as he liked.

Giles switched his hair drier on and waved it over his short hair for a minute. The trick now was to get through to the anniversary next week, the 6th of May, without Leah leaving Barton Townes. On that day he would give Leah the big surprise present, perhaps even introduce her to Catherine, and all would be made clear. Things wouldn't just go back to normal, they would be better than normal. They would begin again. Sort of, he thought.

Dare I wait that long, though, he said to himself? I'm at my best when I'm acting, not thinking; maybe I should do something sooner, he went on. I can't wait nearly a week. He altered his plan, slightly. He would talk to her as soon as he could and tell her the truth about the email. With a little luck she would be at the station working a normal Monday shift where he could buttonhole her. Or, before he went to bed tonight she would actually answer her phone and they could start talking. There. That's a plan, he thought – a good one.

But he wasn't fated to get away with it that easily. Each time he believed he had settled things, the events of the past twenty hours went swirling round his head stirring up barbed circles of thought. He should have done this, then no, he should have done that. He should have done more to cultivate friendships over the years; he shouldn't have isolated himself from people through his obsession with career. But then, he considered, he wouldn't have been so interesting to someone as gorgeous as Leah and he would never have gone out with her in the first place. His job made him what he was. He was certain of that. If he was as charismatic as people said, it was because he was so full of himself on air, so energetic and confident. But it was his success there that seemed to make him insensitive and thoughtless. The Catch 22 pinballed around his head and made him want to scream.

He was still sitting on his bed with his head in his hands when the phone went. He dashed to the bedroom extension and picked it up. It was Leon, his producer.

'Hi, Giles - just checking in with you about the show in the morning.'

'Fine, Leon, erm, good. What's happening, anything?'

'Well, we've got a fire overnight at the Harlon estate, a child's dead and the police suspect arson.'

'Oh, Christ. Nice.'

'I know. Mum and Grandma are in the Royal Bart too in a bad way. We haven't really done anything much on it today according to Sarah so I thought we'd go big with it in the morning. I've lined up the local police guy that deals with this sort of crime and the county chief fire officer...'

'Sounds good, Leon...'

'...Thanks – the cops also think that foul play is likely, so I thought that we'd do a short phone-in session after the news at eight too. That okay?'

'Yeah, Leon, that sounds good too.'

'Or, we could take out the whole eight-to-nine slot with it if you like – there's not a lot else happening tomorrow, as things stand.'

'Okay.'

'And Reg is going to be there all morning and we're going to round up a cop specialist on arson so you can do a live to air with him.'

Giles was pleased - he could do phone-ins standing on his head. He wanted this week's shows to run on tramlines so he could free his mind up for Leah.

'Great. Great stuff, Leon. Sounds like you've been working hard on it. Anything else?'

'One or two things we can take a look at first thing. Oh, don't forget we've got the Culture Secretary coming to Bilt cathedral on Tuesday and I should be confirming an interview for you with her in the morning. I'll email you some stuff about her in a minute. And I'm still working on John Clegg.'

'Really?'

'Yeah. He probably won't come cause it's Tory land, but I know he'll be driving right past us on Thursday morning at about half-six on the way to Hull, so you never know.'

'I wouldn't get excited - the deputy Prime Minister's not going to come here.'

'Since when were you an expert on politics?'

'Thanks, Leon. Anything else?' He wasn't in the mood for taking any shit from his bloody producer, not even in jest.

'No, that's it.'

'Thanks, Leon.'

'Not a problem, Giles. Giles – are you alright?'

'Yeah, why?'

'You sound a little odd if I may say so?'

'Do I? Probably because I've just woken up from a sleep.'

'Oh, right. See you in the morning then.'

'Yeah, see you, Leon. Thanks for ringing.'

'Not a problem. See you.'

Leon might be a bit of a fusspot but he was becoming a real pro – just the sort of producer he needed this week. Something's going right anyway, he thought. Plus, the Culture secretary and maybe John Clegg. Giles liked the higher pressure stuff: it stopped him from getting complacent. If he had plans to get onto the national network he had to show the big wigs in London that he could cut it with the big politicians.

He went to the bathroom mirror to inspect his face again. There was no point in trying to lie it away at work next day – Leah might tell someone about the fight and it would be all round the newsroom in five minutes. Bloody Two Counties was terrible like that. There was no way of knowing what would happen there in the morning, so best not think about it. Giles was exhausted with thinking. Today had been bad enough – let tomorrow take care of itself, he thought. Mind you, he could help things along by getting out of the building as soon as he finished his show at nine. He could make an excuse and they could do the review meeting without him for once.

He phoned Leah's number again at her flat and got the machine. Then he rang her mobile and got the same. He started to text her, wrote half a sentence but wasn't sure he was doing the right thing so he scrapped it. He went to the office and tried to write an email but scrapped that. It was nearly half-past nine. That really was it for one day. He went downstairs and poured himself another big glass of water. He drank some then set it down to go fetch a couple of Paracetamol from the cupboard, his face hurting and his head aching worse than before. He took the rest of the drink upstairs wondering whether to take another shower and debating with himself the wisdom of phoning Leah. Was he sure that what he planned to say would be right? He decided to do neither. Enough, Giles, enough, he told himself; this is enough for one day.

In his bedroom again he pulled the curtains across to darken the room, set the alarm and tried to go to sleep. After ten minutes he got up, went downstairs and took a couple of Ibuprofen and drank them down with a half-glass of squash. He slumped back up the stairs still feeling like a walking tragedy but when he laid his head down and pulled the duvet up over his shoulders he fixed his mind on the past.

He went back to being twelve years in Scotland walking beside the loch with Catherine. He looked carefully at her face again, inspecting the picture like a real photograph. They were sitting in the grass now. He saw all the shapes on it: the slim nose, the freckles, the normal mouth. Normal mouth? Yes, when he was twelve Catherine had a normal mouth and ordinary ears and the same skin as anyone else he knew of his age. But her hair stood out, long and brown and nice. A tiny pang of longing rose up from an ancient cell of memory and nipped him. That was okay. It was nothing. No – it wasn't 'nothing' – it gave him a feeling of comfort. He was relaxing now; very soon he would be asleep. As he fell, one last shred of Sunday April 30th passed across his mind. Monday morning might well be terrible, but he would turn from this Gilles Wilkinson into Giles McAndrew, the BRBC Two Counties Radio Breakfast Show presenter and thought that, maybe, if he tried hard enough, he might convince himself that this day had happened to someone else.

In the night something made him come awake. In this lonely place he thought often about the possibility of being burgled in the night. He sat up, strained his ears, head up, on full alert like an animal. Nothing. He needed to piss and got up with a growl of annoyance. As he let it go, he felt a throbbing from the gash Leah gave him. He wiped himself, rinsed his hands and decided to go downstairs to get some more painkillers. As he trod delicately down the stairs listening again for the sounds of an intruder, something else still troubled him. He couldn't work it out. I'm half-asleep so it's not surprising, he thought. I'll think about it in the morning.

He went to the fridge for the water jug, and to two cupboards for a glass and the Ibuprofen, and the troubling thing was still there. He swallowed the liquid but not the tablets – he'd decided he'd taken enough already - still trying to guide his mind in the direction of the missing thought. Then he caught it. It was something he had to find: a piece of paper. He went back upstairs but instead of taking the stairs to the attic bedroom, he went to his office. He switched on the main light just so he could see the desk lamp, and the brightness of the bulb felt like an attack. He rushed as fast as he could to the desk and flipped the switch – went back to the wall and flicked off the ceiling light. That was better. He turned and looked down at his desk. It wasn't under the keyboard, it wasn't on top of any of the three piles of papers or behind the base unit or the monitor. It wasn't under the magazine. There! There it was, on the floor. He went to pick it up and nearly overbalanced.

'Shit!'

He steadied himself and grabbed the sheet of white A4 paper. The blank side was uppermost. He stood, flipped it over, and knew why he'd woken up.

'Shit!' he said again.

It was page 2 of Catherine's email.

Page 2 of 2

aren't they. But auntie Sooze tells me you're in a big relationship now. Tell me all about it when we meet, won't you.

Have you heard yet about Uncle Ian's 70th birthday party down at Wareham in September? I was wondering if you'll be going. I can tell you that my mum is dying to see you again. But of course I'll see you way before that. In a few days, hopefully. You realise it's 26 years since we last saw each other? When Mum and Dad carted us all off to Ontario? Last time I saw you you were 13 – incredible, no?

See you soon, G.

Lots of love,

Catherine

PS What happened to your name? I don't like Giles – too posh!

> ----- Original Message -----
> From: Giles McAndrew
> To: Catherine Lang
> Sent: Thursday April 27, 2006 07:13 PM
> Subject: Re: That Thing We Talked About

Catherine

Hi. Thanks for the note. It's great to know you're back in the country. I'm really looking forward to our meeting up again.

Okay. Here's what I wanted to ask. Auntie Suze says you're a star artist in Canada. "A risign star" according to a newspaper. Wow. Is that right? That's amazing, terrific. Because, I'd like to buy one! An important anniversary is coming up soon and I want to buy the person a special present. One of your paintings will be ideal. The woman in question likes art a lot. Forces me to go to galleries! I'm a bit of a philistine, though. I prefer riding a bike!

So do you think this is possible? Suze saiys you have some paintings with you in England. I hope so. Get back to me as soon as. Yes, it's been a long time, muchoo long.

Love

Giles

Giles McAndrew
Breakfast Show Presenter
BRBC TWO COUNTIES RADIO
24 Brldges Lane, Barton Townes, Bartonshire, BT3 1TV *0299 451923*

'Bastard!' said Giles aloud. It was unbelievable. He hung his head and shook it for a few seconds. Still, he thought: this is the proof – when she sees this, she'll understand everything. He put the piece of paper on top of the keyboard so he'd find it straight away in the morning, switched off the light and went back up to bed. Feeling better, but not ecstatic about losing precious sleep, ten minutes later his bedroom began to fill with the sound of a light rhythmic snoring.

May Day at Two Counties Radio

Monday May 1st

'You're listening to Early Bird, with Lucie Bastable, on Two Counties Radio.'

'It's almost a quarter-past-five on a Monday Mayday morning here on Two Counties Radio. I can just hear the birds singing already if I strain my ears enough, ha-ha...Okay, today, the TCR Community Bus will be in Talenham market place from ten 'til twelve, so if you've nothing much else to do this morning, why not go along there and see Russell and Heidi who'll be happy to put you on to the internet, helping you to do all sorts of things, finding information, playing games – anything you can think of? So if you're not hooked up to the 'net at home, why not come along and have some fun? Time for Kate Bush – this is 'Running Up That Hill', and you don't want to be doing too much of that today, it's a holiday!'

'Bloody hell, I'm talking drivel again, Sonia...'

['No, you're not – you're okay, you're fine.']

'I can't hear birds from this studio, what am I talking about...'

['No, it was fine, it was fine, people'll like that, don't worry. Okay, I've got Tom Collins, the owl expert ready, okay? You fine with your first question?']

'Hang on – yep, I've got it. Fine. I'm ready.'

In Barton Townes, no one knew where to find Two Counties Radio. When Sarah Billings, the station's spruce and efficient news editor, arrived at the town for the first time, she got off the train, asked some locals for directions and received a reaction suggestive of someone who'd just alighted from a spaceship and was trying to talk to them in Martian. The first one hadn't a clue what she was on about. Two said, 'have we got a radio station in Barton Townes?' The third said, 'Um, it's near Tesco's, I think, up by the industrial park. You'll need to get a bus or a taxi.' Her new place of employment turned out to be nowhere near Tesco's, nor the industrial park and was only three minutes away on foot, two and a half in fact, at Sarah speed.

To find it from the long, ancient high street all you needed to do was take the turning opposite the parish church, Bridges Lane, and it was on your right-hand side about a hundred yards down. But screened by trees and set back fifteen metres from the road, it was as good as invisible. Lacking a big, bright sign to announce it, forty-nine of every fifty persons driving past did so without so much as the tiniest inkling that an award-winning BRBC local radio station was right there under their noses and under the stewardship of managing editor, Simone Pound. The fiftieth would be someone who'd worked there or who'd once been a guest on the air.

In a way it was just as well it went unnoticed. Vacated in 1986 by Biggs Insurance, TCR HQ was a two-storey box of anonymous glass and metal that would only get its day in the sun when someone announced a competition to find the most soulless building in the UK. TCR staff looked up at the edifice once, when they came for their interview, then never bothered again. After that they just headed for the door, sensibly blind to their workplace's architectural charms.

Within this nondescript shell, the bright and hard working personnel did indeed deliver radio output of award-winning quality: the 2003 Sony Award for Best Local Radio Station trophy sat proudly on a newsroom shelf for much of 2004 until it was accidentally knocked off and dented, after which Simone housed it on her desk. Since then, the drab, functional quality of the surroundings had failed to materially reduced the quality of the station's work, *Media Magazine* having described it as recently as November 2005 as 'fresh, innovative and startlingly well in touch with the community.'

On the first day of May, AD 2006, as many of the good people of Bartonshire and Bilt enjoyed a well-deserved Bank Holiday lie-in, it was business as usual. *Radio doesn't take holidays, it makes holidays*, as last week's key jingle had it. Jackie Husband, in the first minutes of her day on the front desk, stifled a yawn as she wiped her work surface clean of dust and coffee stains and prepared herself administratively for a steady trickle of guests and visitors. Giles McAndrew's breakfast show was playing from wall speakers in the modestly sized reception area at a carefully modulated volume.

'And Janice is here with the Bank Holiday traffic news...'
'Thanks, Giles - Bank Holiday Traffic is moving well this morning on the A544 Barton Townes by-pass, but a butter lorry has jack-knifed on the racecourse roundabout and shed its load. This is causing a tailback of about a mile as of two minutes ago on the satellite pictures...'

'Oh, crikey, it'll be messy down there for a while this morning then, Janice.'

'Looks like it, ha-ha.'

'Still, if you've got a loaf of bread handy and a Swiss Army Knife you'll be alright...'

'Ha-ha, probably, Giles, ha-ha.'

'And I reckon if we can get a couple of blow torches down there we can hand round toast while people are stuck in the jam, ha-ha.'

[Ha-ha, good one, Giles,] said Leon into Giles's ear from the Ops Room next door to Studio 1

'Ah well, all in a Bartonshire Monday morning, ay Janice?'

'Ha-ha, don't forget Bilt, Giles or you'll get me shot.'

'Well it's not my fault it's the second smallest county in England.'

'Giles!'

'Only kidding – I love Bilt, 'course I do, and the people over there know it too. I was over there a couple of weeks ago opening the March Gardens Celebration and I had a gr-reat time.'

'I'm sure you did, Giles.'

'What's that supposed to mean?'

'Nothing, Giles, ha-ha - that's it from me, Janice Lemon, Two Counties Radio travel – our next bulletin is at 9.30!'

'Thank you, Janice. I think.'

'The Breakfast Show, with Giles McAndrew –Every Morning from Six on BRBC Two Counties Radio.'

'Noona Reynolds is here with me – so, Noona, what have you got lined up for us this morning on the show after nine, anything good?'

'Of course, Giles, as if...'

'Sorry, Noona, forgive me for suggesting that your show could ever be less than interesting...'

['Easy, Giles...']

'Ha-ha, thank you Giles, I accept your apology. Well, we have a man who talks his way to massive prize winning marrows, turnips and swedes every year at the Bilt Show – we're going to see how his preparations are coming along...'

'You mean he talks to his marrows...'

'Yes, and his turnips and his...'

'Bit of a Prince Charles, then, is he?'

'I think so, Giles, ha-ha, and I'll be also be talking to actress Bonita Barnes whose new one-woman-show, Cancer for Beginners comes to Barton Townes Royal Theatre for two nights starting tomorrow.'

'Sounds great, Noona, how could I ever have doubted you?'

'I don't know, Giles, ha-ha, you're just a nasty individual this morning, aren't you, ha-ha...'

'Am I? Where did you hear that?'

'You know I listen to you every morning on my way in.'

'Ah, that's kind of you.'

'Did you get out of bed the wrong side?'

'Me? No, Noona, no – I couldn't be better thanks.'

'I'm glad to hear it'

'Thanks Noona! Noona will be with you as usual after the news and sport at nine and I'm sure the show will be just as perfect as it was yesterday...'

In the Two Counties Radio newsroom, the scruffy, cluttered hub of reporters, producers and presenters, the atmosphere was quiet and congenial for a smallish but growing number of workers warming steadily to their tasks. Sarah Billings looked intently at the BRBC news database for anything new breaking nationally, with one ear on the Breakfast Show that played on a pair of nearby speakers. Chris Tovey, the chief website guy, was doing websitey things in his corner adjacent to Busy Ian Borage, a reporter who was already working on a news package on a broken gas main in Ingleby for the Drive Time show. Diana Clark, Noona's producer, had she been in the room, would have been distracting others with her usual pre-show twittering and fussing but she was away from her desk, grabbing a last-minute word with Head of Programming Damien Read in his office. The office lights were on but plenty of natural light helped worker-concentration at the far end of the room where two men were quietly conversing. Fairly keen and fairly experienced reporter Marcus Shifley pushed his chair back from his flat screen monitor and looked briefly out of the window with its lovely view of housing estate back gardens. He went back to the screen, which showed the regional database of British ghost sightings that was currently assisting his investigation into the possibility of spirits haunting the crypt of Bilt Cathedral, and, pleased with what he saw, turned to his neighbour.

'So, Dave, what did you do at the weekend, anything much?'

Big Dave Plymouth didn't look up from the running order of Bob Constable's afternoon show on the screen in front of his large head.

'Record fair in Cambridge, Saturday.'

'Any good?'

'Not bad. Sunday I took The Beast for a spin up to the coast. You?'

'Nah. Nothing to report. 'Ere, have you seen Leah Caighton this morning? I need to see her.'

'Strangely no. Unfortunately no.'

'Is she in?'

Big Dave looked up at her empty desk and chair nearby, and looked back at Marcus, clicking the ubiquitous pencil in his mouth against his teeth.

'I don't know – she might be out on a job.'

He scratched his beard and went back to writing cues for Bob Constable, even though he never bloody used half of them.

At her desk by the door, Sarah was distracted by Lynda Purves entering the room with her refined walk to begin preparations for her Midday show, but even more by the arrival of a second woman right behind her. The elfin figure of Lucie Bastable came and stood close to her chair, making Sarah smile, though she tried to look as though she was concentrating on BRBC breaking news stories.

'Did you catch my show, this morning,' said Lucie, quietly.

'You must be kidding. I didn't wake up until a quarter-to…'

'I'm joking,' said Lucie, producing a fetching smile of her own.

'How did it go?'

'Good, I think,' she said discreetly, lest anyone else heard her immodesty.

Lucie Bastable's dark, heartbreak eyes burrowed a silent question about her radio presenting abilities into the thin Two Counties carpet but her doubting thoughts were abruptly interrupted by Greg McKenzie, TCR's deputy boss who swung one half of his body into the newsroom door.

'Lucie – review meeting in two minutes in MR 2.'

'Okay,' she politely trilled back. She glanced briefly behind her to see Greg's slim bespectacled face disappearing at speed again. She turned back to Sarah.

'I need the loo – see you later,' she said and left the room with a characteristic trot. Sarah Billings contentedly turned her thoughts to another probing story about immigrant farm workers in the far-East Midlands, even though she thought she'd probably junk it later on.

A couple of minutes after the 9 o'clock changeover from Giles to Noona in Studio 1, a small group of Two Counties staff began assembling casually in Meeting Room 2 for the thrice weekly review meeting for Lucie's show, the dreaded five am-to six graveyard shift. Greg, only 35 but already the senior male statesman of TCR management, nimbly slotted into position at the head of the table in the

cramped room. Lucie, still slightly nervous about these dissections of
her work, having only been presenting for a short time, entered and
half-tripped over an overhead projector someone had left on the floor.
She squeaked, then managed to sit down beside her producer, Sonia
Van Huisten. Then Marcus arrived, filling in as unofficial deputy to
Sarah Billings and began watching everyone intently, two along from
Luce, covering his interest with aimless doodling on his notepad. The
final arrival was Busy Ian, who liked to lend Sonia and Lucie a hand
with finding daft local stories to keep the local insomniacs and
ridiculously early starters from switching stations or watching TV.

Sarah Billings could easily have led the meeting, but for
reasons currently unknown, this had become one of Greg McKenzie's
pigeon holes. Cynics may have suggested in private conversation in the
newsroom or over a couple of post-shift beers in the Grey Gardens
across the road, that TCR's number two took this much interest in the
show on account of Lucie's petite comeliness; but seeing as most of the
station was at least half-in-love with her, that was probably not the
reason.

The event shambled to a lazy start, which was no surprise for a
meeting with no formal start time and no written agenda. After a few
minutes of casual chat, Greg coughed lightly, said 'Okay, shall we
make a start?' and scrutinised his A4 notepad for self- direction.

'Right: I don't know about anyone else but I thought it went well,' he
said, looking vaguely through slim, trendy glasses with a middling
amount of enthusiasm at the assembled group. As ever, Marcus fought
to stave off the imminent boredom by trying to shape the embryonic
debate.

'What did you like, Greg?' he asked, keeping his tone as light as a
piece of Noreham Summer Fair sponge cake.

'Oh, several things – no disasters or big mistakes to start with, which
may seem silly but…what is this, Lucie, your fifth week?'

'Fourth.'

'Fourth. I've known experienced presenters make bad gaffes, but so
far we haven't had any yet, have we?' Greg scanned the others for
agreement.

'Apart from the morning when she had to do the travel and the line
from Birmingham went dead and she said "a lorry has shit its load on
the A69,"' said Marcus, to much laughter and general approval, though
Lucie's face coloured up like a pretty little red balloon.

'Ha-ha, but that can happen to anyone, Marcus, can't it?' said Greg,
smiling at Lucie.

'In actual fact, I did that when I was subbing for Jonno that time when there was no one else because of flu…as you well know,' she said still flushed, reaching over to slap him on the wrist. Marcus smiled benignly to no one in particular and tried to look cool as he swelled inside with pleasure at the physical contact.

'Um - ha-ha,' said Greg, pulling the meeting round his way again, 'I think the smoothness is coming. I'm thinking that you're getting sharper all round and I'm hearing a much more confident tone.'

I'm *hearing* a much more confident *tone*? said Marcus to himself.

'I'm still worried that I'm talking absolute rubbish sometimes. Like this morning with the thing about "you don't want to do too much of that - it's a holiday," when I introduced the Kate Bush song.'

'It's not rubbish, Lucie,' said Greg. 'It's what the listeners like – it's what we do.' Of course it is, thought Marcus. And therein lies the problem.

'Well, I think she's doing really well,' said Sonia and giving Lucie a large, winning smile of support. Lucie smiled back with obvious gratitude and really, no one around the table begrudged it her.

'And I think, Sonia,' said Greg, 'you're doing a good job too – you feel that Sonia's giving you the right amount of support, I think, Lucie, yeah?'

While Marcus thought he was going to throw up, Lucie refused to answer. The flow of thought and opinion on her work on the 'G' shift came to a temporary halt as the door opened loudly and through it walked Leah Caighton.

'Mind if I sit in?' she said, mainly to Greg, trying to be bright and breezy and missing by metres. There was an unspoken rule at most BRBC stations, that as many people were encouraged to give some input to as many review meetings as possible, so no one minded in the slightest – but eyebrows were raised in surprise as she planted her neat bottom on the one spare chair.

'Of course,' said Greg, his welcome echoed by one grunt from Busy Ian and a clearer, 'Hi' from the direction Sonia, with whom she nominally shared a flat.

'Mind that chair,' said Sonia, 'One of the legs is broken.'

'Thanks, it's okay,' said Leah, rocking it to make sure it would take her weight, still stony-faced. Greg flashed another look in her direction before turning to Lucie, who was now replying to him.

'Yeah, one of the best things for me is that I know Sonia's there for me, and Ian too – I know Ian's been working really hard.'

'So, do you think then that you're beginning to gel as a team, you three, yeah?' said Greg.

There were one or two murmurs of agreement with Greg McKenzie's astute observation. 'So astute,' as Marcus Shifley was to say to Big Dave Plymouth later on that day, 'that I nearly awarded him the National Award for Radio Station Astuteness right then and there.'

'You should have astutely knocked one of his smug teeth out,' Big Dave was to reply.

The meeting went on in an atmosphere of mutual and professional support for another nine minutes. Marcus quietly observed Leah Caighton listening and watching the meeting with much the same silent intent as he. Greg, just once, asked specifically for her views but she declined the opportunity. So what are you doing here, he said to himself? He wanted to ask her whether she'd actually heard any of this morning's show, or any of Lucie's early steps in broadcast radio, but didn't dare. Which he? Greg and Marcus both.

This aside, Marcus Shifley felt as he normally did when meetings went this way: like breaking a window in disgust. He thought about destroying the meeting by telling Greg what he really thought of Lucie's presenting skills so far: that she was a lightweight even for five in the morning when no one out there wanted politics, crime or fatal accidents for at least another ninety minutes; but he didn't. Maybe he'd point this out to Simone at a later date if he could find a way to do it tactfully. But he definitely wouldn't tell her even in passing that he fancied having a crack at the job himself. He always found it hard to speak to the Managing Editor: something about her scared him.

Greg McKenzie still had more notes written down and was going to use them before they broke for their various morning tasks.

'One thing I do want to point out before we finish – and um, I do think it's a good thing, is that I think you're handling the pre-show chat with Giles, um, extremely well.'

This time no one jumped in with a comment. Marcus looked at Leah from the side of his eye but saw her only scratching her arm with three long fingernails.

'Oh,' said Lucie Bastable hesitantly – 'thank you.' The air in the room seemed to turn solid. No one spoke for several seconds.

'Yes. I know it's perhaps a dodgy area, but listeners do like the idea of - ah – Two Counties as part of their family. In fact,' Greg went on, leaning back in his chair, 'I've seen some research which shows that they rather like it if they see their local station as a kind of soap opera.'

What? said Marcus Shipley's face, scrunching up into lines with incredulity.

'So – and I hope this is not being too controversial – you know, I think you and Giles flirt rather well together. There's a chemistry there.'

Greg grinned broadly, hoping to take some of the daring out of his comment.

Marcus gave his superior a look and didn't care what he read into it. He wondered what the hell he was up to. Was he mad or just a totally insensitive cretin?

'Greg!' said Sonia in protest. Busy Ian continued to doodle a flying dragon on his notepad. Leah Caighton looked at a poster about BRBC's target audience on the wall opposite her. No one read what she was thinking because no one dared to look in her direction now, not even Marcus.

'I wouldn't call it flirting, Greg…' said an abashed Lucie, doing everything she could not to look at Leah. Sonia sent Greg the filthiest look she could muster and tutted, hoping this would distract him into looking her way: she didn't care that she was only at the station on temporary assignment. He was dead right of course, but he didn't have to be such a prat as to say it here of all places. But Greg McKenzie, seemingly oblivious to the reaction to one of his pet theories of radio, was determined to establish the fact that this was an important point.

'Okay, look,' he said, as Sonia tutted loudly a second time, 'It doesn't matter what you call it, just keep doing what you're doing – it works, it's strong.' If nothing else he would flatter Lucie into submission. 'You just sound as though you like each other is all I'm really saying and it comes over really well.'

Shame there's no one listening to TCR at ten-to-six in the morning to hear it, Marcus wanted to say, but he wasn't going to do was hurt Lucie's feelings for anything. He silently thanked McKenzie for again showing everyone what a prick he was, thus giving him ammunition to store away for a big laugh with Big Dave later on.

The meeting was nearly over. There wasn't that much to discuss as a group. A genuine consensus would have been positive for Lucie: she was doing well. She was in her mid-twenties, had a fetching voice for radio and displayed an innocence and warmth that might take her a long way. The group would all have agreed with Greg on that. Even Marcus, in a better mood and sober knew that even if she'd never have the weight to do Breakfast or Drive-Time, she would be pushing Noona, Lynda and Jim for one of their positions in the next three or four years or so if she stuck around. And we'd get there quicker, he thought, if we were all brave enough to make some constructive criticism of her in these meetings.

As the group broke, Greg slalomed in between a mess of chairs to catch a word with Leah but as he went to open his mouth her back had already disappeared out the door. Lucie Bastable went back to the newsroom to get ready to go out to interview a group of cyclists who were about to take off for Indonesia to raise money for charity. She felt reasonably pleased with herself. But Leah Caighton – why was she at the meeting with a face like thunder?

She thought there was an on-air chemistry there with Giles too – was that it? Was she jealous? She couldn't be: Leah was drop dead gorgeous and beside her Lucie felt about twelve. But people were weird; working in local radio taught her that. Overall, the chemistry-with-Giles compliment pleased her a lot. It was like a notch on her broadcasting belt. But it was a total embarrassment for Greg to mention it in public, even if it was great to get such support from on high.

A short way across the newsroom, Marcus noticed her smiling as she grabbed her jacket off the back of her chair but didn't think she was smug. He only wished she had a smile like that for him. That lucky bastard Giles, he thought and went searching through the crowded waves of cyberspace looking for ghosts.

9

Easy Come, Easy Go

When she got the idea, she couldn't believe it hadn't come to her sooner.

There was one useful thing about Giles, thoughtless egotistical bastard though he was: since they got together he'd always been free with his personal information. He frequently left his bank statements lying around at home, let her borrow his debit and credit cards and told her all his passwords if she ever asked for them. Stupid, Giles, you should never give away information like that – not even to me. There's an irony there, she thought: maybe he was free and easy like that with his girlfriends because he was so closed up verbally when you needed him to show you his affection or his supposed love.

She moved across the room to the computer with haste. You're just not tough enough sometimes, she thought, or smart enough, even though you were always told you were. She knew his Biscali username and password and using those she could read his emails and find out what he was bloody up to. She logged on and found the website in her favourites and typed in Giles' information. Her heart stopped when she saw his most recent message. A Catherine Garner had sent him something with the message title, 'Meeting.' Heart now in mouth, she opened it with a click, and read:

Hi Sexy Radio Man

I'm still fine for tonight. I'll be there before you. The Coffee Shack, still, right? Don't fret, I'll find it. I'm all set. Can't wait to see you. You got my number if there's an emergency.

Love

Catherine

X

She threw the mouse at the desk and stood up sending the chair flying. The fucking treacherous, deceitful, shithead. She rushed out of the flat, wanting only to get into her car and drive somewhere and think. She drove to the coast, stopping only to buy petrol. Several times she had to tell herself to stop grinding her teeth as she drove. She didn't listen to music – she was too unhappy. She drove to the sea at Marcham, the smallest of Bilt's seaside towns, and sat in the car for a long time on a road just off the parade. Eventually she went for a walk along the promenade. There was still plenty of daylight at nearly eight o'clock. Most of the Bank Holiday crowds had gone but the pavements still seemed full: families eating chips in polystyrene cartons; young blokes and older ones drinking beer in cans. The gift shops looked cheaper and shoddier than she'd ever seen them, and the amusement arcades were loud and depressing. After a hundred metres she crossed the street to the beach. Over the sea wall the tide was out and the sand – it was more like mud - stretched out for miles. A few children were milking the last of the daylight throwing beach stones or scraping the sand with driftwood, but it was mostly deserted. She decided to drive back to Barton Townes.

When she arrived at the flat at around nine, Sonia was sitting behind the glowing screen of her computer. Leah didn't mind her flatmate using it even though it was parked in her own bedroom.

'Hi,' said Sonia. 'My laptop's buggered again. Sorry.' Leah looked a little abashed, knowing that Sonia would have come back from work to find the mouse hanging over the desk and the chair lying on its side where she'd thrown it. It had taken the waste basket with it too, spilling cotton buds, cotton wool balls and all sorts of detritus across the floor. She saw that Sonia had picked it all up and set the bedroom straight. Leah was flustered by this. She should have apologised, but she didn't want to get into a conversation about how she was feeling or a confessional about her and Giles. She felt she looked a total mess as well.

'I'm just finishing,' said Sonia, typing at a frantic speed.

'No, go ahead,' said Leah. 'Have ten minutes at least - I'm going to get cleaned up.'

She went into the kitchen to make a drink. She put the kettle on then went straight to the bathroom and got into the shower. She had to come out looking as normal as she possibly could. Perhaps Sonia had been too preoccupied emailing people to notice that anything was wrong.

Poor Leah, thought Sonia, firing off another email to the background hiss of the shower. She's in such a mess and she won't let me in. Not that she cared so much about that. Leah was okay but she was quite hard to like: she was often unpredictably moody and spent a lot of time away at Giles' place. She was good at her job, but wasn't one of the core of young workers who often went pubbing, clubbing and eating together. She probably never would be. It was no fun sharing a flat with her; Sonia started to think that she should begin looking for another place to live. She logged off and went to the kitchen to make a cup of tea.

Leah, coming out of the shower, didn't want any in the event. She went straight to her room, shut the door and took over the computer.

She had doubts about many things but few now that it was time to start looking for another job. She typed in the code for the internal BRBC staff vacancies site and had a look at what was out there.

10

Giles Tells It Like It Is

Tuesday May 3rd

Marcus Shifley nipped into the Ops Room next to Studio 2 to see if Leon wanted to come to a lunchtime birthday drink and sandwich for Sophie Land, one of the reporters. At that moment, Leon was fully absorbed in producing the show, following the conversation Giles was having with a caller on the subject of the local rat population. Marcus stood next to Leon and watched the great Giles McAndrew in action through the studio window. He saw a slim guy in black, better dressed and better looking than the rest of the male presenter-hood combined. Even sitting down he looked tall. Giles' face was full of concentration as he rounded up the conversation and clicked-in a jingle.

'Giles McAndrew, the Breakfast Show on Two Counties Radio, six 'til nine, every weekday morning.'

'Okay, it's eight-to eight on this miserable spring morning. It's cold and it's rainy, which – ah- is a terrible cue for the next item as we head up to the news: Global Warming. Will Tandridge is the director of the Springwatch project for our region, the coastal-east midlands. Morning, Will. It's that time again – doesn't' seem like a year since we were discussing Springwatch last, well, year...'

Marcus hated the way Giles said 'eight-to-eight'; like it was some unique McAndrew signature or something.

'Morning, Giles. No, it doesn't.'

'So. Spring 2006 – did it come early this year?'

'Yes, we think so. We've again seen birds migrating here earlier than was the case a few years ago, and budding was again early this year.'

'So this cold weather doesn't put you off the idea that climate change is actually happening – you're convinced.'

'If you look at average temperatures for the UK, five of the last six years have been well over the average since 1900. So yes, I'm pretty convinced.'

'But there is some good news in this for us, Will, is there not?'

'Well...'

'Gardeners – and we have millions of 'em here in Bart and Bilt – can enjoy the fact that their plants and flowers are getting into bloom earlier than ever - so they can brighten our lives up with them too, can't

they, as we go about our business? Hanging baskets appearing earlier than usual, yes, cheering up the high street?'

'Yes, that is true, Giles, but-'

'And we'll have a longer growing season won't we? And a chance to grow Mediterranean-style vegetables and fruit? Lemon trees in Barton Townes – I rather like the sound of that, Will.'

'Well, of course we won't be able to do that any time soon- climate change isn't happening that fast...'

'Yes and there's the flooding too, isn't there.'

'The ice caps do seem definitely to be melting, and in time the sea level will rise...'

'Which is going to be curtains for us, isn't it, living as we do in the lowest lying land in the UK.'

'Yes, Giles, if we don't do more to protect the environment we could well be in for some seriously sticky times ahead.'

'We might become pretty good at producing rice though...'

'Ha-ha, there is that, Giles, yes, but it won't be doing the potato crop any favours.'

'...and we'll be rowing everywhere instead of polluting the environment with our cars.'

'In the flooded bits of the UK I should think there's a good chance of that, yes.'

'Which suggests that our rowing chances in the 2050 Olympics should be even stronger than they are now...'

'I can't see why not, Giles, ha-ha.'

'But more seriously, the effects of global warming, if we don't all get our act together, will be pretty catastrophic – the scientists haven't changed their minds since we last spoke...'

'Oh, yes indeed and no they haven't. In the Thames Valley, for example, rising water levels will threaten the very existence of London as our capital city. And the cost of moving the seat of government and millions of people to higher ground would, in those circumstances, be absolutely enormous.'

'So we should all stop moaning about our Council Tax, Will, yes?'

'Well, some consideration of our possible future might just help us to put some of our troubles aside for seeming just that little bit petty.'

'And better still, you and I, William, and many of our listeners will be dead when this all happens, ay...'

'Um, probably.'

'That's a relief then...well, great talking to you again, Will – and do I take it you still want our listeners to contact you with sightings of animals and insects, and plants and trees budding and leafing, yes?'

'Oh, very much so, yes. The number to call is: 0299 445445 or they can log on to our website, Springwatcheast.co.uk.'

'Brilliant, Will. I'll be in touch as soon as my spring flowers start to get themselves going. Or rather, my gardener Maurice will – he's much more aware of this stuff than I am.'

'Ha-ha, thanks, Giles.'

'Thanks for coming on, Will, talk again soon, I hope.'

'I hope so too – bye.'

'Oooaaa-kay then: the Springwatch number is...0299...'

'How does he bloody get away with it?' said Marcus, who'd always had trouble in trying to understand the presenter's popularity. He had an image that was part-playboy, part-Terry Wogan – and no one liked Wogan any more, did they? No one in the newsroom except for Jane, Noona, Sonia, Daisy, Lynda and Lucie. Why did all the women like bloody Wogan? He didn't understand it.

Leon wasn't ready to listen: he was still concentrating hard on the show, where at five-to-eight Giles' energy levels were still high, though they had peaked. He clicked the mouse on a thirty-second trailer for Jim Johnson's afternoon show and took a momentary rest.

'Hang on a minute...Giles?'

'Yes, Leon...'

'You need to fill in for about 90 seconds until the news. Then after the sport, when we go to the segment on pigeon control, steady down, yeah? A little at least.'

'Got you.'

Leon clicked out of radio contact with Giles and attended to Marcus's point.

'The thing is,' he said, leaning back in his blue swivel chair, 'he's popular. If you don't like what he does, go look at his ratings. And he's sharp. Did you hear him thinking on his feet, there? He doesn't sit at home writing it all down. And he doesn't take liberties all the time. He only gets a bit dangerous when he's in a bad mood. It's just that he's been in one all week.'

'Must be his time of the month,' said Marcus, scowling. He started to set off for the newsroom. Leon stopped him.

'Now, now. And look, cheer up - you don't think I'd enjoy doing the show as much as I do if he was just an ego, do you?'

Marcus supposed not. He was disappointed. It was bad enough that Giles had a woman like Leah at his constant disposal; the idea that he might be something more than a lucky, egotistical wanker was enough to ruin his whole day. He killed it off before it took a hold on his mind and went back to the newsroom to write a couple of trails for Lucie.

11

Giles and Catherine Eat Out

Tuesday May 2nd

By the time Giles met up with Catherine at The Coffee Shack in Noreham he was desperate to put a floor under his slide down.

The venue was good for a couple of reasons: firstly, he wasn't so well known in Bilt's cathedral county town – he couldn't afford to be distracted by some old dear recognising him however remote the chance - and secondly, he was fed up with same old-same old Barton Townes. He wanted to get away for awhile.

It was very good of Cath to travel up. He didn't want to go down to London in midweek; he'd been feeling drained of energy since Sunday and didn't have what it took to go down and back in an evening - not the way he was feeling right now.

Since Monday morning when he realised Leah wasn't coming back, Giles had been holding on to the idea of seeing Catherine again like a life belt in a rolling sea. On Monday night he couldn't concentrate on the TV and found himself thinking about his cousin and saying, 'She represents the good times in my life.' He heard himself say it, though, and thought, I sound pathetic.

'Giles, get a grip - there's never been much wrong with your life.' he said aloud as he rubbed his tired eyes.

But the malaise that began on Sunday morning was swamping him by Tuesday evening as he drove out to Noreham. He hadn't been able to reach Leah to plead his case. He'd been phoning her constantly but kept getting her messaging service. He suspected that she'd bought a new phone. It would be typical of her. If she said she never wanted to see him again, then to start with at least, she'd do everything she could to make that happen.

He'd called at her flat in Barton Townes four times, but each time, she wasn't there. He carefully considered the idea of parking outside and waiting for her to come back but decided against it just as he resisted the temptation to knock at her door and interrogate Sonia Van Huisten. That would have been demeaning. He hadn't tried hard to work out where she was. She was bloody minded enough to go check into a bed and breakfast to avoid him. And he wasn't going to crawl, he told himself. Not on his hands and knees, anyway. Then he told himself he would beg her to come back if he had to.

He'd got fed up with telling himself things. But he was determined to soldier on and battle through this. But really, carrying the burden alone was too hard. It was time for someone else to carry a share of it for him if they could and would, if only for a while.

Trying to see Leah at work had been a non-starter. Leon told him about her turning up for Lucie's review meeting on the Monday before disappearing for the rest of the day; the news turned the hair on the back of his neck into a field of frozen erections. Today, not finding her in the newsroom after his show he'd wanted to ask Simone if she knew of her whereabouts, but was too embarrassed. He was Leah's boyfriend; he was supposed to know where she was at all times. He found out she'd rung in sick. Leon had told him. He didn't like Leon knowing about his private life, but in order to find out where Leah was, he'd to open up to him and admit that there was a problem.

The fact that Giles could carry on working through all this was a blessed relief. Getting up in darkness wasn't great when you were feeling low but once he'd opened up the station and got the running order for his show up on the screen in front of him, he slipped into the routine he'd worn like a skin for five years and just rolled forward. Once on the air at six, he was live to the people of Bartonshire and Bilt so he just had to plunge in and be professional. He wondered how long he could keep it up, though, if this went on. After nine he was free for the rest of the day. Monday had been full of wide empty spaces of time and so had today. Tonight he had Catherine to look forward to, but after that? Wednesday, Thursday, Friday? They were like nightmares you knew were coming.

He had just one thing to cling to: cousin Catherine. He was desperate for the evening to arrive. It promised so much: seeing her would be great in itself; she might have a big idea for winning her back or just getting her to contact him, and there was his gift project too. She was bringing a big sample of her work up for him to look at and he was going to pick one. His feelings for Leah and his excitement at the thought of her being pleased with him again fired up his determination. He wasn't going to give in to her loss of faith in him. He was a winner and always had been; he had to trust that he could prove it again.

The one single thing that had fallen right was being able to organise the meeting with Catherine so easily. He'd looked at her website over and over again in the huge empty spaces of daytime he'd had to fill and couldn't get over how impressive it all was, how impressive her career had grown to be. She painted in oils, said the text, specialising in 'abstract expressionism of the now'. He didn't know what that meant, but he made his mind grip the phrase 'smooth swathes of warm colour' and, studying the paintings online, agreed with it. The reviews on the site were amazing but they were all full of guff like 'Lang's languid brushwork describes an ample fetish for life as lived' and 'Lang distances herself from new- Gesturalism...' - it nearly drove him crazy. But he laughed at the fact that this was Catherine they were talking about. Little Cath Garner.

The paintings impressed him too; he may not have understood them but they were undoubtedly attractive. He liked the big coloured backgrounds and the way she added squares, rectangles or circles in contrasting colours, either in lines, wavy or straight, or shaded in, putting them always off to one side or in a corner. He was particularly taken with one painting, *2003 – Indentation II, a* wash of pale maroon and dark purple swirls that sent him into an almost trance-like state. He couldn't have told someone why he liked it; he just did. He wanted to buy it, but it was presented on the site as an example of a Catherine Lang success. It had already been sold for $8000 US in March 2005. It would be worth even more now probably. *Eight thousand dollars!* That was a tidy sum.

So it was turning out to be a great idea, buying 'a Lang' as a big anniversary present for Leah. The price tags were a bit of a shock, though. However, after taking a deep breath, he decided he would bite the bullet. Was she worth two or three thousand pounds worth of his money? If he won Leah back, the outlay would be worth every single penny twice or three times over. And he was sure she'd like one of these. She'd dragged him around enough galleries on holiday the last two summers to know that unless his memory wasn't playing tricks: she loved this sort of modern stuff.

He kept his thinking focussed on Catherine as he drove down the Noreham road out of BT, trying to stay positive. His choosing her as a confidante was perfect: she was a blank background on which to present his problem; she was smart - she had to be, she was an artist, for Christ's sake (and anyway he could tell she was intelligent from her internet picture) - and she was completely detached from TCR, Barton Townes and indeed, his whole adult life. If anyone could give him good advice, she could.

At the major roundabout on the outskirts of Noreham, Giles started to feel pain in the throat each time he swallowed. But as he came into the town centre, feelings of nervousness began to take over. He didn't think he would be tense about seeing Catherine again but he was. Once they met, though, it wouldn't be awkward, he was sure of it. Meeting people never bothered him: seeing old friends, making new friends, talking to strangers or strangers who were fans, it was all the same to him. He thrived on constant contact with people.

He walked down the high street to the restaurant after parking up, pushing all negative thought to the back of his head. I need to get control of my life again, he told himself; it's the loss of control that's doing my head in. Then as he looked up for The Coffee Shack's sign, a slim smiling face bordered by long straight chestnut hair came bearing down on him and made him stop.

'Gilles?'

As soon as he heard the woman pronounced his old name in the French way with a sliding 'G' and no hint of an 'S', the shock of new recognition began. Then he recognized her face from the website: the hair and the thick eyebrows and the friendly smile flashing even teeth. It was almost like meeting a famous person in the flesh. Sometimes they were a disappointment up close, but not Catherine.

'Catherine,' he started to say but had the word crushed in half by her huge hug right there on the street. It was fine; he didn't care what people thought about that; they could go to hell if they didn't like it.

'Wow! Gilles! It's you!' she said, and laughed and hugged him again and the way she held on to him, then looked at him and squeezed his arm, he knew that he'd done the right thing in making this night happen. She looked hard at him, smiling.

'You look...worried,' she said, her hands still holding both his forearms.

'Oh,' said Gilles, trying to make light of it, 'do I? No, I'm fine, I'll tell you all about it when we get inside.'

'And what's this?' she said, touching the plaster on his cheek.

'Oh, nothing. I cut myself cleaning my teeth.'

'Ha-ha-ha.'

They went inside. Giles steered them away from the window on the off-chance that someone would recognise him. They found a nice-looking table in the far corner and Giles began to relax. There was a big window right behind them but it looked out on a side street. Then he realised how vain he was being and felt a dab of shame as they sat down.

'Gilles, God, let me look at you! You look great – apart from the worry, ha-ha. No, you look healthy, like you're doing really well.'

'Thanks.'

'Oh, but except for that plaster – what happened there? Come on, tell me truthfully, if you can stand to.'

'I'll tell you that later too.'

'Okay...'

There was a sudden gap in the conversation. Giles cursed himself for not telling her about everything straight away. Why didn't he? Then Catherine filled the gap.

'Isn't this funny, seeing each other again after all this time?' she said, touching his arm.

'Yeah, isn't it,' he said, smiling, 'and you've got the accent!'

'Well, of course, I'm Canadian now!' she said laughing.

Giles couldn't help laughing back. He'd only just re-met her but she seemed like a lot of fun. In the odd dark moment before falling asleep the last two nights he imagined he might be making a huge mistake and be about to meet some kind of moody artist but she wasn't like that at all.

'But I like it.' He looked at her and shook his head. Yes it was strange to see her again but so great. 'It's so good to see you again, Cath – I can't believe it.'

'Thanks – hey, no one calls me Cath except my mum - but you can!' She laughed again. 'And you're so damn thin, Gilles, I'm so jealous, just look at you!'

Sitting opposite each other at a restaurant table wasn't ideal but they got the general picture of each other pretty clearly, checking out their ageing faces and bodies.

'I knew you'd be tall. You always were when we were young,' said Catherine.

'No, you were the same height as me...' Giles left his sentence hanging and thought for a moment or two - '...weren't you?'

'No, shorter, and you should have remembered that,' said Catherine.

'I'm sorry, ha-ha.'

'It's okay.' It was smiles all round. Giles began to feel really good.

'Can I call you "G" like I used to?'

'Of course you can.'

'I'm not sure I'm ready for "Giles" yet.'

'It doesn't matter. Call me what you like.'

Because of his long legs, their knees touched under the table. He liked the fact that she didn't move hers away. He wanted them to be as they'd been as kids, even though it was silly to expect it after all this time – after they'd inhabited two different worlds for so long.

'Oh, thank you.'

The bread, oil and olives had arrived. Giles' concentration was all over the place. Here he was, excited to be with Catherine again but he kept thinking about Leah every other minute. And he kept thinking he should ring Leon about the show next morning. He couldn't concentrate properly. It was enough to drive you crazy, he thought, which made him feel better, because, he reasoned, if I'm aware of the fact that I might be going crazy, then I can't be.

'G, I can't believe you're on the radio! I love it.'

'How did you hear it?'

'The Internet – what are you, stupid?'

'Oh, yeah,' he said, though he still wasn't sure how she'd managed it.

'You sound so great, you know? I can't believe how well you handle yourself.' She was so excited to see him it almost bowled him over.

'What, you still think I'm stupid?' he said, smiling, revelling in her praise.

'No!' she said, whacking him on the hand. 'I mean you're so damned professional – and you've got one sexy voice, do you know that?'

He felt he may have actually coloured up a little, but he loved her saying that, not least because the women who normally told him were always way past fifty.

'Sorry, I'm making you blush – hey, let's order.'

So they ordered and ate olives, drank a glass of wine each, even though they were both driving, and talked about their families and other soft topics, apart from Catherine's art, which of course was a serious subject. But once their main course plates had been taken away, Giles knew he couldn't wait any longer.

'Cath, I need your advice.'

'Okay...' She looked doubtful suddenly. '...is this what you're worried about?'

'Yeah.'

'Are you sure you want to ask me?' she said very deliberately, as if she were giving herself time to think about it as well as Giles.

'I think so...' He knew so. 'Yes, I do, unless you don't want – '

'No – let's go ahead.' She edged closer to him, gearing herself up to listen and concentrate. There was a determined edge in her voice too, as if she really was fine with the situation. Giles heard it and responded.

'Okay, get ready, here goes...'

'Shoot,' said Catherine, 'I'm all ears.'

The dessert menus came, but it only halted Giles for a few seconds. He began.

'You know I have this relationship with Leah...'

Catherine nodded, her intelligent face scrutinising his.

'...well, we had a massive fight on Sunday. That's how I did this,' said Giles, pointing to the sticking plaster on his cheekbone. 'She doesn't want to speak to me – she says it's over.' He paused and looked at Catherine in case she wanted to ask a question. She didn't appear to, so he carried on.

'It was over a number of things. We…fight quite a lot, because, y'know, we're two strong people who think we know what we want…egos, I suppose is the problem. And Leah doubts, y'know, what I think about her. And so she can get jealous sometimes and she's jealous now about a girl at work. She got it into her head that I was attracted to her. And then…'

Giles was talking fast and needed to stop and take a breath. He let out a big sigh, puffing out a long breath like he was a giant blowing a storm up on an ocean.

'…and then came your letter.'

Catherine looked confused. Giles carried on with the explanation.

'I printed off your email where you said, do you remember? "I can do what you want…I understand the need for secrecy…you have a great radio voice…"' He looked at his cousin. She was looking down at her placemat with a furrowed brow. She looked up when she heard Giles' pause.

'She didn't think…?'

'She does. She's read it all wrong - she only read the first part of it, the first page. She doesn't know you're my cousin.'

'But we did that so that she'd get the surprise!'

'I know…'

'Oh, I'm so sorry. What did it say again? Break it to me gently.'

'"I can do what you want", "understand the need for secrecy" "you sound so sexy on the radio…"'

'Oh, my God - I'm really sorry if it was my fault, I never thought for a minute-'

'I know, I know. It really isn't your fault, don't worry. It's Leah. I couldn't believe she could be so stupid. And I should never have printed the bloody thing off in the first place.'

'Why did you?'

'Why? Because I deleted the email so Leah wouldn't see it but wanted a copy for myself so I could see what I wrote to you and what you wrote back.'

'Why did you want to delete it? Because Leah-'

He finished the sentence for her.

'Reads my email. Or rather, uses my computer sometimes when she's over. It was just a precaution. But now…'

'Oh, viage, viage…' said Catherine quietly.

Giles didn't understand the word but he got the sentiment.

'You know,' she said, 'it was just Leah's mind picking up on what she was worried about – what she was scared of. You know, in those situations, when we're reading our partner's mail, we're frightened we're going to find something terrible so if there's anything that can fit the paradigm we just believe it, it's our deepest fear, isn't it?'

Giles looked vacantly back at Catherine; now it was an English word he wasn't positive he understood. He was past caring whether he looked dim or not.

'Fits the what?' he said. Catherine started laughing. He laughed too.

'The paradigm...if there's anything there that fits into our, um, suspicious way of thinking, we see that and nothing else.'

'Thank you,' said Giles. Catherine smiled back at him. 'Have you done that?'

'Of course – haven't you?'

'Believe it or not, Catherine, I've never been the type for reading my girlfriends' mail.'

'What, never?'

'Nope.'

He wasn't lying; he assumed that if a girlfriend was having an affair, he wouldn't need to read her mail to find out. But this made him focus again on what he needed Catherine for. He gripped himself and let go.

'So, look, Catherine, I need you to help me work out what to do. I haven't been able to contact her, she's gone to ground. But the last time she spoke to me she said it was over. I don't know whether to leave her a message telling her about the surprise before we get to the anniversary day – Saturday - or not. There's a chance that if I don't do something, Saturday will be too late.'

'You mean she'll be gone for good or something?'

'Exactly.'

Catherine looked at Giles doubtfully, then looked down into her placemat. She picked up her wine and took a sip. Giles tried to read her face, but couldn't.

'Wow,' she said and picked up her glass again. She looked terribly serious, suddenly. Her pretty forehead wrinkled up into a little field with four deeply ploughed furrows.

'Cath, I admit it - I'm desperate; I just don't know what to *do*...' he said, expressing his exasperation with hands wide on the table. This was so hard for him. He wanted to say, 'You have to help me' again, but he felt exposed enough already. He felt like he'd just given up two pints of blood.

'Oh, G...' She reached over and mussed his hair affectionately. Then something made her look over Giles' shoulder at the window. It was partly because a shaft of low evening sun was suddenly shining into the restaurant, and partly because a woman's face was staring at her through the glass.

Straight-Shooting Cousin

'The worse thing is, I didn't see it coming,' said Giles. 'I kind of thought I had everything under – y'know – control - that I understood her, I mean…but I didn't.'

'That's an easy mistake you know, Gilles.' She ignored the woman at the window.

'Is it?'

'Oh, yeah. When Michael walked out on me I was packing the bags for our vacation. He came home and said, "What are you doing? Did you really think we were still going?" He'd told me the night before that he was having an affair – and I thought it wasn't important to him and that he still wanted to be with me. Then he said, "It's over." I must have been out of my tiny mind.'

She carefully looked over at the window again. The face had gone.

'That's what Leah said to me! Just like that: "It's over."'

'Well, what he actually said was worse: "It's over, kid," he said, as if I was about sixteen and he was Humphrey Bogart. We couldn't have children, you know.'

Giles was excited by Catherine's story and the fact that it was so easy for her to talk about something that must have been traumatic. He wasn't keen on telling people what he had for breakfast, let alone spilling his guts on the subject of his private life.

'Yeah, I think my mother mentioned it. I'm really sorry about that. Was it…?' He wouldn't normally have been this brave, but Catherine was beginning to rub off on him. She was more direct than the people he normally talked to.

'It was me.'

'Oh, I'm sorry. I shouldn't have asked.'

'Yes you should. I don't mind. And anyway,' she said, looking calm and in total control, patting his hand, 'you're family, G.'

'Where are you staying tonight – you're not driving back? Sorry, I should have thought - you could have stayed with me, I've got a spare room – you still can.'

Catherine didn't hesitate.

'Can I? That'd be great. We haven't even started trying to sort you out yet. And I can show you the canvases I've brought with me.'

'You think we still should? You must be an optimist.'

'Yeah, I'm an optimist, Gilles, and you might as well become one too. You're not going to get Leah back by sinking into the ground.'

'Okay - I'm going to get her back,' he said, giving out a gallows laugh.

'That's it. Take that attitude and you will…Have you seen her since Sunday? Have you tried to call her?'

'Of course, but she won't answer her phone.'

'But you work together, right?'

'She wasn't at work yesterday and she stayed right out of my way this morning deliberately.'

'Can she do that? At the BRBC?'

'They're very good like that at the BRBC - it's not exactly a high powered corporation.'

'It's not?'

'Not at local radio level it's not.'

'Oh – so they're covering for her?'

'Of course – people go off sick all the time. The staff are very good - everyone pitches in.'

'So where is she at night?'

'I don't know – her sister's maybe.'

'Why do you think that?'

'She's done it before and I know what she's like - when things go badly for her she runs or hides out of the way. And she and her sister are very close.'

'And you haven't been over there?'

'No. It's too far to go chasing her over there – it's fifty miles away. More.'

'But you…'

'Yeah, I've been going out of my mind. But I'm not driving a round trip of a hundred miles to find she's not there or won't see me.'

'It might be what she wants.'

'No, I don't think so. That's now how she works. I don't think so, anyway. And even if it is what she wants, I'm not going to do it.'

'So, what's your thinking - that if you get back together again you need to do it on equal terms, right?'

'Exactly. That's better than I could have put it. But I don't know… how long this can go on for. For all I know, she could be about to chuck in everything and leave Barton Townes. For all we know, she might already have left.'

He watched Catherine furrow her brow in concentration, her big brown eyes staring intently at the brick-walled interior of the café, trying to find a solution for him.

'Boy you have got some hard thinking to do,' she said.

'I know, I know. That's why I need you to help me.'

'I don't want to worry you, G, but I think you might need a lot more than just me.'

He hoped she was kidding as he summoned the waitress. When he paid the bill, he got up from the table feeling full, then realised he hadn't really tasted his food.

Giles, driving home to Corumby slowly so that he didn't lose his cousin, yawned several times and worried about sleep. With a four-thirty start each work morning, his iron rule was to be asleep by ten. If they stayed up late talking he'd be a hopeless wreck and the show would be terrible. The last two nights had been bad enough, tossing and turning, dreaming strange dreams and waking before the alarm. It was already ten-past-eight. Still, in his own house he could make his excuses and go to bed. Cath would understand. The normal rules of politeness wouldn't apply.

As he signalled to turn right up the lane to The Barn House, he realised that he felt calmer. Maybe it was the tiredness but maybe it was Catherine. As he checked the rear view mirror to see that she was right behind him, he realised how pretty she now was and how well-proportioned - even though she was tall - and how well she dressed. He didn't really know any arty-farty people, but he liked her blue Chinese-style jacket over a t-shirt – or was it Japanese? - her shiny blue jewellery and her embroidered denims. No one at the station dressed like that.

Catherine loved the house, or said she did.

'Mmm, you've really done a nice job,' she said, walking through the hall into the huge kitchen. 'Is this Leah's doing?'

'No! We don't live together – and anyway, give me some credit. I'm not that dumb – I don't need a woman to pick me a kitchen.'

'Very nice – Scandinavian kitchens we call these back home.'

'Yeah, it is - a Swedish company did it.' He wanted to tell her that he chose it because it matched Leah's cool and elegant looks, but he couldn't. Back in 2004 she was hardly his one, true woman of The Barn anyway. The thought that he should marry her if he got her back, shot into his brain like a lightning bolt from outer space. It shocked him. God. Marry her?

'You keep it really tidy, G. I imagined something messier.'

Catherine hadn't noticed Giles' temporary mental displacement.

'Oh, well, I have a woman who comes in and cleans once a week.'

'Don't tell me, Leah?'

Giles laughed, ironically.

'Oh, ha-ha-ha.'

His cousin had just triggered another memory: that she used to make him laugh when they were kids. It was funny to him how the grown up girlfriends he'd had never had and to be truthful, didn't now.

Catherine smiled back at Giles, trying to show him that he shouldn't take his situation as matter-of-life-and-death serious. They stayed smiling at each other for several moments. Giles wanted to reach out and hold her hand. He looked at Cath and saw approval of him in her face. It gave him a lot of pleasure and some reassurance. They were about to become friends again; that was great. A simple thing amongst the vast complications of Leah.

'So what am I going to do about this woman, Cath?' he said as he slumped down on the kitchen sofa, Catherine mimicking him unconsciously a second later.

'Okay, first, you got to tell me honestly what you've done to her – then we can measure how big the problem is. Then we might be able to see what we should do.'

'I laughed at her.' Giles told her about Sunday's row, tipping everything he could remember about it out of his head, leaving no detail out except for how he felt about Leah's nakedness. Then he asked her a question.

'How much of this is jealousy, Cath? - because that at least shows that her feelings are deep for me, doesn't it?'

'Well, you know I don't know her, Giles, but it sounds to me that she is *very* insecure about you. I'm going to ask you some mean questions.'

'Go on.'

'How do you treat her?'

'What do you mean – am I nice to her?'

'Kind, considerate, thoughtful – do you give her time, do you encourage her in her career – all those things?'

'Christ, I try to be. I'm...we do things she likes doing a lot.'

'A lot?'

'Sometimes...as much as we do things I like doing.'

'Do you take her out?'

'Of course! We go to the cinema, shopping, restaurants. Occasionally we go to the races.'

'Do you shout at her?'

'Not unless she shouts at me first.'

'Really?'

'Really!'

'Do you hit her?'

'No!'

70

'Excessive sexual demands? Or strange ones?'

'What? No! What do you think I am?'

'Does she give you what you want?'

What? he thought. Then he understood.

'Yes.'

'Do you give her what she wants?'

'Catherine!'

'Don't be such a prude, Gilles, for heaven's sake – do you?'

'Yes.'

'Do you argue about sex?'

Sheesh, he imagined Australians might be like this, but not Canadians.

'Look - I'm an artist, G - we're all like this where I come from, I promise you.'

Giles imagined what she might get up to with her artist friends in Montreal – wild debauched parties? Wife swapping, or what was it – Giles had wanted to do a feature on this at TCR but was outvoted – *swinging,* that's what it was called these days. God, he hoped not.

'No, we never argue about sex. We have a good sex life.'

'So you're a normal couple in this respect – this is what I'm trying to establish.'

'Yes.'

'Hey, you don't have to be so bolshy! Don't you know that over half the relationships in Western society break up for sexual reasons?'

'No, I didn't.'

'Haven't you ever done any talk shows on sex?'

'God, no – the listeners don't want to hear about, um, blow jobs at seven o'clock in the morning!'

'Too busy givin' 'em an' getting' 'em, I guess.'

'Catherine!' he said, but laughed along with her. He wished Leah was like this. Giles knew he could be closed up but Leah was worse if anything. He realised suddenly that if he was being honest, they probably didn't talk about sex as much as they should.

'So I'm just getting the sex issue out of the way. I'm trying to see if there's an underlying issue to your problems, a fundamental, that you need to address if you want the relationship to get back on track.'

'Yeah, I understand.'

'So can you see a fundamental problem here?'

Giles was pulled in two directions. He wanted to be absolutely straight with Cath, but as the top presenter on the local radio, he felt that he should be much wiser than this. It showed him how BRBC studiously avoided addressing things that really mattered to people all the time. Great on gardening, rubbish on blow-jobs and matters of the heart. He suddenly felt like a bit of a fool – not so worldly-wise as he liked to think he was. So should I be honest? he asked himself. Can I let go of my pride? He decided he had to. That if he wasn't, his cousin would only see through him and he'd end up looking even more stupid.

'Okay. Look. The problem is that we argue too much. Our relationship is too, um, stormy.'

'Volatile?'

'Yes, volatile. We have great ups but we have bad downs. And I don't know why.'

He watched Catherine's concentration again. She'd picked up one of the cushions and cuddled it as she thought.

'Is it normal to argue?' he said, getting up and starting to pace around.

'Of course it's normal to argue! Michael and I did all the time. Our friends do too – gay couples, straight couples, everyone. It's what you argue about that counts, and how hurt the individual feels when you do it.' Then she stopped and looked Giles in the eye.

'Look. Really, most relationships are about power. You should think about this. If one person in the relationship has too much power over the other, sooner or later there's a good chance that the weaker one is going to rise up one day and say, "enough." Does that ring any bells?'

Giles heart began to sink.

'Yeah, a little.'

'Don't tell me - you're the one that wants the power.'

He didn't answer right away. He thought about the times when Leah got her own way, when she made him suffer. Then he tried to weigh up, essentially, who was in charge in their relationship.

'Yeah, I suppose so.'

'And she makes you fight for the right.'

'For the right?'

'For the right to have power over her...'

'Yeah. She does.'

'Okay,' said Catherine, as if to underline the solution to a Mathematical problem on a blackboard.

'Thanks, Cath – brilliant. So it's my fault. I already feel like shit and you come along and make it worse.'

'No, stop it – you don't see. If you can own up to that, that's half the battle won! Now you go to Leah and tell her what you've learned.'

'And I have to tell her that I'm ready to give ground.'

'Well, obviously! And aren't you?'

Giles stroked his face, ran his fingers over the plaster over the his stitched wounds.

'Gilles, if you're not, then…'

'Then I'd better let her go.'

'You said it.'

'No, you're right.' She was. He knew it. 'I just need to take a moment to, y'know…'

'Assimilate.'

'Whatever.'

Catherine laughed. 'But the present is a good idea too, though. A great idea. Not as important as a revelation of new self-awareness, but still, if she likes it, it'll be a lovely gesture, I think.'

'Do you think?'

'Yeah! And you've such good taste!' She laughed of course, and Giles went and picked up another cushion, moved three steps back, and threw it at her.

Giles watched her take the gesture as it was meant and laughed. At least this has come out of the disaster, he thought. Catherine back in his life.

'Would you like some tea?' he asked her.

'That would be nice.'

He went over to the long counter, put the kettle on and got the other things organised, finding his mind tipping out a conclusion to the evening's proceedings. Well, I got one thing right: I thought. She'd given him a fresh perspective on his relationship. She'd made him feel about fourteen years old, though.

'You're so clever,' he said, after he'd poured boiling water into the teapot. 'And I hate you for it.'

'I don't know about that. I'm a woman who's had one long relationship in her adult life, and that failed.'

'But do you know why it failed?'

'Yeah - we should never have got married.'

'Why did you, then?'

'Because we were young and stupid.'

'What did Michael do?'

'What do you mean, to me, or for a living?'

'A living.'

'He was a theatre set designer.'

'Is he a good one? Successful?'

'Not really.'

'Are you with someone now?'

73

'No.' Her face changed to a frown. Giles saw how little lines had appeared in the corners of her mouth.

'Gilles.'

'Yeah?' he said, feeling his throat. It was okay.

'Does Leah have fair hair? Parted in the middle?'

She must have seen a photo in the hall or was there one in the lounge somewhere? Giles had to stop and think about it.

'And does she have highlights?'

'Yes. But they look natural, I think,' suddenly, instinctively defensive.

'Does she have blue eyes and a kind of snubby nose?'

'What?'

'Quite a wide mouth with nice full lips?'

He looked at his cousin with the most blank expression. Then he nodded.

'I saw her looking through the window at us in the restaurant.'

13

Who Shot the Prairie Dog?

Giles stood in the middle of his kitchen trying to take this in. Leah. Following him?

'And I don't want to worry you, but just as I saw her looking in, I was touching your hair.'

He could no longer quite believe what was happening to him. Where was his luck? It was as if someone had laid a curse on him. A week ago, less, he had been a pretty contented man to whom the fates had been kind: he had a great job; he was healthy; he had a huge chunk of his life still ahead of him and he a good relationship with a beautiful woman. But now it all seemed to have just melted away. The relationship part, anyway. Again he felt the loss of control. Things kept going wrong and he appeared to be completely powerless to stop it.

And how the blazes had Leah known where they were going to be? Was she turning into a witch? He'd told no one about his meeting with Catherine. Oh – he sussed it very quickly – she must have hacked into his email system. Had he fixed the time and place of the meet with Catherine that way? Yes, he had. I should have done it by text, he thought, swearing inside.

Catherine went over to him and put a consoling hand on his shoulder. She would normally have hugged him as she did other people in these situations, but thought she'd better not. If he were crying it would be different. But Giles wasn't even close to letting himself go. He just seemed stunned, and locked up tight with pain and anxiety.

'If you just let it out, you'll be amazed how clearly you're going to be able to think...' She moved her hand to his shoulder blade and rubbed the area affectionately. It was like rubbing a marble statue. Or trying to console James Bond. Here's one who's not a crier, she thought, and felt worry for him growing for the first time that evening.

'Okay, come on,' she said, 'help me get the paintings in from the car.' It was time to try to distract him from the problem for a spell. They could come back to Leah's appearance out the café in a little while.

'Come on, let's go,' she said, tapping his back now.

They brought in four paintings from the back seat of her car. The cloth wrapping on each one was thicker than the actual canvas and frame.

'We'll start with these four - I like these the best,' she said.

They brought them into the lounge where Catherine carefully un-wrapped each one with considered movements of her hands and arms, and propped them against the easy chairs and the sofa in a line.

'Okay, take a look at these babies of mine and give it to me straight.'

Giles sat across from the display on the other sofa. Despite everything, he found himself looking properly, enabling the beauty of form and colour to do its work. He found his eyes moving from one to the other, to the other and to the other, and back again, and his mind becoming slowly absorbed. The more he looked, the more he wanted to keep looking. When he was about to toss the exercise aside and go back to the new development with Leah, he blocked it with the vague feeling that despite her seeing him with Catherine, she was back. Or hadn't gone. He could still win this battle with her. Could still win her over. He knew it. And the painting would help. My God, the paintings, look at them. They're beautiful, he thought.

'I love them.'

'What, all of them?' said Catherine, smiling, encouraging him to disassociate.

'All of them. What's this one called?' he said, going right up to a canvas of melting yellow ochre overlaid with a group of small overlapping circles of dark red on the right-hand side.

'Stand back from it – about eight feet.' She went to the painting, picked it up and held it in front of her, resting the weight of it on her hip.

'There. Look at it now.'

Giles stood up, went and stood behind the sofa and stared at the piece. The rich colour pulled him in to start with; then the circles and then the tear began to insinuate their way into his thought processes. Catherine poked her head around her painting to look at his reaction.

'Like it?'

'Oh, yeah. What's it called again?'

'Oh, sorry.' Catherine looked serious for a moment, and heaved a sigh. '"*Who Shot the Prairie Dog 2*"'

Giles' eyes followed it to the new position Cath place it in against the armchair

'It's a bit obvious, isn't it...' said Catherine, meaning 'arch'.

'Maybe if you live in a mental hospital it is,' said Giles.

'Ha-ha, well - as long as you like it.' She wasn't sure whether she trusted his urgent rush of enthusiasm.

'Like it? I can't believe you're so talented.' He thought about that as an insult. 'Do you know what I mean?'

'I know what you mean,' said Catherine. She picked up *Prairie Dog 2* again and re-positioned it on one of the back sofa cushions and came round to study it, the top half of her hands in tight jean pockets.

'Thank you.' She still looked troubled by her work. 'Do you want it to give to Leah?'

'No, I want it for me. I'll give you any amount of money you like for it.'

'It should cost you six, but you can have it for free.'

'Don't you like it?'

'If you like it, I like it.'

'Don't patronize me, Catherine Garner,' said Giles, but he was smiling kindly when he said it. He was beginning to recover.

'No, I like it – I just prefer *Prairie Dog 3*.'

'You didn't bring that with you, I suppose.'

'No, I couldn't.'

'Why not?'

'I haven't painted it yet.'

'Oh, you artists are such a clever bunch of people, aren't you,' said Giles.

They both laughed again.

'Are you going to choose another one for Leah?'

'You think I still should.' He meant to say, Wasn't it too late? but he was afraid of Cath suddenly telling him it was.

'Yeah. I'm going to take *The Prairie Dog* for me and another one for her. Mind you...'

'Yes?'

'She would love this though. I have no doubt about that.' *Prairie Dog*'s abstract depths were again starting to mesmerise him. 'No doubts at all.'

'What sort of art does she like?' said Catherine, starting to re-wrap the *Prairie Dog*.

'Um – oh, all sorts.' Catherine's face gestured for him to expand but he didn't really know what to say. And he was afraid of talking so as to make a complete idiot of himself.

'Does she have a favourite painter?'

He thought of Picasso but that was only, he realised five seconds later, because she'd dragged him round a museum in Paris a year or so before that was nothing but Picasso. He didn't really know. He made a quizzical face at Catherine.

'Style of painting? Period?' He still looked vacant. She laughed.

'Don't laugh at me.' He was smiling.

'Does she like modern art?'

'Yeah, oh, yeah. I was going to say that, modern art. I'm still a little...you know.'

'I know, that's why I want you to take your time, you don't have to rush.'

'It's alright,' said Giles, still sitting in an attitude of admiration for Catherine's painting. 'I know what I'm doing.'

'How do you know she likes modern art?' said Catherine, a step away from giggling some more.

'We usually go to see modern stuff. Look, we went to see a thing in London, at the new Tate. By that American guy that did the one of the diner at night.'

'Hopper.'

'Yes! That's the one. Hopper. She loved it.'

'So that's why you think she'll like *Prairie Dog 2*?'

'Yep. She'll like it – trust me.'

'But he's not an abstract painter, G,' she said, chuckling to keep him onside.

'Yeah. I know. But it doesn't matter. Just trust me. She'll love your work.'

'And did you like it?'

'What, the Hopper thing?'

'The exhibition, yes.'

'It was okay. I liked the one of the diner. It was very green.' He was smiling, at ease with ignorance. Why should he try to be clever sharing the same room as an expert?

'Very green.' Catherine wanted to laugh really loudly at that but she wasn't sure he could take it.

'Yes, it had a green glow over it. But he's not as good as you, Cath.'

She laughed out loud at that. Was he stringing her along for laughs? Did he know more about art than he was letting on? She didn't know him well enough yet to be sure.

'So here's the key question,' she said, 'Are you really going to take one for Leah?'

'What do you mean?'

Catherine thought she knew now what she wanted to say.

'Do you want me to be honest with you?'

He looked at her in such a way as to suggest he'd strangle her if she was anything but.

'There's no point choosing her a painting if she isn't coming back.'

'You think she might not come back?'

'I think you should be prepared for that.'

'Oh.'

Giles began to well up.

'Does she tell you she loves you?'

'Pretty much.'

'Pretty much?' said Catherine, unimpressed.

They sat down on the floor.

'Pretty much.'

'Okay. I'll take that as a "yes," for the sake of the discussion. If she does, and you don't do anything stupid in between, here's what I'd do. But don't get your hopes up here - I haven't got anything inspirational for you.'

'Just tell me what you think - it'll be a lot better than nothing.'

'Okay. Well, you asked for it. Try to text her and phone her tonight before you turn in. And try her again in the morning. But if she's still blocking you, leave it. Wait it out. See if leaving her to stew for a little while brings her to you.'

'Hah.' Giles' laugh was desert dry.

'Hear me out. See what she does and keep waiting it out. 'Til Saturday. If she hasn't shown up by then, I'd go find her, wherever she is and however long it takes, and give her your present, the painting, or whatever you want to give her. Find her and tell her exactly what you've been going through and, most importantly, how you feel about her. If she won't listen, then sit outside her door and write everything down in a letter and push it through the letter box. And if that doesn't work, then you'll just have to get real and move on. If she won't listen, she either simply doesn't want you any more or clearly isn't the person you should be with.'

Giles stared hard at the French doors, thinking.

'Hmph,' he said.

'You don't like what I said or can't wait until Saturday?'

'Didn't I tell you? I'm the least patient man in the world. That's how I get things done, Cath, and how I got to where I am.'

'But you haven't run after her so far - you've let two days go by...'

'I've phoned her and texted her twenty times, more.'

'But you didn't knock on her door?'

'No.'

'And you haven't got in touch with her sister. Her friends...'

'No.'

'Well, you haven't tried to contact her, then – not seriously.'

'But...but.'

'But what?'

Giles seemed about to burst. Cath waited for a loud explosion, realising the lengths he must have gone to all evening to keep his emotions under control, but it didn't come.

'I'm not sure I can throw myself at her like that.'

'Well, it's up to you, kid.' A little of her sympathy for him began to leak out from the reservoir. Men – so much pride, she thought.

'I'll sleep on it.'

'And you never know, she may come back when you don't expect her to.'

'Yeah, and she'll probably be carrying a gun.'

'Are you serious?'

'No,' he said, and this time they knew they couldn't make a laugh out of it.

Then there was a knock on the door. They looked at one another as if it could only be one person. It was gone nine o'clock. Giles didn't get casual callers at this time of night. He went to the front door, leaving Catherine in the lounge – and opened it.

'Hi, is that your car outside? If it is, you've left your lights on.'

It was Mr Freeman from next door.

'I was out walking my dog. The battery will be flat in the morning.'

'My heart nearly stopped,' said Catherine a little later on in the kitchen. They were sipping some hot chocolate together before going up to bed.

'I nearly crapped myself. Literally,' said Giles. He wanted to laugh, but his laughter muscles were frozen. This still wasn't a time for laugher.

Catherine read a small 'thank you note' Giles had left by the kettle the next morning. It made her smile and then made her drop into a deep pool of reflection. She thought about his description of this girl, Leah, and wondered what she would be like to meet in real life. She thought about his choosing one of her paintings for her and had doubts about the decision all round. And she thought of her own choice of coming to England. But put against her cousin's situation, the decision to venture across the Atlantic Ocean now seemed no more complicated than a walk to the corner out to buy a bag of sugar.

She hadn't meant to wake up on a bright English morning and fill herself with this pessimism. Not when she was so pleased to have got her cousin back. She made herself some breakfast and coffee and switched on the radio while she did it. It was tuned to Gilles' station and there he was, talking to his local people. Gone was the fractured, uncertainly of the night before. Now he was confident, controlled and very much in control. He was good. Serious at one moment, then lighter the next when a change of mood was needed. Slick. Zipping from interview to banter with a weather girl, to directly addressing his audience without a glitch.

He might be in awe of her painting but she didn't have what it took to do his job either. She was proud of him.

She left a note for him, written on the back of his, careful this time not to leave a trail of destruction behind her.

'Thanks for the bed, Gilles. Let me know how things go with Leah. I've left the other paintings for you. I'll need the rest in about a week – do you want to come and meet me in London the weekend after next? If not, I'll come to you and pick 'em up. Keep them safe. Call me later on my cell phone won't you.

Catherine. X.'

She thought one kiss was harmless enough, and anyway, the state the man was in, when he found it and read it later, he'd probably eat it if it meant keeping it out of Leah's sight. She had an image of Leah frantically scrabbling through Gilles's dustbin in the dead of night, torch in hand, filthy faced. She thought again what a mess the two of them were in. She wondered if she would ever see for herself what this girl was like; she wanted to, she thought.

She placed the note on the table and stood for a moment taking in the quiet and the emptiness of a strange kitchen. It was warm and smelled good, coffee and oranges. She listened to the hum of the fridge and watched the sun streaming in through the windows colouring everything a bright golden yellow. Nine o'clock on a spring Wednesday morning. It was time to leave Gilles behind and look after her own situation. She took a quick look around before she left, checking that she hadn't left anything behind.

She thought about his relationship with Leah again and saw that it was doomed. She didn't like the smell of the whole thing, unless Gilles had fed her bad information out of pessimism. She was famous among her tribe of friends back home for being uncannily right about these things. She could feel Leah not returning, and feel her now, already far, far away.

14

Leah's Misery

Wednesday May 3rd

'*Elton John there, with "Philadelphia Freedom." I thought when that started it was going to be the one he did with George Michael. Bob Constable on The Afternoon Show here with you until 4 - my guest today is the Reverend Alan Marlin of St John's, Balby, lovely spot there up in the north of Bartonshire. You an Elton John fan, Alan?*'

'*I quite like him, Bob, yes.*'

'*Do you have a favourite of his?*'

'*"Better Off Dead," I think.*'

'*What, better off dead than have an Elton John favourite, ha-ha?*'

'*Ha-ha, no Bob, a friend of mine had one of his records at college, and it's the one I remember.*'

'*Oh, right. I suppose that's appropriate for you, isn't it, that song?*'

'*How do you mean – oh, right. "Better off dead." Well, actually, Jesus said we should love God so we can have a life lived to the fullest. So...*'

'*And I don't suppose he meant buying lottery tickets and watching Big Brother.*'

'*No, I don't think so, Bob.*'

'*Okay, it's eighteen minutes past one on another glorious early May day here on Two Counties Radio, and in a few minutes it'll be time for Mr Al Green, or to be precise, The Reverend Al Green, which I would say is rather appropriate with my guest today being none other than the Reverend Alan Marlin. But first we're going to do a couple of questions on the phone. So, here we go. First, on line 1, we have Deirdre from Welt-on-Sea. Hi, Deirdre.*'

'*Hi, Bob.*'

'*What are you up to this lunchtime?*'

'*Just making a sandwich.*'

'*What are you putting in it?*'

'*Lemon curd.*'

'*For lunch? Lemon curd?*'

'*I've just had a bag of crisps.*'

'*What flavour?*'

'*Pickled onion.*'

'Ooh, one of my favourites. Right. Deirdre – what's your question for the Reverend?'

'Well I want to ask him – are you there?'

'Yes, hi Deirdre, I'm here.'

'Okay – good. I'd like to know, do you still get a problem with people stealing the lead off your roof? Only I was doing some research in Barton Townes library the other week about my Dad who used to win competitions showing vegetables, and I saw an article in 1969 about the lead being stolen from a lot of church roofs that summer.'

'Well, Deirdre...'

Leah switched the car radio off and drove in silence. Heaven knows why she thought it would distract her from replaying the sight of her boyfriend in a restaurant with another woman. It didn't. The cinema in her head replayed the film again. The pictures tortured her, but she was fatally attracted to the pain at the same time. How dare another fucking woman lay claim to Giles; and how dare she touch him. Only one woman was allowed to touch him like that and it was Leah Caighton, not some desperate, middle-aged hippie slut.

So that was the woman from the email letter. She's a lot older than me, she thought, and was surprised. How could he possibly want a forty-year-old body when he can have mine? But she knew Giles: that bit didn't add up. She bit her lip in annoyance at the thought that he wanted a more mature woman. God, I'm twenty-nine, not seventeen, she said to the cross-examining barrister in her head - and in many ways I'm much more mature than he is. Men could be such kids, even at 39. Neither could this be a question of brains: it was obvious – though a subject they didn't openly discuss – that she was the brighter of the two of them – she had the paper qualifications to prove it. So that's it, she thought: he feels threatened by my brains and the strength of my personality. He wants someone less threatening. She recalled the woman's face and admitted that although it was ten years older than hers it was an intelligent and an attractive one. She felt a hurt just below her stomach and a fuming sense of outrage in her head created by the possible answers to two differing questions: Don't you have to just admit that you're not the only attractive woman in the world, Leah? and How can you lose your man to a woman as old as that?

After storming off on Sunday, Leah had regretted throwing the email at him. She'd had to find it in his inbox on her computer to read it again. She read it over and over in the forty-eight hours after the bust-up, and each time it whipped her into a frenzy of jealousy that was like a thin white-hot reed of poisonous toxicity in the middle of her mind.

They say jealousy is green, well it isn't, she thought: it's burning white, with gun metal grey behind it. It almost left a metallic taste in her mouth. It was one thing giving in to painful thoughts about Lucie Bastable that could be explained away as paranoia – the evidence against Giles there wasn't conclusive, she had to admit – but this long-haired woman was wholly different. This new threat was there in writing - and now she'd experienced the reality of seeing them together, and seeing them touching. Touching him, Leah, touching him, went the barrister, the word touch a humiliating tap dance on her rawest nerve. Where else has she touched him, Leah? I rest my case.

She pulled over at the next lay by and threw up. She hadn't eaten all day but she'd drunk a lot of water. Most of it came flying out of her mouth on to the grass. She felt shockingly bad; then while still bending down on the edge of the ditch, suddenly felt better.

A woman came over to her, older – she'd stopped too. 'Are you okay?' she said.

'Pregnant,' Leah replied, 'but I'm fine - I'm used to it.'

Only later did she realise that the woman must have known she was lying. It must have been about half-past three when she stopped and as far as she knew, you didn't get mid-afternoon sickness with pregnancy. She drove on, thinking about a place where the present met the past.

Once, when she was like this as a young girl growing up, her mother had said to her, 'Leah, one day you're going to suffer so much, thinking you're the Queen of Sheba,' and for once in her life had sounded truly angry with the beautiful daughter with the charmed existence. Leah was frightened for a second then confused for several while she scanned her brain for knowledge of the Queen of Sheba and got nothing. She shrugged the challenge off. What did parents know about being young in the 1990s?

Mind you, her contemporaries had never understood her either. She was a target for the school bitches for being superior, aloof and distant – in the end, to survive, she'd had to out-bitch them. She got her strength to do so from the knowledge that she drove the boys crazy with her drop-dead looks. She wasn't being big-headed: it was the plain truth. It had been that way even at primary school. Even then grown men had stared at her slyly wherever she went. Then when she grew breasts and grew taller she would walk down the school corridors, and the streets come to that, swinging her hips with her head in the air not giving a damn, knowing the effect she was having on the male population around her. The words, 'you're going to suffer so much one day' followed her down the years in silence in some distant recess of her mind, observing her every deed, waiting for the day when they'd drop down into her here and now, speaking to her clearly again and truly meaning something. It would take the experience of a personal catastrophe for it to happen. Leah drove onward fighting the notion that the day had arrived.

She'd hardly had girlfriends growing up. No one wanted to throw their emotional lot in with a girl who had everything her schoolyard rivals wanted, like the starving wanted food. She had one friend when she went up to big school and who stayed loyal to her for the next seven years, mostly because the pair of them had the same characteristic of possessing sexuality and beauty rolled into one. They called them The Bitch Twins. So all the other girls had hated her guts, so what? What did it matter when the boys wanted her and the men too?

It was heavenly to be thirteen and have the older lads in the school coming to her, teasing her, making her laugh, paying her attention. She had never looked back from there. She knew most girls suffered all kinds of problems because she saw them crying in the school toilets, read about it in magazines and saw it in the plots of TV soaps. She suffered none. In her mind, boys were lined up in dozens waiting to drop everything for her. Naturally, she responded. Each time she felt her heart strings go *twang!* for a guy, she would just make a point of passing his way in the corridors and looking at him in a certain way and sooner or later he would come to her. Almost always sooner. So her teenage experiences of the opposite sex were easy and plentiful. Some lasted months, some weeks, some one long evening. Only she never really fell in love – how could you when boys cried so easily? But the great thing was, the great consolation, was that no one ever dumped her. She always dumped them. She was irresistible.

And if it wasn't enough that Leah Lisa Mary Caighton was blessed with the power of some tarantula of love, she was intellectually gifted too, and was good at sports. She was a key player in the hockey and netball teams from the age of eleven. Out of school she danced, took examinations and always scored merits and distinctions. When she reached the GCSE stage at 16, the only relevant question was 'how many A grades would she get?' Teachers fawned over her to get her to take their subject at A level.

Then the problems began, and soon it seemed that she had finally been sent the bill for the golden years of her youth. Just after her GCSE's she fell off a horse, tearing ankle ligaments and damaging her back. Sport wasn't so important now, but she cried at the thought that she would have to stop dancing. Then, by way of compensation, she dreamed of being an actress, and the following autumn auditioned for the school play. She was so good she was asked to play Juliet. But her back got worse and she had to go into hospital for an operation. It was fairly minor, but she was no longer Romeo's lover.

Her bad luck seemed to develop the quality of a curse when she contracted glandular fever a month before she was due to start university, and it was such a bad case she couldn't go out and couldn't even read a magazine; all she wanted to do was sleep. She tried to start her English degree at Exeter, but quit in distress before Christmas. She took the rest of the year off and re-started at the same place, the following October, but she still wasn't right. She had felt weak and listless for so long she could no longer tell whether the problem was physiological or psychological. Even after the blood tests no longer showed traces of illness, she would suddenly feel tired and think, Shit, it's still there.

Her confidence was affected. She no longer sashayed through life with unbreakable self-belief. Funny how life goes, she thought. Just as confidence begets success, so the same thing worked in reverse. Now Leah's intelligence enabled her to appreciate what it had been like for her fellow school pupils to deal with the world and all its painful uncertainties. She came to realise what a wretched, stinking individual she'd been all those years and how badly she'd missed out on friendship.

The biggest thing she had looked forward to at Exeter was getting back into drama. If she had the talent she'd been told she possessed at school, she would take lessons from a really good professional. If it meant dropping out to go to RADA or somewhere nearly as good, she would do it. So she had some lessons but it was clear by the end of the first term that she didn't have the talent she thought she had – not enough to be a professional anyway. At least, her teacher didn't think so. Now Leah Caighton walked around the campus and the town with a sour, disappointed expression and was no longer so attractive. Now only half the men she came into contact with fell in love with her on sight.

She still effortlessly had love affairs and one night stands if she felt like it, but it wasn't the same now she her innocence was gone. But still, no one had yet broken her heart. She went all the way through her schooldays, through her degree and her two-year post-grad course in broadcast journalism in London unscathed. No one, she knew, had truly won her until she met Giles McAndrew when she was 25.

By then her career plans were sunk in the mire as far as she was concerned. Pleasant thoughts of a job at the BRBC Centre in London or in television at the start of the course became the miserable acceptance of having to start in the invisible twilight of local radio. Her mind and body were both still dogged with lethargy. She was unable to shine, incapable of making the spark that might re-ignite her. And so she accepted the easy placement into one of the career world's mediocre pigeon holes. Still, the reporting work was a doddle and she was always busy - never chained to the desk. She enjoyed reading the news when they let her and doing live reports from the field. She liked that she could chase a story herself, develop it on the phone, in person and in her head and find that another working day had flown by not unenjoyably. Life could have been a lot worse, she knew very well, not least from her working life. And she was only in her mid-twenties. One day she would gather up what was left of her strength and do something to match the dreams she had once had. But not yet.

So she liked working at Burb stations despite the times when she despised the scruffy dress of her colleagues, the ditchwater-dull furnishings and the constantly trivial output. The music was boring, the stories were sometimes plain pathetic and most of the presenters were vain and uneducated. She knew she was a terrible snob, but she didn't care - she'd stopped caring about anything with any feeling of passion a long time ago. Then along came Giles McAndrew.

She was only working a six month attachment contract in the lonely backwater of Two Counties in Bartonshire when he arrived one wet July in the middle of Wimbledon. She wanted him from the time she heard a brilliant interview he did one morning with Kenneth Branagh, who they'd only got to come to the station because the head of programming knew his sister. Hearing Giles making this famous star laugh and be so enthusiastic on air, obviously not thinking for one second that he was the guy's inferior, made her neck hair stick out on end in admiration. But before she could do anything about it, they weren't extending her contract and she had to go back to Radio North Yorks. She was utterly miserable at first - she'd already decided that she had to have Giles McAndrew - but one day in the first week back in Harrogate while rushing to meet a tight deadline on a story about a brewery, a colleague said,

'Leah, what's got into you? I've never seen you working so fast.'

She knew right there that she was right again, that the fever's fatal poison had finally left her.

It was a whole year before a reporter's job came up at TCR, but she got it. She hoped like hell Giles wasn't about to up and leave when she arrived because there wasn't much in Bart and Bilt to hold anyone who wanted something exciting out of life. It had a muddy coast, brick and tractor factories, a solemn cathedral, miles of potato fields and nothing much else. Thankfully Giles McAndrew didn't seem to be going anywhere - though she didn't yet understand why - and it wasn't long before she got her claws into him. The bird of prey image wasn't a particularly accurate one because for a long time he brought out the gentle side of her. She had never been in awe of a man before but she was of Giles. All she wanted to do for a long time after they got together was to work near him for some of the day, spend time with him in the evenings and be there for him on weekends.

But time was passing. She had begun to hear her biological clock ticking more loudly, causing her to reflect hard on children, marriage. She was 27 when they finally got together, had passed through 28 and was now fast-crawling in the waters of 29 and about to reach 30. As far as she was concerned her time for motherhood was approaching; was scooping her up like a stray dog that needed to be brought back home and cared for. She feared it, but feared the consequences if she refused the call even more.

He was worthy of impregnating her, she had never had any doubt about that. And love? She'd always felt differently about Giles. Always. She was slow to admit that the hunger she had for him was love, but deep inside, she'd known from the moment she heard him talking to Branagh. Has all that faded now? she thought, when the front door opened and her sister arrived back from the supermarket with bags full of Waitrose shopping. Were her feelings for Giles dying? Or being eroded by their incompatibilities? Or was it a phase they were going through? The hatred she felt for the woman in the restaurant made her think that her love was still real, still a live, pulsing thing. But then again, was it just the green-eyed monster attacking her pride? She was miserable and she was confused, but she wasn't going to put up with it for long. There was a madness happening at the moment. She didn't understand it but she it was there, sure enough, and it had to be resolved one way or another very soon.

15

Leah and Neale

The chances of Leah Caighton going to a bar alone and staying that way were non-existent if that was the way she wanted things to go.

On Wednesday night, tired of retreating, she took an eight mile journey by taxi from her flat in BT up the north road to the fashionable village that was Lichester Barton. Here, much diversion was enjoyed by Bart and Bilt's young professionals and aspirant yobbos in the form of chi-chi bars, new restaurants and several examples of the good old English pub. She took off just to look into the possibility of a distraction from her misery, nothing more concrete than that.

She'd heard *Crush* being discussed at work as a great place to go, so she avoided it and went to *Bar 00* instead. For a Bartonshire hangout it looked pretty swish from the outside. She slinked inside on three-inch pin-dot heels wearing an expensive jacket over a short, black sleeveless dress that wasn't cheap either. It wasn't the sight of her bare legs that burned the eyes of every door watcher, though they were good, but rather the effect of the whole package: the way the clean hair, the long torso, the beautifully shaped rear and the shapely legs came together as one. She didn't notice the impact she had on men in social situations like this because it had been a given for so long. At work this could be a complete nuisance; like when she wanted her words to be taken seriously in meetings only to find the likes of Greg and Marcus gazing at her face like misty-eyed goons.

As she made for the bar and scanned its length for a good empty stool, this wasn't on her mind. She just wanted a bloody drink. But when she ordered a double vodka and tonic as she lifted her bottom on to black leatherette, she saw the smile the barman gave her and was pleased to be reassured that she looked good tonight.

She saw her target when she looked for a barman to re-fill her empty glass. He was about her age, scruffily good looking with an open, honest face wearing fashionable stubble. He wasn't tall and lean like Giles and didn't look like he had much money. He looked like an acoustic guitar singer or a guy from an off-tour indie band, only fitter, tougher and properly fed. At a push, he could be her type - for a night anyway. She took this in before he saw her. He drifted over to slot into a space at the bar that had opened up right beside her, trying only to make eye contact with one of the bar staff. But then he was distracted by her, giving her a single look that said, 'bl-*loo*dy hell' before going back to trying to get a drink. However, she could see in his expression, even from the side, that the damage had been done. This was too easy, she thought.

'Hi,' she said.

'Hi,' he replied, turning his head, thinking, She can't be interested in me: I'm not in her league and I'm too scruffy. Leah read his thoughts almost before they appeared, and realised that if she really did want to pair herself up with this one tonight, she'd have to make some of the running. She didn't mind that, not at all in fact, the mood she was in: she was now certain that before the light came up on another day she would scoop him up, suck him in and spit him out downwind.

'Can I buy you a drink?' she said.

A knot of excitement appeared in her gut as she realised that Leah Caighton was thinking like a single woman again, back on old territory. She felt safe, at home in an arena where she knew she exercised more power than she knew what to do with. It was a long time, though, since she'd played the game.

'Isn't it supposed to be the other way around?' said the stranger, but he smiled to show that he was kidding. 'Yeah, I'll have a Bud.'

She was off and running. Leah looked for a free bar keeper but they were all busy. She kept the ten pound note raised between her fingers where it could be seen, but turned her attention to…

'I'm Leah.'

'Neale.'

'Hi, Neale,' she said grinning at him without trying to be too keen, trying to come over as a nice person rather than a starved man-eater.

'Hi, Leah,' he replied, wondering what the fuck was going on.

'Yes?' said a barman, looking from Neale to Leah and back again.

'A Bud and a double vodka and coke,' she said.

'Oh,' said the barman, adjusting.

'Cheers,' she said when the drinks arrived. She couldn't remember the last time she'd done this. Had she ever done it exactly like this, ruthlessly hunted a man down? She hadn't been single for nearly two years, and before that, she'd hardly gone out after she'd finished with Baz, and that had started when she was on the rebound from Chris. So the last time she was out on the pull, she would have had to have been about 23. But even then she hadn't been confident enough to sit up at a bar like this, like…like…like the Queen of Sheba, buying the first drink at the start of a blatant pick up.

'Cheers,' said Neale. 'I was going to say, "I haven't seen you in here before," but that would be too stupid for words.'

'It's okay – you're right, I don't normally drink in the village.'

'Which begs the question, why tonight?' said Neale genially, grimacing at the sourness of a beer that wasn't cold enough.

'I'm celebrating my new found freedom.' She decided she wasn't going to waste time waiting for diffident blokes to make up their mind whether they dare make an approach.

Blimey, thought Neale, wondering whether she'd dumped the unlucky so and so into a passing Fenland dyke from a moving vehicle.

Leah hadn't made up her mind where this was going to go, but was fully prepared at least to consider the possibility of shagging him. The chance to hurt Giles had an almost irresistible quality to it, even though he might never know. But she would. A shag would just go nicely to prove to herself that she could still meet men on unequal terms. And what the hell, why not? She hadn't had a one night stand in years, and furthermore, Neale was pretty fit, the more so for immediately displaying the fact that he wasn't a chinless half-wit.

Suddenly she had a premonition of what might happen here and shuddered. She saw an evening bag colliding with her face, swung by a jealous girlfriend, and her jaw crunching and cracking as it made contact with the parquet wooden floor. The images formed an old repeating nightmare. The girl sat on her stomach spitting obscenities into her face as she lay there with her dress around her waist, her crotch on full display to a bunch of leering male punters holding lager bottles in grubby hands. Then an ambulance, then a hospital, x-ray machines and a drip, then realising she had no one to phone. She blinked at the mirror behind the bar and saw herself: 29, no close friends, no husband, no children. What have you done with your life, Leah?

'Are you okay?' said Neal

'Yeah, fine.' The daylight nightmare, a cloud formation of headache grey had passed over her. She turned her head slightly to meet the evening sun was still shining through the plate glass window behind her.

'Someone walk over your grave?'

'Something like that.' She moved closer to Neale's jacket and had the feeling of wanting to be lying on the bare chest of a man who'd just spent his lust on her, but who she could just walk out on, free of obligations. She looked at his left hand – no ring.

'So, what do you do, Neale?' she said swigging half her drink down in a gulp that puffed her cheeks. 'Let me guess – car salesman.'

'No,' said Neale, laughing.

'Good, I hate car salesmen. Erm, internet designer thingy. Web-bloke. You know what I mean.'

'No, not one of those either.'

She was dreading him asking her the same question. How would it sound: 'I work in local radio?' Terrible, she thought.

'Okay, let me look at you.' She so had the upper hand, she thought. Neale had something nice about him, the way he let her dominate the conversation, not needing to take control of things as a lot of men would. She picked up her glass again and dumped the rest of the drink down her throat. She didn't need it to boost her confidence; she was beginning to feel as right as rain, the best she'd felt for weeks.

'Yeah, I've got you wrong, haven't I – there's something nice and artie about you. Teacher, art teacher.'

Neale laughed louder this time, showing nice straight teeth but a couple of silver fillings. Not silver – she knew what she meant. It was okay – she didn't want a perfect Neale.

'I'm an artist.'

'Wow…' Interesting, she thought. 'You don't look the type for an art smock and nude models, ha-ha.'

'No,' he said smiling, 'I'm not a fine artist – I was kidding you a little – I'm a graphic designer. I work with logos and posters, stuff like that.'

'Well, that's still good, isn't it?'

'Yeah – I do a lot of the original designing where I work, so – yeah, it's good…creative.'

I could easily shag him, thought Leah. She thought about condoms - she might have one in her bag. Neale, meanwhile, put his thinking on high speed alert. He'd wondered two minutes ago whether she was a prostitute, but there was something way too soft about her, and real. She was coming on to him like someone trying to win a bet that she could get shagged by a stranger less than thirty minutes after their first contact. There was something not real about that, though, he sensed. She clearly wasn't that kind of woman.

'So what do you do?' he said.

'Spy. But don't tell anyone.'

'I thought you looked tough, ha-ha,' he said.

'Yeah?' said Leah, grinning with pleasure.

'Yeah, like I wouldn't want to be the guy that tries to chat you up when the, um, attention isn't wanted.'

'Ha-ha, you're not wrong there, Neale,' she said winking an eye at him and clicking her tongue.

'What do you say, or do you just kick 'em in the balls?'

'Ha-ha. The excuse about being in a "big relationship" almost always works. Or, "before this goes any further, I want you to know I've got my period." That normally sends them away screaming.'

'And what about if that doesn't work?'

'When that doesn't work? I just tell 'em, "I'm sorry, darling, but I'm a lesbian." And if they don't believe me, I say, "do you want to see my strap-on?"'

'And that works?'

'It's never failed yet.'

Neale looked through the huge window behind them, out at the village scene: a car getting a lucky space just outside; a group of girls in short dresses laughing so loud he could almost hear them through the glass and the music that had just started to bang away in here.

'Let me buy you another drink, Neale,' she said, raising her voice and not remotely caring about conventions.

'No, thanks all the same. I have to go in a minute. I just stopped in here for a quick one. I'm meeting someone.'

'Why didn't you say so?'

'Should I have done?'

'I thought you were...' She looked vacantly across the bar – it wasn't appropriate to say, 'up for it.' She wasn't a whore.

'Sure, but I'm meeting someone.'

'Oh,' said Leah, almost frozen with shock; this just did not happen to her.

'Okay. Well, it was nice meeting you, Neale,' she said, trying to regain an impregnable composure. She stared dead ahead at a bottle of Sambuca.

'Yeah, you too,' he said, finishing his bottle. 'Maybe I'll see you around some time.'

'Yeah, sure,' she said, looking at him again and giving him a tight smile. She couldn't fucking believe this, her insides swaying between anger and embarrassment.

''Bye then,' he said putting his bottle on the counter-top. He looked at her and smiled politely one final time. As he did so, Leah looked at his left hand again for a ring, in case she'd made some bizarre mistake. No, no ring. Bloody, fucking hell, she said to herself, what was happening here? She was sure he was lying. Everything about him said 'single.' The same barman as before was suddenly free right in front of her.

'Vodka and tonic,' she said, trying to smile politely but she couldn't.

'Double?'

'Please.'

93

She continued to fragment. What was this? I'm 29 and losing it? I can't be, thought Leah. She wasn't taking this. She ran after him. She grabbed her bag, swung down off the stool and made the door as fast as her heels would allow. When she got outside she looked left first and saw him immediately. He was just twenty yards down the street towards the village green where knots of drinkers from The Bell, their pockets full of money, were guzzling their way through the dusk and making lots of happy noise. As he waited to cross the road, she caught up with him and pulled at his arm.

'So what is it, ay? What's wrong with me?'

Neale turned round with a 'what the hell's going on?' expression.

'What? Nothing. Nothing's wrong with you – I...what do you mean?'

She read his face. He didn't want to be there talking to her. He wasn't interested in her. She was stunned again as if she'd taken a blow. Her mind raced, even though she was halfway to being pissed. Am I really going to say, 'Don't you fancy me?' For God's sake, Leah.

'Look – I'm...' she was lost for the right words, but had come too far to say nothing. 'I thought,' she said moving as close as she dare so she could speak quietly enough so no passers by would hear. O *fuck*, she went inside. 'I thought you were interested.'

He looked at her with frank eyes, and Leah could see that she could really get to like this guy in a proper, serious way and that it wasn't the drink doing the thinking for her.

'Look, can we...come over here,' he said. He drew her to the bench in front of the war memorial and sat her down. Leah looked at him, waiting for the verdict like a girl waiting for a crucial exam result.

'Um, look – I'm sorry. You just picked the wrong guy - I'm just not looking tonight. Sorry.'

She couldn't believe she was hearing this. Not from a man. She was even more convinced there was some horrific mark on her, or odour, that she couldn't see or smell herself. He saw her face, and decided to let her have it with both barrels – he didn't know why.

'Leah – it's Leah, right?'

Christ, was there no humiliation she wasn't going to have to endure? She felt her face burning.

'There's something manic about you. Something desperate. I'm really sorry. I didn't want to sound selfish or anything or, um, uncaring, but I've got enough problems of my own to deal with.'

He felt bad now, sorry that he didn't have what it took to try to have a serious conversation in the bar there with this woman. She was stunning to look at, but something told him that the baggage she carried would be way too much for him.

The light finally dawned on Leah.

'You're not meeting anyone, are you?'

'No,' said Neale, 'I'm not.'

'You know what? You're the only man who's ever rejected me.' She had to claim some pride back even if it was the last thing she did and even if it wasn't much to claim.

'You should try being a man, Leah,' he said and smiled ruefully across at the crowd on the green, talking loudly, laughing happily, celebrating the imminent arrival of summer. 'I don't want to sound patronizing, but you look too beautiful to me to be out man-hunting.'

Why shouldn't I fuck a man when I want, she thought. What's wrong with power coming to women at last?

'Look, I'm sorry, I'm going to go. You're going to be okay, yeah?'

'Yes, of course,' she said, finding a note of haughtiness. But she couldn't hold on to it. She felt herself softening. 'Thanks for being so honest, Neale.' And she held out her hand for him to shake. He didn't know whether to laugh or feel sorry for her. He took it and shook it.

'I hope,' she said, 'that if we meet again I'm less manic.'

'And I hope I'm less head-up-my-own-arse,' he said.

Leah missed his lie, already back deep inside herself again, and went back to the bar. Someone else had her stool. Her jacket had fallen on the floor. She looked at her drink, still sitting there, went over to it, grabbed it and threw it into her mouth. The girl who had her stool glanced at her. Leah glared back. The girl turned away and carried on talking to her friend.

She found a taxi easily. They were still coming into the village dropping off more revellers on the main street. She gave her address to a rare woman cab driver. That was enough for one night. Look at me, she said to herself, as the dusk settled into darkness over the fields of root crops and rape: I can't even go out and get a free fuck and a re-booted ego. Avoiding conversation, she thought about life-after-Giles and wondered how she was going to deal with it; that things might have changed so much since she was last truly single that she wouldn't be able to operate any more. What was she going to do if being beautiful wasn't enough when you got to 29? She shivered, wondered if she was cold. She wound up the window that the last passenger had left open. She felt a soft headache appear at her left temple as they passed the Barton Townes sign and it immediately began to get worse.

She got home and drank a lot of water. Then she sat in the living room and watched TV without even looking at it. She went to bed and lay there in shades of depression, regretting the fact that she'd promised Sonia she'd go into work in the morning. She wished she had some dope, but she'd always avoided it – at that moment, she regretted it. Then she thought about booze and wished she could get into the idea of getting smashed on her own, but she'd never done that either and good sense told her that this wasn't the time to start. You're too bloody sensible, Leah, that's your trouble.

She needed something to take the edge off the deep, desolate place she was in. She lifted her buttocks to pull up her dress to the waist, then put her right hand in between her legs, closed her eyes and rubbed herself gently. It was speculation. She waited to see if her body would override her mind. As one minute passed into two, the messages the nerve endings sent to the brain were green-lighted and returned. Pleasure began to develop in her crotch that quickly developed a momentum of its own and she was away. Passing a point of no return, she pulled the gusset of her knickers aside and felt her lips part from the wetness coming through from inside. As she stroked herself up and down gently in rhythm, she began to lose herself in her biology, the metallic poisonous emotion falling away into the darkness. She reached up with wet fingertips and rubbed her clitoris softly until she croaked slightly in the throat, then began to moan softly. Four, maybe five minutes later she was completely lost in sweet oblivion.

Afterwards, satisfied but still upset, she wanted to cry, but absolutely refused. Giles kept wanting to get involved in her thinking, but she wanted nothing to do with him, so shut him out. 'Let me in, Leah,' she could hear him pleading, but she was having none of it. He wasn't coming back to her yet no matter how badly he wanted her. Not after tonight.

16

A Visit from John Clegg

Thursday May 4th

It started with a headache he woke up with that morning a few minutes after four. Another day and night gone by and still no sight nor sound of Leah.

Many was the time doing the breakfast show Giles wondered how the hell he managed to keep going considering the insane hour he had to get up on a work day. After six years of it though, dragging himself out of bed in the dark had become second nature. He hated it for maybe ten seconds - twenty in winter – then just accepted his lot and got on with it. The monotony of the daily routine would often trouble his mind, but once trails of hot water had unglued his morning eyes he was fine. As he buried his face in a warm towel he would begin to focus on the show ahead of him, and once he started doing that, he was as good as off and running.

He loved it more than he could tell anyone. He didn't care that he wasn't Big Time; that he wasn't on Radio 5 – yet – at least not when he was live on air to the people of the two counties. He loved the studio, the equipment, the metallic smell of the enclosed space, the guests, the sliders, the headphones, the cardboard boxes in the corner, the notices on the wall, everything. He even loved the unglamourousness of it sometimes. He loved clicking the mouse on to jingles and trailers; loved reading texts and emails that Leon sent through, even the crap ones; loved the phone calls from listeners, even the ones about gardening, farming and what was the world coming to; loved the fact that with the mike hanging down in front of his face, he was free to be himself.

Of course, this was something of an illusion. To be a radio presenter he had to be an actor, he had to present a part of himself to the microphone and to the public that wasn't the whole Giles McAndrew, never mind the real Gilles Wilkinson, but it was the part of him that sometimes he loved the best. Driving the studio desk was like being at the controls of an aeroplane or an air-traffic control system, only better. The show revolved totally around him and depended entirely upon his ability to listen, think and talk all at the same time, entertaining and educating people, the real, salt of the earth folk of these flat lands of farms, roads, dykes and coastline. He was right in the middle of them -

he'd seen it on the map. The Two Counties Radio building was smack dab in the centre of the built up area that was Barton Townes, which was smack dab in the middle of Bartonshire and Bilt if you looked and thought of them as one. He was the heartbeat of the counties. Who else had the ability to talk to the people like he did?

Whenever he drank too much, or got too animated in a meeting and verbalised these feelings, people of course thought that Giles McAndrew was off his head and that his ego had finally blown up and out so far that it had burst; for wasn't it obvious that there were fifteen presenters all told at TCR? And that Giles, with a show that was 'talk only' for just the last two hours of his six-to-nine slot, spent no more time with the good folk of Bart and Bilt than Jim Johnson on Drive Time? Who was he kidding?

Giles didn't give a damn if he got too animated and passionate about his job. It was this depth of feeling for the job that made him the most listened-to radio presenter in the whole of the East Midland counties of England, and though he loved to be liked, anyone who didn't like his attitudes could go to hell. They were all driven by jealousy anyway.

However, on Thursday May 4th, two days before the second anniversary of his first date with Leah, at 4.35am, as Giles picked up the milk and turned the key in TCR's front door to open her up for the day, his passion for radio was nowhere in sight. Already, thoughts of Leah were burning a hole in his head as he switched on the reception area light, ran behind the desk to switch off the alarm, then made straight for the kitchen cupboard to get some Paracetamol, switching on more lights as he went.

At this time of the morning, the glamour of radio broadcasting wasn't anywhere to be found. Though Lucie Bastable was the first on the air at five, Giles was always in first, so the opening-up duties were his. BRBC's budget for local radio didn't extend to an all-night security guard or phone operator. He found a big bottle of water in the fridge and swigged a load down with the tablets and thought about starting work. Despite the pain from this time of trial, he was implacably determined to prove to himself if no one else that he was nothing if not a true pro. Short of slicing him clean in two or shooting him, Giles McAndrew would be in that studio chair each weekday morning at six come what may, and eight o'clock on Saturdays.

He put a kettle on for his second cup of coffee of the day, then opened up the newsroom where he had a desk next to Leon. He leant on the mouse to fire up the computer and switched on the monitor; made a series of rapid clicks to get through to the running order that Leon had left him, noticed three post it notes on his keyboard, two from Leon and one from Sarah Billings, then went back to the kitchen. He wasn't fully awake yet by any means but he was getting there.

He came back to his desk with a mug of coffee and sat down. He took off his coat and got an energy bar out of a pocket on the way, put the coat on the chair behind him and ripped open the packaging and took a bite. He opened his desk drawer and saw a cellophane pack of dried apricots next to a pack of chewing gum and pulled both out onto the desk. Then he started looking over the running order and reading his notes on the show ahead. There was plenty going on, what with the Regional Picturesque Town of the Year announcement due by fax at 7, an interview with the deputy Prime Minister John Clegg a little further on and Barton County Hardware's first game in the League 2 play offs to yak about, so there'd be no problem delivering a show full of energy and interest. Giles slipped an apricot in his mouth and went to the BRBC internal news service for the latest on Clegg and the local elections and got ready to study Leon's questions for the interview, his head still splitting.

Lucie Caighton arrived at the station ten minutes after Giles at 4.40am, her programme carefully and precisely worked out ahead of schedule as usual. Stomach only slightly knotted, she re-boiled the kettle and went to studio 2 to get the desk ready for her show. Giles had already switched on the regional live feed, so she could hear a record from national station 5 Live playing softly from a speaker as she turned on her monitors and worked the mouse so that the three computer screens faded up into coloured light. She found her running order, checked that the faders were where she wanted them to be and went back to the kitchen to get her camomile tea.

The door to the toilet corridor banged open and Leah Caighton was on her before she knew what was happening. A push in the chest from a braced palm sent her flying backwards into the work surface at an awkward angle. She stayed on her feet but gasped from the pain that shot through her backbone. Her assailant hissed at her with demented eyes from a distance of inches.

'So tell me what the fuck is going on between you and Giles - anything? Eh? Tell me – what is it?' said Leah, sprinkles of spit hitting Lucie's forehead and hair in embarrassing splodges. 'Because if there is,' she said, giving her adversary no time to answer, ' you little slut, I'm going to tear your fucking face off for you, d'you understand?'

The face in question, which didn't hold much colour anyway at this time of the morning, was deathly white. It gaped back at Leah in shock. Lucie's mind floundered, unable to process an event way out beyond her expectation, but Leah still stared back at her, breathing heavily, wanting to hit the smug little cow. Then she saw the fear in the girl's eyes, noticed her slender frame shaking, and realised she'd made a dreadful mistake.

'Nothing,' said Lucie, but too late to materially affect the situation. Leah had already turned and exited the door through which she'd entered less than sixty seconds earlier. She ran to the emergency exit door at the end of the corridor and pushed at the bar with a grunt 'til it gave, letting her out into the emerging dawn. She put her key in the lock of her Polo and stood for a few moments, panting as if she'd run a mile. She could feel sweat running down her armpit hollows.

'What the hell am I doing?' she said softly to the empty Barton Townes dawn. Then she carried on silently: 'and what the fuck have you done? You must be mad.' She felt her heart racing as she opened the car door. Once she'd driven for a few minutes, her mind began to turn slightly. Still, she thought, I fixed that little tart. She'd never really liked Lucie at all, she realised, even though everyone else seemed to, especially the men, if you could call the blokes who worked at TCR 'men.'

It was done. She couldn't go back into work later on now. In fact, it was bloody obvious that she'd burned her boats at TCR. Her time there was over. She drove for several miles just letting that sink in.

After a while, the implications of her actions began to sink in. Unless she managed to find a way to wheedle some sympathy out of boss Simone so as to get a good reference, she might be done with local radio for good. She pictured the plain, boring building of plain, boring TCR and at that moment, didn't care if that was the result of all this shit she was going through. It was Giles's fault, it was love's fault and it was her own fault. We could all do with a good thrashing, she thought as she drove on, believing she was seeing things more clearly. She wiped tears away with her left hand quickly, then changed gear as she slowed to the roundabout for the dual carriageway heading further west.

In the kitchen, Lucie wiped her tears dry with a peach tissue and through the rings of shock around her mind, realised she had to deal with the situation in some way or other. She rushed down to the newsroom and found Giles and Leon talking, Sonia looking at a screen and Busy Ian putting his bag down on the desk. Sonia looked up immediately and saw her distress, stood up and started over towards her.

'I can't do the show,' said Lucie, motionless, 'I'm sorry, I can't,' and she dissolved into tears in Sonia's arms. She pulled back and looked at Sonia, her make-up running.

'Leon can do it, can't he?' she said, feeling terrible to be letting the side down.

'Of course he can - tell me what's the matter?'

Leon and Giles broke off their conversation and came over to Sonia's desk.

'Are you okay, Lucie?' said Giles, all concern.

'Sure, Lucie, I'll do the show,' said Leon, head jerking with electricity at the chance to step in and show what he could do. 'Are you okay?' he said, hoping she wasn't going to change her mind.

'My running order's on the screen there, Leon,' said Sonia flicking her head towards the screen.

'Right,' said Leon eagerly, and sat down to study what she'd been planning to do.

Sonia took Lucie across the room and out to the kitchen to find out what had happened. Only a small corner of Giles mind contained the thought that this might have something to do with him. He went back to the Clegg interview discussion with Leon.

'Giles McAndrew – every weekday morning on Two Counties Radio from six – gateway to the new day!'

'Okay, it's just coming up to twenty-two minutes past seven and we're *extremely* pleased to have John Clegg with us in the studio this morning! G'morning, Deputy Prime Minister, thank you so much for coming in.'

'Pleasure to be here, Giles.'

'You make an early start in the mornings, don't you?'

'Yes, I get started very bright and early – and it's an election day of course, and that means an even earlier start to the day – the working day, that is - than normal. In our democracy, today is a very important day. People in past years, you know, had to fight very hard and long to get – to win the right to vote and of course, this is something that in the Labour Party we take very, very seriously, and enthusiastically, trying to tell people how important it is to come out and vote on an election day.'

'Yes, it's local election day and you're here in Barton Townes campaigning for the party or are you just passing through?'

[*Giles – careful now,* said Leon into Giles's ear from the Ops Room]

'Ah-ha, well, yes, actually, I am just passing through, making a stop on my way north in the midst of my very busy schedule, but I'm sure I'll be able to find some time to talk to some of the good people of Barton Townes about the, ah, issues that are going to be important in their making their minds up to vote today. And perhaps more importantly, just trying to impress upon them the importance of turning out and making the effort to vote. As I'm sure you know, turnout in local elections is not as high as we in the government would like, so I'd like to do something here in Barton Townes about that in the short time I have in my day.'

'Yes? Well, that's lovely. Do you think you can avoid an electoral disaster today?'

'Well, you say, "disaster". Of course, it's traditionally very difficult in the mid-term for a government to maintain its support from a general election, but we'll see if we can do something to get out supporters to the polls so that doesn't happen. But even if the results aren't quite what we would like, then so be it, we'll just have to put our backs to the wheel and work harder for the people of this country.'

'I see, and in case any of you are worried about bias here at TCR, local Tory MP Trevor Howarth will be appearing on Lynda's show later, and Liberal Democrat...em...'

[*'Tim Fern, Giles, education spokesman.'*]

'...Tim Fern, their education spokesman is going to be with Noona at around lunchtime. So, John, why do you think that the people of Britain are deserting you party in droves?'

'Well, you know, as I just said, it's mid-term and governments always have to deal with the-'

'Because the government's had some troubles recently, haven't you, what with [*'Careful, Giles, give him a chance to finish'*] the release of immigrant criminals into the community by mistake and the problems you've had-'

'Well, of course, we deeply regret the releases, and we know how unfortunate the whole thing is [*'Remember what we said, Giles, whatever you do, don't mention his dicking around'*] and we're doing everything we can at the Home Office to put it right.'

'Do you think Charles Darke should resign over the releases?'

[*'Nicely put, Giles, good.'*]

'No, I don't. Charles is doing an excellent job and...'

'How can he be? Sorry to butt in, Mr Clegg, but how can you say that when convicted criminals, men who've committed crimes like rape and murder, have been let out of jail, with the man in charge not having a clue what was going on? He's supposed to, isn't he?'

[*Nice, Giles, nice.*]

'Well, what I think you have to understand is that we live now in a very difficult world where it's very hard to keep track of the inflow of legitimate workers, which we need very much to fill the jobs in our expanding economy.'

'With respect, John, that's a lot of rubbish isn't it? [*Steady, Giles*] These are not just immigrant workers we're talking about, but-'

'I think the problem here is that you don't understand government, um, Gill. Here out in the wilds, perhaps you aren't as clued in to things as you should be.' [*Ouch! Don't rise to it though, Giles, take it as a compl..*]

'Can you tell me, John, what's difficult to understand about you being unable to keep your hands off your diary secretary, [*No, Giles...Oh, no.*] never mind what's so hard to understand about your government not knowing how to run prisons in a basic way.'

'Right, thank you very much, but this is not a line of questioning that I think is acceptable.'

Clegg ripped his headphones off and threw them at Giles, missing his right ear by a couple of centimetres, saluted him with a hand on which only a single, middle finger was raised, and muttered, 'little bastard!'

'Ouch! Mr Clegg,' said Giles, in a matter of fact sort of way, 'has just thrown a pair of headphones at me, listeners. And I think you'll find, John, that rather than being a "little bastard" as you just called me – I don't know if you managed to get that, listeners - I'm about six foot-three inches standing up in my stocking feet.'

'Get stuffed!' said Clegg from the corner of his mouth, marching across the room, a minder already holding open the studio door, ready for a speedy exit. But Giles heard it.

'I'd get un-stuffed, if I were you, Mr Clegg. Mr Clegg leaving us there, well worth his weight in potatoes and pasta [*Jesus, Giles!*] Yes, John Clegg, the minister for local government and deputy Prime Minister, showing there why I won't be voting for his crowd in today's elections... [*Giles have you lost your mind?*] I hope Lynda has as much fun with her Tory later on as I just had with Mr Clegg. [*Shut up, Giles, click on to a song or I'm going to do it for you.*] And no I won't put on a record, Leon – my producer here, the excellent Leon Dilkes, wants me to put a record on so he can give me a good telling off about my performance with Mr Clegg, but – I'm sorry, Leon, I'm not going to do that - it's about time the politicians of this country realised that the folk out here in the regions are not going to be treated like fools. [*No, Giles,*] *no – I'm overriding you!*] And I want you to ring the station and let me know what Leon should say to me - should he shut me up or should he support me and the people of Bart and Bilt? Ring us now on 0299 445445. Come on and let's hear some democracy at work here at Two Counties Radio. Here's the number once again - 0299 445445-'

A song cut in before Giles could further galvanise the democratic energies of his listeners. Tina Turner's 'Simply The Best', may or may not have influenced those tuning in to pick up their phones to show their solidarity with him, but her raunchy tones rang out across the two counties to them at 95.7 on the FM dial, immediately breaking BRBC's code of practice concerning the amount of speech its local stations had to broadcast each week.

Leon burst into the room.

'What the hell, Giles, you stupid idiot! Have you gone crazy? What's the matter with you?'

Giles McAndrew didn't quite know what to say in the circumstances, two minutes and forty-five seconds left and counting down from the end of the song, and his career suddenly heading in the direction of the Bartonshire sewage system. Leon saved him the bother.

'I've just had one of Clegg's minders telling me that we'll never have a government spokesman on again and Clegg shouting in my ear that what you've just done will cost TCR a year's funding – what the hell is the matter with you? I can't believe it. You've...you've...'

'Oh, stop whining like an old woman, Leon, he can't do that. And anyway, I'm the one who's going to get carpeted - you're only the producer.'

'Thanks. Well, you can get out of that seat, I'm taking over.'

'No, you're not – I promise to be a good boy. And you have to get out there and count the votes – that is if anyone's fucking interested.'

'Enough of the language, Giles.'

'Oh, fuck off. I'm having the worst week of my entire life and suddenly I'm sick of not being able to say this and say that on the radio, and now you're telling me I can't say "fuck" with only you and me in the room?'

Giles could see that Leon was on the verge of blowing a gasket so tried to calm him again, holding both hands in the air, leaning back in his seat. Leon, meanwhile, in a big enough flap already, was now wondering what on earth his presenter was talking about. Worst week of his life? He knew he and Leah were having some problems, but 'worst week of his life'? So far this week, apart from being a touch grumpy on air, it had been business as usual - until now.

'I'm sorry, I'm sorry, I'm sorry. Look – I'll say it again: I promise to be good. We've an hour and forty minutes to go. Let's get on with things. Is that Dog Owner's Association bloke still on the line?'

'Yes,' said Leon, just coming off boiling point, arms folded like an outraged pantomime dame.

'Put him on when the record's finished. Come on, Leon.'

'Alright; but no more buggering around, alright? No more!'

'Ah'ht! Language!'

'Giles,' said Leon, 'you've had it. Do you know that? Had it? I don't know what you thought you were doing; I just-'

'Ah, just get back to the Ops room.'

Giles put his headphones back on and looked up at a screen to see how long it would be before Tina and her song came to a stop: fifty-three seconds and counting down right in front of him on the screen. Giles took a deep breath and looked through the running order for the next half an hour. He was still seething inside and knew he had to pull himself together to save himself, if it wasn't too late already. As the song faded, Giles pulled down his fader and began again.

'People of the two counties, I do apologize for that outburst, that…that tirade of mine just now. I had no right to lose my temper with Mr Clegg and I apologize to him unreservedly right now, and to the Labour Party as an organization, and to my superiors here at BRBC. I don't know what got into me. I could tell you about some of the, er, personal problems I've been having this week, but you won't want to hear about that. Now, dogs! The chairman of the National Dog Lovers Association said on breakfast TV earlier this week that we in Britain are the worst dog owners in Europe, and we have him on the line right now. David Lehmann, welcome.'

'Hello, Giles.'

'Hello. So, you…'

'I enjoyed your interview with John Clegg very much, by the way.'

'Oh, well…'

'Yes, it's a refreshing change to hear some real, genuine passion on the radio.'

'Thank you.'

'You're welcome. Frankly, I think Clegg's had it coming for a long time-'

'If that's your view, Dave, it's certainly not mine. Now, to dogs and what you said in London this week - do you really think we as a nation, are worse, crueller than the French, or the Swedish or the Germans?'

'Well, Giles…'

Outside in the operations room at the desks of Leon Dilkes and broadcast assistant Mary-Jane, the phones lines were queued down to the thirty-two limit, a figure unmatched in the twenty-one year history of Two Counties Radio even by last spring's mid-morning programme direct from the Chelsea Flower Show.

'That bastard,' said Leon, just under his breath. How dare Giles McAndrew break about five of the most sacred of radio's fundamental rules in one go – and half look like getting away with it? But he and his assistant Mary-Jane had begun taking calls and all of them were squarely behind the presenter. In they came, one after another, all supporting Giles. Leon was furious: they were getting jammed. He wouldn't be able to brush this under the carpet. They would have to make the results public or at least say something. He'd have to run straight to Simone at nine o'clock to see what they were going to do.

He stopped taking calls and tried to listen to the dog interview. He couldn't. He turned to hear Mary-Jane saying,

'You support Giles McAndrew? Oaa-kaiieee,' and watched her make another stroke in the 'For Giles' column on her pad and start to write a note down on what the caller had to say.

'The bloody people in this county,' he muttered, forgetting for a moment that they were covering two. He expected support for someone attacking a Labour government in one of the most Conservative parts of the country, but they didn't have to show that they loved Giles McAndrew so bloody much. Or was it that they really hated the Labour government so much? He didn't know. He wasn't sure he knew anything any more.

At the end of the two-way on dogs, as a three minute-twelve second report package on tractor theft played, Giles popped into the Ops Room.

'How's it going?'

'Great,' said Leon, 'everyone thinks you should take over the running of the country.'

'Mary-Jane?'

'Same,' she said, punching through to another caller. 'Thank you for calling Two Counties Radio, Mary-Jane speaking on the Giles McAndrew Show, what would you like to say?'

Giles turned and went back to Studio 1. Mary-Jane stared at his retreating body in admiration before noting yet another 'It's about time the people of this country...' call in favour of Giles' demolition job on the deputy-Prime Minister. She made another stroke on her packed left column.

As the volume of calls practically busted the telephone system in two, Giles took the show down to nine o'clock without further incident, agreeing with Leon during a later package on the impact of eastern European workers on alcohol crime that they should take no calls live on air. His head was still hammering for mercy at the pain that still throbbed in waves at the front of his skull.

17

A Meeting for Leah

Simone Pound heard the interview but wasn't going to rush into work and get everyone flustered. She'd avoid Jackie on the reception desk and slip into her office through the back door and let the fall-out come to her.

TCR's managing editor was, on the surface of things an unremarkable woman of fifty-one who liked plants, gardens and Elton John. Male colleagues down the years had dismissed her as being 'too nice to be a news editor,' 'too nice to be a head of programming,' 'too nice to be a deputy managing editor' and finally, 'too nice to be the boss of a station like this'. All the while, they watched while she rose up the chain of command, leaving them bitter and fallen behind. It was all too easy to misunderstand and underestimate her.

Maybe it was something about BRBC culture that allowed her type to prosper. She was laid back in a manner only BRBC management could be in the two-thousand '00's. She 'wouldn't be seen dead in a business suit' and her collared tops were never crisp. In fact, everything about her seemed soft almost to the point of blurred. Her face was easily forgotten by those who only met her once and even those who'd worked with her for years could never say later what she'd worn that day at work, even if they'd sat in an afternoon meeting with her for two hours. She wasn't pretty, and her hair was a bit of a mess and she was carrying a little spare flesh around the middle. She had no hips and her bust wasn't worth mentioning and never had been. And yet, when people really got to know her, they had a tendency to fall under her spell. Men too.

The newbies fresh up from their broadcast journalism post-grad courses especially couldn't understand that someone who could easily be their mum was the person in charge, the young males especially. And though there was some sense of authority about her they were surprised that she wasn't the deputy-managing editor, or the boss merely holding the position on a temporary basis until a proper manager took over.

The older men at Two Counties had learned their lesson. At first, they – especially those suffering from a touch of testosterone overload, were amazed that such an ordinary woman had levered her way up the greasy pole of local radio and after a first encounter marked her down as fluffy at best. When presenters who didn't deliver on the ratings front were moved on they assumed that it was Greg McKenzie who pulled the strings. It took a little time before they realised where power truly lay.

The change would usually come when they, themselves made a gaffe, ran up against the corporation rules or found to be generally not pulling their weight. This would result in a gentle summons to her office for a coffee and a chat. Fearing nothing they came out the other side of the experience feeling as though they'd let the station down, their colleagues down, themselves down, their parents down and, worst of all, the people of Bart and Bilt down. By the time they'd got back to the newsroom, they had resolved to change their ways. Though too embarrassed to admit it to their work-mates at any price, they'd been *Simone-d* and knew it. Within a couple of days they'd accepted the situation and began to treat her with a new respect.

Of course, there were rogues who went through the process still feeling contempt for Simone Pound. It happened with great frequency however that within six months, a terrific attachment position across the other side of the country appeared as if from nowhere which the recalcitrant grabbed with alacrity. They left TCR swearing to God that if it had a good reputation it was all down to the talent of the presenters, the diligence of the reporters and the professionalism of the producers, not Simone Pound. Over the five years of her time in charge, however, the gaps between such departures had widened and now rarely occurred – and now Two Counties Radio, broadcasting to the broad and lonely flatlands of the obscure eastern edge of midland England, was an award-winning station.

Greg McKenzie's view of Simone Pound was closer to the rogue than the typical TCR female who uniformly loved her to bits. He wasn't being unkind; he simply knew she wasn't cut out for radio in the digital age. Now that the podcasts and up-to-the-minute local websites had arrived, he would watch her fall further and further behind the trends that were hurtling towards the medium at fearsome speed, until she would have to be put out of her misery. You could hardly run a modern organisation like TCR now with a plant spray and a recipe for shortbread, so what chance would she have in two years time? For the past two years or so, he'd lived by a policy of maintaining his reputation as the driving force of the station, the new ideas as well as the implementation man, and biding his time.

She did have an uncanny ability, just when you thought she'd finally reached the point of being visibly and provably ineffectual, to pull a tough fibre out of her being and defeat you. Or do it by sheer luck.

But when the newsroom stopped work and listened with a mixture of horror, glee but mostly total disbelief, Reg Gunfire, who'd had a deep affection for station politics for many years, turned to Noona Reynolds and said, 'Forget the end of Giles. This will be end of the era of the Pound. The rule of McKenzie is nigh.'

When Greg entered her office at 9.03 a.m., sliding into her office without knocking on the half-open door, TCR's managing editor was quietly relieving a blue PVC bag of her lunch: a sandwich; an apple; an Innocent smoothie; a Picnic and a can of Sprite, onto her cramped desk.

'Have you heard the big news?' he said, having slid into the room without knocking on the half-open door.

'Oh, did the Hardware win last night?' She tolerated football but knew her colleague hated it.

'No! Giles! Giles McAndrew did an inter-'

'It's okay, Greg, I heard it. And Leah's already rung me, so I know her side of the story. Then I rang Lucie at home.'

Simone struggled to hold her enthusiasm for disabling Greg's smugness as she rattled through her bulletin.

'Oh, you know about Lucie and Leah?'

She didn't even bother to refer to that episode.

'...and Ian Jagger rang me about it – so what else have you got for me - Bilt Cathedral hasn't collapsed, has it?'

'How did Ian Jagger?' The man's mind appeared to be in such a whirl that he couldn't even construct the sentence properly. 'Labour party chairman?'

'Oh, you know the bosses, they gave him the number probably – that's if the party hasn't got all our numbers stashed away somewhere handy. I'm sure they have.'

'Oh. Right.'

'So what do you want to talk about first? Politics or women's politics?'

'Well, I was thinking about Leah Caighton,' said Greg. 'Do you think we might take steps to take her out of harms way?'

'Has she joined the army?'

If there's one thing Simone Pound was not in the mood for on this particular morning was Greg McKenzie trying to bully her.

'I'm sorry?'

Greg didn't get the reference, which surprised her.

'I think,' she said, 'we should listen to what Leah has to say when she comes in for the meeting.' She rearranged her hair unselfconsciously with a brush, missing Greg's surprise.

'Oh. I rather thought we were going to have to let her go.'

The 'we' made her laugh. She was surprised to see him enthusing for Leah to be fired. All the men loved her. I wonder if he really knows how to satisfy a woman, she thought? Or maybe his cock doesn't work properly. Something wasn't right with him, anyway. She let him play his little game.

'I may agree with you, Gregory,' she said, knowing that he hated the long version of his name, 'and I may not. The Code-'

'Says that we should go through the agreed procedures and give her a full hearing. I know. But I thought...'

Simone was already half way out the door, heading for the kitchen to fill an empty coffee jug with water for a brew. One of the many things she liked about being Number 1 at the station was the ability to take social liberties like this and get away with them. She often left the room without a word when Greg was desperate to get the upper hand on her.

She filled the jug at the sink and looked briefly around the kitchen where she knew Leah's incident with Lucie had taken place. She guessed how awful it must have been and wondered at innocuous, institutional rooms like this hosting such dramas.

'Oh, hi,' said Sarah Billings, her News Editor and number one fan at the station, walking in behind her, trying to be bright.

'Hi, Sarah - how's things?'

'Fine,' replied the trusty Sarah, looking smart as per usual in clean white shirt and beige chinos. But not fine, thought Simone. 'Y'know. Within reason. What about you?'

'Good. We need to have a talk about the Clegg incident.'

'I was going to mention it - are we going to have an extra review meeting?'

'No – we'll sort this out more quietly. Did you hear Giles and Clegg?'

'I did – you?'

'No, but I had the bloody Labour Party chairman on the phone at home about ten minutes after it finished, would you believe. We need to work something out.'

'Oh – okay - no problem.'

'And can you track Giles down for me? Is he still here?'

'I'll go and check.'

'I need your brains on this, Sarah. If I don't have some sensible advice from somewhere I'm liable to say something I shouldn't to England Management, never mind Regions, or even Tony Bliss if he rings me up.'

'I thought Greg was good at calming you down,' said Sarah, indulgently, knowing full well he did the opposite.

'As I said, if I don't have some sensible advice from somewhere I'm liable to end up in bigger trouble than Leah. I'm going to meet Giles later in my office. I'd like to see you before then. Could you come and see me in about half an hour?'

'Sure.'

'Hair looks great, Sarah – mine's so rubbish.'

'It's not,' said Sarah, effortlessly cheerful, despite herself. 'And I need to do something with mine, actually – I'm bored with it.' She ran both hands through a layered, boyish mop of centre-parted straight fair hair.

'What? I'd have killed to have hair like yours at your age. And you're so tall – I'm so jealous. You're what, five-nine?'

'Five-seven-and-a-half,' she said, flicking her mop one more time.

They batted hair and height around for a bit, then stood back to back and asked sports reporter, Alan Barker, who'd wondered in, to judge the difference in their heights. It was agreed that Simone wasn't so much of 'a female short-arse' - as she put it - as she thought and that she shouldn't worry so much about herself because she looked really good. They felt guilty for lying, though would have pitied her less had they known that a man nearly ten years her junior had been enthusiastically seeing to her bedroom needs on and off for most of the past month. But the men at the station didn't know. In fact, the thought wouldn't have occurred to a single one of them in a month of Solid Gold Two Counties Radio Sentimental Sundays.

The banter eased Simone's own mind at the start of what promised to be the worst day in TCR history. Her next task would be to deal with Greg's annoyance at being kept waiting all this time, but that would be near the least of it, she was sure. But after seeing Sarah, she was properly ready for him now. She came back into her office in her customary slow, unflustered way.

'Now, Greg, what were you saying?' She poured the water into the machine and got a canister of ground coffee from the cupboard behind her desk.

He watched Simone fiddling with an odd-looking plant on her desk. I wasn't saying anything, you silly cow, he thought, and thanks for keeping me waiting.

'Oh, um, no, well, so...'

'What I thought we'd do, is meet Leah and see if we can't sort it all out without the official blasted hoo-ha,' said Simone, stroking a leaf on her Preacher-in-the-Pulpit gently.

'So you don't want to get rid of her,' said Greg, trying to stay neutral.

'I don't really know what I want,' said Simone, truthfully. Which was why she wanted a heart-to-heart with Leah if that was possible. Then she might work out what was best for her and do it, though that would depend on the grace of Lucie Bastable.

'This might cause us a lot of trouble. It might be easier to lance the boil by letting her go.'

Lance the boil, Simone thought? What boil? Leah hadn't been anything remotely approaching a problem until this morning.

'Well, let's hear what she has to say. There might be more going on behind the scenes than we realize,' she said.

'Even, God forbid, if her mother's got terminal cancer or something, it hardly justifies threatening a colleague with physical violence,' said Greg, sitting on a chair with legs outstretched and crossed, arms folded. For nearly a full minute they didn't speak; the only sound in the room was the coffee machine's drip and gurgle. Then Greg McKenzie decided to sum up.

'In the end, we'll have to do what's right.'

No, thought Simone: I'll do what I think is right for Leah and the station, and we'll see if we can't get both those things coinciding.

'We'll see later,' she said.

'What time?'

'Ten.'

'Right, I'll see you then – if you need me, I've got to go and talk to Lesley about the community bus.'

'When does your bus stint finish, tell me?'

'A week today. But I can cancel it to help you with the fallout. I'll cancel today, shall I?'

Simone was having none of that.

'There's no need for that, yet. We'll do the meeting at ten and you'll be able to get to the bus before it goes.' The bus was being fixed at a local garage. 'It won't be ready until eleven at the earliest.'

'Then I need to see Damien about the website.'

I don't need your bloody timetable for the day, thought Simone. You're not the bloody Prime Minister.

'Where's it off to today?'

'The bus? Prama Farthing Primary School.'

'Okay – well, see you later,' she said, pouring herself a mug of coffee.

'I'll be there,' said Greg, and left.

By the time Leah Caighton drove carefully into the cramped station car park for her meeting with Simone, having changed her mind about quitting before she was pushed, she had managed to remain outside Giles' reach for four days.

At the same moment, Giles was in town, visiting the bank and buying one or two bits and pieces. By now he had become sick of the dispute and sick of Leah in a way. Standing outside Costa, paper mug of coffee in hand, he rang Catherine and reached her. He wasn't pestering her; she'd asked him for progress reports.

'Where are you, if you don't mind me asking?' he said.

'The streets of London. You remember that song?'

'Yeah,' said Giles. 'Whereabouts?'

'Just outside the Royal Academy. In Piccadilly. It's lovely.'

He updated her on the Leah situation once again. Not that there was anything to say. He told her nothing about the Clegg incident.

'There's something grotesque about her,' he said to Catherine.

'Hmm, maybe. Have you ever checked out her star sign, Giles?'

'No,' he said, surprised. He'd suddenly thought of her embroidered flared jeans. 'Should I?'

'Sure – it could be interesting. What's her sign?'

'I haven't a clue!' Cath laughed at the way he said it, as if she'd asked him for the average height of a yak.

'You should check it out, Giles – you're such an Aries.'

'What does that mean?'

'Look it up on the Internet. Look – I got to go.' She was in London seeing dealers. 'I got a meeting in ten minutes and I got to walk faster than this.'

Giles didn't know either what he would have done by Thursday if he hadn't had his cousin to talk to. He wondered, too, how he'd waded through the sludge of all those fights with Leah, going back almost two years, on his own. To be without her for four days made him wonder how they'd both put up with it all this time. If he and Leah got back together, he wasn't going to go back to that; they had to come to some kind of new understanding.

By the time he started the short trek back to the station, Leah was already standing in the corridor outside Simone's office hoping like hell she didn't run into anyone. She ducked into the Music Library to avoid Big Dave and Marcus, whose loud voices she heard coming from the direction of the newsroom, not realising that their likely destination was...

'Oh, hi, Leah – um...'

...the Music Library. She should have known.

114

'Hi, Marcus.' She thought Marcus was quite sweet, but barely looked at Dave, who wasn't her scene at all.

'You looking for a CD?' said Marcus.

'No, waiting to see Simone,' she said, lacking the energy to explain the detour.

'Oh.'

'Yeah,' she said, hands in pockets drifting out to the corridor. The scene was embarrassing. Maybe I haven't any alternative but to leave, she thought: they don't want me around, obviously, now I've attacked their precious Lucie.

She wandered the few steps back to Simone's office when she heard someone's striding steps behind her, which stopped abruptly behind her. She turned around and Giles was standing there.

He looked terrible: gaunt in a face which was thin anyway, and pale. I probably look even worse, she thought. She suddenly felt lost without him. She looked at the floor, not knowing what to say. Giles came right up to close to her and was about to speak when Simone's door opened in front of them.

'Oh, hi, you two,' said the managing editor, as if they were a pair of school children. 'Do you want to come in?'

Neither Giles nor Leah knew what to say, until Giles got a hold of himself.

'Have I got the time wrong? Ten, you said, I think.'

'Did I?' said Simone. 'Hang on,' she said moving out beyond the doorway to the corridor, 'I need a wee.'

The couple watched her skip past them then turn the corridor corner where she ran into someone, then both voices disappeared and the space around them was quiet.

Giles tried to make eye contact but Leah wasn't playing. He spoke.

'I've been trying to get hold of you, but...'

'I've been out of range - you know what I'm like. Sorry.'

'Why?'

She finally looked up at Giles. She looked awful, but still wonderful.

'Why am I sorry?'

'If you like.'

'I'm not really sorry – well I am. Oh, look, Giles, this has been really difficult for me...'

'And for me – if you'd let me talk to you or text you I could have explained things and we could have sorted this out.'

'Could we?' she said, and his heart sank. So she didn't want him any more. It was over.

'Yes. I don't suppose you opened my emails either.'

'No. Sorry.' But I opened one of yours, she thought. I wonder if he knows.

'I don't understand you, Leah.'

'I know.'

'No, listen.' She was being so hard. His morale just kept dropping and dropping with each sentence out of her mouth. And now she folded her arms and dabbed her foot on the carpet - he wasn't going to get anywhere.

'If you still...still...' He couldn't say it. '...want us to be together, why didn't you let me in to talk to you?'

'I don't know.' She didn't. She suddenly saw how awful she was being but was helpless. She thought of her mother's words, 'Queen of Sheba' again then thought, I'll never change, and was suddenly horrified of what she'd become.

'You drive me crazy, Leah – all this could have been explained.'

'Really? The letter? And the woman I saw you with?'

'Yes. Both.'

I'm driving him into Lucie's arms, she thought. I'm such hard work for him. He really wants a woman who'll look up to him and nothing more.

'How will you do that? How could you have done that?'

Giles thought of his next words, already ready to come out of his head and mouth, and was shocked. He tried to stop himself, but at that moment, all he wanted to do was hurt her.

'I'm not sure you deserve an explanation any more after what you did to Lucie.'

Then voices were heard again. Simone was turning the corner with Greg McKenzie in tow: the conversation was over. Giles made a quick decision. He moved a half-step closer and spoke quietly.

'It was my cousin, Leah. That was Catherine you saw, my cousin from Canada. And the email was from her. It was nothing, a misunderstanding - you didn't read the second page!'

'What?' said Leah.

'Sorry,' said Simone to them, brightly and a little breathless. 'Have I messed up the times of our meetings? Didn't I say eleven o'clock, Giles? Hi, Leah. Are you okay?'

'Um, yeah, fine.'

'No, it was ten, Simone, but it-'

'No, it does matter. I'm so sorry. I'll tell you what we can do. I'll see you now, Leah, and Greg, could you take Giles into your office and talk through the Clegg situation? Then I'll see you about it straight after I'm done with um, Leah, Giles. If that's okay...'

116

It was okay with everyone except Greg, but Simone had Leah inside her office with the door closed before he could say anything. The men went round the corner to Greg's office and began to talk politics.

Simone didn't go back to her desk. She stayed with Leah in the space in front of it and took both her hands in hers.

'Leah – my dear. Whatever is the matter?'

Leah was taken aback by Simone's directness, and the physical contact, too. In the normal run of things they had little to do with each other. Her immediate boss was news ed. Sarah; her line manager, Greg. It occurred to her that this was the first time she'd been alone in her office like this. She felt Simone's hands on her and began to feel something coming up from deep inside her.

'I...' She looked into Simone's soft grey eyes. 'I...I've got myself into a terrible mess.' She could say no more than that before she folded into tears. She let herself drop into Simone's arms and felt as though she'd found a mother. She seemed to be there a long time before Simone spoke.

'Come on, my love, let's get these tears dried and start doing some talking.'

Simone let go of her gently and sat her down in a chair.

Leah didn't like talking about herself to anyone, not about how she really felt, but before she knew what was happening she began to pour out half her life story. She found herself admitting things she barely accepted herself.

'I'm just not capable of believing that Giles really does love me.' She felt a huge weight fall out of her and was surprised almost to the point of amazement. She suddenly realised that she could feel a sense of freedom inside if she chose to. The relief was overwhelming.

'The trouble is, you don't love yourself, either enough or at all.'

This was another bombshell for Leah. She didn't have anyone to speak to her like this. She recognised the truth of it as soon as Simone said it, but it never would have occurred to her alone.

'What was it like for you growing up?' said Simone.

'My Dad was always very hard on me. Wanted me to achieve a lot at school – a *lot*.'

'And did you? I can't remember what you did.'

'I worked really hard. Then I got glandular fever and things went downhill from there, really.'

'It's obvious you're very bright, Leah. I'm sorry it hadn't occurred to me that you needed telling. But I suppose even at your age – what are you, 28?'

'29.'

'Huh,' Simone grunted, thoughtfully. 'Even at 29, I think we all need telling how good we are at things, how clever we really are.'

Leah thought of Giles. She began to see that maybe his life wasn't as simple as she'd always thought it was: the local hero presenter; the supremely confident, slick guy who seemed to have everything figured out.

'Do you think Giles is insecure?' said Leah.

'We all are, love, about some things. I doubt that Giles is any different. But you know him better than I do, dear. You tell me.'

'I don't know that I really know him – isn't that stupid?'

It sounded highly intelligent to Simone Pound.

'Well now, why don't you talk to him and try to get to know him again, as if it's the first time?'

'I don't – I don't know. When I – when I'm difficult, when I give him trouble, it always seems to bounce off him. He just goes off into that studio as if nothing's happened, and sounds like the most confident man in England. I don't know how he does it – I couldn't do what he does if I trained for it for a hundred years.'

'Ah, you're confusing two different things. Presenters, when they get in there in their chariot, especially the men, they become another person. When they're "on," they can forget the rest of their lives, no matter how bad things are, and be brilliant.'

That, too, was obvious when you had it spelled out for you, but Leah hadn't understood that about Giles. She realised that she'd never talked to him about his presenting properly once. She felt guilty. I should have taken more interest in him, she thought.

'I'm jealous of him, Simone,' said Leah, as if a moment of brilliance had struck her brain like a shaft of white light. 'I didn't realise it but I am.'

'Do you resent him?' said Simone.

'Yes, I think I do.' The revelation didn't make things much easier. 'I resent how important he is – around here. And I think I feel threatened by it. I've taken what he does for granted – how good he is, I mean. I suppose I should be proud of him. And that troubles me - why don't I?'

'He is brilliant, for local radio. We could still easily lose him. But – I understand why you don't feel proud of him. Until you truly face up to each other, really want to understand each other, you won't.'

'Simone, what am I going to do?' Simone was no longer her employer, Leah realised. Not when they were like this, talking about Giles.

'I don't know. What do you want to do?'

'I'm not sure. I still love him, but I'm starting to think that we're just too different for the relationship to work. What do you think I should do?'

'I think you should leave Two Counties Radio.'

Leah looked up from the carpet at Simone open-mouthed.

'I should say, "You have to leave for disciplinary reasons."'

'And are you going to get rid of me, then?'

'No, of course not. Do you think we would have had this talk if I was going to do that? I know I come across to people as a bit batty, but I'm not cruel. I think you should leave because I can't promote you. You're a good reporter on the way to becoming truly excellent, Leah, way brighter than those around you – though for Christ's sake don't tell them I told you.'

'God, thanks,' said Leah, feeling warm all of a sudden.

'And you have a lovely radio voice. But, you should be doing my job in ten years time, and you can't afford to hang around here. You need an SBJ job, a head of programming or news-ed job, and you haven't even been on any courses yet, have you?'

'No,' she said, looking at Simone with a sense of wonder.

'Well, we need to get you on a couple of management courses and then you need to start looking for promotion opportunities elsewhere.'

'But...'

'"But why haven't I said anything to you before"'?

'No, that wasn't what I was going to say.'

'Oh, well, you perhaps should have done. If I was really on the ball in this job, love, I would have said this six or nine months ago. A year, maybe. I'm really sorry.'

Suddenly Leah found herself feeling for this woman who until ten minutes ago she hardly knew. She was still relatively young at 29, but there was something about Simone that spoke of a failure that made her sad. Station boss at a local BRBC was bloody good though.

'It doesn't matter. I'm just so glad you're not going to sack me.'

'Thank Lucie Bastable,' said Simone, composing a look of forced neutrality. Leah went cold at the thought of saying anything more to Lucie, and felt instantly miserable at the thought that in the next day or so she might have to find a way of doing it. If she could find a way of sliding out of it, she would.

'Be grateful for the fact that Lucie wants to forget about it – put it behind her. She's a very nice young woman, Leah...'

Don't tell me that, said Leah to herself.

'I know,' said Leah. 'I'll find a way to make it up to her.'

'No matter how difficult it is for you, do just that.'

119

Leah stood up – she could see Simone's body language telling her it was time for her to go.

'Now – if you think you're ready, go back into the newsroom and ask Damien what's going on. You need to catch him before he leaves. He's only here for the morning. With a bit of luck he might send you out for the rest of the day.'

Leah didn't get to hear the alternative. As she closed the door behind her, she realised that it was her job to quit messing everybody around and get back to work. She'd get over the embarrassment of being amongst everyone again, and she'd tough out the Giles situation if it came to a split. She really felt tough again. What a woman that Simone, she thought, and got excited about the compliments she'd been given. Managing a station in ten years? At 39? The thought hadn't remotely occurred to her. Nor indeed had moving up the scale at all. She'd been without a career plan, or a life plan for so long now. Maybe it's time for me to change direction. Maybe I should take a leaf out of Giles's book and become a go-getter, she thought, as she slipped into the newsroom as unobtrusively as she could and went up to Damien Reed, the head of programming.

'Hi, Leah – are you on now?'

'Yeah, I'm back, what do you have?'

'Great. Um, well, you can have haemorrhoids at the council offices, or World Cup Fever breaking out amongst the cows at a farm in Long Shatton.'

'You're kidding…'

'Um, yeah I am: it's either haemorrhoids at the council offices or concerns about falling milk yields in Shat.'

'I didn't think we had any cows round here.'

'This is possibly why the yields are dropping like flies. Go and find out for us, will you?'

'Sure.'

'And you can take the new gizmo to try.' He turned to pick something up from his desk. 'Don't worry – it's simple. Same buttons for record and playback. When you get back Marcus or Sarah will show you how to edit with it. It's fantastic.'

She took the neat little Baby-Corder, the state of the art recording and editing machine they were piloting, from the hand of Damien Reed and went to find out some more about cows.

18

A Meeting for Giles

When Simone had finished her time with Leah she went straight into Giles and Greg, but knocked first.

'Hi, come in and sit down, Simone,' said Greg.

'Are you okay, Giles?' said Simone.

'Yes, I'm fine,' said Giles, though his mind was crashing about all over the place, like an amusement ride out of control. He was scared about what he'd done earlier and when he managed to get his mind off that for a few moments, it crashed into Leah again. What a fucking mess I've got myself into, he thought. He was angry because he'd so stupidly let his emotions get out of hand; let the personal spill right over into the professional. It was unforgivable, he kept telling himself. He should have known far, far better. He was practically forty.

'We were talking about the problems with the Labour Party,' announced Greg. 'What's the latest – any more calls from Central Office?'

'Only from Alan de Cameron asking me to pass on his thanks to Giles.'

'Y'joking,' said Greg, suddenly jerking forward in his chair.

'Yes, I'm joking. But I bet he's doing exactly that if news has reached him,' said Simone.

'Is there going to be serious comeback, do you think?' said Giles.

'No. Don't worry – they've got their hands full down there dealing with Clegg's bonking and immigrant criminals running around on a crime spree. They're not too worried about us. Chairman Jagger rang me at home this morning but his heart wasn't in it – he was just going through the motions.'

She felt like crossing her fingers behind her back.

'What did he say?' said Giles, still a mite anxious.

'He said that rumours of Mick's marriage being on the rocks are being greatly exaggerated,' said Simone.

The joke was appreciated by Giles, at least.

'He actually said that if we weren't careful, not just us, but all local radio stations would be told to go to hell the next time we want to interview someone in the Cabinet. And the next time and the time after that.'

'Meaning?' asked Giles.

'Oh, Christ,' commented Greg.

'Meaning he's just blowing a load of hot air - if he was even considering that, he wouldn't have come right out and told us.'

The phone rang, and Greg picked up.

'Hi, Greg McKenzie...Yeah, okay. It's for you, Simone – Alyson Knuckle from the Today programme, Radio 4.'

'Tell her I'll call back,' said Simone, and I know the Today Programme's on Radio 4, Greg, you bloody pain in the rectum, she thought.

The phone rang again. Greg and Simone tutted simultaneously.

'Yeah, Greg McKenzie? Uh-huh...Simone, 5 Live drive-time show, they want to do an interview this afternoon live.'

'With me?'

'Yes.'

She made a face. 'Tell them I'll be in all afternoon, and to tell me what time they want me and I'll be in my office.'

'They also want Giles.'

'They can't have him.'

Giles raised an eyebrow.

'Bad for your career if you go blabbing about it to Piers Allen, Giles. I'll tell them what a bloody brilliant and fearless presenter you are, and I'll tell them how sexy you are, how's that?'

'Ha-ha, fine Simone, fine.'

Greg McKenzie sat with folded arms at his desk and scowled.

19

Another Meeting for Giles

As the tumultuous day passed twelve o'clock, Giles still hadn't left the building. He was in the relative gloom of Simone's north-facing office. He was slumped in a chair. He felt exhausted.

'You need some sleep. You look…well…'

'Like I've been up since four o'clock?'

'Ha-ha, thank God you haven't lost your sense of humour.'

'There's not much of it left, I can tell you that.'

Simone Pound filled a filter with ground coffee for the third time that day.

'What? You were lucky this morning – that ought to bring some of it back.'

'Lucky?' exclaimed Giles.

'Yes. Only the part of the Labour party that likes Clegg hates you, but the rest of 'em, the Tories and the Lib Dems love you, we've had a record number of phone calls and 91% of them think the town should put a statue of you up outside the town hall. I'm worried I'm going to lose you to 5 Live or somewhere if this has leaked out.'

'Funny how life goes, isn't it.'

'Well, I'd have to say "no" to that at the moment. But I know what you mean.'

'Yeah, well, I'm sorry. That would all be my fault.'

Simone went over and ruffled his hair.

'Don't worry. You're going to hate me next, anyway,' she said. 'Cup of coffee?'

'Please. Why? What have you done?'

'I told Leah that she ought to leave.' Giles panicked inside. So Simone thought she and he were unsuited to each other – that finishing was the best solution.

'You could have sacked her anyway – but tell me what you mean.' He'd mention the panic in a moment.

'I can't push her forward here in the next year unless something odd happens. She has a lot of talent, you know.'

'I know,' said Giles, admitting it only not to appear dim to his boss. He knew it but had always tried hard to avoid accepting it as truth.

'And a great radio voice. But she needs to get out of reporting and into management. Either that or go hell for leather at a national job presenting speech radio.' Shit, thought Simone. I forgot to tell her that.

'You're joking,' he said, trying to pull back her advance, 'she can't get on with people.'

'She can learn that as she goes.' She walked round her desk to give Giles his drink in a bright yellow beaker.

'Are you sure?' He knew about the talent but the idea that Leah could ever present was outlandish to Giles – she seemed to completely lack empathy with other human beings.

'Yes – I am.'

'But she doesn't even seem to like people, Simone.'

'Ha-ha.'

'No, I'm serious.'

'So am I. She's got really strong qualities that everyone will see if she can get out from under one big problem. She can.' - Giles was shaking his head – 'She's got passion and brains, Giles – just like you.'

'You're telling the wrong person.'

'Have you ever thought really hard about why she finds it hard to get on with people?'

'You're kidding, Simone, aren't you?'

'Not with you, silly, I mean with the people around her at the station.'

Giles assumed it was for the same reason they rowed a lot: that she was a strong-headed cow who at certain times insisted on having her own way whatever the cost.

'Go on.'

'She's has very low self-esteem.'

'Simone, I don't think you know her.'

'You think you know everything about her, but when we get very close to someone, we can lose sight of what's right in front of us.'

'Go on.'

'She loves you. Envies you. Is jealous of you. Resents you.'

'Thanks.'

'Love's a big thing – but I know what you mean. But the simple reason for all the negatives is that she thinks she isn't worthy of you.'

'You have to be kidding, Simone. She's so difficult with me – she treats me like crap sometimes, y'know.'

A couple of excruciating examples started to play in his head.

'And you're perfect, I suppose. None of it's your fault...'

'Hey – I thought you were a fan of mine.'

'It's her way of defending herself, Giles. And she's just being perverse because people are perverse, aren't they? Her way of dealing with thinking she's not good enough is to pull you down. Or to destroy the relationship with bad behaviour. She probably thinks better that than you leave her because you realise she's not good enough for you.'

'Blimey, Simone.'

'What?'

'Why didn't we talk about Leah like this a year ago, a year and a half ago?'

'Ha-ha, I don't know. We're all busy. Don't make me feel guilty.'

'I never knew you were this…insightful.'

'Well, if I am being insightful it's because I've had a lot of my own problems to sort out. I've done a lot of reading in the last couple of years – oh, I might as well tell you – since I went into therapy.'

'Really? I know your marriage didn't work out.'

'Oh, there's a lot of stuff I've been through that I've never told anyone. I've been very late doing something about it.' She looked out of her window at the sunshine and thought of summer holidays in hot France.

'Well, I can honestly say you've stunned me, Simone. Low self-esteem? Bloody hell – I didn't see that one coming.'

'I'm right, Giles: I realised when we were talking this morning and she agreed with me.'

'What? Can I carry you around in a bag with me and pull you out when I need Leah to agree with me?'

'Ha-ha.'

'How did you pull that off?'

'It's a woman thing, I think,' said Simone smiling.

Yes, it would be, thought Giles. He hated that smug Sisterhood thing. He feared it – it meant that understanding women would always be beyond him.

'So tell me what I should do now – about Leah,' said Giles, but he sensed that she was slipping away from him already.

'Here's an irony for you, Giles, "the great communicator" – start talking to her.'

'I'm not sure I know how any more.'

'I think she's ready to give you a chance.'

'You think? She's told you?'

'Pretty much. Yes - pretty much.'

'Well, I need her to start answering my calls. She's kept everything switched off since Sunday – refused to open my emails.'

'Try again.'

'Will you be our referee if I can get her to talk to me?'

'Ha-ha. A mediator? I don't think that's the answer,' she said, looking out into the sunshine again. She was getting hungry. Food was far from Giles's mind. He sipped the last of his coffee, still looking weary and forlorn.

'You need to sit down together and make sure you properly open yourself up to each other. Do you think you can do that?' said Simone.

'I have no idea,' he said slowly.

'Why don't the two of you try at first on your own. Then if it's not working, and you both want me to help, I will.'

'Christ, Simone. You don't know what she's like,' he started to say then realized she knew her now far better than him. 'Well, you know her as a woman – I can see that obviously, now, but you don't know her as a man.'

Simone smiled.

'Ha-ha, no, and I don't want to. Which is why it's better that you two patch this up on your own.'

Giles chewed the whole thing over, trying to focus on not letting himself be overwhelmed. He cursed himself for his Clegg outburst. Now Simone had opened up a chink of light in the Leah darkness it was the last thing he needed, a negative distraction like that.

'People are bloody weird, Simone, aren't they.'

'What do you mean?'

'Or, maybe they're not weird.' The situation seemed to be running way out beyond his control. Being honest with himself, he hadn't seen any hidden depths in Leah Caighton. And now Simone was bringing her back to him but taking her away at the same time.

'It's maybe that I just don't understand them.'

'All of us have that problem, you know. I'm not a genius.'

Giles didn't answer. He'd begun to think she was. So Leah was incredibly bright and had a great future in radio, did she? That was something that had slid right past him. He thought her unpredictability and self-centredness proved the opposite: that she didn't have the intelligence to realise that in between the good times she caused their relationship massive problems. As for her reporting, he'd never seen her in action and didn't talk to anyone she worked with who might have told him. Suddenly he found the sense to see that he was going to lose her. Even if he could show her how much he loved her, she was going to leave him, if not sooner, then later. If Simone was right about her career potential, then they weren't on the way to becoming a husband and wife presenting duo, they were destined to separate definitively, permanently.

Giles put his fear aside. He could just as easily be wrong. So he wasn't a brain of Britain – so what? Lots of couples had different levels of intelligence. If she really did love him, it could work. They'd go to London. They didn't have to work at the same station. There were loads of stations in the south-east: London; Sussex; Kent; Essex; Three Counties; Reading – talk radio, commercial radio, there were loads of opportunities out there.

Simone had been pottering about around her desk while he was thinking.

'Okay, Giles, time to press on. So we'll leave it like this: let me talk to 5 Live and 4 about Clegg. The press'll find you, of course.'

'I don't want to talk to them.' He did, but in the circumstances, it just complicated things. 'I can put out a statement.'

'Yes, do that. Why don't you write one here or fax it to me if you do it from home. What are you going to say?' She was pretty certain he didn't need tutoring.

'Oh, you know, regret upsetting the deputy-Prime Minister, uncalled for, all that stuff. Shall I mention being under personal pressure?'

'No, it'll only get them interested in you. You don't want them prying into your private life.'

'No.'

'Just call me if you're not sure about anything. And back tomorrow as usual, yes?'

'Of course.'

'Your time will come, you know. When this dies down a little bit, you'll still be getting offers if they find out how good you are. If they bother to listen.'

Giles thought about moving on. He'd enjoyed being a big fish in a small pond. If the attack on Clegg was going to lead him to a lucky break, then maybe he'd take the chance to really make it. He was kidding himself. Of course he'd take it – this is what he'd always dreamed of: the radio big time. Was he good enough? He'd find out.

'And if you want that help with Leah, let me know.'

'Okay, Simone.'

Giles got up and left, thinking about his boss. What a woman. That's the sort of woman I need. He dreamed on for a few seconds before allowing his thinking to drop back into its normal equilibrium position. He knew he only felt safe when he was in control of the relationship. He needed to be the boss, the driver, the pilot. He had to feel as though he had the upper hand. He felt bitter at that; why wasn't he more grown up? It's time you became a man, he thought; time you let someone right in and be your equal. I'm not sure I can, came the reply from deep inside his being, and for the first time, he thought about his real self with a sense of panic.

When he got to the newsroom to pick up his memory stick he was assailed by colleagues wanting to congratulate him for his humiliation, as they perceived it, of a big politician. Figures of Clegg's stature didn't come out to TCR that often, and when they did, weren't shy about patronising them: sweeping in and out of the building in three and a half minutes, refusing hospitality, as if a visit to a local radio station was like stopping off at a public lavatory.

'Giles,' said Jim Johnson, TCR's straight-laced, model aircraft-obsessed, lunchtime presenter, 'you did us proud.'

'Too right, well done, mate,' said Marcus, who didn't talk to Giles often, but sort of liked him when he did. 'Pity it wasn't Bliss.'

Lucie came over and stood smiling on the edge of a crowd of four or five, looking dark and lovely in fresh-looking clothes and discreetly re-applied make up. Giles couldn't help noticing, despite himself. He instinctively looked around for Leah, scared for a second, but as he'd been told by Simone: she was out on a job.

Had anyone bothered to carefully scan the rest of the room, Sarah Billings would have been conspicuous for her refusal to let the general buzz of excitement visibly distract her from her work. She continued to look at her computer screen, but listened in on the conversation and laugher just six feet from her desk, she alone wondering whether the darling son of TCR's striking a blow at the politicians for the people might not have serious consequences.

Meanwhile. Giles McAndrew continued to revel in the attention and felt bad that he didn't spend more time with these people. I'll start putting that right next week, he decided. Leon came into the room looking as pleased as hell with life, and they went off to talk about Friday's show.

'Have you forgiven me? I was rough on you this morning - I'm sorry,' said Giles.

'Don't be daft. The phones are still going mad,' said Leon. 'You might have started something,' he went on. Giles couldn't be bothered to think too hard about what he meant. An anti-politician backlash? Politicians were despised already. Where might this lead: assassinations of Bliss and others by middle-aged Volvo drivers from towns like this? Little old ladies throwing smoke bombs at Gordon Green?

Later on, at the garden table round the back of The Barn House near the apple tree, Giles sat at his laptop with the umbrella up to shield his eyes and the screen from the sun, writing his press release and thinking about Leah, thinking about everything. His phone hadn't stopped ringing and throbbing, and emails were piling up. There was no wind in his chimes, but the blackbird sang on in the tall tree behind him with an inexhaustible energy that never seemed to run dry.

20

Press Release

Fax to Simone Pound, Managing Editor, Two Counties Radio. 4/5/06
Press Release – Thursday 4th May 2006
From: Giles McAndrew, Breakfast Show Presenter, Two Counties Radio (Bartonshire and Bilt)

As you may already know, an incident occurred on my Breakfast Show on Two Counties Radio this morning which resulted in the Deputy-Prime Minister, Mr John Clegg, prematurely ending an interview.

I wish to state quite categorically that the situation that developed was one entirely of my own making. In the circumstances it was perfectly understandable for Mr Clegg to leave in the light of my making inappropriate comments of a personal nature. I now regret having made these very much.

I was unforgivably rude to Mr Clegg and for that I wish to apologize unreservedly to him for breaking with the ethical rules of broadcast journalism. I would like to extend that apology to the Labour Party and to Tony Bliss, the Prime Minister. And his wife, his mum, his hairdresser, his brothers, sisters and goldfish. Blah-di-blah-di-blah.

I would finally like to wish Mr Clegg well in his future career, what he has left of it, and hope that he can remember to keep his dick in his trousers, for his wife's sake and for the country's for the next two weeks at least.

Giles McAndrew

Is this grovelling enough, Simone? Could you smarten it up for me? Change anything you like. Love Giles.

21

Reconciliation

When he went to his office at two o'clock to send the fax, he saw 'Leah Caighton' in his inbox in bold black. 'Call me,' said the message headline. His insides reverberated. He called her immediately and she answered inside three rings.

'Hi,' she said.

'Hi. It's me.'

'Hi. So, do you think we should meet?'

'Yes. I do.'

'Me too. Where?'

'I don't mind.'

'Shall I come to you,' said Leah, 'or do you have bad memories of me there now?'

Giles winced. She wasn't wrong – but she wasn't quite right: they'd had some fantastic times at the house.

'If you have, let me come and break the spell. Let me make it up to you.'

He heard a voice shrunk to something small and tinny saying something so large, he found it hard to contain himself. These were words women said to him in dreams. This was wild stuff for Leah; he began to get excited.

'No. It wasn't just your fault. I know I'm bad. I know I'm arrogant, and I treat you like a kid sometimes.'

'If this is the new Giles, I like it.'

'Come over and you can find out for yourself whether I'm new or not.'

'What time – when I finish?'

'Yeah, what time are you finishing?'

'Um, I started again mid-morning. I can get away by six, I should think.'

'Get here when you can.'

'I'll be there by seven at the latest.'

'Great.'

'See you then.'

'Yeah, see you then.'

131

Fantastic, thought Giles. Leah, on her way back to the station to start editing her interview with a friendly but worried farmer, smiled as she folded her phone and tucked it in her bag.

Giles's afternoon dragged while Leah wrote her introduction, her links and her wrap, and inserted them around the best bits of the interview. She could have done it with the new magic gizmo, the Baby Corder, as everyone was stupidly calling it, but she didn't want to risk screwing it up and wasting time she didn't have while Damien explained to her how you used it. So she came back to the newsroom and got on with the job using the computer. She worked away her afternoon alone in a corner with the headphones on, listening, watching the green wavy lines on the black screen with intense concentration, cutting and pasting, until she was happy with what she'd done.

By three she'd sent the material to Sarah's computer, job finished. Half an hour later, Sarah called across the newsroom to Leah. Leah turned in her swivel chair to see Sarah smiling slightly and holding an erect thumb aloft. The news editor nodded her head a couple of times and mouthed the word, 'great' to her. Leah smiled back, feeling very, very good to know that she could produce a good package on a day like this, never mind do it with a minimum amount of fuss.

At twenty-to-four, Daisy Smith who was doing the news reading shift came back into the newsroom after throwing up in the toilets. She was white and sweating. When she went home two minutes later at Sarah Billings' insistence, Leah volunteered to fill in.

'You sure?' said Sarah, who could have done it herself, and would have rather enjoyed doing some work at the microphone again.

'Yeah, I'd like to,' said Leah.

She looked at what Daisy had left, re-wrote a lot of the text and brought in an item about Iraq that hadn't been used all afternoon and some breaking news about Rooney's metatarsal. She loved doing this. At four she went into the NPA booth on her own. She sat at the desk, slipped the headphones on, hit the mouse a couple of times, opened up the fader, waited until she heard the words, 'And now the three o'clock news and sport, read to you by Leah Caighton,' then started to read from the screen in front of her.

'Police have announced the arrest of the so-called Kilburn Killer, after six months of investigation. Charles Clewbury of Cricklewood was charged this morning with the murders of...'

Simone Pound listened in, breaking off pieces of banana with her fingers and popping them into his mouth as she went.

'...and that's the news this afternoon. Next bulletin at four-thirty. Now the sports news with Alan Barker.'

132

'Lovely work, Leah, lovely,' said Simone aloud, getting up to drop the banana skin into the bin. She took out a tissue and wiped her hands and smiled.

Though I say it myself, I've still got it, thought Leah, as she walked out of the building at a quarter to six. She found herself feeling excited about her job for the first time in a long time. And she was seeing Giles again tonight.

In the shower at six, she pulled the attachment off the hook and let it play over her crotch, enjoying the tingle and thinking about later on. She remembered the phrase, 'make up sex' from a TV programme, but couldn't remember which one it was. She thought about that for a bit and felt good. She felt herself smiling. It seemed like forever since she last laughed. She spent a long time drying her hair and making it look just so. She checked her underarms and decided they didn't need re-shaving, and inspected her pubis in the mirror and liked what she saw. She sat down on the edge of the bed and checked herself underneath and decided that a little manicure work was needed. Then she did some work on the nails on her feet, clipping carefully, then filing off the burrs. She put on her best, sexiest underwear, and inspected her rear in the mirror, twisting her neck to see. I'm nearly bloody thirty, she thought, and felt a bit dismal momentarily. It still looked good, though, she considered finally, though it was never round enough for her liking.

She put on clothes in the colours Giles liked: a subtle shirt in green, plain, set off with a silver periapt that was so clean and bright you could almost see it in the dark. Her trousers were plain too, expensive, olive green. She thought for a moment then took the trousers off, then the knickers, then put the trousers on again. She found the sandals she bought in Italy and put them on, and was satisfied that she felt and looked good, maybe great. She changed her earrings, had a drink of water, remembered to put a pair of sensible knickers in her bag with the rest of the stuff she needed for tomorrow, and left just as Sonia was coming in from the station.

'Blimey – out on the pull?' said Sonia.

'Yep,' said Leah, smiling.

Giles whiled away an afternoon that lasted for a week. He took out his bike and cycled for over an hour down the lanes of Bartonshire. He took it easy, enjoying the feeling of his legs rotating the pedals in a soft whirring on the tarmac below him. The sun kept shining, as it had for the past two days, and when the lanes were quiet, really quiet, and he could see for a mile in front and behind, he lifted his face to the sun, eyes closed for a few seconds at a time, loving the feeling of warmth and light. Vitamin D, he thought, realising he was reducing some rarely grasped moments of inner peace to an item from an almost long-forgotten show. The habit was so ingrained though. He hadn't won that many awards that he could measure his life out in them. Instead the past five years seemed sometimes to consist only of one continuous interview with Bart and Bilt people broken into hundreds of pieces. He lifted his face to the sun again and let his mind go blank for as long as he felt safe. Better.

He passed a turning to the right signposted 'Tower Hill 3' and decided after all to give a miss to the only high point in the county. The view was spectacular, and on a day like today you might even see the sea, but he didn't think he had enough time.

He went home and showered. He watched his penis swell and rise at the thought of Leah in his bed, but he only washed himself thoroughly. Drying himself standing in the centre of his room, he thought he could do with some sleep. He put on his night trousers and a t-shirt and opened a window. He set the alarm for five-fifty, lay on top of his duvet and went to sleep, feeling that it had been an amazing day, not least because he'd survived it – and now Leah was coming. He'd call Catherine when he got the chance – maybe before she arrived. Which reminded him of the painting – it was still in its studio wrapping in his living room: he still had to hide it. He thought of giving it to her a day or two early. It might be the best idea he'd had all week. He closed his eyes, changed his thinking completely to a favourite scene from his past, a regular trick, and within two minutes was asleep.

When the alarm went off he woke easily, used to an afternoon nap, and went about organising the next part of the day. He went to his fridge and pulled out some curry and rice and put it by the microwave. He got a bottle of white wine from his hall cupboard and put it in the freezer. He should have started chilling it earlier. He had some cold beer in the fridge though.

He called Leon, and spent too much time talking about the fallout from the Clegg interview. They chatted about whether they should follow it up on the show. Giles said he should make a profuse apology which suited Leon down to the ground. They decided that they'd made more than enough waves than was good for both of them and the station. It was also useful for Giles to bring work right back to normality. He wanted to concentrate on Leah.

He called Catherine but couldn't get her. He left a short message, telling her to listen to the five o'clock news programme on Radio 4 or buy a Friday national paper. He didn't think it would make the TV. He knew she'd get a thrill from seeing his name in The Guardian and The Times. Giles thought about his probably making the nationals and the

134

requests for interviews that had already started and began to like himself again. Maybe my career is going to take off after all, he thought.

Six o'clock. He went to the kitchen and surveyed the dessert situation. The M & S tiramisu was still there from last Sunday. He studied the carton for the sell-by and use-by dates. They were okay. He put on some music in the living room and turned the volume up high so he could hear it wherever he was in the house. The advantage of a detached house, he always thought when he did this, and he thought it now, as he waited interminably for Leah.

And so the time passed by, drifting towards seven.

At ten-past, Giles began to think that Leah might have changed her mind and he started to panic from the feet up, but then he heard a car coming down the lane, having not put on another CD, and watched it turn into his drive. It was her. Seconds later she walked in the side kitchen door.

At first they smiled at each other a little sheepishly. Giles felt something in his head take off or give way the second he saw her. Then a pang from his heart made him feel part-elated, part-helpless. She looked very beautiful to him, but not right. Tired, he thought, and wondered whether, though he'd pinned the responsibility for Sunday mostly on her, what happened had cost her as much as it had cost him.

'Hi,' she said, still smiling self-consciously, but feeling happy as she looked over his shoulder as they hugged each other. Her teeth, tending slightly towards large, flashed white at the world for the first time that week, though Giles missed the spectacle. She closed her eyes momentarily then pulled back and away so she could kiss him.

'You look great,' said Giles.

'And you, you git,' she said, slapping him playfully, 'might have made more of an effort.'

'I wasn't sure whether to put on a suit of armour,' he said, causing Leah to say 'hey!' and go to thump him again, but he stopped her by holding her tight and they both laughed.

'I've never liked this shirt much,' she said fingering the collar with a frown, 'but I like the jeans though.' She rubbed his thigh for a second and Giles knew that things were going to be okay, they would be good. 'Have you got some wine?' she said.

He got two glasses and the bottle of golden Australian wine from the freezer and they both thought of the dreadful past few days in the silence.

'The freezer? It isn't too cold is it?'

'No, I forgot to put it in the fridge.'

135

She tutted, then remembered herself. 'Sorry,' she said.

Giles poured them each a good glassful.

'Cheers,' said Leah, clinking glasses. They made small talk and work talk until Giles felt it was time to face up to what had happened over the past few days.

'Do you think we should talk about what happened?' said Giles. I'm going to get this over with, he thought, quickly, if that's possible.

'Yeah, okay.'

'Shall we go outside?'

'No, it's getting chilly.'

They went into the living room.

'Hang on, said Leah, 'I've got to go and get my clothes for the morning.'

She went back to the kitchen for her bag which she'd put on the kitchen sofa, pulled out trousers, vest, top and knickers, and took them back to the living room where she laid the trousers and top out carefully to try to avoid creases. Then she went and sat with Giles on the long sofa, laying down and putting her outstretched legs across his thighs. He was grinning like a Cheshire cat at the knowledge that she was definitely staying.

'Alright, then – I'm ready,' she said.

'Good,' said Giles, ready to do this. He began the proceedings. It feels like a court case, he thought. He proceeded.

'I want to say sorry for everything – I just…I just want everything to be okay between us.'

Giles had a sudden appreciation of how long a time they'd been together. It felt like a premonition: that if they had to do this after two years, something was fundamentally wrong with them.

'Do you know what I think,' said Leah, 'Six-foot-two, eyes of blue?'

'What do you think? – and it's six-three, actually.'

'You always say that – I think we should discuss this after we've been to bed. You can tell me about your cousin later.'

Giles was little less than amazed at her. She was rarely playful like this, Leah. He couldn't believe his luck. So if it's to be as simple as this, he thought, then so be it. Maybe in the grim first days of May, they'd crossed a Rubicon without knowing it. God, maybe out of disaster can come a new 'us'.

'What's up with you? Have you won the lottery, or something?' he said.

'No, not exactly. I'll tell you later.'

'No, tell me now.'

'No, big guy, come down here and kiss me.'

136

Giles let himself drop down. He met Leah's mouth in a wet kiss that went all the way to showing him that everything was soon going to be right back to normal. Giles felt his groin swelling quickly, as Leah's animal sensuality began to pour into his cerebral receptors like hot water filling a bath.

'Mmm,' went Leah. 'Come on, take me away from all this.'

'Would you like me to? Seriously?'

'Time for talking later. Take me upstairs.'

Leah lifted up easily into his arms. He didn't imagine he'd be doing this so early. He'd expected initial tension, the pair of them batting around their recent hostile thoughts about one another, all the bad feeling still hanging in air like noxious gas. Something had happened to Leah since...since...since he didn't even know when. He wondered what it was, but she was right, the talking and the analysing could wait. He got almost to the top of the first set of stairs and threatened, cackling like a pirate, to throw her down to the bottom. Leah screamed,

'No!' then 'No, Giles!' when he threatened to do it a second time. He thought she might be annoyed but then she brought her face up to his and laughed, and kissed him. Both their mouths opened to receive each other, before he dropped her onto her slim feet on the landing carpet. The next stairs were too narrow for play. And yet. As Leah went on ahead of him, Giles reached a hand out for her bottom and plugged his open hand between her legs, stopping her. He kissed her hair and rubbed her gently, making her go 'mmm' again with closed eyes, then lean her head back into him, rubbing like a cat. She felt warm on his hand and he squeezed her soft under-flesh, loving the feel of it, enjoying the ability to take all the toughness out of her. He took his hand away and pressed his stiffness into her buttocks and began to wish he'd worked some of this off in the shower earlier.

Stepping into the bedroom, Leah turned and would hardly let him move forward. She clung on to him, kissing his neck and reaching down for his behind, as if she couldn't wait, as if she was verging on desperation. Giles pushed at her again from the groin and pulled her shirt out at the back wanting to get it off in one go, but the buttoned up front stopped it going over her head. He began undoing it but was too frantic. Leah quickly got hold of the top one and undid it, and the second, and Giles had it up and off, the cuff buttons being undone. He threw the shirt to one side then reached down for her bra sides and flipped them up and off the superb rounds of Leah's breasts. He reached inwards and gripped each nipple, loving the feel of both at the same time, before flicking the still hooked bra over her head and away.

Her naked top half was a glorious thing to him: her skin smoother than any man could want; her breasts hanging there deliciously, making him feel as though he could lose it and go crazy any second; that he might bend down and bite them off. He wanted to frame them, hold them, watch them all day, take pictures of them and possess them in a way that was beyond imagining. He felt himself getting a little out of control. He saw that it was probably the fact that for days he thought he'd lost her. It was okay now, he told himself; he could calm down; she was back.

Leah had the top of his jeans undone now and Giles let her have some space. He was in dreamland, only also in difficulty, being too excited for his own good. He kicked the denims across the carpet a foot and took off his socks as Leah got rid of her shoes. Then she stroked him through his pants but he had to stop her. He grabbed at the top of her trousers, still noticing her breasts waiting there, the nipples pointing at him. He calmed himself for a second, slowed himself down, and pulled the zip down sensibly, as if he were undressing a mannequin in a shop, and slid the material downward. Where her knickers should have been was the immaculate flesh below her neat navel; he looked down and saw the top of her pubic hair and he thought he was going to lose his mind. Leah held her legs stiffly together to let the trousers drop to her feet, before pushing them away with her right foot. Then she put her hand on his length and rubbed the smoothness of it underneath but Giles again pushed it away.

'Oh,' she whined slightly in jest.

'No, it's too much – I'll come.'

'Okay,' she said, and let him take her between the legs with his fingers. As Giles felt her wet flesh he tried to concentrate on her enjoyment to take his mind away from an imminent explosive anti-climax. His kissed her neck and watched her face reacting to his careful friction, eyes closed in apparent pleasure. He slid up to her clitoris and hoped she was ready. He found a place he knew she liked, remembering to be gentle. He felt Leah jerk upwards, then fall down again, moaning once. Then he rode his finger up and down softly and steadily, trying to maintain a good rhythm. He relaxed to know that he could still do this to her, relieved too to have her back in this way. If I could make our time like this, we would have no problems, he thought. Each sign of her pleasure as he moved his wet finger back and forth gave him hope. His kissed her mouth, then her cheek, then her earlobe, admiring her. He was in a safe place now, as Leah went deeper and deeper into the ride. He went to her neck again and smelt her perfume, pungent and enjoyable. He looked down at her breasts again, at the nipple area and he felt his stiff penis twitch in response. Leah was making more noise now, but his arm began to ache above the wrist, making him lose rhythm. He changed positions to try to ease it, but it was difficult. He gritted his teeth and tried to relax his arm. No good. He changed positions again so a part of his right arm was supported by Leah's hip. That was better. He picked up some more fluid from below, and noticed how her lips were fat and the area now a-flood with liquid. Okay, so good. He got another steady pulse going and Leah became more noisy, making sounds as if he were twisting her arm behind her back. He loved her making a racket – and the house was so isolated, no one was going to hear.

He was sure there was no turning back for Leah now, but he didn't want this to go on for much longer. His arm was hurting again just above the wrist but he couldn't stop. He moved up to lick and suck her earlobe again, knowing she always liked it at this point. He slipped down and licked her neck too, and she felt so light suddenly, he thought she might be suspended in mid-air. The pain in his arm had gone. He kept going down. He put his mouth on her nipple, then licked it with his tongue and she groaned and said,

'Oh, Christ, yes,' then, 'Oh, Giles, go on, then.' Giles wondered what he'd done to make her take off. She was louder and more intensely into it than she had ever been before, as far as he could remember, and he remembered everything.

Her groaning went on and got louder still. 'Make me,' she said; she was almost shouting. At last, amid the action, Giles could relax: she was over the tipping point. 'Agh, go on! Giles, oh! Make me!' she said, then broke into a final wail. Giles watched her face as she went into spasm, loving the sight of her eyes screwed up tight as if in pain. But then he had to concentrate as her bucking groin made him lose his place on her. He worked hard to hold on, almost laughing at her loss of control, not wanting to lose his hold on her, to squeeze out every last second of pleasure for her, for himself, but she was pulling away.

'Keep it there, keep it there,' she said, still riding a long wave of intense pleasure, and he did as he was told as always, holding on tight as she reached the end and let her body drop and relax. He looked down at her pubic hair, loving the fact that it existed, loving the fact that it was right there in front of him, with only him to see it and feel it.

Then he began to think of himself, as Leah began to rest. He was still hard and stupidly ready to come. He'd always had this problem with her. She was way too sexy for his own good. I should have eased myself off in the shower, he told himself; you're such an idiot.

139

Leah began to come for him, pushing his hand away and moving into position so she could reach down and get hold of him. He rapidly thought about which position would keep him going the longest and decided he needed her on top. Then he realised he was in danger of getting this completely wrong. He was thinking too much; being too deliberate. He could still spoil the moment, the occasion. Oh, sod it, he said to himself, and guided Leah at the hips so her head rested on the pillow, and he moved up with her, above her. He looked down at her, her legs already spread wide, and got into position. He looked down at her carefully, and got his length into what he hoped was the right place and pushed. It went right in. It was heaven, but he had to hold himself still to stop the scene descending into ridiculousness.

'Giles, it's okay. It doesn't matter.'

She'd told him this before and though he still felt like a let down, he tried to trust her. He looked down at her eyes and he felt hopelessly in love with her. He began to move and he watch her close her eyes again. He forgot about the fact that he couldn't grind away for however long a great lover was supposed to and gave himself up to his heart and soul. He forgot about counting his thrusts, ignored the temptation to think about documentaries about Egypt or images of old women with grey perms on buses, and gave himself up to the sensations his brain sent out from being inside her lovely, velvety vagina. He cursed her. Why did she have to have, on top of everything else, the power to make him feel like this: incredible, but falling apart at the same time? It just wasn't fair.

Up and back he went silently or noisily, he had no idea, the pleasure was so impossibly good. This is unbelievable, he wanted to tell her, but couldn't, through concentrating on a pleasure so big it was a wonder it didn't kill him right there on the spot. He looked down at Leah Caighton and felt overpowered by her, but it was a feeling, of love, of terror, that lasted only for a second, for he exploded inside her and his brain melted into liquid and he was blind and deaf to everything except his head shooting into the endless universe. The feeling seemed to last forever, then it was gone, and he found himself still thrusting gently, and Leah looking as pleased as anything, but watching him with concentration.

'God, Giles, are you okay?'

He couldn't and didn't say anything – he just smiled and let himself drop down on her.

'Ow!'

'Sorry,' he said.

'Just – that's it.'

They found a place soon enough where they could both remain locked together, comfortable, at peace.

Giles closed his eyes and rested, still inside her, feeling perfect. He was emptied out completely, of all emotion, of all tension, of all worry. He heard the word 'bliss' in his head and he stayed there right with it, lying in the long warmth of her sublime body.

'I love you,' she said, but he didn't hear it. He was sleeping. His unconsciousness was a magical dead state, dreamless and floating. It seemed he was there for a long time, but the bedside clock had only moved from 7.39 to 7.44, when he heard,

'Wakey-wakey, darling, you'll have to move,' from Leah's lovely mouth. He heard himself grunt 'hghmm?' as his girlfriend got up from the bed and nimbly made off for the bathroom with a clump of tissue between her legs. Giles watched Leah go, a flap of white under the vertical line in the centre of her rump, unable to take his eyes off her.

Less than a minute later he leapt off the bed and went downstairs to get a drink for them. As he stepped into the kitchen his phone went off on the counter by the microwave. He picked it up and looked for the caller's name – it was Catherine.

'Hey, Gilles. How are you?'

'Really good.' It was exciting to know he had good news to tell her.

'That's great, G, *really* great – I'm *so* happy for you,' she said when he told her he and Leah had got back together. 'Now you'll be able to give her the present,' she went on, her voice rich with excitement too.

'Yeah. I think she's really going to like it.'

'I hope you're right,' she said, chuckling richly, 'my ego will be in pieces if she doesn't.'

'You sound full of the joys of spring, what are you up to?'

'Oh, I couldn't possibly tell you that, ha-ha!' she said.

'Hmm, don't tell me you've met a man already?'

Catherine studiedly hummed a nonsense tune down the other end of the line.

'Or did you have one stashed away the whole time?'

'Gosh, I'm not that clever, Gillesie. But listen – I phoned to ask you about Clegg. I saw it in the paper just now, in the Evening News. Are you okay? Are you going to be punished for that?'

'No, I don't think so,' said Giles dismissively, his mood still up.

'No? Aren't you worried?' said Catherine.

'No. It'll be okay. Really.'

'Really? It sounds like you broke some pretty big rules there – and have you thought about the government? They might do something…'

'You're forgetting something,' said Giles, smiling broadly.

'What's that?'

'I'm Giles McAndew.'

'What?' she replied, her voice still light.

'I'm Giles McAndrew. I have fans. A load of them rang into the station today supporting me. I'll be fine – they won't touch me.'

'You're Giles McAndrew, pah! Ha-ha.'

'You wait and see'

'I hope you're right,' she said, her tone falling away and becoming serious.

'You'll see. Look, I have to go.' He heard Leah padding around at the top of the house.

''Bye, then, stay in touch – and watch your mouth!'

'I will – 'bye.'

Giles closed the phone and trod merrily back up the stairs to Leah.

22

Afterwards

The premonition had melted away, forgotten. Giles stayed there on the bed feeling thoroughly content with life, secure, at least for a while, from the demands of the station, and in recovery from the lacerations sustained in four days of Leah traumas. Dusk was coming on outside. Giles listened for his blackbird, but the windows were closed. He lay there naked, his arms folded comfortably behind his head, his groin warm and glowing. He could feel a throbbing there, gentle, like a pulse from a machine way deep within his body. He wished the feeling of well-being could last and last. Leah came back from the bathroom and they lay there together for another quarter of an hour, content, hardly speaking.

Eventually, they went downstairs to the kitchen to eat and drink, and talked, at first about nothing much, in the contented shadow of their physical togetherness.

'Do you want more sauce?'

'No thanks.'

'Shall I shut the back door?'

'Yes please, I'm getting cold.'

'Okay.'

The glasses and cutlery that clinked on the table reverberated in the big kitchen with its tall ceiling and hard floor. Giles knew that they'd have to do some talking at some point, but not yet. He ate his chicken and relished it, suddenly finding an appetite for the first time in days. He still felt clean and new, and he glanced up at his girl as they talked, and he believed again in the future.

He thought about the two of them turning over to a new chapter in their story, and he couldn't stop himself thinking of marriage. His first attempt – to a schoolgirl sweetheart – had led him to believe for two decades that his brush with the institution was a calamity not be repeated, and further, that to have made such a decision was intelligent, mature and still, just about, modern.

Why did he need it? And as for children, after his divorce he'd just decided, 'no'; flipped the switch in his head marked 'Kids' to the 'No' position and there it had stayed. It was rusted now. But there was something so overwhelming about being back with Leah again. He only realised now what it meant to have been so close to losing her; now she was here in front of him, and with such optimism in the air. If he and Leah were married, then it could be a super-glue to hold what they had firmly in place; if they made a precise, permanent commitment to each other the problems they had would have to be worked out – there'd be no running away from them. Whatever troubles they ran into, whatever arguments that flared up, if they were married, after what they'd just been through, they would have to be resolved. Compromises would have to be reached and would have to stick come what may. No excuses. He should ask her now.

'What are you looking so serious about?'

'Did you know – it's two years on Friday since our first date.'

'Is it?' Her face showed puzzlement. She was amazed that Giles had registered the event. Last year she'd had to remind him. No, tell him.

'I might have known the wicked witch in the west wouldn't have time for such sentimental stuff, ha-ha.'

'Oh, "ha-ha" yourself,' she said. She was used to his taking the mickey out of her, but not in such a poetic way – what had got into him, she thought?

'Hey - you tell me off for eating with your mouth full.'

'Sorry. You know…' she took a sip of wine. '…sometimes you still take me by surprise.'

'What?'

'You know you're not much of a romantic.'

'Maybe you still don't know me as well as you like to think.'

Leah frowned suddenly, memories of the days she'd just endured coming back to her.

'What's up?'

'Giles, we do have to talk, don't we?'

This was what he wanted to hear - but he could still see a conversation in his mind's eye where they examined what was going wrong, with Leah going into a strop then refusing to communicate.

'Yes, of course – I wanted you to say that.'

Leah hesitated then recovered.

'I have to know that there's just going to be me.'

'You mean you still don't know if you can trust me?'

Leah thought hard. She was prepared to trust him, but was scared to lose him. She was so tired of carrying that fear around with her all the time.

'After this week, I really don't know. I think so – but oh, I don't know.'

'Tell me what would change your mind,' he said.

'Change my mind?'

'You know – make you believe you can trust me.'

If you proposed to me, Giles, she thought; if he did that, everything would be a whole lot easier; in fact, it would be completely different. She couldn't say this to him though. I'm not going to play the girlie-girl for him, she thought, even now.

They were heading for a difficult place again. Giles could feel it. Why don't I mention marriage? Do I want to marry her? He needed time to think. What if getting married only made things worse? What if, when we had an argument, Leah felt trapped? It would be a disaster; she'd be gone in a year.

Leah took a last mouthful of rice and sauce and leaned back in her chair. She was about to speak, then realised she had to come closer to him to say this, not move away. She leaned forward across the table and took his hand lovingly.

'Giles, just – why don't you just be more attentive to me?' She'd messed up what she wanted to say. She nearly said what she really thought: why don't you fucking tell me you love me without me having to drag it out of you all the time? Then, bugger it, she'd propose to him!

'I mean, if you were just a little bit more considerate of my feelings, you know?' she said trying hard to be sympathetic. Giles frowned and tried not to call her a hypocrite. 'Like with...' It hurt her to even say the name, '...Lucie Bastable. I went to her review meeting the other day.'

She did what!

'Oh? Why did you do that?' He made sure his face was turned away as he said it; he pretended to be interested in the garden behind her through the windows.

'Because I can be a paranoid, troublemaking cow when I want to be.'

'Blimey...' said Giles looking at her face again.

'Don't start.'

'If you're going to be like this, I think I could give you anything, my darling,' he said, stroking her cheek.

'Funny man,' she said, moving away, but gently, so he wouldn't take offence. 'Look, I went because I wanted to unnerve her. I'm sorry, but this week I've been going crazy.'

'Why?'

'Hold on a minute – and you have too, don't forget. I went to be a nuisance, although, as you know, I had a right to be there, and I heard Greg McKenzie saying how great it was that you and Lucie flirted on air so brilliantly.'

'What? He said what?'

'You know what he's like.'

'Someone needs to chin the bloke. He – flirting? Pff - he can call it that if he wants, I suppose, but it's ridiculous. Is this – do you – is this why you think I've got a thing for Lucie? It's - this is me being professional,' he said throwing a napkin down on the table. 'I've done it with hundreds of people on air down the years.'

He took a breath to see what response Leah gave him.

'Yes, fair enough, I suppose you have to...'

'There's no suppose about it. I've "flirted on the air" with women old enough to be my grandmother, never mind my mother, and ugly enough to put in a bloody museum!

Leah tried hard to sympathise with his anger, but only wanted to hear him helping her to dismiss the threat of Lucie from her mind. She tried not to smile as he raved on.

'Christ – this is all I need!'

'Calm down, dear.' Giles had got up and was pacing back and forth in the space between the counter and the washing machine.

'Don't try to be funny. It's not funny. That…that bastard. I'll bloody sort him out if I ever hear of him doing that to me again. In fact, tomorrow…'

'No, don't! You'll make me look really bad if you say anything.' Giles walked up and back, up and back, until Leah came across to him, put her arms around him, kissed him.

'Ssshhh,' she said, putting her forefinger on his lips. 'Ssshhh, hey, enough. It's nothing – it doesn't matter. I know you're right – you have to do it. It's okay – I work in radio too, you know.' She kissed him again, then reached down to the crotch of his trousers, feeling him.

'You'd better not be too tired later.'

'There won't be much later – you'd better make it soon. It's a working day tomorrow.'

'You're such a creature of habit. Have you not ever thought of doing your show on three hours sleep? It might be interesting.'

'It might be a total disaster like this morning and I'd be out of sync for the next five days.'

'You're getting old, cowboy.'

'And you're going to get a smack on the bum if you don't shut up.'

'Oooh, yes please, mister.'

He grabbed her and she squealed, right there in the kitchen where cups and plates had flown in anger a few days earlier. Leah's kiss, he thought, had to be the best kiss in the world. I'm ten years older than she is. Ten years! How have I got away with it for so long? What does she see in me?

'Do you think you could persuade me to change my mind about wanting to be a Dad?' Straight away he was scared – he hadn't meant to say that. He'd meant to start a careful conversation about getting married.

'What?'

'You heard.' But something inside made him carry on. Something was opening up in his head.

'Am I hearing you correctly?'

'Yes, you heard what I said.' Now he wanted the thought vindicated: he needed her approval straight away.

'I think you should sleep on it.'

'What?' Don't let me down, Leah.

'Seriously. Don't look like that.' She kissed him. 'Okay, tell me what brought this on.'

Good point, thought Giles. He thought about it.

'Just us being back together,' he said and shrugged.

'I think it's more than that, dear - I know you.' Leah yawned. At ten-to-nine she was ready to crash until the morning. Some day it had been.

'Okay, I'll level with you. I don't know why, but it – I – this is going to sound silly.'

'No, it won't, go on. Stop being so bloody Giles,' she said. She was holding him, stroking his arm.

'We have a biological clock too, you know.'

'God, you're really pathetic, you men,' she said, then realised that she didn't really mean it.

'What do you mean?' said Giles mortally offended and moving away.

'You're only bloody thirty-nine. To hear you talk anyone would think you were fifty-two.'

'Look, I don't want to be seventy when my kid goes to university.'

Leah was smiling inside but was still loving having the upper hand on him.

'A few hours ago you thought you never wanted kids.'

'Yeah, but you always hoped I'd change my mind.'

'But I never thought you would,' she said, only half lying.

Later on, after Giles finally felt that he'd made enough love to his woman, for her, not him, and they were lying together again skin to skin on top of the duvet as it got dark outside, Leah stroked the hair on his forearm and brought up the subject again.

'Giles...'

'Yes?'

'Were you serious about what you said earlier about having kids?'

Giles hadn't changed his mind, but would have admitted under oath that he was still trying to get used to the idea that he might fall into a domesticity he'd always associated with giving up and giving in.

'Yeah - I think so.'

That would do Leah for the day. Yes, what a day alright. It had begun with her attacking a work colleague, passed through the best career boost she'd ever had, and ended with her nearly ex-lover promising her to give her a child. She was totally done in, and decided to quit while she was rounding the back straight in the Olympic Stadium, her nearest rivals sixty, seventy metres behind. She patted Giles' hand.

'I think you're lovely,' she said. 'And now I'm going to sleep.'

Giles thought about fathering a boy, carrying spears and wearing war paint in the jungle, and wondering how old they would be before he would be able to make love to Leah without having to picture old grey women or polar bears attacking him to stop himself coming too soon. He was struggling to stay awake. I should have proposed to her downstairs. Why didn't I?, he thought as his mind dissolved into clouds and air.

Leah turned over and laid her other cheek on the cool cotton pillow and sighed. She smiled at Giles remembering their anniversary. She thought there'd been no chance of it, but she'd been wrong. She thought back to May 6th 2004, a warm Thursday night sitting outside a Church Longfordham pub holding hands for the first time, looking at this tall, cool, handsome, radio presenter guy and thinking, you're all mine, I can tell. She'd been so happy that night. She closed her eyes and fell quickly away into dreams.

23

Bad Medicine

Friday May 5th

Night passed by over The Barn House in Corumby, turning to daylight around five o'clock. By then, Giles McAndrew was at the station checking the running order of his show with an already energised and excited Leon Dilkes. They mulled over the interview of the day before and still wondered whether they should steer clear of it today, Friday, 5th of May or not. Very much so, thought Giles. 'Go there if the listeners take you,' said Leon.

'Have you grown another pair of balls since yesterday?' said Giles.

'Maybe.'

Leah woke up to the alarm Giles had re-set at seven. It felt only a tiny bit strange to be back in the familiar routine of a night spent at her boyfriend's house: leaping out of bed before she could fall disastrously back to sleep; checking she'd taken her pill as she had a wee; getting in the shower and thinking of the working day ahead. This morning she also woke with the memories of the discussions of the night before fresh in her mind.

She went downstairs in a towel to get her bag and her morning clothes, but slipped into the kitchen first to make a drink. She noticed the radio when she lifted the kettle to add some more water, and found herself reaching over to its 'on' switch with an eager hand. She heard Giles in the middle of an interview.

'Isn't there a line to be drawn between police investigation and police intimidation, Chief Inspector?'

'Yes, you're right, there is; but the Bart and Bilt Constabulary is proud of its record in the treatment of suspects…'

She listened for ten seconds more after settling the kettle back into position, then went to the living room to pick up her clothes before racing upstairs to put on some make-up; she was running a little late.

As she skipped back down the main stairs she saw a white envelope on the mat. She didn't think it was there when she came out of the living room five minutes before. Or was it? No, she would have seen it; it was quite large and quite thick. She detoured to the door and bent down to pick it up. Odd: it was for her, 'Leah Caighton', but there was no address under her name, which was typed. She immediately ripped it open, sensing something wasn't right. Who the hell would post her a note by hand to Giles's house? She felt her insides on the turn from solid to liquid as she pulled out three pieces of folded white paper. Opening them out she quickly realised that the point of each sheet was to show her a drawing. They were skilled markings in ink, all three showing a man and a woman having sex. The drawings were separated into individual pieces in two ways. First, in each, the couple were shown in a different sexual position. Hang on, no, there weren't three, there were four. The fourth piece had got stuck to the third.

Leah was looking from one sheet of paper to the other, all her emotion condensed to a pulling sensation in her diaphragm and a rocketing heart beat. She couldn't move her jaw, and couldn't move her feet. She felt her knees twitching then gently knocking. It was the labelling of the drawings. On three of them a small arrow led away from the man's groin to the word, 'Giles.' On one of these, an arrow from a woman's long straight hair was the word, 'Catherine.' On another, where the woman was being taken from behind, the arrow led from her breasts to the word, 'Lucie.' The girl had her short boyish haircut. Whoever drew this knows her, she thought. The third Giles drawing had a woman on his belly. From the backside a line led to the name, 'Leah.' It was her alright: the artist had the hair length and the style exactly right. And her body shape.

Leah felt as though she might fall over, then suddenly she found herself sitting on the floor without really knowing how she got down there.

And then she turned to the fourth drawing.

A couple were again drawn in sexual congress. From the woman's eyes was the arrow again, and to her again, 'Leah'. From the man's groin was the word, 'Neale.'

Leah didn't know how long she sat there with her mouth gaping. Then she got up and walked into the kitchen and sat down on the sofa still gripping the drawings in her right hand. She didn't understand. Neale? The spelling looked wrong. Not Neil? The awfulness opened her up in the stomach. What had someone done – followed her to Lichester Barton? Fucking followed her? Who? Who had stalked her? This was a stalking. Oh, God, she screamed inside her head. Was it Neale himself who had done this? No. How would he know about Giles and his cousin? And was he that stupid to put his own name on a drawing? No, it couldn't be him; she'd met Neale and he wasn't that kind of guy. He just wasn't. She remembered his face, the moment she noticed him – she saw openness and honesty. It wasn't him. So it was someone else? At Two Counties – it had to be; you had to be there to know about Giles

150

and Lucie, Giles and her, Leah. But Catherine? Who at TCR knew about Giles's cousin: someone he told? But Giles didn't mix with people at work. Leah was confused and still her stomach hurt with panic and uncertainty and horror. The words, 'followed me' kept appearing in her head. Someone followed me to Lichester Barton. It was horrific. Me: they followed me there. Where from? From home? Followed me and I didn't see them? Didn't notice it? And then they spied on her and Neale. It was the detail that was horrific. The quality of the mind that would plan so carefully and go to such lengths. She felt nausea coming up from her gut in a rushing wave and before she could reach the sink a mixture of liquid and solid flew out of her mouth on to the floor. The second half of the batch fell safely into the sink on top of mugs and plates. Leah ran the tap and leant right over so her mouth caught the stream of water that jetted out. She looked around for a cloth to mop the floor with, then saw the roll of kitchen towel on the counter. She used that to scoop up the disgusting mess. All the time her mind was racing. It wasn't in her body. She wasn't in her body. That's how it felt. The real Leah was somewhere else, away from this horror.

She threw the fat wedge of sodden, squelching towel into the bin, then retreated to the sofa again. Get a grip, Leah, you're stronger than this, she said to herself. Come on, now.

She fought back at the panic well, but into the space came pain. Why would someone at Two Counties Radio want to hurt her like this? What sick bastard would scare her too? In her distress she couldn't focus. She had no idea. A blink of her mind said, 'no one': no one I know at work would do this; was capable of it. She felt weak in the calves, even sitting down. Then there was the sheer sickness of the drawings; and the invasion of privacy. Who did she know who could be so disgusting? Who hated Giles that much? But no: it wasn't about Giles, it was about her; who hated her so much? The envelope was addressed to her, not Giles. She was the one that was supposed to be hurt.

And was it true? My God, Giles and his cousin? It wasn't true about her and Neale, so it wasn't true about Giles and this Catherine. But I saw them, and she thinks his voice is sexy. Cousins could marry, cousins can marry, cousin do marry. Don't they? Giles made me trust him but can I? Are the drawings what the spy had seen? Was it possible? No, he was a sick fuck. A fucking evil sick fucker. But was it possible? A stream of news flew across the front of her mind in a tearing rush, all the bad things, the nasty things, the extraordinary things that the people in ordinary towns likes this did to one another. Anything was possible these days, anything.

151

Still she felt unable to move, unable to do anything except think like this in a constant rolling panic. It was impossible to stop. She couldn't slow it all down so as to catch her thoughts, study them properly, never mind stop it completely.

Think of something, Leah, she told herself. Do something, for Christ's sake!

She would take this to Giles; they would work everything out together. But then she thought of the fourth drawing and realised she couldn't show it to Giles. She'd keep it all secret. She couldn't admit to Neale. Not in front of Giles. He might not believe her truth, and he might leave her. But she hated secrecy, she hated sneaking and deceit. She wanted to find the person that did this – it was Lucie. No. It was Catherine. No, it could still be Neale. She was coming apart. I'll have to deal with this alone. For the first time the thought of running came into her head. Calm down, Leah, and no, don't cry, don't cry, you'll make it worse. Calm down - *I'm calming down!* But she didn't and she started to cry. She didn't want to but she didn't have the strength to stop it. She keeled over slowly to lie on the sofa, like a woman shot down with a gun in cold blood in slow motion. She told herself the tears would act as a safety valve, come to her as a relief, but they didn't and they weren't. She cried and cried out in a wordless howl of agony and as she did the only answer was to run, to get away, as fast and far as she could, and start again somewhere. To get in her car and drive away and never come back to Barton Townes or the radio station, places that only seemed to bring her problems and grief. She was 29 and there had to be a simpler life than this, life with a man who didn't bring complications, jealousy and this new misery.

Then she had to run to the downstairs loo, flinging her towel away as she went. She ripped open the door and sat down. Brown liquid came out of her anus in a rush. She sat there with her hands over her eyes, struggling to focus, but this time feeling a sense of something being released in her head by the release of her body.

Shutting her eyes made thinking easier, and thoughts came, tumbling towards her. This is such a mess. *Such* a mess. I have to go – I can't cope. Yes, you can, Leah. What about love? What about Giles? You love him. Maybe she did, but she stared at the obvious lesson this week had taught her: that life would be easier without him. I need someone I'm not scared of losing, and I'm going to be a presenter and he won't be able to bear the competition – it'll kill him. I have to leave to move on. I love him but I have to leave him. The pain was excruciating: the pain of leaving, the pain of staying.

The logic came pouring out of her. I'll write to Simone for a reference. I'll phone her. What about today, Leah? Can you work? No, she couldn't work. But she had an idea that popped into her head and decided to run with. As fast as she could manage, she got dressed and washed her face, trying to move fast enough to stop her thinking about anything beyond the specific thing she had to do right now.

She was in the car with her stuff in two minutes, not really caring what she looked like. It seemed to take forever to get to Bridges Lane but it was less than ten minutes. She drove fast. She turned into TCR and went through to the rear car park. There was one space there still. She parked and got out. No one arrived at the same time to see her. Focus on the one thing, she kept saying to herself over and over again. She almost ran to the back station entrance and in seconds she was knocking on Simone's office door. Please be in, Simone, please be on your own. She felt her desperation and gritted her teeth trying to hold back tears.

'Come in.'

Leah opened the door, trying not to make too much noise. She stood in front of Simone Pound and tried to speak, but realised she had no breath.

'Leah – whatever is the matter?' said Simone coming over to her. Leah reached into her bag for the drawings.

'You have to help me, Simone, you have to help me.'

She handed the drawings over and tried to carry on, but she was gasping for breath. Simone looked down at the papers and tried to make sense of them. She didn't know who Catherine was and didn't know who Neale was either, but it was painfully obvious that someone somewhere was making terrible mischief. Bad medicine, she thought, bad, bad medicine. She looked at Leah, who looked back with a wild look of desperation.

'You have to let me go, Simone. I can't work and I have to get away.'

'Come and sit down, darling,' she said and tried to steer Leah to a chair, but she was brushed off.

'No, I'm sorry Simone, I have to go, but I need you – I need your help. Can I phone you? Please? Can I phone you later? I need someone and you're the only one.'

'Of course you can.' Simone tried to remain calm as she went to her desk and wrote her mobile number down on a piece of scrap paper, her own horror at the drawings beginning to open up. She put them on her desk determinedly not looking at them, then folded the scrap of paper in half and gave it to the girl whose mouth hung open in such a way as to make Simone's heart squeeze against itself. She felt herself about to cry but bit her lip hard. She waited two seconds while the urge dropped down again inside her then got hold of Leah's hand.

'Look, wherever you go phone me when you get there.'

She watched Leah nod at the floor. The girl couldn't speak.

'Are you going to be okay? You're not going to do anything silly, are you?'

'No, that's the last thing I'm going to do. I've got to go to make sure that's the last thing I do.'

It was working. Leah felt the excitement of escape coming like the cavalry to save her. She could hardly believe it – how easy this was. Then the guilt began.

'I'm letting you down, I'm so sorry,' said Leah. A tear of self-pity fell from her eyelid on to her top. Simone hugged her and rubbed her back.

'Leah, do what you have to do, but here,' she said, pulling away, 'write your mobile number down for me. If you don't phone me I'll phone you, and if you play hard to get I'll find you and throttle you, so help me.'

Leah laughed through the film of liquid and wrote down her number, crossing out a digit where she made a mistake. She looked at it carefully before she gave it to Simone.

'Love, can I keep the drawings?'

'Keep them?' It seemed too much for Leah to think about.

'Yes. In case I can find out who sent them. Or do you want to...?'

'I never want to see them again. You have them.' She looked over on the desk where Simone had put them, then looked away again. At that moment Simone didn't know what she could do about them, but she felt Leah's revulsion and sensed a black dread coming up from behind her.

'I'll keep them safe – in case you change your mind.'

'Okay,' said Leah, but Simone could see that she already had her mind on other things; that she was already three-quarters gone.

'Simone, I'll never forget this, and I'll repay you.'

'I'll remind you of that when you're on national radio, or the TV,' she said putting her arms around the still young girl once more. Leah buried her face in her boss's shoulder, laughing once while still crying.

'Go on, then, go,' said Simone. 'If that's what you have to do, get out of here. Go on, don't think about us, we'll manage without you.'

'Okay,' she said.

Leah Caighton left the office, walked down the empty corridor to the rear station entrance out into the car park and got into her car. She found a tissue in her bag and blew her nose. Then she found a dry corner to dry her eyes on. She started the engine then after a deep breath slowly guided her Polo through the narrow exit, signalled right, waited for a minibus to pass then moved out into the road. She drove for a hundred metres, steadily, and came to a junction. Left was the high street; right was the turn she wanted. Turning right again at the next roundabout in less than a minute she was on the ring road heading west, away from Two Counties Radio, away from Barton Townes and away from Giles McAndrew.

24

Sweet Painted Ladies

Friday morning came also to a striking looking woman of around forty, seventy miles south of Barton Townes. She laughed into a glass of morning Champagne, fully naked half-under bedclothes smelling of sex, and thought, there's something so right about this. London. There was something frightening about this capital city with its vast giant breath but there was no mistaking this feeling: she hadn't had so much fun since she was twenty-five.

Poured from a bucketed bottle, the drink was a little too cold, but it was still nice. Propped up on one elbow, she took another sip and another look at the stripped torso next to her. Then she looked up at his face – his eyes had closed again. She moved the glass to a hovering position over the somewhat hairy chest and tipped the angle of the glass slowly, deliberately, carefully, watching the liquid slide ever-nearer the lip. When it reached the tipping point she held the glass in suspense, checking his eyelids again for movement. Nothing. She noticed his breathing just becoming regular and soft. Restraining a giggle, she tilted the clear, fizzing liquid over the edge of the glass. She watched the first splash hit his chest then pulled out of the way as the man sprang up into shocked life and yelped.

'Argh! Hey!...You little...' he started, but realised he didn't know her well enough to decide what playful insults he could fling back at her for that.

'You...' he started again then stopped, not least because he wasn't serious. He liked a little bedroom horse play as much as the next man. 'Don't move,' he said, to the woman who was now lying on her back, laughing, her Champagne flute held high. The man, now awake, did some careful tipping of his own. He watched his own stream of melon-coloured liquid go slowly drip, drip, dripping onto Catherine's stomach. She giggled and as a trickle of wine slid quickly south down past her navel into her dark hair; she didn't mind that at all, in fact.

Two minutes short walk away from the Two Counties radio building in the sleepy backwater of Bartonshire's county town, a youngish woman in smart, crisp work clothes was frantically trying to make something of a breakfast for herself. Short of time after sleeping past the alarm, she gobbled some toast and slurped as neatly as she could, given her hurry, at a mug of hot tea. She didn't do a good job of it.

'Oh, piss!' she said, as liquid flew up over the rim onto her white shirt. 'Shit!' She put the mug down and, scowling, threw the stained shirt in the sink and scooted upstairs to change. As she was buttoning up a fresh shirt in the mirror and checking her hair in the long mirror she heard a key being hurriedly jiggled around in the front door lock before the door itself opened. She walked to the landing to check.

'It's me!' came a voice.

'What's the matter?'

'Nothing – I left a folder in the office,' said the returner speeding up the stairs.

'How did it go this morning?'

'Oh, you know – not bad.'

'I bet it was okay - you're much too hard on yourself.' The woman had to raise her voice to give herself a chance of being heard. She checked her reflection again in the mirror. Then she turned; The Returner was in the bedroom.

'And *you* are much too sexy.'

Before she knew it, Sarah Billings was being forced back against the bed. Her calves hit the box drawer edge and she fell back with a scream.

'I haven't got time! I'm late!'

'Go on, give us a quick snog, my delicious one,'

'No! You're getting to be a right little problem, you are.'

'I know, ha-ha, but I can't help it: I can't resist you.'

'And you're creasing this flippin' shirt – I've just put it on; I spilt tea all over the first one.' Sarah sat on the edge of the bed and finished off the buttoning up.

'Do you want a ride in?' said The Right Little Problem.

'Might as well – we're coming home together tonight, yeah?'

The Right Little Problem leaned over and kissed her on the mouth. Sarah kissed back, allowing her partner's tongue to do just a little bit of mischievous, playful delving.

'Yes we are,' said Lucie.

Around a couple of corners in Bridges Lane, a popular radio presenter removed his headphones and hung them neatly from the large black angle-poise microphone after signing off on his one hundred and ninety-first Friday show at Two Counties Radio. A noise at the door made him turn his head to see Simone Pound, the station's managing editor, sliding quietly into the studio. She hushed the song she was humming almost inaudibly as she crossed the threshold; she had nothing to give her favourite boy, nothing but bad news.

Four miles to the west as the crow flies, above The Barn House in a sleepy fenland hamlet, a blackbird still sang his effortless love song, calling the news to all females round and about that he was right here, whistling fit to burst for a mate, as the countryside of eastern England continued its effortless journey into spring. The wind from the south-west was just strong enough to ripple the wind chimes outside Giles McAndrew's back door, sending out a discord that quickly died away on the spring morning air into nothingness.

Part Two – The Destruction of Giles McAndrew

1

Engineer Horizon

Friday May 5th – Evening

The man in the navy Nike singlet and long navy Nike shorts and white Adidas headband jogged at a decent lick along the bank of the Crichton Causeway that ran east away from Barton Townes in the direction of Tellingham and turned off his ipod to think. He panted evenly, hardly feeling his gently ageing legs, watching the path stretch off in front of him to the horizon in an engineer-straight line. Normally he liked the numb monotony that took over his brain on this part of the run but he needed to get his mind in gear. Things weren't going to plan.

Love, he thought, o love. Such a fine thing but maddening at one and the same time. His love was gone and might never return no matter how hard he tried now to fix things. The plan had looked good on paper. Not foolproof perhaps, but not far short – it should have worked. But he'd pushed her too hard, stretched her to a breaking point then pushed her beyond it. He snapped her like a twig. Too clever, he told his Air Zoom Elites with the laterally oriented longitudinal flex groove and the torqueable shank – you over-reached yourself, buster.

Then he made himself shut down the negative thinking and tried to plot out a way to get her back or failing that, a route to the place she was headed next. He could be patient, he had that in him. He would bide his time and make a second plan. She wasn't likely to emigrate as far as he could see. But if that did happen, well, he would focus on another candidate. A song came into his mind and he sang it to himself as he ran, breathily, intermittently, between the rise and fall of his diaphragm and lungs.

'I got...myself set...on you...I...got myself...set on you.'

The evening wasn't warm but as he pounded the hard ground he felt warm and comfortable in his body, his pace even, steady. Positive...thinking - don't be...negative. Think...Positive...get her...back. Soon, when the blue light above the engineer horizon had faded a little more towards a bluey-grey, he would cross the bridge and cut through the field path to his house, cutting only a moderately moist swathe as he went.

2

England Calling

Giles dragged himself back to The Barn House after finishing the show and a short one-way conversation with Simone in Studio 1. He went to the cupboard under the stairs and from the musty darkness right at the back carefully retrieved the wrapped painting. Made by his cousin, the talented Catherine. He carried it to the sitting room and propped it against a fat easy chair, then stepped back and stared at it. A portrait-shaped rectangle of white plastic-foam sheeting looked back and struck his mind with an appalling blank thud. Part of him wanted to open it up to refresh his memory of the lovely object but the rest of him didn't have the heart. What was I doing, he said to himself, thinking I could solve everything with a present? A stupid little present. His mind was lit by a momentary revelation of pathos at his puny attempt to hold back the ceaseless mighty tide that governed human relationships. He wanted to cry but didn't let himself. She was gone, apparently, so what was the point?

He sat down and stayed put for a very long time as the innocent mid-morning air moved slowly across the room to the sound of a quietly ticking clock. Giles didn't hear it. He heard nothing. After a while he felt nothing save a thickness inside his head that hung inside his thinking like a cloud of cement.

At some point he changed position, leaning back on the sofa to rest his head. He closed his eyes without sleeping and stayed there for he didn't know how long. He had nowhere to go, and nothing special to do. His mind lay down with him and let itself be wrapped in a beige, nebulous cover that sent him eventually to the temporary protection of sleep.

At Two Counties Radio, Simone Pound's desk phone gurgled futuristically at her. She really didn't like the sound but hadn't yet got around to ordering a new one.

'Simone...'

'Hi, Jackie.'

'I've got an Ian Bakerson on the line for you.'

'Oh?'

'Says he's from "England."'

Oh, buggery, thought the chief of Two Counties Radio. Here comes a bollocking from the national head of BRBC. She wasn't sure she was ready.

'Hi – Simone?'

'Speaking...'

'Ian Bakerson, assistant head of BRBC England.' Assistant head – not so bad.

'Hi, what can I do for you, Ian?' she said, swivelling around in her chair to look at the level of coffee left in the jug.

'I've just called to give you a heads-up.'

A 'what?' she thought. 'Oh, yes?' she replied, bluffing.

'They're coming for you, Simone, have no doubt about it.'

'You'll have to tell me who you mean, Ian. If you mean the press, I know already – I've had my front desk girl blocking over ten calls since I got in.'

'Start taking them.'

'What?'

'If you don't talk to them, more of them will come up and camp themselves outside the station – and they'll go to your house, you know. They'll stop at nothing until you deal with them on their own terms.'

Simone heard the howl of wolves in the back of her head and suddenly felt an almost overpowering urge to gag in her throat.

'Simone?'

'I'm still here, don't worry. Ian, I can't believe they're so interested in us, in Giles – it's only us, Two Counties Radio - we're nobody.'

'You *were* nobody, Simone, but now you're news. How big a 'news' you become depends on what you do and what you do about your man there, Giles. But it's not so much the press I came to warn you about - it's the government.'

'What, all of them?'

'Ha-ha, no – well actually I'd better be accurate: Number 10's putting a whole load of pressure on us, which also means you.'

She was surprised. She rather thought they'd have other things on their mind.

'I thought they might be a little preoccupied with other things, you know, like the prisoner releases and such like - and local election results.' Not that I've bothered to look for them yet this morning, she thought. 'And I've already had Jagger, the party chairman, on the phone giving it to me – did you know that?'

'Forget Jagger, he's no one. They have a special unit at Number Ten to deal with situations like this and people like you - the "Media Monitoring Unit."'

'They do?' said Simone, feeling about six years old.

'You have no idea what the government machine is like. They're ruthless. You won't be interviewing a minister 'til after the next election, I can tell you that, but that's only for starters. Remember no one votes Labour where you are anyway. They don't need to care about you one little bit.'

'So why are they doing this, then?'

'Because it's what they do. They've been doing it for a long time, this lot – it's reflex.'

'Oh,' was all Simone could think of saying, so she shut her mouth and rummaged around in her bag with her spare hand for some sort of distraction. More than anything she wanted to refuse to take this seriously, but in the end she knew better. She tried to sound grave and professional.

'What do you think I ought to do with my man Giles then, Ian?'

'At the moment I don't know quite what to say.' He paused with exaggerated exasperation at the other end, as if his morning's work involved having to save the world from ecological disaster and suicide terrorism as well as this. 'It depends on what they do next. If they put a hit squad onto it, keep watching all the tabloids for something about Giles and a lap dancer or Giles with a large male donkey.'

My God, thought Simone.

'You're not serious?'

'I am. Then as far as the press is concerned, it's the toss of a coin. Forgive me if I frightened you - what actually happens next all depends on whether they've anyone more important to destroy. If it's a quiet day they might go for him full on.'

'Or?'

'Or they might just forget about him. You have to be ready for anything.'

Simone didn't know what to say in reply.

'Look, what he needs to do, your guy, is to keep his head down for the next month. Tell him to play a straight bat on his show, and away from the studio go nowhere, talk to no one. If you can stick him in a monastery or a nunnery, do it. Actually, better not make it a nunnery, ha-ha.'

'Ha-ha.' Funny man, she thought. 'Is there any chance that there'll come a point where you'll want me to take him off the air.'

'If it comes to it, Simone, it won't be your choice, it'll be ours, I'm sorry. But I don't think it'll come to that. As long as he keeps his head down, I think he might be okay. Oh, and as long as he's not doing anything daft right now.'

Anything daft? She found a toffee in her bag and wanted to eat it but realised she couldn't yet.

'Um, excuse me for being thick, Ian, but spell out "anything daft" for me, would you?'

'He's not gay and married is he?'

'He's neither as far as I'm aware.'

'Affairs?'

'Nothing as far as I'm aware of.' She cringed at her sin of omission. Then in an instant felt better: she believed in Giles.

'You're so full of doom, Ian. I've got to tell you, we've been flooded with calls from listeners supporting him. They love him for what he did to Clegg.'

'Simone, listen - I'm very pleased for him, but where I am no one gives a damn about that. The more – look, how shall I put this?' The assistant-head of BRBC England, now sounded like a patient professor in a seminar room full of freshers clutching A level certificates still wet. 'The bigger the kerfuffle the interview kicks up in the press down here, the bigger the kick in the balls we're going to get from Bliss.'

Simone felt herself shrinking where she and sweating under the armpits. She began looking in her bag for her spare deodorant.

'You're not saying he's going to be involved?'

'God, no – he'll get a ten second briefing if that from one of his team today and maybe one tomorrow if the press is still interested overnight.'

He meant it metaphorically, of course he did. You're so dim sometimes, Simone.

'You may have forgotten, Simone, but he's got a war to run and a reputation to salvage before he resigns. If he ever does, ha-ha.'

'Ha-ha, right.' I'll have to start reading the politics pages, she thought.

'Which reminds me: I've got one crumb of comfort for you.'

'Oh?'

'Thank your lucky stars Gordon Green isn't Prime Minister.'

'Yes?'

'Yes. They'd have mailed your bloke's balls back in a plastic envelope by now if that bastard was in charge.'

'Alright, well thanks for phoning, Ian.'

'I haven't finished. They may want some of you too.'

F-f-f-fiddle-faddle, went Simone.

'You're not joking about this either, are you?'

'No, I'm not. Go very carefully, Simone. How broad's your back?'

'Broad.'

'It might need to be if they decide to crucify you for not controlling Giles.'

'Look, I thought all the papers hated the government?'

'Well, ha-ha,' said Ian Bakerson utterly without mirth, 'two things there - they've still got The Sun, just, and two, the other tabloids may want to make Giles a champion of the tax-paying classes, and if they do, then your guy can expect threatening phone calls, his bins ransacked, the lot.'

'Calls from the government...'

'Exactly. Not that they're going to be saying "Hi, we're the Labour Party." But what I'm trying to say is, ah-huh...' - Bakerson's guttural laugh wasn't a signal of amusement – 'that you might have Tony and the red tops on your trail at the same time.'

I'm so way out of my depth, she thought. Way out.

'Then,' he continued, 'you could have journos and TV crews hanging round you for about a week. Now, that might be your cup of tea, but if it isn't...'

Simone said nothing.

'That's the nightmare scenario...' She still said nothing. 'Look, Simone, it might still be okay – just hang on to your hat. I'll be back in touch if I hear anything. Are you still there?'

'I'm just listening to you.' She began to quietly fiddle with her car keys.

'Are you okay?'

'Yes. I'm just taking in what you're telling me.'

'Look, if you feel you're struggling, just give me a call. And I'll stay in touch anyway. If I hear anything I'll be straight on to you, I promise. Be handy to have your mobile number.'

She reeled it off.

'Great. Phone me if you have any questions.'

'I will.'

'Hold on the line and my PA will give you my mobile number.'

'Okay.'

'Right. Thanks, Simone. 'Bye.'

''Bye, Ian.'

She waited while Ian Bakerson's flunky came on to give her his number and she duly wrote it down on her pad. She replaced the phone and carefully typed the number into her own phone, feeling for the first time since getting over her separation and subsequent divorce that the world was just too much for her to take. She instinctively went to reach for the plant sprayer, but fussing with her babies again wasn't going to help her think this one through. Wise up, woman, she said to herself.

'Bloody well wise up!' She couldn't keep the words inside.

There was a knock at the door but by the time she'd looked up, Greg McKenzie was already across the threshold.

'Will you PLEASE wait for me to answer you before you come into my ROOM, Gregory!'

Greg McKenzie was completely taken aback, his whole body visibly rocking back onto his heels. Then he evened himself out again. 'Sorry,' he said, looking extremely affronted.

'Sorry, Greg,' she said, immediately feeling a spasm of guilt for blasting him, but only a spasm - he'd had it coming for a long time. 'I've just had England on the phone.' Damn! She hadn't wanted to tell him but it slipped out.

'Oh,' said Greg, 'perhaps we should have a chat about that.'

Bugger, went Simone inside.

'Later, Greg.' She had to get away from him. 'Look, I've got to go into town. We'll talk about it later.'

'They're upset, I suppose.'

'Yes, but we'll talk later.'

'Okay,' said Greg. He watched Simone as she walked to the door, opened it and left with him still standing on her carpet.

Blast him, he's getting worse, thought Simone Pound as she walked at urgent marching pace from the building veering immediately left towards the main street of shops. She heard a whirring click to one side of her as she went, the unmistakable sound of a camera. She stopped and looked. A tall, slim, good-looking man with a shaved head in a grey hoodie and low-slung jeans held a Pentax loosely in his right hand. He smiled at Simone as she turned away and carried on walking into town.

3

Bike Around The Barn House

He was cold when he woke up a minute or two before midday. He opened his eyes and saw the same scene – the painting and his living room. His mind re-opened, unshuttering the morning's payload of the devastating bomb. He waited for his feelings to appear and unfold over him with dread. What he found emerging inside him was unexpected - a strength and a determination to recover. The pain was still there but he was going to deal with it.

He forced himself to get up, get moving and to try to go about his normal afternoon business. He went to the kitchen to make a drink. The taste in his mouth forced its attention on him: it was rank. It was metallic, awful. Then he thought he needed to smoke but shook the feeling off. He hadn't smoked for over ten years. No, he was not going to retreat or shrink - he was going to bounce back. I'm a leader after all, he told himself, and leaders don't quit; they don't get depressed and they don't fall apart. They get back up on the horse; they fight and they recover. A quitter never wins, he thought – and a winner never quits. I'd forgotten that, he said to himself. If I can remember things like that at a time like this, I can't be too bad.

She's gone, but who said she was gone for good?

The house phone rang but he left it. The machine could pick it up. It wasn't Leah – he knew it wouldn't be. As the coffee brewed he went to the computer and checked his email. Six new messages. One was from Catherine. He didn't want to read them. He'd look at them later. He went upstairs to look for a farewell letter from Leah. He went to his bedroom: nothing. He went to the bathroom even though it was a waste of time: she wouldn't leave such a thing next to a bar of soap or leaning against his razor. He scanned the landing, went down and searched the living room again but there was nothing; not a letter, not a folded note, not even a 'fuck you' on a torn scrap of newspaper. He rushed back upstairs to his bedroom and looked under his pillow, under the bed and down the side of the bed by the window, the side Leah slept, but there was nothing to see but clean wood and carpet.

He went back to the kitchen feeling old, feeling forty still looking for the note. His mobile buzzed at him from the kitchen counter next to the back door. This time he looked at the sender but ignored it when it wasn't Leah. He scanned every work surface again and again for a note, then looked behind the bread bin in case it had slipped down the back, but he only found crumbs. The sink just had water droplets in it, the fridge only food. The cupboards were as normal: just cupboards. He knew he was being crazy, but he had to look everywhere at least three times, just to be satisfied in his mind. After three circuits of the house he stopped. Leah had gone without leaving a single word behind her.

He was going to get through this but he wasn't ready to talk to anyone or listen to anything they might want to say. The desire to communicate would come back soon enough. He wasn't that badly damaged – he was mending himself already. He had decided upon it and it would be so. He asked himself whether he was going to be able to do the Saturday morning show and the answer came back, 'Yes, I can do that - I have to do that. The people expect me not to buckle.' His inner voice spoke again: 'My people need me,' it went and he wanted to laugh at his egotism, but he felt that he would never laugh again. I need it, though, he told himself - I need to be arrogant to get through this. I need Giles McAndrew to help Gilles Wilkinson beat the pain of this. The phone rang again and he went across the room, looked at who was calling then switched it off.

He drank some coffee, then a glass of water. Then he went to the utility room at the back of the house and unlocked his bike. He made up a bottle of water from the fridge jug then made his way upstairs to get changed but stopped halfway thinking, Sod it, I'll go like this. He had trainers on, he'd be fine. He pushed his bike over the threshold and leaned it against the wall while he locked the door. Then he mounted it and eased it slowly to the road, where he looked and as usual heard no traffic. He let his machine roll a little further then began to pedal. His mind rolled on. I'm going to deal with this. I'm going to be my normal self from right now and nothing is going to stop me.

The weather was doing nothing. The sky was grey, but the cloud cover was thin and high. A breeze blew, not a wind. Fine, I don't care, he said. Suits me. He came to a country crossroads and turned right towards the distant sea. Not that he wasn't going to go to the mud flats of the Bilt coast - he never went that far east. For nearly two hours he pedalled, in a slow melancholy way, thinking about Leah, thinking about himself and what life was doing to him. He met almost no traffic, keeping to the back lanes of Bartonshire that ran past lonely farms and dykes. He smelt cut grass and flowers when he passed through villages and hamlets. The sun came out, and when clouds gathered thickly enough, went in. His inner voices kept him company with their incessant dialogue.

'A summer of this is going to kill me.'

168

'No, it isn't, don't be silly.'

'I'm not being silly.'

'Look, your girlfriend's left you - you're supposed to feel like you want to die.'

'I don't want to die.'

'So what are you worried about then?'

'What am I worried about? My woman's left me.'

'You and a million others.'

'There aren't a million Leahs.'

'They all say they that, bud, don't worry.'

'I don't care what they all say - I'm me. She was mine, I loved her, Leah Caighton, not a million women.'

'She wasn't good for you.'

'But I still loved her. I wanted to marry her.'

'You were kidding yourself.'

'No, I wasn't – well, okay, I may have been, but maybe not. And I wanted to have a kid with her.'

'"A kid?" What kind of father would you have made, calling it "a kid"'?

'Shut up and leave me alone.'

'No. You want to get over her, right?'

'Right.'

'Then you have to deal with me first.'

'God help me.'

'Now there's a thing.'

'What?'

'When are you going to deal with your mortality?'

'What?'

'You're going to die, Gilles.'

'I know.'

'No, I'm not sure you do know, not really. You're going to die and when are you going to deal with what's going to happen to you when he comes calling for you, The Grim Reaper?'

'I'm going to live to be a hundred and ten, and I'm still going to be banging women when I'm a hundred and two.'

'You're scared – when are you going to deal with it?'

'Not while I'm dealing with Leah.'

'Okay – but it'll come back.'

'What will?'

'The fear, stupid.'

He turned down a familiar lane signposted 'Corumby 4' and pedaled on, at about half his normal speed, dragged down anyway by his mood.

169

He barely heard the birds twittering contentedly in the dense peace of a spring afternoon now settled heavily on the countryside. It nearly helped his mind bear the pain. He thought of his house that would soon be coming back into view with dread. He thought of leaving. Not just the house, but Barton Townes. The dread began to lift. He took his mind to a place of ideal escape, the place he'd always wanted to live, to be: the Cornish coast. The Atlantic surf would forever be crashing in on idyllic sandy beaches dotted with bleach haired surfers. There'd be barbeques there at night, beers with friends, a fire, kisses with easy-going good looking women. Easy life, easy loving, easy times. A job at the local radio station. They'd scoop him up, a talent like him. It didn't matter which one. Any would do: Radio St Ives, Radio Polzeath, Radio North Cornwall. He'd do it for two hundred quid a week, a hundred and fifty - it wouldn't matter. As long as it paid the rent and fed him. He wouldn't even need a car; he would bike everywhere and for longer journeys he would take the bus or the train.

'You're kidding yourself, Giles. You're nearly forty - you're much too old to be a beach bum. They'd laugh at you.'

Maybe. But he didn't need that crowd really. A walk on the beach with a dog and my voice on the radio - that would be enough. "Hi, Giles McAndrew here comin' atcha on Surf FM. The sea is a brilliant blue on this beautiful Cornwall morning. I'm just above the beach here and a white-sailed yacht is crossing the horizon in the far distance and the sun is rising in the sky - it's going to be another lovely day." In his dreamy Cornish town back street the artists were quietly painting the days away, the air was heavy with the sweet meaty odour of pasties baking and out of oven range it sang with the heady tang of ozone. It would be sunny every day. Well, most days. And of course, he would learn to surf properly, even though he'd soon be over forty.

Each day would be a celebration of his decision to come to a life fantastic, by the endless, mysterious sea, sand forever in his toes. And in the winter when the tourists had all gone away he would go to the pub for real ale and honest conversation and there would be laughter and at weekends music and he would be accepted by everyone after a couple of years, be a part of something real. He would marry a good, kind woman and have children, finally. With his own precious family he would see out his days there until one day he dropped down dead.

Giles felt that he'd already begun the process of getting over Leah right there, but it didn't mean he couldn't think about her if he wanted to. So when she appeared on the edge of his mind again he let her in and his whole being was encased in her loss. Why, Leah, he moaned as he passed the Corumby sign?

Then his memory produced a thought up a siding: the drawings. Simone hadn't brought them to the studio to show him; they were left only to his imagination. It didn't seem remotely possible that someone he knew, who they both knew, had tried to destroy what they had and had succeeded. He had to see them. He drank a glass of juice quickly but didn't taste it. He would take the pictures to the police – they had equipment to do with forensics now that practically boggled the mind. They would find DNA and so, the evil, sick bastard who did this would be revealed.

Then, as his mind was on the verge of being swept away by a fever, sense returned.

'Giles - no crime has been committed. Nobody has broken the law here.'

'It should be against the law – how could it not? It's not against the law to send obscene drawings through the post? It must be.'

Two pairs of voices battled for supremacy in Giles's mind: febrile versus calm; negative versus positive. A fifth voice was like an arbitrator. There might actually be something in that, it said. I should go to the police just to enquire.

'You're wasting your time; they'll be much too busy to deal with stuff like that,' came the reply.

He felt the cold reality of the present in the stomach now, then in the colon. Someone is out to get me. He looked out of the kitchen window that looked out on his front garden as if the perpetrator might be out there. Then he walked back across to the sofa, kneeled on it and looked out on the back garden, as if his enemy might be skulking there with more tricks up their sleeve. In broad daylight, Giles, he said to himself? You're crazy. Stop it.

The twinge of fear passed quickly. Such miserable sneaking around was done by weeds and cowards, not men with true bottle. He set his dream future against the pleasure of beating this loser to a pulp when he found him. He hadn't hit anyone since school. No, since a fight outside a pub - when he was what? – he remembered the year and counted forward – twenty-five? He saw himself kicking this person laying on the ground, a faceless body. He was kicking it in the ribs, in the thigh, stamping on the groin, but leaving the head. Whose face? Who hates me? He could feel everything beginning to fall apart. His positive voice spoke up:

'Pull yourself together, Gilles.'

'What?'

'You have to go forward now.'

'I know.'

'You have a show to do tomorrow - at least get to the end of that.'

'I know.'

'Then you can re-group.'

'You think I can?'

'Of course you can – you're Giles McAndrew.'

'Yes,' he told the voice, 'I'm not a fucking loser - I'm fucking Giles McAndrew.'

4

A Unit of Media Intelligence

On the first Friday morning in May near ten o'clock, London was glorious for those who loved cities. Fleet Street, even with its newspaper offices long lost to the cheap open spaces to the east, carried an atmosphere that was hung heavy with a dense, pungent whiff of history. In the present the air was cool and the atmosphere hummed with the compressed intensity of the working people who buzzed to and fro. From the millionaires to the minimum wagers, they ached with a subconscious longing and invisible skein of desperation which only the gigantic capital city could inflict upon them.

Rob O'Donnell walked past the sandwich bars and solicitors offices appreciating none of this. He came out of Nero with an Americano Grande in his right hand and held it aloft to hail a taxi. Thanks to the congestion charge instigated by the once-hated Mayor Stone, in less than a minute the black cab had already reached the Aldwych and was ready to glide down the Strand toward Trafalgar Square. Diesel fumes offended the noses of the citizens crossing the street on their way up to the National Gallery and the Charing Cross Road but the odour was broadly neutral inside the cab. Rob scanned the sports section of The Times for the rugby and the racing results and waited for his coffee to cool down.

At the square the chariot turned south, resisting the gravitational pull from the enclaves of Mayfair and Soho and smoothed down Whitehall where about half way down the cabbie pulled into the curb opposite Downing Street. Rob paid the man and wasn't bothered in the slightest about leaving a mere 30p tip. There was minimal traffic as he crossed the road, an amazing fact when for those important or intelligent enough to hear it, the heart of the nation state thumped undyingly beneath his feet. He loved this part of his day so much it was a wonder he hadn't yet been caught in a fatal dream state and swept under a 219 bus to Vauxhall Park Road while crossing the road.

At the tall wrought iron gateway to the seat of executive power he flapped his ID at the duty constable and began the short walk up to Number 10 as if he was the King of the World. By the time his urgent footsteps had left the gates twenty metres behind them he was in a different city. The tall buildings on each side of him closed out so much noise he could have been in the most tranquil suburban street in the

173

South-east of England. Well, perhaps he exaggerated a bit there seeing as Downing Street had no gardens and no garages: was utterly urban. But still, the sudden quiet always surprised him and he always liked it. Robert Charles O'Connell was too preoccupied with his own thoughts to hear birdsong but it was there nonetheless. Often, when the mood in the office wasn't too stressful he heard it fine.

It irked him that he had to walk right past the door of Number 10. He wanted to be one of the ministers or senior civil servants who owned the right to saunter casually up to the policeman on the door to whom they could smile and offer a polite 'Morning' as they smoothly penetrated the great portal of English political power. My time will come, he told himself.

Instead of joining the elite that touched shoulders with the PM as a regular part of their working day, he walked thirty metres further on, past Gordon Green's Number 11 and turned right through a narrow, gated gap in the railings, and dropped down the short flight of steps to a side entrance. He nodded to the lone security men, his card at the ready. After noting the blank stare of reply, he was surprised when the man took a step towards him and said,

'I need to take a look in there, if I may.'

Rob didn't know what he was talking about until the man held out a hand towards his coffee carton.

'Oh,' said Rob, feeling stupid and indignant at one and the same time.

Security removed the lid, peered down into the steaming contents and sniffed. He looked up and handed the cup back to its owner, replacing the lid as he did so.

'Thank you, sir.'

Rob gave the man a gravely serious nod as he turned to swipe his card through the machine. Hearing the beep, he pushed at the door, felt it give under the pressure and went in.

Shazana sat at the tiny desk that did its best to form a reception. Mid-phone conversation she swivelled her chair around to look aimlessly down the corridor as she spoke. Rob noticed the shiny beauty of her dark hair then felt his stomach pinch a little when he heard her laugh. He was still gazing when she turned back to register him with wary, rich brown eyes, the mouth still forming a smile for the caller. She turned away again as he walked past her.

At the end of the corridor he came into the wide hallway singing with bright natural light. But its charms: the teak parquet flooring; the Queen Anne chairs and tables; the Tang vase and the rich smell of beeswax polish were lost on him. A distant morning Hoover sounded as he

174

passed a wall portrait of Marlborough and turned left down a narrow corridor. At the third door on the right he stopped. He turned the round polished doorknob and walked in.

'Ah, Rob, at last,' said Simon Barnett.

'Sorry I'm late,' said Rob, putting his coffee down on the table.

'Don't worry,' said Tanya Howe, 'we gave up on getting any respect from you a couple of years ago. What kept you?'

Rob frowned and sat down. With his presence, this sub-division within Number 10's Media Monitoring Unit could now proceed with its morning's business.

'Personal,' he said.

'That'll be the divorce, then,' said Simon to his female colleague with a satisfied smile.

'Chill out, Rob,' said Tanya, 'it's common knowledge.'

'Fine. I'm chilled, don't worry. Right, where are we starting then? Oh – where's Chilton?'

'Ill.'

'Really...' said Rob, who didn't believe in days off.

Tania gave him a briefing paper.

'Item One, Two Counties Radio – Giles McAndrew.'

Rob laughed, not reading the sheet. 'Local radio; what a bloody joke,' he said. Simon joined in on it but not Tanya. Rob hated her. She came on poised in life between postgrad student and matron. The fact that she had a great face was irrelevant; the fact that she was a 'nice person' vaguely disgusting. He couldn't believe he had to work with her.

'Give me the story then,' he said, already peeved beyond belief.

'Haven't you seen it in the paper this morning? Breakfast show jock out in the back of beyond, but really quite on the ball took Clegg to the cleaners yesterday morning on his show. Went completely barking for no reason. Clegg had no choice but to walk.'

'Details?'

'Oh, the jock took liberties,' said Tanya, 'completely broke protocol – he was supposed to stick strictly to the local elections – but he asked about Darke, about the affair.'

'Cheeky bastard. Well, we'll have to fix him.'

'Yes,' said Simon, 'we need just to decide quickly on how much grief to give him.'

'That should take all of ten seconds,' said Rob.

'Ha-ha,' said Simon. 'What, removal?'

'Oh, I think so,' said Rob casually.

'Do you want me to lean on his boss at national level?' said Simon.

175

'What's the position?'

'Andrea Potter-Symons – pretty amenable sort of woman. I've sorted her out a couple of times, just with some tickets and an invitation here and there.'

'Does she owe?' said Rob.

'Um…yeah, just about.'

'Oh – hang on – thanks Katty,' said Tanya.

Coffee and biscuits had arrived.

'Yeah, thanks Kat,' said Simon. The door closed again.

'So what do we want? Seriously…' said Simon, 'do we definitely want to shift the guy?'

'Okay - what do we know about him?' said Rob, looking and beginning to relax. He took off his jacket.

'Um, right – he's Two Counties' top presenter,' said Tanya. 'Confident, personable, great looking, good at running campaigns on behalf of his listeners…'

'*Coh* – don't tell me - shopping trolleys in the road, recovering Mrs Johnson's stolen washing…'

'Um, no, Rob,' said Tanya patiently, 'reducing bullying in the local secondary school by 60% thanks to a campaign he started, raising money for new cancer equipment at the local hospital. The station raised three quarters of a million quid last year for CAT scans.'

'What's this – local radio turning into Blue Peter?'

Tanya gave him a withering look.

'Don't you ever listen to local radio?'

'No,' said Rob, snorting, scandalized. 'Do you?'

'Occasionally,' she said, lying.

'Enough, you two. Look, this is not someone we want to take on lightly,' said Simon.

'I agree – we should absolutely squash him.'

'Okay, then Rob, go on, give it to us.'

'A couple of smears to feed to the papers - just to make sure he doesn't get ideas above his station.'

'Oh, ha-bloody-ha.'

Rob hadn't intended the joke but wasn't going to let on. He ignored the coffee on the table, obviously, and inspected his carton of Americano. He sipped contentedly at the last third of the drink and thought about the meeting after this one and about how much his divorce lawyer would be screwing him for when he sent him his bill.

'What have you got in mind, Rob, Internet porn? Doing young kids up the rear in the local woods, ha-ha,' said Simon.

'Something like that,' said Rob, allowing himself a smile. 'What about this morning's papers? What did it get?'

'Hang on. Look at the briefing paper - page one, halfway down. It missed The World at One but PM ran an interview with the station boss. She did one with 5 Live too. They ran it second story.'

'Not the man himself, then,' said Simon.

'They're obviously keeping him out of the firing line. Running scared,' said Rob.

'Did you hear a tape, Tan?'

'Look, it's just as much your job as mine to do the bloody donkey work. No I haven't.'

'We should hear it.'

'I'll get a lackey on it in a minute,' said Simon.

Tanya was annoyed. Bloody blokes in the unit always expected her to do the leg work when it was just as much their job to check these things, as it was theirs to at least scan the morning papers on the way in.

'So what about the papers, Tan?' said Rob. She rolled her eyes but briefed him anyway from her notepad.

'Quite wide coverage this morning, but nothing really developed. Angle is what you'd expect – Clegg the unsuspecting buffoon mugged by heroic small town DJ. Short but favourable story in the Telegraph, The Mail loves him, as does the Express and The Metro. Sun, nothing much – two paragraphs. Made The Guardian - page 9 - but not The Independent. The Standard didn't use it. They'll no doubt all be doing some digging today to see if there's anything else they can squeeze out of it.'

'Times? Chronicle?'

'Times - smallish but enthusiastic – page 7. Chronicle, quite interesting. Small story but they can't make up their mind whether to get behind Clegg for us or give him a kicking because they think it's time Tony replaced him. The big picture is basically the same - they're not far from really getting behind the guy but they can't make up their minds. They either don't know what to make of local radio or they despise it like you two.'

She waited for a response to her insult but all they gave her were looks of bemused contempt. She sighed inwardly and carried on.

'They ignored the press releases we put out.'

'As expected,' said Simon. 'They want to smash us. Home Office shit, Iraq, Clegg's screwing - they just want more and more.'

Rob grunted. 'What's Clegg's office done so far?'

'I was on to Paddy last night. They delayed as long as possible to gauge the reaction and now they're putting out the "had no choice" defence.'

'Are they using it?' asked Simon.

'Where they are they're just ridiculing it. I think it might be a very good idea in the circs to beat a retreat,' said Tanya. 'If we go hard on this bloke, we may get a storm.'

Tanya had no takers for that. Rob despised her for being unable to say 'shit storm.' He liked women who weren't afraid of the f-word.

'I just think the press might be ready to really get behind the guy if we push them. We have to tread very, very carefully.'

'Look, Tan, this wanker's done us over. He needs to pay.'

Tanya often wondered where the party had got Rob O'Donnell from - straight out of the script of *Lock, Stock and Two Smoking Barrels* via Winchester public bloody school by the sound of his stupid voice. She still absolutely refused to pay him the compliment of asking him a single thing about his private life or his background. He'd been back in the unit after a six-week training stint with the Policy Unit for two days and she was sick of him already.

'What if the papers don't bite on the smears?' said Simon.

'Then there's nothing we can do,' said Tan.

'Yeah, fine, bollocks to them,' said Rob O'Donnell, 'but we do what we can. We're getting no change out of them, but there's no harm in just putting out some stuff. You never know, the Screws might be interested for Sunday if we dig up something that smells; The Peephole, too maybe.' Tanya nearly laughed aloud at his attempt at commanding the local cabbie slang.

'Any fallout down there in, what is it, Bartonshire?' said Simon.

'Massive support from listeners. Too early for local papers of course but one of us should make some contact, see what they're doing next week.'

'Christ, Tanya, do you get up at five every morning?' said Simon.

'Just doing my job.'

She works too bloody hard, thought Simon, feeling her threat.

'Get a lackey on to that one,' said Rob. 'And would you two like to come up with a couple of things for the tabs this morning?'

'Who are you to give out orders, O'Donnell?' said Tan. She thought of Simon in the chair next to her - he was a bloody pain too. Wishy-washy. She wondered what on earth he was doing here.

'Sorry,' said Rob, realizing with annoyance that he still couldn't manipulate Tanya half as much as he wanted to. 'It's just that David wants me to take on something quite important. I'm seeing him later.'

178

If that bastard was going to get promoted already, thought Tanya, I'm out of here.

'Okay, look. We'll sort the details of this one, but you've got to do the bulk of Item 2,' said Tanya.

God, thought Rob, the sooner I stop pissing around with trivial shit like this…

'Okay. Done. So let's finalize, can we? You gonna smear this guy or not?'

'What do you think, Simon?' said Tan.

'We may as well - you can say our leverage is disappearing, but if we show them we know we're losing the fight, they'll just kill us all the more.'

'Blimey, Simon, have you been reading Campbell's autobiography?' said Tan. 'That's really quite smart.' He wasn't half bad looking too, she admitted to herself, and he had a good bum on him. Pity he was a prat.

'He hasn't written it yet,' said Simon; surely Tanya knew that?

'Okay,' said Tan, sighing, 'how about we smear but go light. Just an affair or two, maybe with the station boss? Can we find out if that's plausible?'

Rob didn't like mucking about like this but wanted this piffling job off his hands.

'Okay. You can find that out. There'll be a photo of the boss on file somewhere. This Terry Wogan, too. Try the website.'

'I've already seen his picture, Rob. Mr McAndrew is a sex God compared to Wogan,' said Tanya.

'Fine. So, a couple of smears for the piece of toss, then, nothing too heavy, if that's what you want. But if it begins to blow up, we'll have to put the boot in.'

'Understood, Rob,' said Simon. 'Leave it to us this morning - we'll get things going then see what develops. But at least ring The Chronicle.'

Rob had a very good line into one of the bad boys there for some obscure reason connected to one of his father's old jobs.

'Okay, but you do the rest,' Rob said to Tanya.

'Okay.'

'Right. Let's get on, then,' said Rob O'Donnell, looking at his watch.

'Item 2,' said Tanya. 'David Filcher MP, marital affairs of.'

'Ah, a very interesting case,' said Simon.

'He hasn't been buggering his cat again, has he?' said Rob.

'No, his secretary, ha-ha.'

'I bet she wasn't laughing, ha-ha.'

Such little, little boys, thought Tanya Howe, and made up her mind right there that she had to get out of the unit as soon as she possibly could whether O'Donnell was on the verge of promotion or not. It was time they found some other mug to keep the kids under control.

Ten minutes into the discussion of how they were going to stifle the sexual proclivities of the MP elected to the mother of Parliaments by the good people of Leicester South, the door opened again without a knock.

'Everything okay, you people?'

Each of the trio had already straightened their spines and transferred their attention by the time he got to 'you.'

'Yes, David,' said Rob O'Donnell loudly.

'I need to give you a little brief on Filcher. I'll be back in about ten minutes, okay?'

'Okay,' 'Sure,' and 'Yes, of course, David,' came a chorus of replies.

When David Richard left, Tanya and Simon burst out laughing; and when Simon went, '"Yes, David,"' Tan spat out a noise like sofa upholstery ripping.

'What?' said Rob, cheeks reddening and jaw clenching. 'Oh, fuck you.'

Yes, fuck them. They'd still be here when he was having the front door of Number 10 fucking Downing Street opened for him every morning. We'll see who's laughing then, he thought, draining the last of his coffee.

5

Simone Makes a Speech

On her return from Superdrug Simone was approached by a young man in the station car park, who asked,

'Simone, could I possibly have a word?'

'You can have one - "arseholes."'

She went inside with an attack of pins and needles hitting her behind the knees. She didn't know where the smart-Alec burst came from. She didn't know she felt that angry about gentlemen from the press hanging around her station. A woman got out of one of the seats for visitors and said,

'Miss Pound, I wonder if I might have five minutes of your time.'

Simone turned to Jackie Husband at the desk.

'Jackie? What's she doing here – get rid of her. And what's she doing wearing a visitors badge?'

Simone walked round to Jackie's space behind the desk and through the gap next to the partition wall into the main body of the building. When she was out of sight of the reception area she beckoned Jackie to her with a twitching finger. Jackie began her defence.

'I'm sorry, Simone. She said she was on Lynda's show.'

'What's her name? She can't have been on the list!'

'She was - Alex Tandy. She's on Jim's list, last guest.'

'Alex Tandy is a man – he's the county champion rat exterminator.'

'Oh,' said Jackie. Shit, she thought – I've done it again, while Simone made her feel worse by shaking her head.

'And didn't it strike you as odd that she turned up two hours early?'

'She seemed so convincing, though.'

'Get rid of her.' Then Simone felt guilty, even in the wild circumstances of the unfolding day. 'I'm sorry if I seem annoyed at you.'

'It's okay - really,' said Jackie. 'I'm bloody stupid sometimes.'

'No, you're not. Well, yes, you are,' she said, and they both laughed.

'But I still love you, don't worry,' said Simone, touching Jack's forearm.

Jackie smiled and went back out to the reception area to eject the fake rat catcher.

'Then lock the door,' said Simone as she went. 'We'll use the intercom for the rest of the day.'

She was back in less than a minute. She was a little breathless.

'Okay?' said Simone.

'Yes, fine, I've done it. She's gone.'

'Do you who know you're expecting for this afternoon's shows?'

'Yes, I think so.'

She got a look from Simone.

'Yes, I do.'

'Fine, but check again. Don't let anyone in unless you're sure they're on a show or have got an appointment. If they say they have, check them twice as thoroughly as usual. Get them to show you a credit card through the window. Or driver's license.'

'That's a bit strong isn't it?'

Simone gave Jackie another look.

'Okay, Simone, I'll do that, no problem.'

'And from now on, if anyone from the national press calls me, put them through.'

Jackie was confused.

'It's okay, Jackie, I know what I'm doing.'

Do you, thought Jackie?

Back in her office, Simone rang Sarah Billings' extension number.

'Hello?'

'It's Simone. Sarah, could you come and see me right away?'

'Sure.'

Ninety seconds later, Sarah was there.

'Come in.'

'Hi, how are you?'

'Ask me in a couple of days – right now I'm up to my neck in it. Look, I really need you to be here for me – there for me? Whatever it is – I need you right beside me in the next couple of days. Can you do that?'

Sarah nodded.

''Course,' she said, looking serious and supportive.

'Great. Right – first, I want you to go and find a phone in an empty office - take a Yellow Pages with you – and find me a security firm in Barton Townes. I need them to get a man round here as fast as they can. Better yet – ring Detective Sergeant Alan Dowling at the cop shop, tell him I told you to phone him and ask him who he'd recommend. Okay?'

'Okay.'

'And I'll tell you what's going on when you've done it.'

'Okay.'

'Right,' she said, 'tell you what – sit here – use my office. Sit there,' she said, pointing, 'Make yourself at home – grab a coffee from my pot if you need one. I'll be back in a bit.'

She took a notepad from her desk and put a pen behind her ear.

'What shall I say if the phone rings?' said Sarah wheeling the chair into a position she liked.

'Don't answer it. Better still-'

Simone turned round to the wall, found the socket and pulled out the male piece. She left and followed the corridor path through two fire doors back to the reception area. She eyed the scene just outside the front door. She saw four figures just outside the front door talking to one another now: the photographer in the hoodie; the fake Alex who asked to talk to her and two men she didn't know. Jackie Husband looked at her expectantly from behind the desk. The reception chairs were empty except for one.

'Who's he?' said Simone doing a fair impression of a first-time ventriloquist.

'Astrologer bloke for Jim at 3.'

'Anyone else try to get in?'

'Those two blokes outside.'

'What did they say?'

'Can we come in to see you?' said Jackie, pointing her pen at Simone.

'What did you tell them?'

'I told them to beggar off back to wherever they came from.'

'You didn't!'

'No, I said you weren't seeing anyone under any circumstances this afternoon.'

'Good girl. The woman – she was just braver, I suppose.'

'I suppose,' said Jackie.

'From now on, tell them-'

The phone rang.

'Shut that up for a minute.'

Jackie lifted the receiver, put a digit on the retractable button for three seconds then left it on the desk. Then punched another that switched the system to answerphone.

'From now on, tell anyone who comes from the press that I've left via the back entrance.'

'Oh – are you going home?'

'No, I'm not going home. I'm going to be in here until tomorrow morning the way things are going. Next. I want you to put all my calls through to Studio 2.'

'Alan's in there recording a piece for tomorrow.'

'I'll chuck him out.'

'But...'

'He can go and do it on the moon – this is much more important. Put all my calls through there until I tell you otherwise, okay?'

'Okay.'

'Wait ten minutes.'

'Wait ten minutes...'

'Yes. I'm going to get everyone together in the newsroom.'

'Should I be there?'

Simone held on to her patience with a sigh.

'No. You're needed here.' Simone placed a firm hand on her receptionist's forearm.

'I need you to hold the fort for me. Okay?' she said, boring her eyes through Jackie's lenses, cornea, retinas and right through the back of the sockets into her brain, hoping that it might seal the issue.

'Okay,' said Jackie, who rather than being worried was, loving the excitement. 'Can I ask a question?'

'Of course you can but make it quick.' She wanted to get on with the emergency briefing.

'Why are we being besieged by journalists?'

'There's only three of them.'

'And there're all the calls.'

'They just want dirt on Giles.'

'Oh. They've asked me about him.'

'Who have?'

'Journalists. On the phone.'

'What did you say?'

'I said "Giles is a really nice bloke."'

'What else?'

'Nothing.'

'Good. Are you sure?'

'Positive. And that he gets on well with everyone.'

'Did you?'

'Yes.'

'Good girl.'

'I lied.'

'Well of course you did. Are you sure you did?'

'Yes.'

'You didn't tell them anything about the fight...'

'What fight?'

'The – oh it doesn't matter.' Simone was now in a tearing hurry.

184

A smug grin appeared on Jackie Husband's face.

'Oh. Ha-ha. Very good, Jackie. You didn't tell them though...'

'About-' she lowered her voice and looked around at the otherwise empty reception. 'Leah and Lucie? No.'

Simone, mildly scandalized by how much tittle-tattle about the station employees Jackie must carry around in her head all day, asked herself, 'I wonder what the bloody hell she knows about me?'

'And finally...'

'Yes, Simone?'

'Next few minutes, any one of our lot comes in, tell them to come to the newsroom immediately, okay?'

'Okay.'

'And remember...'

'Calls through to Studio 2. All of them.'

'Not all of them – you screen them. "Yes" to the press, "Yes" to my family, "Yes" to any of the big wigs from above, "No" to everyone else. That's basically it.'

'Right.' If only it could be like this all the time, thought Jackie wistfully as she took the system off answerphone. It rang straight away.

'Two Counties Radio, Jackie speaking, how can I help you?...Sorry, no, she's in a meeting. But if you call back in ten minutes she'll – hang on, make that twenty minutes. In twenty minutes she'll be ready to speak to you...No, really, she will...I promise...twenty minutes...'bye then.'

Simone bustled her way to the newsroom sweeping meeting rooms, offices, both toilets, the kitchen, every room bar Studio 1 and its Ops Room for staff as she went. She didn't wait more than a few seconds before she called everyone to attention. This was a necessary job but she wanted it over with quickly.

'Okay, everyone!' The electric buzz of conversation immediately ceased. 'This is just going to take a minute. I just want to put you all in the picture. I just wanted to tell you that we're officially right smack in the middle of the firing line of the national press...' Pause. '...and the government, because of yesterday, because of Clegg walking out of the interview. It's the press that most immediately concerns us.' She kept going without a pause, noticing two or three workers drifting into the room as she spoke. She saw someone turning off the station output, heard its music fade. 'Thank you,' she said. She wasn't sure how she was going to say this: what to leave out and what to leave in. She was just going to go for it and hope she didn't upset anyone, especially Giles later.

'The fallout from the interview with Clegg yesterday has been worse than I had any idea it would be - much worse. The national press are here in Barton Townes, besieging us, really.' She paused to make an inadvertent nervous laugh as she noticed many of the faces in front of her turning into frowns.

'And they're constantly on my phone asking me to talk about Giles and about what happened. So far I've told them nothing, but when I finish this meeting, under advice from on high I'm going to start taking their calls.' She paused and looked at the sea of faces again. She'd never seen the scruffy old newsroom so crowded. She drew a big breath and carried on.

'They might be ringing you too if it starts to get any worse - if they haven't already - or they'll be at you when you leave tonight and it'll no doubt be the same tomorrow. I want you to tell them nothing. Absolutely nothing. I'm relying on your nous and experience as reporters and journalists yourselves. I want you to be your own worse nightmare when you're on a job - give them sweet bugger all - absolutely nothing.'

Someone had their hand up.

'No, Ian, you can't go to the toilet.'

There was a burst of laughter, not least for the boss's wit being so unexpected. Where did that come from? said to herself. She hadn't meant to say that. Busy Ian was less than amused. Then the crowd looked at the boss to see a deadly serious face.

'In a minute Ian - I've got something else I must tell you before we go any further and before I forget. For those of you who don't yet know, we've lost a fine journalist today.'

In the pause that Simone left hanging in the air, some of the workers thought someone had died. Whoops, that came out wrong, thought Simone.

'Leah Caighton has left us.' Simone suddenly sensed the tension. 'No, she hasn't died. Sorry...' There was laughter again, but this time it stopped quickly as the crowd waited for the managing editor to continue. 'She asked me if she could leave on compassionate grounds, to which I of course said, "Yes". However, I expect that leave to become permanent, if you see what I mean.'

Simone wiped her brow with the back of her hand. She thought she could feel body moisture leaking out of every pore.

'Which brings me to Giles.' She hoped to God she wasn't making a mistake now.

'Giles has had a very tough time recently. Which explains why he made his – why he upset the deputy Prime Minister yesterday. Now -

whatever your personal feelings for Giles, whether you know him well or whether you don't, I want you, please, all of you, to protect him.'

She spelled the next bit out slowly.

'As I just said, please do not give the press any chance to run his good name into the ground. He is one of us. What has happened to him could one day happen to you. Even some of you who don't present now, in the future, you never know, it might be you in that chair – in that studio, letting – making a mistake that might later come back to haunt you.' She looked at her audience and saw them staring intently at her, listening, thinking. 'They're not like you, these people. I know it's tempting to think that these types from the Mail and the Star and what have you, are just the same as you, just young reporters trying to gather up information to make a good story. But they're ruthless. They don't care who they hurt. And they don't care how much. They're cold-blooded. You're not. You're good people – they're bastards.' Are they, she thought even as she spoke? Aren't they really just us? She suddenly realized that in front of her a lot of people were laughing again.

'So what we need is to get together, act together, stay together.'

Then she was struck by an uncomfortable sensation: as she was speaking she was suddenly outside herself and she could hear this person trying desperately to make a good speech. She saw her speaking with hands in furious motion. Yet on she went talking, listening to herself as she went. God, how am I doing this, she thought? Watching and speaking at the same time?

'We're an award winning station. We know we can do great radio. Now we need to prove that we're a class act as a group of people.'

The sensation left her. And now I'm going on too long, she thought. I've got to shut up. And I've got this bloody pen behind my ear. She took it out self-consciously and laid it down on top of the notepad that she put on Sarah's desk when she came in.

'Now - if I've left anything out, please tell me. Otherwise, I'll answer any questions.'

She let out a huge sigh of relief and opened her eyes wide for a second before letting her face recompose itself. Busy Ian's hand was immediately in the air and a lot of people laughed again.

'Yes, Ian? I'm sorry about that remark just now, love.' She let a smile flicker on her face before looking serious again.

'What sort of questions do you think we're going to get asked? Only I haven't been outside the station all day.'

'I think I can answer that, Simone,' said Alan Barker.

'Go on.'

'A number of us have been approached outside, front and back, and on the phone. They want us to tell them about Giles's personal life. I was asked, "was it true that Giles beat up his girlfriend?" I was asked, "Did I like Giles McAndrew?" Also, "Did I not agree that he was out of his depth as a presenter?" And they're also looking for dirt about the station. "Is it a bad place to work?" "Is the managing editor doing her job?"'

'I can back that up actually,' said Greg McKenzie, interrupting and ready to take the floor to make a small speech of his own as the station's second in command. 'I've had calls from a number of the nationals asking me the same sort of thing. The Ex–'

'Thank you, Greg – anyone else?'

'-press asked me – '

'Greg, it's okay. Unless you've anything different to tell us...'

Simone felt the sudden silence hit the room. She felt an immense excitement there too, though.

'Sorry, Greg - I just want the others to speak, as you and I speak a lot together...Yes, Noona...'

'If I happened to kick one of them in the balls by accident on my way out of the car park, will that be okay?'

Laughter erupted again. Then Big Dave Plymouth indicated that he wanted to speak.

'Dave...' said Simone, gesturing to him with her hand.

'Boss.' Big Dave always called her 'Boss', feeling that just uttering the word 'Simone' out loud was a threat to his masculinity.

'I get the point of us saying nothing to the press, but wouldn't it be better if we came out with a show of strength and told them how much we support Giles, tell 'em how good we think he is? It might really help the situation...push 'em onto the back foot...'

There were several murmurs of assent, which surprised her. Perhaps she'd mistakenly assumed the worst about Giles's level of popularity at the station.

'That's a good point...' That was a good point. She should have thought of that. However...

'...the thing is though, that if you all start saying your piece about Giles – it isn't that one of you is going to say he's an egotistical so and so...' Laughter again. '...or worse, it's just that something might slip out by accident without your realizing you've done it. It's far easier if we have a simple, basic rule, Dave. If we agree on "nothing" then there should be less chance of an accident occurring.' She waited for a reaction. There seemed to be no dissent.

'So let's all agree then, folks. As I said - give them nothing, tell them nothing. Oh! And be polite. They're bad enough as it is without provoking them. So no kicks in the balls, Noona, or anyone else. And no swearing at them. Only one person is allowed to swear at them and that's me.' Again there was laughter, but she cut it off.

'Well,' she said, warning them, 'it's funny and all that, and it might make you feel better, but it might get you in trouble later on with the powers that be. And more to the point,' she said, having another thinking breakthrough, 'it might only wind them up enough to start poking their noses into your life.'

The body language of those assembled seemed to show agreement again with the ed-in-chief.

'Okay, I think we're done.' No one put their hand up. 'Right then everyone, thank you so much. Business as usual then.' It was over. Simone let out a final sigh of relief that could have blown up a balloon. Then Greg McKenzie was sidling up to her.

'Shall we talk it through?' he said.

'No,' said Simone. 'I've got–'

'I think we need to talk through a strategy.'

'No, Greg, thank you,' she said quietly. She didn't want any of the staff to see her like this with her deputy. It wasn't good for morale. 'Not for the time being. I'm going to take a load of press calls now, but I can see you at 4 o'clock. Don't come and find me - I'll find you. And I'm sorry I was rude to you just now, Greg, I didn't mean to be.'

The job's getting right on top of her, thought the deputy with pleasure. She's going under.

Well, that was a disaster, Simone Pound, she said aloud, but quietly as she shot away in the direction of Studio 2 not waiting to monitor Greg's reaction to the apology.

The phone was quiet when she got there. She sat down in the dingy, airless room and was glad for the silence. She blew a stray hair away from her left eye and opened the notebook. She thought it a miracle that she hadn't left it behind in the newsroom. She found a clean page and folded the pad back neatly in front of her. She wrote the word, 'Situation' at the top and underlined it as neatly as she could. She was going to try to sum up for herself where she, Giles and the station stood. It would clear her head. After she'd written that up she was going to write 'Strategy' underneath and try to figure out what to do about the bloody mess they were in. She began working her mind over the events of the past thirty hours or so as clinically as she could, before she realized that she had to start further back, at the story of Giles and Leah.

For a few minutes the studio was quiet. As she began to concentrate she felt the coolness of it and noticed how stale the air was. She noticed the metallic smell of equipment mixed with dust and perfume. Noona would have done her show in here at lunchtime. She realized how much she missed reading the news and travel, and for a minute or so regretted launching herself successfully upwards into management. As each second passed, the thick quietude of the room pulled Simone more deeply into herself. In the midst of the fury into which Two Counties had been propelled she began to appreciate for the first time in a very long time how much she loved radio, local radio. It made her feel, in the eye of the storm, really quite warm and cosy.

Then the phone rang, and the spell was broken.

6

Dirt Never Sleeps

'Hi – Derek? Tanya.'

'Hi, Tanya, what's going on?'

'Just a small something.'

'Ha-ha – small? At the moment your lot could get a poodle to produce a pile of shit an elephant would be proud of, ha-ha. Don't tell me - Clegg and the radio bloke.'

Tanya Howe was only mildly surprised but any surprised was too much for her this morning.

'How do you know that?'

'Just a wild guess.'

'You're supposed to say, "the MP."' She started to frown. How did he guess so easily?

'I'm psychic - don't worry about it.'

'I won't, Derek – you could never make me worry.'

'No, I'm sure. Listen, something interesting's happening up there you should know about.'

Shit.

'Oh, yeah?'

'Nothing bad for your lot, don't worry. Quite the reverse as it happens.'

'Go on.'

'Well now, ha-ha, if I was to pass this on to you, I'd have to have something in return.'

'Have many favours, Derek, or how big a "one"?'

'Ooh, I should say five normal-sized ones or one very big one, heh-heh.'

Nuts, thought Tanya. I ring up The Chronicle to dish some dirt on some Nobody from Nowhere land and I get a hack who's miles ahead of me and trying to take me out for a ride.

'Look, we can work out the price later. Give me what you've got.'

'Okay – are you listening?'

'I'm listening.'

'Right – it's a nice little love story for you, Tanya. Seems this bloke's got himself into a pretty big mess up there in the wilds of wherever it is.'

'Oh, yeah? What?' said Tanya, tapping her pen on her pad over and over. Get on with it Derek, you bloody prat. They were mostly all the same these male journos, milking every situation to death. It was so boring.

'A nice little love triangle, or rectangle, to be exact. A girl that left him over not one but two others.'

'And?'

'A bit of fighting in public, a bit in private.'

'What, fists?'

'Yep, fists, or nails to be exact, and a slanging match or two.'

'Big deal, Derek, happens all the time.'

'One of the women is his cousin.'

Blimey.

'They're not...'

'That would be telling.'

'Who's your contact up there?'

'You might say it's family.'

'Oh, really?'

'Something like that, ha-ha.'

'You lucky sod,' said Tanya, just playing along. Derek would no more reveal a source than reveal his...She choked that line of thinking, because that's just what blokes like Derek were itching to do.

'So, Derek, McAndrew and this cousin - are they doing it or what?'

'Well, what do you think?'

'I just think you should tell me, Derek.'

'Word has it, yes.'

'What else?'

'Oh, just a few more details. Seems like his woman is a bit barking ...'

'Which woman?'

'The girlfriend...following him around a bit. And going out looking for sex in between.'

'Why is it none of my friends aren't as interesting as this, Derek?'

'They probably are, but just aren't telling you, ha-ha.'

'You're making half of this up.'

'Not a word, I promise you. With this one, we don't have to – the truth'll do us just fine. Nice little human interest story.'

'You said "rectangle" – who's the fou...the third woman, then?'

'Oh, just some girl who works at the station.'

Tanya was familiar with a lot of bizarre goings on in the lives of MPs and senior politicians, information she'd found difficult to deal with when she first joined the unit, but she liked to think that outside in the real world people's lives weren't quite so grotesque. That said, the bloke had to be some sort of minor celebrity, so perhaps that had gone to his head. At the grand old age of 27, she was slowly coming round to the sorry conclusion that the slightest brush with fame and fortune turned ordinary people into monsters.

'So what are you going to do with it?'

'We're chewing that very thing over right now, as it happens.'

'God, you're going to have a field day with this, aren't you.'

'Ha-ha, not really. The readership isn't really going to be interested in a two-bit disc jockey no one's heard of in some corn-chewing county. If he was a Someone he'd be front page and every page halfway to the sports section.'

Tanya didn't know whether to fall for that or not. If the details were lurid enough, the punters from Lands End to John O'Groats lapped it all up. For about half a day, then they forgot about it. The poor bloke at the radio station, though – he won't know what's hit him, she thought. She hated the press. Carnivores, parasites, whores. No morals whatsoever. She really had to get out of the unit as soon as she could.

'If you're lying, and you're really going to do this bloke, leave him something, Derek - don't ruin him completely.'

'Not my decision, ha-ha. And you know how this business works now, Tanya - we're only doing what we have to do to earn our money, keep afloat – it's a tough old world.'

'Yes, Derek, I've heard it all–'

'And anyway, if we do this bloke, you'll be the ones who benefit, so what are you complaining about?'

Poor girl, he thought - she wasn't cut out for this at all.

'I know, Derek. When are you going to print with it?'

'Tomorrow.'

'How near the front?'

'Oh, somewhere near the middle, just a page, actually, nothing special.'

'You said you were still chewing it over!'

'Okay, so I lied, ha-ha.'

'And what about Clegg – you're leaving him alone, then?'

'Wouldn't you like to know…'

You're such a wanker, she thought. 'Come on, Derek…'

'Just the page next to your disc jockey.'

'Angle?' She asked the question though she knew the answer.

'Mad Cleggie, losing his grip, can't even control a situation at radio sheep shagger – come on, you know how it goes.'

'Yes, I'm learning fairly fast thanks to your tutelage. You're giving Clegg only a page, Derek? You're letting us off scot-free, then – what's got into you?'

'Not into me, into the bloke who runs Pop Idol, ha-ha. Or rather his wife. Then there's Moss and that pop Herbert she knocks around with.'

'Why bother covering politics at all? Why not give the whole paper over to celebs – your sales'll go through the roof.'

'That's what I keep telling the bosses, ha-ha, but they won't have it.'

'Your day will come, Derek, don't worry. By the way, they don't have sheep in Bartonshire. It's vegetables.'

'Yeah, whatever.'

'There's no way, I suppose, that I could threaten you into not printing this junk about Clegg at all?' She knew she was wasting her time but it was her job to make the effort at times like this, however futile.

'Ha-ha, I don't care what they say about you, Tanya, I think you're doing okay,' he said, lying through his whitened teeth. If you could do this for real, Tanya dear, he thought, you'd be giving me a couple of blow jobs in return for slaughtering this DJ to keep some of the shit away from your Clegg.

'You're only saying that because you know how to walk all over me.'

'Ha-ha, you know that's not true, ha-ha,' He was beginning to hurt for lack of a cigarette. It was such a bastard these days having to go and stand in the street like a common yobbo.

'Anyway...' said Tanya, fed up to the back teeth with the conversation.

'Yes, anyway, when are you going to buy me lunch?'

'I'll let you know.'

'Oh, hang on - what were you ringing me about, exactly? Trying to feed me some of made up stories about the disc jockey, ha-ha?'

'No, Derek, we've found out some stuff about the local hero that isn't very flattering. Really.'

'Don't tell me: you've got family up there too...'

'No, just some quality research I've done, as only those with an education know how to do.'

'Ha-ha, ooh, we are feisty today. What have you got then?'

'I won't insult you - you've got more than enough on the poor sod already.'

'No, come on, fair's fair - I've shown you mine, now you show me yours.'

'Oh, nothing much – just some bad gambling debts and a bad attitude at the station, loving himself way too much, treating everyone like crap.'

She felt herself going hot on the inside with embarrassment. It was obvious she was making this up.

'And don't tell me - women.'

Tanya could feel herself adding a scowl to her festering mood. The job was so preposterous. Here we are in government, and we're running around spreading lies about people, which is bad enough, but we go round spreading such stupid, obvious lies. She wondered whether the Tories would be as amateurish as this, or the Liberal Democrats. She decided the Lib Dems would be as bad and the Tories worse, but it didn't make her feel any better.

'I'm not even going to go there, Derek, because you've got all you need to ruin the guy already, and in actual fact, because you're a lucky swine you're obviously way out ahead of us on his love life.'

'Ha-ha, there you are, y'see, you should always leave it to the professionals.'

'Is that what you are?'

'Ha-ha, so, lunch, Tanya.'

'When I'm having a good enough day to be able to cope with seeing your ugly face. Which isn't today.'

'Ha-ha, when will that be, then?'

'When we're in such a mess we need The Chronicle to win us an election.'

'See you in thirty minutes, then. How about The Wolseley?'

'I thought you never ventured further west than St Paul's Cathedral?'

'For you I'll make an exception.'

'Bye, Derek.'

'Ha-ha, bye.'

Tanya sighed for about the twentieth time that morning. At least The Chronicle's luck is ours too, she told herself. She thought through the dynamics: if the Tory press goes big tomorrow on Giles McAndrew - the hero of the small man against Big Bad Tony and his Screw-Up Crew - The Chronicle's going to blow them out of the water with the full story of his shagging three women at a time. If Radios 4 and 5 want to keep talking about the Clegg interview they'll lose interest fast when they find out that the presenter can't keep his cock in his pants.

Fine, she thought: that would save her some time tomorrow, then. She and Simon would ring the other nationals and the Burb after lunch to make sure they knew that The Chronicle was going to break a story on a wild radio presenter's taste for incest, though. Their drooling over that would no doubt end their interest in taking Clegg to the cleaners, she thought. They had to be bored with his ineffectiveness by now, anyway, didn't they?

But it was never ending. If scrabbling around on telephones threatening, bribing and muck-raking for a living wasn't bad enough, the sheer relentlessness of it all sealed her view that the whole scene was putrid. Dirt never sleeps, she thought. They're only humans, the politicians. Doing this job had brought it home to her. For sure there were some bent, nasty and monstrously self-seeking characters in the trade, but 90% of them were honest, stupidly hard-working and served the country in a way the moronic people of Britain didn't deserve.

They worked crap hours too; had crap marriages and died young. So if they wanted to shag each other and blow off steam when they reached the end of their rope like the rest of the human race why the hell shouldn't they? Why did the press have to chase them around because it couldn't be bothered or didn't have the brains to write intelligent political stories? It wasn't fair. But the radio presenter stuff left an even more bitter taste in her mouth. He wasn't a politician and outside of a bunch of pensioners in a town no one had heard of he was totally unknown; and yet he was going to get well and truly screwed. On the other hand, she thought as she put on her jacket and made her decision about where to grab some lunch, if Derek Bailey wasn't lying, he had it coming. Blokes. They were so bloody predictable. It's a rum world, her grandmother used to say. And the dirt in it never sleeps, she'd tell her in reply if she were still alive.

7

Simone and the Fourth Estate

I don't know how I'm going to handle this, she thought.

'Yep?'

'Cissy Wilson from The Express for you...'

'Put her on, Jackie.'

'Okay.'

She stared at the scratches in the surface of the studio desk as she waited for the voice to click in.

'Hello, this is Cissy Wilson of The Express- is that Simone Pound?'

'Yes.'

'And you're the boss of the station, yes?'

'The managing-editor.'

'Managing editor, fine, thank you – may I ask you a couple of questions, Simone?'

'About what – our new Marks and Spencers, ha-ha? The Bilt Flower Show?' She tried to sound bright to cover her hostility.

'Er, no, it's about your breakfast presenter, Giles McAndrew.'

'Fire away.' Be nice, Simone, be nice, she told herself.

'Fine. Ah, how do you feel about his upsetting of John Clegg yesterday?'

Crikey, thought Simone, is that the best they can do?

'I don't think it's our job to insult politicians live on air.'

'Oh, so you're not supporting your presenter, Giles McAndrews?'

'McAndrew. Giles McAndrew.'

'Sorry, McAndrew.'

'Giles is an outstanding radio presenter, the best this station has ever had, one of the best in the whole country at his job.' Take that.

'Oh. So, are you happy with his growing status of champion of the ordinary people of Britain in the face of an, um, over-mighty, arrogant government?'

'No.'

There was a silence at both ends as Cissy waited for Simone to flesh out her answer.

'Um, could you, Simone...'

'Could I what?'

'Um, develop that a little bit.'

'Tell me, Lily, which of my answers so far haven't you understood.'

'Oh, come on – and it's Cissy, by the way – we both work in the same business - can you just give me a little more?'

'Give me one good reason.'

'We're just trying to provide our readers with a service. And this is a story that's full of interest, and if everyone we interviewed was as - gave us this much information, we wouldn't be able to fill a newspaper.'

'Okay, ask me another question then.'

There was a deep sigh down the line in the capital that made Simone feel about three feet high; like the captain of a team of amateurs who weren't good enough to make it to the big time. She blew the strand of hair away with a sigh.

'You must, surely, be able to tell us more how you feel about one of your presenters calling the Deputy Prime Minister a lazy, fat slob who can't keep his willie in his trousers on live radio.'

'What?'

'Sorry to put it like that, if...'

'Where do you get this from? You want me to stop messing you around but you can't even get your facts right. Giles did not call Clegg a lazy, fat slob and did not use the word "willie."'

'What did he use, then?'

Simone thought about it and realized that she didn't know.

'It didn't matter what word he used. I've already told you that I do not approve of my presenters insulting any of their guests, whatever the provocation, under any circumstances. I have also told you that I don't think because of that, Giles McAndrew should be some sort of, er, "People's champion" as you put it. Now why don't you ask me an intelligent question, Cissy or stop wasting my time.' Phew, that was better, she thought.

'Do you think that McAndrew's outburst shows that you're failing in your job to keep your presenters under close control?'

She'd expected this one.

'Of course not.'

'Why?'

'Isn't it obvious?'

'Tell me.'

My God, thought Simone: they're hassling and hounding me and they want me to do all the work for them. Is this what we do too, she thought?

'In front of a microphone, a presenter has freedom of speech. If they have a bad day or...or...or...they're not feeling well, they may make a mistake and say something they later regret. It happens.'

'McAndrew was under some personal pressure, wasn't he? We know he's been having problems with his partner, right?'

'I'm not prepared to comment on that.'

'Oh, come on, Simone, everyone in the press knows that your guy's got some issues in his private life. Now, isn't it your job to make sure that if one of your presenters is going off the rails he doesn't go on the air?'

'Well, yes, I…'

Simone began to go empty at the front of her brain. The thoughts dried up before she could convert them into words. Yes, it was my fault, she said to herself - I should have known that Giles was under a lot of pressure and I ought to have done something about it.

'Look,' she said, 'it's, er, my job to know my presenters…'

Yes, it's my job to know my presenters.

'…but I can't be supposed to know every single little detail about them. They obviously want to keep some things from their bosses and that's quite okay. But sometimes one thing leads to another and they go over the edge when you least expect it.'

She was in deep water, scrambling like a two year old for sand under foot.

'So this happens a lot at Two Counties, does it?'

'No, it does not.'

The memory of the time when a local radio presenter committed suicide flashed through her mind. She scraped the loose strand of hair away from her face with her hand this time and felt herself sweating. The studio's coolness seemed to have evaporated.

'Look, Simone. I don't mean to put you under pressure here - we're actually looking to write something positive about Giles for tomorrow's paper…'

This was unbelievable. Why was she being so fucking awkward, then?

'…could you give me some of his strengths?'

Simone took in a deep breath and began a speech outlining her man's good points. Cissy interrupted her three times with 'hang on' as she took notes.

'That's lovely. And can you tell me, is it characteristic of Giles to lose his rag on air?'

'No, but he didn't lose his rag on air.'

'Well, whatever you want to call it. "Lose it" would perhaps be better.'

'Look, if politicians didn't just blether when we interviewed them – surely you must know this – if they actually answered our questions, then presenters like Giles wouldn't lose their temper.'

'So you're saying that Giles's personal life had nothing to do with his outburst?'

'No, Giles is working under a huge amount of pressure at the moment through absolutely no fault of his own and unfortunately he just cracked suddenly. For God's sake, we're all only human.'

'Thank you, Simone, that's lovely. Thanks for your help. 'Bye. Enjoy the rest of your day.'

There was a click in her ear and the line was dead. She felt her gut contracting. She'd screwed it up, first call. The hack had wrapped it up in about a second and a half out of nowhere as soon as she'd got what she wanted. Simone felt cheapened, exploited and weak. What have I done, she thought?

She dialled Jackie in reception.

'Jack, stop all press calls 'til I ring you back. And I need a tape of Giles's interview with Clegg. Could you get Allan and ask him to get in here as fast as possible…Thanks.'

Before she spoke to anyone else she had to listen to the interview. She hadn't actually heard the real thing yet. She'd relied only on second hand accounts. God, I'm hopeless, she wailed inside. After all that effort I told them that Giles cracked on air - out of my own mouth. Then Allan Ruzinski came through the door.

'Hi, Simone,' said the tech, smiling, 'what do you need, the Clegg interview?'

'Yes…please, Allan, if you don't mind.'

'No problem. It won't take a moment; I've been playing it for people all day.'

Simone pushed her wheelie chair out of the way to let Allan get at the mouse. In twelve seconds and seven clicks, he had it. They listened together.

Simone looked up at the tech.

'What do you think?'

'What do *I* think?' he replied, surprised. 'I think Clegg got what he deserved.'

'But why? What did he do wrong?'

'He's Labour,' said Allan. 'So I just don't like him.'

'But what do you think of Giles?'

'What he did, you mean?'

'Yes.'

'Do you want me to be honest?'

'Yes, of course I do.'

'I think he's good at his job, but he made a mistake. Nothing more, nothing less.'

Allan Ruzinski was a bit too gruff for her liking at the best of times but today his attitude was like someone scraping a cheese grater across her brain. She let him get back to the newsroom where he was downloading some software for Noona's computer. She rang Jackie again and within two minutes the phone rang again. She looked down at the machine as she went to pick it up and felt her mind go numb. It was a mistake doing this, she realised, but it was too late to go back.

'Hello?'

'Hi, is that Simone?' said an alarmingly confident voice.

'Yes.'

'Hi, this is Adam Williams from The Independent.'

She cursed Jackie for putting him straight through. A couple of moments to take a few deep breaths would have helped.

'Yes?'

'Oh, are you okay?'

'Of course I'm okay – get on with it, I'm busy.'

'Oh.' There was a pause. 'I just wanted to ask you a couple of questions about Giles McAndrew and his interview with John Clegg. If that's okay.'

'Right. First question?'

'Oh – um, could you tell me, are you supporting Giles?'

'What is he now, a football team?'

'I mean in terms of what he's done.' The confident ooze had gone out of his voice.

'Of course I don't condone him insulting a guest, but he...' God, there was no way out of this, though there had to be, surely. '...he just had a temporary misfire. That's all.'

'Could you expand on that, do you think?'

'Look, Adam. What do you want me to say? I've got a whole line of you people waiting to grill me about this. Just listen to what I have to say, here: Giles McAndrew is a brilliant, brilliant local radio presenter. He's bright, he's sharp, he's funny, he cares about the listeners, he initiates campaigns for local hospitals, local schools, all sorts of things. He's worked here for five years-' - was it five? She'd have to check that too – '- and on one, just one occasion, he made a slip of the tongue. And now you want to crucify him. Well, I'm sick of it. You can all write what you bloody like and you can all go to *hell while you're doing it!*'

'Are you okay?'

'*What?* Of course I'm okay! What is the matter with you people?'

'I'm sorry, Simone, but I think what he did was great. I want to write a piece in praise of Giles McAndrew. I just wanted to get some information straight from the horse's mouth, so to speak.'

'Well, why didn't you bloody well say so?'

I'm going mad, she thought. I never swear like this. Look at what these people are making me do.

'Look, I'm not going to be sworn at down the phone. If that's–'

'No, no, I'm sorry. Adam. Please. I'm sorry. It's just…'

'It's getting on top of you too, it's okay, I can hear, ha-ha. I understand.'

Simone's whole being plunged into a dead pool of deep water. What a *mess*, she thought. I can't do this – I can't do this job. Not this part of it, anyway.

'Look, as I say, I'm sorry. Look, can we start this again.'

'Yes, of course we can. I suppose this isn't the sort of thing you're used to.'

'I don't need to be patronised.'

'Ha-ha, look, I'm not patronising you, honestly. I can imagine what it must be like to suddenly have to confront the newspapers. It must be like an inferno. It's okay, don't worry, it's not something that's remotely easy to deal with.'

A feeling of calm began to appear at the edge of Simone's anger and frustration. Wow, some people can be so nice, she thought, relief beginning to trickle into her.

She ended up having a perfectly nice conversation with the guy from The Independent and this time didn't produce any gaffes - none that she was aware of anyway.

'Ha-ha, I might have to start buying The Independent after this, ha-ha,' she said at the end of it.

When she put the phone down she thought about calling a press conference. Damn, she thought, unnerving herself again, that's what I should have done. Why didn't Ian Bakerson advise me to do that? She stood up and stretched. She was so tense. She was sweaty under the arms and had a sweaty crotch. What the hell was she wearing tights for on a warm day? Then she remembered that actually, it wasn't that warm out in the open air, beyond the madness she was in.

She had a vision of a press conference, surrounded by a hostile media from the capital city, exposing her for the naïve idiot that she was, and shuddered mightily. Phone calls it had to be.

It went on for three hours. She left the studio after The Yorkshire Post, The Telegraph, The Sunday Telegraph and the Glasgow Herald, and took The Guardian, The Star, the Associated Press, the Western

Mail and The Times in her office with the door locked. By six-fifteen just gone, she was a zombie. Then the phone burbled horribly at her once again.

'Hello?'

'Hi, Simone.'

'I thought I told you to go home?'

'It's okay - I'm going in a minute.'

'Good. Jack, are those hacks still at the door?'

'No, they've gone.'

'Back door?'

'No one there last time we checked.'

'Thank God. That's one thing that's gone right, anyway.'

'Shall I tell the security blokes they can go?'

'Yes, yes, they can go. Are they going to invoice us?'

'I don't know, you'll have to ask Sarah.'

'Of course.'

'Actually, I'll do that. I'll see if she's still here.'

'Thank you, Jackie – you've been terrific today.' She really had.

'Thanks – it's what I'm here for, don't worry. I've got a bloke from The Chronicle on the line for you. Shall I tell him you've gone home?'

'How many more waiting?'

'Frank from The Gazette's going to call in tomorrow. He said he understood you were up to your ears.'

'That's fine. Put The Chronicle through, then, Jackie, and go home. You've done a long day.'

'Okay, I will. See you tomorrow.'

'Yeah, see you.'

Simone waited. One more, then she was going home too.

'Hello? Is that Simone?'

She couldn't be bothered to answer.

'It's Alex from The Chronicle.'

'Could you give me your second name?'

She'd taken to writing each name down in full after the disastrous call from that smart-arsed tart from The Express.

'McKeen, Alex McKeen.'

'Thank you. Sorry about that but I like to be clear about who I'm speaking to.'

'That's alright. Very wise.'

'Thank you. Thanks for waiting.'

'No, that's okay, that's okay. Look, Simone. How shall I put this? Um, how do you feel about having a presenter who's got three women on the go right in front of your nose?'

'What on earth are you talking about?'

'I'm sorry if that sounds a bit rude - but come on - let's start with the office romance. What's your policy on your workers having office romances that disturb the smooth running of the station?'

'That's none of your business.'

'Isn't it? Don't you think this is in the public interest when an elected politician gets attacked for no reason by an unelected radio presenter?'

'You enjoy this sort of work, do you?' She was way, way on the back foot. What was this nonsense – three women?

'Sorry, I don't know what you mean.'

'You ring me up here – you don't know me and you ring me up and talk to me like something you've just trodden on.'

'Look – I'm sorry, but we're covering the story about your bloke and John Clegg – and I just thought your reaction to what happened might be interesting. That's all.'

'Oh – so you've already got it written, then.'

'It's all here ready to go.'

'So what am I, then? Just some add on? Thanks for bothering.'

'I just wondered how you felt having someone on staff – sorry, I forgot, he's a freelancer, isn't he, your man Giles – how you felt employing a guy who has a partner, an affair with a work colleague and sex with his cousin all at the same time?'

'How dare you ring me up and–'

'Simone, it's the way of the world. I just wanted to know how you feel about it. And whether you're going to sack the guy?'

She slammed the phone down. She wanted to do what she'd seen them do in the movies, pick up the whole set and throw it across the office, but she didn't have the nerve. She kicked the waste paper bin instead, and stubbed her toe on it. She sat down again and put her right foot up on the edge of the padded seat and gave it a hard rub for ten seconds. She needed the distraction from the growing alarm at what she'd just heard.

The rudeness of the bloke from The Chronicle was like a slap she could still feel across her face. Was he serious? If this was for real it would destroy Giles. She thought of the nice guy from The Independent, whose name she could hardly remember, and how he at least was going to write a nice piece, a supportive piece. But if The Chronicle were going to – she tunnelled her thoughts inward onto the thing. How the bloody hell did they know about Giles and his cousin? About Giles and Lucie? About Giles and Leah? Only she knew about this, surely. She thought again of the pictures and the alarm turned quickly to horror.

This is hell, she thought. Hell is going on around me. It was unbelievable. Right here at her award-winning station. Someone spreading malicious lies that they themselves had spread to the national press who were going to spread it, this poison, all around, across the whole nation. She felt her emotions rise, felt the beginning of tears. Poor Giles, my God. She wondered how he was dealing with everything and where he was. He had to be warned. He had to be prepared. He had to be talked through it if the blow fell and some sort of terrible article was printed.

She got up, grabbed up her bag and rushed as fast as she could toward the back entrance of the station and into the car park with evening coming on. She fired up the engine of her Honda and took off in the direction of The Barn House in Corumby.

8

Simone Makes Spaghetti

There was no answer when Simone rang the front door bell so she went round to the back of the house and looked in through the windows. In the living room she saw Giles staring at the TV from a sofa. His eyes were glazed over and his body motionless as she stood there for what seemed like an age. Then she tapped on the pane loudly. During the third bout, when the tap had gone halfway to a bang Giles suddenly turned his head to the window. A scared face looked back at her she didn't recognize at first. Then its expression fell away to one of resignation as he rose, motioning her towards the side of the house. Simone smiled brightly at him but she didn't think he'd noticed. As she walked round she heard Giles turning a key to unlock his back kitchen door. When it opened, a Giles she'd never seen before looked at her from two feet away. She was appalled and roused to pity.

'Oh, my love, my love,' she said, embracing him. Giles fell limply into her, arms by his side, bereft of energy. She held him there trying to show him that everything would be alright. She stroked his hair as she imagined his mother would have done if she could have been there. She had to stand on tip-toe to do it. She listened for Giles breaking down but there was nothing there; his limpness was like stone. Giles pulled gently away and stepped aside to let her in.

'Thanks, Simone.'

'I haven't done anything yet. But you wait.'

Giles's helplessness was stiffening her resolve. She felt the iron in her soul rising like mercury up a thermometer, as if to balance his falling down.

'Can I get you a drink?' said Giles.

'No. When was the last time you had a drink?'

'I don't know.'

'You don't know? Do you want one now?'

'I don't know.'

Giles sat down on the kitchen sofa and stared across the room into a cupboard door. Simone sat beside him.

'Giles, look at me.'

'Hmm?' he said, still staring, his mouth turned down, his eyes gone.

She took his face in her right hand and pulled it firmly around to face hers.

'Look at me,' she said, but she looked at him, at his eyes, looking for a sign of life.

'Giles, we're going to start fighting this, right here, right now.'

He looked back. She saw a face that spoke without the mouth moving.

'How?' It said.

'I don't know how, but we're going to work it out, you and me.' Still Giles said nothing, but Simone caught the effect of his breath in her nostrils. It stank.

'Speak to me, Giles. Say something.'

He pulled his face out of her hands gently and looked as his bare feet. He shook his head.

'I can't.'

'Can I turn that off?' said Simone. The TV in the other room was up loud and with the doors both to and from the hall wide open it was distracting. She pricked up her ears to hear the words coming from the machine and got up suddenly. She couldn't believe it. She walked into the living room and stood in front of the set. Peter Kay in a blue shirt was reducing an audience to hysterics in his home town. She looked behind her and saw the remote. There was a red button at the top on the left. She punched it hard several times, making the end of her finger hurt in the process. She was beginning to get angry with it when the noise came to a dead stop. She went back to Giles. He hadn't moved. She went to look for the kettle. She found it, filled it, set it down in its cradle and pushed down the switch. Christ, I need a coffee myself even if he doesn't, she said to herself. Then she sat beside Giles again.

'Peter Kay?'

She had to get him talking.

'Peter Kay? What are you doing watching a Peter Kay DVD, ha-ha. You're crazy, Giles McAndrew, do you know that? Crazy. Off your onion.'

'I thought it might cheer me up.'

'Why do you think you need cheering up, my dear?'

'Because Leah's left me.'

'What about work?'

'What about it?'

'Have you had any reporters here today?'

'A couple. They were there when I came back from my bike ride. I told them to go away.'

How the blazes did these people get his address, thought Simone? These bastards much have secret access to names and addresses of the whole population.

207

'And did they?'

'One of them opened the back door and came in.'

'What?' Bloody hell.

Giles nodded.

'I grabbed her by the throat and pushed her out into the garden. Then I came in, bolted the doors and went up to my bedroom.'

'When did they leave?'

'No idea.'

'What did you do in the bedroom?'

'Laid down on my bed. Had a shower. Got changed.'

Simone went to get up.

'Coffee or tea?' she said rising.

'Don't care.'

'I'll make-'

'Coffee.'

She didn't bother asking Giles where things were. It would be less fuss poking about for things on her own. She opened a coffee canister on the counter and found brown sugar in it. The coffee canister with the same label in the fridge had coffee in it. The cafétiere was there on the drainer. She made the coffee, found two mugs and some milk then went back to the sofa.

'Has anyone phoned?'

'One, but I disconnected it from the wall. I took all the sockets out of the wall.'

'Mobile?'

'I've had it switched off all day.'

'Have you eaten?'

'No. Sorry.'

'Sorry? It's alright, ha-ha, I'm not your mum.'

'Ha-ha.'

The laugh was dry but he'd reacted. Simone was fired with hope that she could pull some strength out of him. It was only the beginning of something, but it was something.

'Would you like me to make you supper?'

'No, it's okay.'

Simone looked at her watch. It was twenty-to-seven.

'I'll make us something later.'

'How long are you staying?'

'As long as it takes.'

'To do what?'

'To get you on your feet.'

'I'll stand up for you if you like.'

'Are you trying to get rid of me?' She was smiling at him. He turned one eye to her and she could see he wasn't far from smiling himself.

'No. Don't be silly.'

'I've decided – you and me - we're in this together. If you've got someone else who can come round here and sort you out, fine, then I'll go. But until then, I'm going to be right here. Is that okay?'

He was looking at her now.

'I don't deserve you to do this for me.'

'Yes, you do. And unless you physically throw me out like your reporter, you're stuck with me.' The line, *I got you into this, so I'm going to get you out of it* shot into her head. Had she? She hadn't given Giles the presenting job at Two Counties for a start, so she was off the hook straight away. And it wasn't her fault he and Leah had split. Not the original split anyway.

'What have you got in mind?'

'Hmm? Nothing. Yet. But something'll come to me.'

She got up again and poured them each some coffee.

'Got any biscuits?'

Giles looked up from the floor.

'Cupboard above the fridge…No, to the left.'

'Ooh, I like these,' she said coming back to the sofa. She took one out of the white packet and bit into it, a fancy galette. Giles reached across and took one. Simone watched him bite a piece out of it and begin to chew as if he were a mental hospital patient. She saw herself, saw them both in her mind's eye, and she nearly laughed out loud. It was so absurd what life did to you.

They sat and drank their coffee. It was five-to-seven when Simone looked at her watch. She put the empty cup down on the floor carefully, out of the way of her feet. A crow cawed outside, distracting her. Through an open top kitchen window she tuned into birdsong. He really did live in the middle of nowhere. She sat back in the sofa and rested herself. A long shaft of evening sunlight suddenly appeared across the floor. She followed its length to the fridge then up the kitchen cupboard where it stopped by the ceiling. Then it disappeared as another bank of high, rainless cloud covered over the evening sun. She closed her eyes. Beside her Giles was still quiet. This would do for now, she decided. And she had all evening and all night if that's what it took to take the situation by the scruff of the neck. Or if they couldn't do that, make some sort of plan in the face of this…this… - 'situation' didn't do it justice, and 'disaster' was too negative. It wasn't a disaster yet. 'In the face of these monsters' fitted her thinking much better. Or maybe just one single monster, the one that was causing all the trouble. The sofa was comfy and she could have gone to sleep given half a chance.

Giles got up.

'Where are you going?' said Simone.

'To the loo.'

'Oh,' she said. She watched him move away and was frightened for him.

She knew she was a bit naïve but it was obvious that this series of events could easily end with his being crushed like a cat under a lorry. The media attack might prove to be a two-second hurricane but when it blew over there might be nothing left of Giles McAndrew but his teeth. And that might be the end of him. She saw him in her mind's eye as a shuffling figure in his fifties, grey and balding coming out of Sainbury's in the middle of the day in the middle of the week, carrying a plastic bag with a few odds and ends of shopping inside: a carton of milk; a jar of instant coffee; a packet of Digestives. She shook her head from side to side as if she could send the image out through her ears. It was unthinkable. This was Giles, Two Counties' presenting power player. The doer, the achiever.

She heard a flap of feet and turned to see Giles sort of slopping his body back into the room. Despite his mood he was still tall, still had dark hair and was still handsome.

'What's the matter?' he said, coming to sit down again. She felt like cuddling him again.

'Nothing.'

'What are we going to do, then?'

'I don't know. Help me think about it while I make us some dinner.'

'I'm not hungry.'

'Doesn't matter – I am. You can leave yours if you like but I'm making you some anyway. You do have a packet of spaghetti, do you?'

'I dunno. I might have.'

He got up and she followed him over to the business part of the room.

'Where's your vegetable rack?'

'The drawer, here,' said Giles, bending to open it. Simone bent to pick an onion out of a plastic container then the remaining cloves from a head of garlic and a lemon.

'You haven't got any parsley, I suppose. Or basil?'

'Maybe in the fridge. Have a look. I don't think so.' Giles got a big saucepan out of a cupboard and took it to the sink to fill it with water.

'No – let the water run hot first.'

Simone organized Giles to do more fetching and carrying and had him crushing and chopping some garlic. It was almost like dealing with a child. But she still tried to find a way to tell him what he was in for in the morning.

'Giles,' she said, as the water came to the boil, holding the pasta ready.

'Yes?' Giles was grating some cheese.

'I've got some bad news for you. Do you think you might be ready to hear it?'

'It can't be worse than Leah leaving me,' he said. Don't bank on it, thought Simone, separating the strands of spaghetti in the saucepan.

'The Chronicle is going to print details of your love life.'

'When?' He lifted his head back up and turned it to face Simone.

'Tomorrow.'

'How do you know?'

'One of their sodding journalists phone me to tell me.'

'What details?'

'That you're a total shitbag who cheats on his girlfriend with a work colleague and has sex with his cousin on the side.' There. She'd done it. He might as well know.

'Oh.'

What?

'I'm sorry?' said Simone.

'So am I,' said Giles.

'What do you mean?'

'I feel sorry for them. If that's what they get off on.'

'But don't you care about them dragging your name into the mud?'

'No. It's not true.'

'But our audience is going to know all about it.'

'They won't believe it.'

'Giles…'

He looked at her and again her heart went out to him for his innocence.

'What are you saying, then, that'll they'll desert me? Stop listening to me?'

'They might.'

Giles stopped grating. He was gradually becoming himself again. She felt his presence swell inside the room.

'My ratings will be a disaster. Then you'll have to sack me.'

'You know I'll have to if they're really bad. I'll fight for you though.'

But he knew that if his audience deserted him in enough numbers for enough weeks, there would be nothing she could do to save him. He was great, but he wasn't the station. Simone wanted to tell him, so he was fully prepared, that way before it ever got to that, her bosses at BRBC Midlands, never mind England might terminate his contract. They just had to take one look at what The Chronicle had to say, decide that he was dirtying the name of the corporation, and it would all be over.

'It might not come to that.'

Oh, Giles, said her weary heart.

'They might sack me anyway. If they believe what they read in the papers. Don't worry, Simone, I might be depressed but I'm not stupid. I know if they make me look like...well, bad enough, some kind of monster, England will fire me.'

Thank God for one thing, she thought: he's switched back on.

'Don't you care?'

'You know what? I don't know. All I know now, Simone, is that I've lost Leah, and I want to die.'

'You don't.'

'No, I don't, but now you know roughly how I feel, right?'

She wanted to hold out hope to him as far as Leah was concerned but she looked inside her mind and her heart and found none there to offer him.

'I knew anyway, Giles. I saw you through the window when I got here.'

Giles grunted in reply and went and got himself some orange juice from the fridge. Simone's phone went. It was muffled because it was inside her bag, but she still caught it before the voicemail kicked in.

'Hello?'

'It's Ian Bakerson, Simone.'

'Hi.' She held the phone to her ear but went out into the hall, shutting the kitchen door behind her.

'Look. I've had a tip off about one of the papers. There's an article going to appear tomorrow that dishes a load of dirt on your guy, Giles.'

'I know, I–'

She felt her anger rise, first red, then purple, then finally white. She thought she might get in her car and drive to London, to The Chronicle.

'Hold on, Simone. I want you to pull Giles from his morning show tomorrow.'

'Hang on, Ian.' She was now in the living room. She shut the door and walked to the window to the back garden. There was no way Giles could hear.

'I can't, I'm sorry. We're not going to have Giles spouting on while his audience is reading about him screwing his cousin over the cornflakes.'

'Is this you, Ian, or your boss?'

'Both.'

She'd thought for a mad second that if she could somehow contact Andrea Potter-Symons she could pull things back. She thought hard and fast while she was trying to deal with Bakerson.

'What about Monday?'

'No, come on, Simone, don't be silly. If what I've just heard appears tomorrow, this could be the end of him. Line up a replacement for the whole of next week and we'll look at it again next weekend.'

Simone felt each word like a fresh smack across the face, but she was almost glad to get to the worst that could happen straight away. At least now she didn't have to sit around all weekend and early next week watching things slide away bit by bit. A slow death of Giles's career at Two Counties would be unbearable.

'Will you promise me, that–' She remembered something. She nearly forgot. 'Sorry, Ian, I nearly forgot to tell you - while The Chronicle is trying to smear Giles, at least one other paper is going to be writing a "Giles is a big hero" story.'

'Which one?'

'The Mail and The Independent. There may be others too.' Her hopes soared.

'Hmm. Well, like I say, we'll review it next week. I'll be in touch, you can be sure of that. But for now, get him off the air.'

'But there's no truth in what The Chronicle's going to write.'

'How can you be sure?'

'What the hell do you mean? I've known Giles McAndrew for four, five years and I know him bloody well. This man's been through hell in the past week because of things going wrong in his personal life but it doesn't involve him screwing his bloody cousin!'

Simone felt her head throb with anger.

'Calm down, Simone, calm down.'

Simone heard a squeak and turned to see Giles walk silently into the room.

'No I will not be bloody calm! Why aren't you supporting my presenter? Why are you ditching him? Why are you being so bloody spineless? Have you *no* sense of loyalty down there?'

'Simone. Look. All we're doing is removing him until this thing dies down. If the Mail supports him tomorrow, if they're going to write what a champion of the people he is, then fine. We may well be putting him back in place at the end of next week.'

I've won, she thought. He's backing down.

'Okay,' she said.

'Yes? Look, I like the way you fight for this bloke.'

She froze. I know that tone of voice, she thought. It means you don't like it. That you think I've gone too far, that I'm being rude and therefore – this was the worst of all - unprofessional. Oh, shit, she said inside, and stamped her foot on the carpet without realizing what she was doing.

'No, I've been rude. I'm sorry. I've probably–'

'No, no, you haven't, Simone.' She didn't believe him. 'Look, I'll call you on Monday. But you will take him off the air for tomorrow, won't you...'

'Yes, Ian, of course, yes - of course I will.'

'Good. Okay, Simone. Look, have a good weekend. Or are you working?'

'In the circumstances, Ian, I'll be working, whether I'm there at the station or whether I'm not.'

'But you'll be–'

'In tomorrow morning, certainly. Early.'

'Okay. Well, good luck, Simone – we'll talk Monday.'

'Okay, Ian.'

Suddenly a light switched on in her head.

'Hang on! Ian – you said you got a tip-off? Who from?'

'I'm sorry, Simone, I can't tell you that.'

'Why ever not?'

'I just can't. It came to me in confidence.'

That was it: he really didn't like her. Shit.

'Look...'

'Yes, I'm sure you want to push on.'

'Well, it's late...'

'Okay, 'bye.'

''Bye...'bye.'

'*Bastard!*' said Simone, when he'd gone.

At BRBC headquarters in Shepherd's Bush, Ian Bakerson looked again at the briefing notes from one of the phone conversations he'd had earlier about this Giles McAndrew. Below the notes on this fool's philandering, with his cousin, for God's sake, he saw and read,

"Arrogant. Disruptive. Strongly disliked by fellow staff. Bad team player. Too friendly with female staff. Upsetting morale. Behaviour with

214

women caused fighting amongst staff – physical. Complaints made to senior staff by number of workers. Rumours of harassment incident."

He decided that he'd done the right thing in not mentioning this to Simone Pound. It was too late to ask Heather to file it carefully away in the cabinet with the rest of the Two Counties Radio material but it was too important a piece of paper to leave on his desk until Monday. He opened a drawer in his desk by his knee, placed it carefully underneath the other documents the resided there and re-shut it. He got up from his desk to prepare himself to leave the office for the weekend. He chuckled to himself as he gathered up a few things. Local bloody radio, he thought: what entertainment value. He pocketed his phone and looked forward to getting up early in the morning to get the papers, thought about his Friday night curry and began to feel hungry.

9

Glad To Be Simone

Simone, fuming, closed her phone. However, a new idea had just popped into her head. She was going to try to distract Giles with it.

'Get your phone, could you, love?'

After a short moment he turned and left the living room for the kitchen to get his mobile. Simone hoped against hope that she could somehow keep her man from going under whilst mulling over a suspicion that occurred to her whilst talking to Bakerson.

Giles returned, looking down at his phone, thumb already pressing into the surface facing him. Simone stepped between the sofa and an armchair to meet him.

'Giles, go through your messages would you, and read out to me who's called you. Don't read the messages, just tell me the names.'

Giles looked at her with a face she couldn't quite read.

'Don't ask why – I'll tell you in a minute…go on,' she said.

Giles looked back at the phone and made the necessary clicks.

'Catherine…' he said, still looking down into the tiny screen. 'Andy Reed…Sally Giffen…'

'Tell me when you read out each name whether you know them or not, could you? Sorry.'

'Catherine's my cousin,' he said, looking up with a terrible but determined face. 'Andy Reed - don't know him. Sally Giffen - never heard of her.'

'Good. Go on.'

'Erm…'

Simone waited patiently.

'It's okay, there's no rush. Sit down if you want, while you're doing it.'

Giles perched himself on the front edge of the armchair next to him and frowned down at his phone.

'…Leon…' he looked up.

'Yes, that's our Leon, yes?'

'Yeah…Rob Ashburn - don't know him…Frank Quigley…'

'Frank, okay…' Frank Quigley was a friend of the station from The Bart & Bilt Gazette.

'…Cissy Wilson - don't know her…Catherine – again…' Giles looked up:

'You,' he said and carried on.

'Leon again...Steve Brackenfield - don't know him...Greg McKenzie...Kevin Twombly - don't know him...You again,' he said not looking up, '...Paul Drinkwater...there's still loads to go – do you want me to carry on?'

'Just a few more.'

'Associated Press...Frank again...you again...Cissy Wilson...'

'Okay, that's enough. Could you go back and find Kevin Twombly and listen to his message and read it to me.'

'Okay,' said Giles, and began his search.

'Kevin Twombly.' Giles put the phone to his ear and waited for the voice to kick in. Then he began to recite the message as he heard it, in a flat monotone.

'"Giles...Kevin Twombly here from The Chronicle...I'd really like to have a supportive chat with you about the Clegg incident yesterday...Do you think you could call me? On 0711 345 978. Cheers. 'Bye."' Giles looked at Simone expectantly.

'Okay. Hang on, I'll tell you in a minute. Could you go to your texts?'

Giles nodded.

'And, open up all the ones from people you don't know, and tell me if there's a newspaper after the name. You know, Kevin Twombly, The Chronicle, something like that.'

There was excitement in Simone's voice.

'Okay...right: Elaine Tennant, The Star...'

The wait between each name was excruciating.

'...Andy Reid, The Sun...'

Yes, thought Simone, I'm right. This gave her satisfaction, but it was a grim one.

'...Kevin Twombly, The Chronicle.'

'The Chronicle,' echoed Simone. 'Okay, Giles, that's enough. I might ask you for more in a little while, but that'll do for now.' Her eyes were alive with a mixture of pleasure, determination and fury. In her stomach too, she felt a tightness that was pure anxiety.

'What is it?' said Giles.

She sat down.

'How do these people know your mobile number?'

'What?'

'Okay, listen. Are you ready for this?'

'Go on,' said Giles.

'Someone at the station's betraying us. Someone at the station's a mole for these people.'

She looked at Giles who looked as though any new information was way too much for him. She tried to explain.

'How have these people got your phone number? It's private, right?'

Giles just looked at her intently.

'You don't give your number out to people, do you?' she said.

'No,' said Giles, 'of course not. Well, I give them to friends.'

'Right, so - someone we know has got hold of your number and given them to the press.'

A nasty thought occurred to her. It might upset Giles, but she couldn't be doing with being super-sensitive; it would just get in the way of progress.

'Giles…' She waited for him to make eye-contact. '…do you think Leah is capable of doing this.'

'Phoning the press you mean?'

'Mmm-hmm.' Simone watched him thinking about it.

'No,' he said, 'do you?'

Simone had already thought about it.

'No, I don't. We had to consider the possibility though.'

Giles nodded.

'Sure. Of course,' he said.

The room was quiet while Simone put her chin in both hands and chewed the matter over. She was narrowing down the field. One of her workers was the enemy. One of them drew the pictures and posted them at The Barn House. It was obvious. For how many people in Barton Townes, in Bartonshire, in Bilt, knew where Giles lived?

'Giles…'

'Yes?'

'Have any listeners ever just dropped by your house?'

'No.' He thought about it some more. 'No, definitely not.'

'People stopping to look up at the house?'

'Who am I, David Beckham or somebody? Of course not. And remember, it's in the middle of nowhere.'

'Okay. The room was quiet as Simone walked up and down the room for over a minute. Giles sat there fiddling with his phone.

'Giles…'

'Yeah.'

'Don't take this the wrong way - you don't have a lot of friends, do you?'

'No, Simone,' he said, giving her a hostile glare, 'I don't have many friends here, no.'

'When you came here, you didn't know anyone, did you…'

'No.'

'Then you met Leah.'

'Well, no, I was here for three years nearly before I went out with Leah.'

'But you had girlfriends before Leah.'

'Er, yes.'

'Friends?'

'No, hardly any. What's your thinking?'

She looked into his eyes and saw concentration.

'I'm narrowing down. So how many people would have known where you lived? In the first, say three years you were here?'

Giles thought. He'd had two or three girlfriends here before Leah. No more than that. It was difficult to meet people in the area when you were new; you met them at work, or through friends of friends. Giles had met one in a restaurant, the manager of the restaurant, and he'd gone out with a couple of reporters who'd only been on assignment to Two Counties for shortish periods. And he'd had a fling with Jane Landings. But friends? No, apart from his girlfriends and a couple of one-night stands, and Leon, and Leah, of course, no one had been to The Barn House.

He told Simone this.

She sat there thinking, head in hands, staring at her bony knees. It began to sink in with a deeper sense of reality: somebody was out to get him. They were really out to get him. It was incredible to her. Leah had left Giles and part of the reason, most of the reason perhaps, was that someone at Two Counties Radio, someone she knew and worked with every day, was evil enough to want to coldly, deliberately destroy his relationship with her. And if that wasn't enough, they wanted to destroy his career as well.

It was like the lights being switched on all over a huge building. The one who did the drawings would be the same person feeding the numbers to the press and feeding them lies about Giles's personal life. Simone wasn't sure whether the news was going to make him feel better or send him over the edge – but she had to tell him.

'So,' said Giles, 'someone…'

Thank God, thought Simone, he's cottoned on.

'…is out to get me.'

Simone thought of the field of suspects. It had just widened. Someone at the station, yes, but it could be a pair. A pair of practical jokers? She thought of Marcus and Dave. No, this wasn't joking around. But she had to check it from every angle. What do I know about being a detective, she said to herself? Not much: so I have to think very carefully, very slowly. I've already decided it's someone at the station but I could be wrong. It could be someone who used to work at the station or who knows someone there now and casually gets gossip and news from them.

What, she thought, would cause someone to go this far, to conspire against a man, to go to the extreme length of drawing obscene pictures and posting them? This wasn't far from something she ought to take to the police. Or something she should take to them straight away. But no, she didn't want the police involved. Her first theory was that someone hated Giles for his success but it couldn't be that: that was too trivial a motive for something this serious. More likely someone from Giles's past wanted revenge on him; for dumping him, say. A woman's passion turned to jealousy could be a powerful thing - she knew that alright. She tried to imagine a woman at a desk drawing really with quite a lot of skill a man and a woman copulating and making the act absolutely explicit, lewd. It was hard to think that a woman could do this to Leah but then an image came into her head of women screaming and spitting at a police van taking a child murderer away. Could that much hatred come from a woman for the ending of a relationship?

Then it hit her.

'Simone, God, you are so stupid,' she said inside her head. Someone sick and twisted enough to do this thing didn't have to work with Giles or have gone out with him; to find out where he lived any listener could follow him home from the station any six days of any week; anyone who'd met him casually.

Her head was spinning. This was too grim for words. She was struggling to keep her concentration. I've got to get myself some time to think this out properly. I can't do it here and now. She looked up again at Giles. He was slumped back in his chair, his mind a picture of confusion too. Simone went over to him, pushed him to one side of the cushion so she could plant herself right against him. He didn't smell too good, but she didn't mind.

'What have I done, Simone?'

She pulled away to look at him; he did the same to re-make his point.

'Am I that bad a person? Do people hate me that much?'

'No, no, Giles. Don't be daft. You might not be Mr. Popular, but unless there's something you're not telling me, whoever this is, is a crank, a nutcase.'

He looked at her with a face blazing with indignance.

'There's nothing I haven't told you. Nothing big. Nothing that...I've never upset anyone so badly that they'd want to...' It was incredible; he was beginning to see it - '...do something like this.'

'Okay, Giles, okay. I have to ask you things I don't really want to.' The seriousness of the situation was still fixing itself in Simone's mind too like a virus, like an infection.

'Giles. Look at me. It's okay. We're going to find out who it is. We'll prove it – we'll find proof of what they've done to you and they'll be...'

What, she thought, brought to justice? Sacked? It didn't seem much in the way of justice if all this ruined Giles's career and he couldn't get it back, and if it ruined his relationship with the one he loved.

'...fired or...something.' It definitely wasn't enough. She looked at Giles's face and he looked confused and ready to give up.

'You're taking me off the air tomorrow.'

It wasn't a question.

'Giles, I have no choice. But when I tell them at England that someone is – that there's a conspiracy to, um, drag your name through the mud, you'll be back in no time.'

She was losing hope but she had to be defiant for his sake. He nodded, looking at the floor.

She'd forgotten the positive stories again until her ailing memory dragged the information back to the conscious part of her mind.

'And don't forget - tomorrow you're going to get good things written about you too. The Tory press is going to make you out to be a hero. Shame you don't vote for them.'

Simone watched Giles fail to react and felt her heart sinking with his. Then almost imperceptibly he shook his head from side to side.

'I knew it, Simone. I let them pat me on the back, tell me how well I'd done. But I knew it. Talking to Clegg like that - it was a complete screw up. I haven't got a leg to stand on.' He shook his head again still looking down. 'Not a leg.' His voice trailed away.

Simone thought she would have been happy to see Giles smashing his house to bits. There was no anger in him. No fight. She was lost for something to say; she felt as though she was out of gas. She put her back to the chair's vertical support and took Giles's hand. She started stroking it.

Then she stopped and stood up.

'Giles...' she had to say something. 'When I find out who this bastard is that's trying to destroy you, I'm going to get his testicles in my hand and I'm going to rip the bloody things off, then I'm going to get someone to open his mouth and then I'm going to shove them right down the back of his throat.'

Giles stared up at her with sorrowful, glassy eyes, and it was all Simone could do to stop herself bawling her eyes out like a child.

221

Giles watched and silently thanked her inside for her efforts but he couldn't say any more. He let her come over to him again and put her arms around him. He hugged her back gently, wondering about her, her life. She now knew his intimately, but he realized he knew almost nothing of hers. Then he was wondering where Leah was. He tried to put the thought away - because she was gone and wasn't coming back. He knew this was true. It was a reality he could smell all over the place. In the air. In all the rooms of his house.

By ten o'clock they were both exhausted but Giles asked Simone to stay a little longer. He hated to admit it but he didn't want to be alone.

'You go up to bed,' she'd said, 'I'll come up in a while, and if you're asleep, I'll leave.'

'Okay. Lock the back door behind you with the key that's on the inside - I've a couple of spares.'

Twenty minutes later Simone tiptoed up the narrow stairs to Giles' bedroom and through the half-open door saw that the light was off. She stepped into the room and trod as lightly as a fifty-one year old Elton John-loving fairy could a few steps across the carpet, stopped, listened, and heard the regular breathing of one fast, fast asleep.

She drove down the Noreham road to her own home village feeling strongly that she had to thank God for one thing: that she wasn't Giles McAndrew.

It seemed clear he didn't much want to be here either. It all seemed to stack up: He doesn't want to be here because he senses we're on to him, she thought. Either that or the three of us need to see a good head doctor.

10

The Cathedral Bell Loop

Saturday May 6th

Next morning Giles woke before seven. He tried to get back to sleep to escape his conscious mind but kept being pulled up into rude daylight. He finally decided to try to be strong. He was Giles McAndrew after all. But then he found himself screwing his eyes shut tight and wanting to scream. He didn't. Though part of him thought it might do a lot of good, another part was frightened of what might he might find inside him if he did.

He lay in bed on this new Saturday morning with no show to do for once. Realistically, unless he was going to drink a bottle of Vodka there was nothing to do but dwell in his predicament and try to work out how he got there. He played the details over in his mind - he couldn't help it – lacerating his consciousness with the mistakes he'd made with Leah. I could have stopped her worrying. If I'd treated her right, if I'd looked after her properly, she would have seen the drawings and showed them to me – asked me about them – and we would have sorted the thing out together. Together they would have hunted down the evil postman or woman and set things to right. But I didn't treat her right, he told himself. She didn't trust me. He thought of the painting downstairs in the cupboard. The day had arrived, the second anniversary of their getting together, of their first kiss. Both the idea and the actual buying of it from Catherine was simply too little, too late. I'm thoughtless, and I'm shallow, he thought. I'm vain too. And I can't change.

He decided to get out of bed. He stood up, dropped his night trousers to the floor and went into the bathroom. He turned on the shower – let the water run hot - and stepped in. He let the water hit his head, shut his eyes, and the thoughts came rushing in again. A sound went off in his head, something like a large bell. *Clang!* it went. Then he heard words being spoken to him: *Pride Comes Before a Fall.* And his memory shot back to Thursday night, his phone call with Catherine, causing an acid sea to break over the rocky coast in his mind. He heard himself speaking to her.

'You're forgetting something,' he'd said

'What's that?'

'I'm Giles McAndrew.'

I'm Giles McAndrew. What in heaven's name had he been thinking? He was *who*? He was Giles McAndrew? What a joke: he was Giles McAndrew and he was nobody. That's who he was. And the people at Two Counties: God, what must they think of me if I'm capable of saying that to Catherine? Is that what I'm like every day?

*Clang! w*ent the cathedral bell again, and again the proverb, and again the acid sea and the conversation with Catherine. Over and over he reproached himself and thought of the man he'd become, looked at him, hated him. No wonder I've no friends. The process went on and on, looping round and round endlessly. No matter what he did he couldn't stop his mind and his memory torturing him. Then he was replaying his mouthing off at Clegg, shivering in embarrassment at his arrogance. He forced himself to listen to his blasé reaction to Catherine's concern and *Clang!* went the bell again. But it got worse: this Giles McAndrew was such a pain, such an arsehole that more than disliking him, someone wanted to actually destroy him. So I've brought this on myself, he thought.

He didn't bother to wash himself. His mind was so consumed with pain, he just couldn't bring himself to lift his arms to take the soap out of the dish. He dried himself and got back under the duvet and lay there, his skin feeling as if it were burning and twisting all over his body, while his mind got back to the loop and began the masochistic pummelling all over again. He tried to fight it. In desperation he found consolation in the fact that this misery dulled the hurt of Leah's mere departure. Perhaps I'm only capable of concentrating on one source of anguish at one time, he thought, and maybe that's good. Maybe I've got defence mechanisms in me that I didn't know existed. But these were hardly able to stop the memory replay and the horrendous work of a self-created Torquemada.

He forced himself to think about the press and what they might be doing to him this morning. He hadn't bargained for the assault on his character via his personal life, but each time he thought about it, it didn't really bother him. Let the tabloids say what they like. He had no respect for them anyway. Years of reading out snippets from their stupid stories and nasty tittle-tattle had seen to that. Everything they wrote was drivel. Fuck them. Simone thought it might be his tipping point but she was wrong because she didn't really understand him. He'd been catatonic last night because he felt broken from losing Leah. Besides that, his career suddenly seemed like it was nothing. He'd never told Simone about his Cornwall dream; indeed, he'd never told anyone. But now he felt another layer of discomfort above his original predicament and his bearings slip further. The cathedral bell had come in this morning and taught him that his capacity for pain was a room that could be pushed outwards indefinitely. 'Giles McAndrew' being a vain fool was one thing; underneath 'Giles McAndrew' what am I? What's left? The answering thought was horrifying: just the schoolboy failure and the unhappy kid I used to be.

His mind continued in a turmoil that was like surging, festering lava. New thoughts sliced into the soft, wet tissue of his brain like a chef's knife. The worst cut was this: how has this happened to me? To *me*? I never get down like this, I'm never depressed – so this can't be happening. It was shocking, it was wrong, but he had to admit it: So I'm like everyone else - I can fall down just like they can. And there was me thinking I was different, that I was a winner. The image appeared in head of a giant boiled sweet cracked wide open into two, with its liquid centre spilling out.

Still in bed, the torment went on. It was eight o'clock; then it was nine o'clock. He might have dozed off a couple of times, he wasn't sure. Then he felt something new happening in his head. It was the pain: he stopped feeling it. He looked at the television and his mind didn't blur – it focussed. He felt a clarity reappear in his head. He felt the fog clearing. He tried to feel the pain again but couldn't. He was suddenly afraid. I'm numb, he told himself, I can't feel the pain, but I should be able to. He was in a place he hadn't been in before. He didn't recognize it and it scared him. There was no set of rules here that he could refer to and no language that he could understand. He felt nothing when he knew he had every right to feel suicidal. By the facts of his life he ought to be next to dead, but here he was in a clear and conscious state. His stomach began to feel shaky and he wondered whether he could contain it. It was fear, pure fear. Maybe this is the bottom, he thought. Maybe this is as bad as it gets. Then it occurred to him that beyond numbness and fear there was a land that he thought he'd never come within a thousand miles of approaching: the land of the breakdown.

He had to get out of this. In a state of panic he rushed out of bed to find his phone. It was on the kitchen counter where he always left it at night. He rang Simone. He had to be with someone and she was all he had. Wherever she was, whatever she was doing today, she had to let him be with her.

While he heard her phone ring he looked out of the window to the front of the house and saw some people. Shit, he was naked. He backed away. After four rings she answered.

'Hi, Giles.' Giles listened for her tone of voice – noticed the fact that he could find the concentration to do it and was encouraged.

'Simone, there are guys with cameras outside. Paparazzi, I think.'

'How many?'

'I haven't counted. Hold on.' He moved a step closer to the kitchen window in a half-crouch and scanned left and right as far as he could.

'Two. And a woman without a camera.'

'What do you think I should do?'

'What do you want to do? Do you want to go to your bedroom and hide? Watch telly? Read?'

Inside he laughed ruefully. Had she lost her grip of what he was going through? He liked the idea of hiding - saw waves on a beach in Cornwall in a momentary flash of light in his mind, then went back to his desperation to be next to Simone.

'No. Can I come to the station?'

'Hang on, let me think about it.' He waited for a long time. He understood. He was off the air. He was an embarrassment to the station. If it got back to the regional and national bosses that he was hanging around the station it wouldn't look good for Simone. He heard these thoughts riding above his panic and was grateful.

Her voice came back.

'Sure, yes, come in. As long as you're not thinking of doing anything stupid like throwing Bob Constable onto the floor and taking over the microphone...'

'No, Simone,' he said. God, he wasn't that stupid. And anyway, he didn't have the strength or the energy.

'Fine, but come in the back way and go into my office. If I'm not there, stay there until I find you. Okay?'

'Yes. Thanks, Simone. Thanks so much.'

'It's okay, it's okay. Oh, Giles - have you seen the papers yet?'

'No, I haven't been out of the house yet.' And he didn't care anyway. He should have told Simone he didn't care about what they were saying. He thought about it – no, he still didn't. But he still didn't tell her in case she was disappointed in him.

'Drive carefully, won't you, Giles...'

'Look, Simone, I'm fine. Really.'

'Hmm,' he heard her say, not buying it for a moment. 'See you soon, love.'

'Yeah – 'bye.'

''Bye.'

He felt better. He ran upstairs to get dressed, and as he did so he realised that the idea of numbness was his brain and body's idea of a joke; but the movement of his limbs seemed to push away the cathedral bell loop. I can function, he said inside. He would concentrate only on surface things. He was going to Simone and she'd help him work out what to do next. No, she'd tell him - because he realised that he had no idea what to do.

11

Saturday Morning Search For a Name

'Here are the news headlines at eight-thirty with me, Daisy Smith. A fire broke out last night at a grain store in Barton Townes in the early hours of Saturday morning. At approximately two thirty a.m. flames were seen shooting into the air by a police patrol car at Hobble and Crowther Grain Company. Fireman spent over two hours bringing the blaze under control. This is the second fire suffered by the agriculture company this year. Managing Director Martin Van Brucker rushed from his bed to the scene.

"We are devastated. We have insurance, of course, but the disruption to the business is going to cost us huge disruption. Thankfully no one was inside, but still, it's terrible for us, a real blow."

Police say that they are not yet treating the fire as arson, but neither are they ruling it out. Detective Sergeant Andy Winding:

"The circumstances certainly give us suspicions but until the fire service fully investigate the cause and sent us their report we're obviously not in a position to say one way or the other whether the fire was an arson attack."

The Deputy Prime Minister John Clegg is facing calls to resign this morning following the disclosure in a national newspaper that he laughed about knocking over a 72-year-old patient on a hospital visit in Lincoln yesterday...

Saturday morning was a time of ease for the small number of workers required to keep Two Counties Radio open for business. The newsroom had a quiet and relaxed ambience then, a world away from the atmosphere of hard reporting and earnest digging for new stories it contained during the week. Management was absent presumed tending early spring barbeques or indulging in some other bourgeois comfort whist technically still on call. In the engine room of Bart and Bilt radioland only the football crew rushed around in a state of committed animation as they got ready for their long two 'til seven stint. Sport aside, the weekend brief was to set the tone for two days of rest, relaxation and hard shopping. Airtime was seriously devoted only to records and idle, light, frothy chat.

If you weren't actually at the mike or producing there wasn't much going on. The news had to be written and read and a phone had to be manned for each show but that was about it. The one reporter on duty would be in the radio car charging about from fete to church bazaar to antique sale, so the social and working hub of the place would be virtually empty. One or two evening or weekend people might be in to prepare the music for upcoming shows, and the next presenter up would probably be at their desk and their producer hanging around too, but no more. The reception was Jackie-less, her desk and counter looking bereft without her. When the door buzzer sounded inside the station it was down to whoever was nearest to jump to it and see who wanted entry.

TCR's first Saturday in May of 2006, however, disrupted the pattern. As the clock hit eight-thirty-seven and Jane Landings eased into the last twenty minutes of her show in Studio 1, still wittering about the downturn in the weather just confirmed by regional staffer Olivia Tetrabani in Birmingham, there were enough bodies in the newsroom for a well-grooved working Wednesday. Sports anchorman Alan Barker was already at his desk altering his script and moaning about the lack of peace and quiet, while Big Dave Plymouth was in five hours early to prepare for his weekend music show, 'Big Dave's Big Hits Special,' a two-hour extravaganza of chart smashes from fifty years of pop music. Daisy Smith, TCR's youngest, freshest reporter quietly began sprucing up her eight o'clock bulletin for another at nine suddenly noticed him.

'What are you doing in this early, David?' she said.

The man in question didn't look up, not least because he hated being addressed as 'David'.

'And what are you doing at Lynda's desk?'

'Fuck me, have you seen this?' he then said to Daisy Smith, butting in on himself. The Chronicle wasn't his normal morning read but he made sure he picked one up today on the way in having been tipped off by Marcus who'd picked up a Friday afternoon rumour from Noona's producer, dippy Diane Clarke, that you had to buy it this morning if you worked at TCR.

'Language, Dave.'

'Sorry.' She waved a newspaper at him. 'Oh, you've got a copy.'

'Yep. He's not in today, is he?'

'Giles? No, of course not. He's been pulled.'

'Are you trying to be funny?'

'Ha-ha-ha. No, I wasn't.'

'Daisy, I didn't know you had it in you.'

'I hope that wasn't a joke either.'

'No, ha-ha, bloody hell, you're a razor this morning...who's doing his show?'

'I am,' said Bob Constable, TCR's stalwart afternoon presenter, lover of vegetable growing and model trains, walking through the open newsroom door. 'I have selflessly answered the call.'

'Oh, hi, Bob,' said Big Dave.

'Morning, BD. Hello, Daisy.'

'Hi.'

'You seen The Chronicle?' said Big Dave.

'Oh, is this why Giles has been pulled?' said Bob. 'Why are you laughing?'

'It doesn't matter - come and look at this.'

Bob Constable plodded over in his sensible size elevens to Big Dave.

'Good God,' said Bob half a minute later, reading over BD's shoulder. 'And I wonder where they got that picture from?'

'That's outside here. Press were here all day yesterday. Didn't you see the photographer?'

'No – or rather yes – so that's what he was doing. So, we're worth a paparazzi now.'

'Have you just got in?'

'Yes.'

'Anyone outside now?'

'Not that I saw.'

Both men frowned.

'The poor bugger,' said Bob, reading on.

'Yep.'

'How did they get their information?' said Daisy, her face an incredulous question mark.

'That's what we'd all like to know,' said Big Dave, waiting for Bob to finish so he could turn to the sport.

'Terrible…' said Bob.

'There's one thing I do know,' said Big Dave. 'Giles is finished.'

'We'll have less of that talk, thank you very much,' said Simone Pound, sweeping into the room at top speed.

'Boss! What are you doing here? I mean–' He went to hide the paper but the she made it easy for him, replying as she sprayed a pair of plants on the windowsill across the other side of the room.

'It's okay, Dave, I know exactly what you mean.' She began walking back, still at pace.

'You can imagine why I'm here, I think – and it's okay, I've seen the article already.'

Big Dave's face dropped into neutral and stayed put.

'And if you can't work it out, keep going, you'll get there in a minute.'

Daisy looked up at the Boss with a pleased smile. Simone felt a twinge of guilt for chiding Big Dave when she only made rare appearances now at weekends. But he could take it. And he wasn't stupid; he'd realise soon enough that she had to be here on this particular morning. Like the captain of the ship as it goes down, said a sudden thought popping into her head. But it's not going down, she said back. She turned to her stop-gap-Giles.

'Hi, Bob – you okay?'

'Yes, boss, no problems anticipated – have yo-'

'It should run on tramlines. If you run dry – no, of course you won't run dry, will you,' she said, patting him on the shoulder.

'As if,' said Big Dave Plymouth; 'the seas'll run dry before Bob Constable does – isn't that right, Bobby.'

'I suppose you'd be right about that,' said Bob dubiously. They were all mystified by the conversation, Simone included: none of them had ever known a presenter to run dry on air.

'Plenty of gardening, I suppose, today,' said Simone, pulling an election notice off the wall.

'If it's okay with you…'

'Bob, I'll bop you one if you don't!' she said turning to face him as she scrunched it into a ball.

'Yes, sorry, Simone, I forgot you were a big gardener.'

Simone looked at him.

'Oh, sorry, I didn't mean…' Daisy was laughing and Big Dave was mildly amused, though he would be happier when the boss left so he could re-read the Giles article in the bloody Daily Chronicle. It was incredible. As far as he knew, the nationals had never given TCR a single line of space in the past, apart from when they won the award two years ago when it had been just that: a line.

'It's okay, Bob – I'm kidding with you,' said Simone. She smiled to herself as she sprayed a spider plant that was doing well on top of the bookcase. As Bob Constable began thinking of a radio show full of marrows and marigolds in a contented sort of way, Simone looked at Big Dave from the corner of her eye and found him greedily staring down at his paper. Then his expression changed; he was wondering what the fallout was going to be. He was about to ask Simone what she thought of the article but her phone went off nearby before he could get the words out. As she attended to it, he started humming *Born To Be Wild* without noticing the irony and felt a sense of uncertainty in his ample gut.

'Excuse me,' she said to the small company of workers, and walked to the newsroom door on the way back to her office. She looked down at the caller's name again as she went.

'Sorry. I'm not taking calls on this today. No, sorry. No.' She closed the phone feeling bloody annoyed. It was starting again. It rang again right on cue.

'Hello,' she barked, nastily, trying to scorch their ears off. But the line went dead.

'Bugger you, then,' she said to the shiny metallic object. She disliked the bloody things intensely at times.

She finished the journey to her office, noticing how quiet the station was.

Her office felt different too when she walked into it. She went back out to go to the kitchen to fill her coffee jug with water, meeting no one. She felt her frown in the forehead and consciously unscrunched it, wondering if she could make it stay straight. She felt her jaw too and realised she was clenching it, though she wasn't yet grinding her teeth. She flipped the switch on the coffee machine and saw the red light come on. She stared at it, deep in thought, then sat down heavily.

She looked for the notepad she'd taken to the studio yesterday to write her plan of action. It wasn't there. It didn't matter, she thought; she remembered that she didn't get to start the list anyway. Instead she picked up a letter of not much importance and turned it over to the blank side. Then she took a black fibre tip pen that was lying there next to the stapler and again wrote a heading for the task: "Action". She smoothed out the piece of paper which had been folded twice before being put in an envelope, on the desk. It would do. The coffee machine began to hiss and gurgle. She crossed out "Action" and wrote "Problem" next to it instead. She thought for a few seconds, chewing the end of the pen, then started to write.

1.   Mole. Someone is out to get him. Who?

She crossed out "Who?"

1.   Mole. Someone is out to get him. ----
2.   Who?
3.   Why?

She set her thinking to chasing the whole bloody thing through. Someone is trying to destroy Giles McAndrew. She quickly decided she needed to make another list. Half way down the page she wrote

232

"Damage" and underlined it. She decided to remind herself of what had actually taken place. She yawned suddenly, before she wrote.

1. The drawings – posted to Giles for Leah to see
2. Same stories told to newspaper. Chronicle.
3. G's number leaked to papers.
4. Lovers. Leah – Catherine – Lucie.

The third in the lovers list didn't fit and probably neither did the cousin, but it didn't matter that much and Simone was too tired to change it anyway. She thought about the fourth drawing and added,

5. Did Leah have lover too?

She didn't think that very likely but then again what did she know? She thought back to the two conversations she'd had with the girl in here. She felt sure her intuition would have informed her if Leah had been involved with another man. Mind you, you never knew with young people these days - they had sex like we used to have cups of Ovaltine, she thought, then wondered what on earth made her think of Ovaltine. But no, she was right. She didn't think Leah had another bloke. What of Giles? She trusted him too. His feelings for Leah were as transparent as glass. An image of a naked Giles and a naked woman that was his cousin flashed across her mind and vanished in the distance. She went to write a fifth point. It wasn't Lucie? No. Highly unlikely if not completely. Or am I naïve? I've turned fifty, am I now right out of touch with younger people? She put the thought aside and wrote again.

6. Someone is behind all this!!
7. Who?

Her list had no real structure and the numbering was wrong, but she didn't care. She was clear about the important thing: there was an anti-Giles conspiracy going on. The thought that would complicate things appeared in her memory from yesterday.

8. An old lover of Giles? – Revenge?

She'd have to follow this through with Giles when he got here. She wrote a ninth point.

9. Is it the whole station?

Then she crossed it out.

9. Is it a group?

She knew Giles wasn't popular. Was it possible that a whole gang of her staff had got together to ruin him? The thought was killing. Not my staff, *surely*. If this was what was happening, all her knowledge about human nature would be rendered meaningless. No, it couldn't be that: you've read too much bloody Agatha Christie, she said to herself. She liked her staff. You couldn't like everybody but in terms of a bunch of radio station workers they were for the most part great people, great at what they did and great at pulling together as a team – an award-winning team, lest it should be forgotten. And that was remarkable given that all the presenters had an ego and that rivalry for jobs was a natural consequence of the station having young, talented people inside it. They wanted to get on and that was fine.

She was wasting her time: no one she knew would do this monstrous thing to Giles. She put the pen down and leaned back in her chair, arms folded. She pursed her lips into a hard nodule sticking out of her face. Then again…

The grotesque news stories they'd had came into her head: *Chilham man murders daughters, commits suicide…Barton Townes man commits £2m fraud in City of London…tortured, neglected baby found dead on Townes estate – police shocked.* The fact that she didn't personally know the perpetrators of these unthinkable crimes seemed to push them into an unreachable, parallel dimension. Why? Why couldn't something terrible happen right here? No reason, she considered, only it never had, that's all, so why would it now?

This turned her mind to presenting. Who gained most from – she wrote it down, more quickly now.

10.   Who gains most from Giles leaving? – the other presenters.

The breakfast show presenter was top dog in a station, so what about the others who would love to be in Giles's shoes? She grabbed another scrap of paper, an envelope, and scribbled the list down as they appeared on a week day.

1.   Lynda Parvis
2.   Noona Reeves
3.   Bob Constable

4.   Jim Johnson

Oh – she forgot Lucie who went on in the graveyard at five. No, not
Lucie. No, but she had to be a good detective: she added Lucie to the
list

5.   Lucie Bastable

Then she added the weekenders. She had to think harder. Jane did the
six-'til-nine after Lucie.

6.   Jane Landings

Then it was Giles again, then Lynne again, then another Bob.

7.   Bob Pilcharde.

Now she was writing down names she wanted to cross off as soon as
the last letter hit the paper. Bob, the presenter of TCR's weekly one
hour farming show was unlikely to be attempting to drive Giles
McAndrew to suicide to get his bum on a studio seat at six o'clock
every morning. Not when he had his own farm. She left it anyway in the
name of consistency.

8.   Alan Barker.

Pointless – Alan was the sports presenter and wasn't exactly 5 Live
material. He was fifty-four and had an allotment and a fetish for
greyhound racing. Simone heaved another big sigh and carried on. Next
there was Max and his 60s and 70s music show, 'The Scene' that they
touted as 'hip'.

9. Max Rifford.

Max at least was young enough and ambitious enough to want
Giles's job, but she thought she knew that he worked four nights a week
doing his own disco show or whatever they called it now; she couldn't
imagine him seriously wanting to switch to a breakfast news
programme. This was getting her nowhere, but she wrote the Sundays
down anyway.

9.   Revnd Rory Selestra

She made a face at the whole list. Then she started putting a line through the names. Martyn played saxophone three nights a week and smoke pot so he went straight away. She knew life was strange but she couldn't imagine the vicar doing it. Rory was crossed off. Then she thought of those who couldn't possibly know Giles well enough to know what was going on in his personal life. The rest of the weekenders went, apart from Big Dave. Jane Landings and Giles had once had a thing going on, but she didn't see how she might be hell bent on destroying him when she'd subsequently got married and opened a bed and breakfast with her husband. A cross went through her name. That just left the weekdayers. She studied their names but didn't like the look of any of them as candidates for manic skulduggery. Bob Constable was eccentric but he would go to Russia to be an astronaut before he'd put himself up for the breakfast show on a permanent basis.

This was ridiculous, she thought. Of course none of them were candidates - she knew them all well enough to know that. But she thought she had to be scientific – she thought of *CSI Miami*, and the Vegas one, of *Waking The Dead* and the *Inspector* Thingy *Mysteries*. They all did their ruling out consistently – and sometimes the most unlikely suspect was the guilty one. You had to go through the process.

Lynda and her husband were going through fertility treatment so she was out. Noona was an experienced local radio presenter and superb at her job. At 45 she had time still – just – to develop her career further. But she was perfect for the afternoon job interviewing guests and chatting to the audience in that woozy sort of relaxed afternoon way, so she just didn't fit the bill as a would-be Giles. Even less did she have it in her to drive out to Giles's house poking lewd drawings into his letter box. That left Jim – no: he was too old and as happy as Larry with his Drive-Time position, presenter number two to Giles, and he was trying to get a move to BRBC Cumbria because he wanted to retire to the Lake District. And finally Lucie, who was just starting to present. She crossed her off and there was only Dave. He was a million miles away from serious presenting, but he was known to think badly of Giles so she left him in.

She looked at her list of crossed names. She frowned again. She got up, poured herself some coffee before it got lukewarm and stale, and went to her printer to get some A4 plain paper. She brought back a slim

236

wad of ten sheets. Now she cast her mind over the other station workers who might have wanted to do Giles down.

She wrote 'Possibles' on the top sheet and underneath wrote

1.   Dave Plymouth.

The reporters didn't like Giles much but did any of them hate him? Had he upset any of them? She couldn't think of anything. As far as she could see, Giles kept himself to himself and wasn't in the station each day for very long after his show finished at 9. She liked Giles so felt sure that if the reporters actually got to know him they'd like him too. Same with all the producers and techies and website people and broadcast assistants. Jackie Husband liked him. Fancied him too, she'd admitted, and had since he walked through the door five years ago.

She went through the women on the staff. Daisy? Of course not: it was all she could do to wash up the coffee mugs properly let alone plan a campaign of malice against someone. Could she draw though? Simone imagined the whole station being forced to take a drawing test - it would eliminate many of them at a stroke. She realised of course that she couldn't possibly organise something like that: she wasn't a police inspector and anyway, anyone could pretend not to be able to draw as easy as anything. God, she really was stupid. She went back to her list.

She reviewed the lower grade people, the cleaners, the phone-answerers and the broadcast-assistants. Then she went through the reporters, scouring her memory for all she knew of their personalities. She admitted that there were a few she hardly knew but she trawled her mind for a motive and couldn't find one. It just didn't add up that someone who only knew Giles casually, distantly at best, could plan and execute something like this. It simply had to be someone more closely connected to Giles or to personal ambition.

Leon! She'd forgotten Leon, his producer. No one was closer to Giles professionally. But he couldn't be a candidate: they were too tight a unit as presenter and producer. Plus, Leon really liked Giles, more than was good for him, perhaps. So no, not Leon either. She now went upwards in the hierarchy, knowing she was beginning to run out of names.

2.   Damien Read.

Senior Broadcast Journalist and head of programmes, Damien was a candidate because of professional jealousy she thought. Damien was gagging to present. But he was ineffectual. He might dream of doing Giles's job but he was too mild- mannered to draw pictures of couples in the sex act. He might have a connection or two in the press, but he wasn't the type for this sort of thing – didn't remotely have it in him. She'd met his parents and they were lovely. She drew a line through the middle of his name. And he'd been off sick for a week with a dislocated knee. Next.

3.   Sarah Billings.

Her other SBJ, her news editor. No. Just no. No way. She knew Sarah way too well. Then again, might she want rid of Giles so Lucie might be suddenly be propelled into his job? She wondered if there was any way she'd let Lucie loose on the breakfast show even as a stop-gap but knew she was too inexperienced. And anyhow, she really knew Sarah. Still, she was pleased at her thoroughness. She crossed off Sarah's name. One name left.

4.   Greg McKenzie.

12

Four Bonkers Radio Hell

There was a knock at the door.

Simone looked up at the door hoping whoever it was would go away, unless it was Giles. The knock came again. She got up and opened it herself.

'Hi, Simone.'

'Sarah!' She could come in. Simone opened the door wider and flicked her head towards the window to indicate that she was welcome.

'Have you seen it?'

Simone looked at the bag on Sarah's shoulder.

'No,' she said. She thought back to the lie she'd just told Big Dave Plymouth and made her pact with herself to be bloody careful she told no more.

'You should.'

'You've seen it...' said Simone, more statement of fact than question.

'It's terrible.'

Simone looked for something to fuss and fiddle with but saw what a weakness it was for a leader and stood still on the middle of the carpet.

'Would you read it to me?' she said to Sarah Billings.

'Yes – are you sure?'

'Yes. Sit down there.'

Simone went back to her desk chair and banged her backside down in the seat. It squeaked loudly but she didn't notice. Sarah took The Chronicle out of her bag and found the page – 27 – with the help of the yellow Post–it that peeped out, breaking the straight line of the paper's edge.

'How bad is it?' said the boss.

Sarah looked up. Her expression scared Simone right in the stomach.

'How terrible?'

'Truly terrible,' said Sarah.

'Go on.'

'*SEX IN SLUMBERLAND* – that's the headline,' said Sarah, reading Simone's face as she spoke.

'O-kay,' came the response. Sarah saw how drained and white Simone's face was and thought with some dismay that she suddenly looked about sixty.

'Shall I carry on?'

'Uh-huh,' said Simone, nodding.

'*GET YOUR CLAWS DOWN!*- that's the sub-headline.'

'What?' Simone didn't understand.

'You'll get the meaning in a minute.'

'Oh, God,' said Simone, hiding half her face in her hands.

'Ready?'

Simone nodded. 'Hold on – I'm going to switch my phone off while you do this.' She switched her phone off. 'Go on.'

Sarah took a deep breath and read.

'*Crazy Love Triangle of People's Champion causes sack threat at Four Bonkers Radio* – that's another sub-heading before the –'

Simone waved her get on with it. Sarah looked down at the page and concentrated on reading steadily and accurately.

'*Tormented Bartonshire BRBC breakfast show presenter Giles McAndrew*

faces local radio disgrace after his crazy, IMMORAL lifestyle was revealed to The Chronicle yesterday.' She looked up to see a Simone whose eye-whites seem to have grown to twice their normal size.

'Carry on?' said Sarah.

Simone nodded.

'*After SLAMMING Deputy Prime Minister John Clegg on air on Thursday, the SCANDALOUS personal life of Giles McAndrew emerged yesterday.*'

Simone interrupted.

'Hang on – why did you read "slamming" and "scandalous" out like that?'

'They're in capital letters.'

'Are they?'

'Um – do you never read the tabloids?'

'Not when I can help it, no. Sorry, I'd forgotten they did that. Do you read them?'

'Yep – I –'

'Of course you do. Sorry.' Oh, God, she thought: she knew well that it was part of Sarah's job to know in detail what the red tops were up to. I'm really losing my mind now, she said inside.

'It's okay. Carry on?'

Simone nodded once more.

'*Now it's Radio Three Lovers for McAndrew after...*'

Sarah halted. Simone looked up at her face looking into the paper.

'*...luscious girlfriend Leah discovered he was bonking COUSIN Catherine AND station... reporter dishy... waif...*'

Simone began to get out of her chair.

'...*Lucie...Bastable.*'

Simone took the paper from her lap and placed it on the floor beside them, put her arm around Sarah and watched a couple of tears drop down on the last fold of her white shirt.

'Hey. Come on now. There's nothing going on,' she said, shaking Sarah's left shoulder in reassurance. She looked at the ceiling and shook her head. She looked back at Sarah. 'Nothing going on, come on, now. Nothing.'

'I know, I know.' Sarah dabbed her eyes dry with a tissue.

'I feel bad now – I should have told you more. I should have seen this coming.' But Sarah knew that she couldn't have. If the boss didn't read the red tops regularly she obviously wasn't in touch with the way these people operated.

'No,' said Sarah, wiping her eyes, 'it's okay. I'm okay.'

'Come on, read me some more,' said Simone, going back to her desk.

'Okay. Um, where was I?' She sniffed a couple of times, dabbed her nose, and read on. 'Oh – Oh, you'll love some of this...*Jilted lover Leah Caighton, 25, hounded graveyard shift presenter Lucie at work at five in the morning, viciously carrying out an amazing DAWN ATTACK on her bitter rival in the studio!*'

Sarah looked up.

'Carry on?'

'Yep,' said Simone, grim-faced.

'And you'll love this: *Terror bitch Leah left FOUR INCH CLAW MARKS on the face of McAndrew's pouting new mate as the dawn jock smirked gleefully from the sidelines. She then drove away and vanished into thin air.*'

She looked up again.

'Great, isn't it...'

'Go on.'

'Get this bit too: *A source revealed to The Chronicle that wild behaviour is now an every day part of radio station life. The steamy TCR newsroom is awash with "gagging for it" reporters, newsreaders and weather girls. Said one station source who cannot be named, "local news is boring so staff has to look for ways to kill the tedium." With love rat McAndrew leading the way, the situation at the ex-snoozing station is out of hand. And bosses are unable to control the situation as locals race to rename the station, RADIO SHAG*'

Sarah stopped again to check on her boss. She was pacing up and down a four metre track of carpet on her left-hand side looking fierce.

'Is that it?' she said stopping to look up at the reader.

'No.'

'Continue.'

'Okay – we're now coming to the bit about you – are you ready?'

'I thought that last bit was about me.'

'Not compared to this bit.'

'God help me. Go on – read it.'

'Are you sure you wouldn't rather read it yourself?'

'No, let's have a good laugh together.'

'Okay, but you asked for it: *Station supremo…*' She paused to sniff and wipe her nose again with the tissue. 'At least they got that bit right.'

'Go on.'

'*Simone Pound, the woman responsible for the over-sexed staff, went into hiding at the station yesterday morning...* Get ready…'

'I'm ready.'

'*…barricading herself in a studio from embarrassment and refusing to come out.*'

Simone exploded into laugher. Sarah gladly followed. It was funny, if you looked at it the right way.

'How can I get upset about that?' She wished she'd said, 'How can they expect me to get upset about that,' - it was much braver.

'And even if I was going to, I'd cut my arm off to deny them the pleasure. What…what…' She couldn't find the word spluttering instead.

'Shit?' said Sarah, helpfully.

'Exactly.'

'Ha-ha,' laughed Sarah. She would tell Lucie how the boss took the paper absolutely ripping her to pieces and it would be all right – she would read the stuff about her, take the blow and absorb it.

'Is there more?'

'About you? No.'

'Oh. How much more of this garbage is there, for Christ's sake?'

'Um,' said Sarah re-finding her place, 'one long paragraph and one of a line at the end.'

'Finish the job off, then we'll know where we stand.'

'*The parts of this bizarre sex rectangle now face disciplinary action. McAndrew's career already faces ruin after THREATS from 10 Downing Street for his assault on Clegg. Now he is a certainty for THE SACK after regularly getting into the sack with colleagues. Gorgeous scratch victim Lucie, too sweet to bite back, faces hostile questioning after breaking the corporation's controversial NO SEX WITH COLLEAGUES rules-*'

'What are they bloody talking about?'

'- *Meanwhile, McAndrew's reckless cousin and rumoured SHAG PARTNER, artist Catherine Lang, is set to get off scot-free. She is said to be heading back to Canada trailing smashed careers in her wake, including the station boss who is set to take a Pounding from her bosses next week...*' – 'that's got a capital 'P', "Pounding".'

'Obviously.'

'"...*when she comes out of hibernation.*" And the last bit: "*It's all in a day's work for a Two Counties Radio station that has already passed through the nickname RADIO SHAG to FOUR BONKERS FM!*"'

'Give that thing to me.'

Sarah held out the paper to the TCR supremo, who took it, screwed the whole thing into a big mess and hurled it with as much force as she could at the door, grunting with effort as it left her right hand.

'"Four Bonkers"? What is that? How *dare* they! How *bloody* dare they do it to us! It's such a load of f-*fucking*...' Simone lost the words again, she was so mortally offended. '...*urrrh!*' There wasn't a word bad enough to express how she felt. She had to pinch her thigh to stop from crying, with rage much more than anything else.

'Sorry,' said Simone, breathing heavily and sweating.

'No, for goodness sake – you have to let it out.'

Sarah thought she'd better use her discretion and leave for a few minutes.

'I'm just nipping to the loo.'

'Okay,' said Simone.

Simone got a chair and propped it under the door handle so the door couldn't open from the outside. She picked up the ruined paper to her desk, smoothed it out as best she could, found page 27 and re-read the article. Half way through the exercise she picked up a pot of pencils and was about to throw it at the window but was stopped by the sight of a car crossing the car park. She was glad she stopped herself. She thought of that...that '*fucking* bastard' she'd spoken to yesterday at The Chronicle. 'I'm not going to give you the bloody pleasure,' she said to herself. She still felt awkward using the f-word, but had to admit it felt good to let herself go for once.

'Fuck,' she said quietly to the window. 'Fuck!' she said again, a little louder. 'Fuck!' she said a third time, her head nodding at the floor as she went. She screwed her eyes shut. When she opened her eyes, nothing was moving in the car park now. She felt foolish. She got up and trod almost on tip-toes to the door. She quietly removed the chair. She pressed her ear flat to the door surface until it almost hurt. Then she pulled back and opened it carefully and peeped into the corridor. No one there.

243

She closed the door again and went back to her desk. '*Fucking bastards!*' she kept repeating under her breath. She hadn't realised what the word 'rage' really meant until now. There was a gentle tap at the door and she hoped it was only Sarah. It was.

'Are you okay?' said Simone.

'I was going to ask you the same thing.'

'I'm okay – I'll get over it.'

'Me too. Mind you, there's nothing there about me.'

Simone decided it was time to tell her about the drawings. First she said,

'But you've Lucie to worry about. How is she?'

'She hasn't seen it. I left her sleeping.'

'Don't you think you should get back to her before someone phones or texts her?'

'Do you think?' Sarah looked at her watch. It was five-to-nine.

'Yes. You didn't have to come in, you know.'

'I want to be here to see what I can do.'

'You're such a sweet one, you know that? Go home.'

'I want to come back. What are you going to do?'

'I don't know yet. There might be nothing I can do.' But she knew there was. She was going to work out who'd shafted them all. 'You go to Lucie. And if you really want to, come back, but I can manage.'

'Okay. But no, I'm coming back. Are you sure I can't help you? Otherwise I just want to be here. There's stuff I can do for next week while I'm here.'

Simone moved up close to the girl and touching her arm said, 'actually, before you go, there's something I want to tell you.'

'Oh. It's nothing bad, is it?'

'Come and sit down a minute.'

Ten minutes later, Sarah had become the fifth person to see the drawings, Simone gravely taking the contents from the envelope, careful to touch only the very edges of the pages with her fingertips.

After Sarah left having re-composed herself, Simone went back to her desk and read the article again. This time it didn't seem quite so bad. The style actually gave the piece a comical tone that defused its explosive initial impact. However. While she was dragging her mind through its implications the phone went off beside her making her jump.

Be brave, Simone, she said to herself. You've done nothing wrong.

'Hello, Simone Pound?'

'Hi, Simone – it's Daisy.'

'Oh, hi, Daisy, everything okay?'

'Yes, fine.'

'Everything okay with the news?'

'Yes – ha – I think so.'

'Good.'

'I've got Greg on the line for you.'

'Put him through.'

'I'll see if I can - I haven't worked this before. I'm trying now.'

There was hissy silence, then a click.

'Simone?'

'Yes?'

'Greg.'

'Oh, hi, Greg.' She told herself to be natural, which immediately provoked the knowledge that she was now bound to sound tense and awkward.

'Hi. I'm ringing to see if you're okay. Have you seen the article?'

'In the Daily Chronicle?'

'It's The Chronicle, now.'

'What?'

'It's called "The Chronicle"– it used to be "The Daily Chronicle" but not any more.'

'Thank you for that.' My God, he was such a pain.

'That's okay.'

'Yes, I have, Greg, I've seen it.'

'What's your thinking?'

'I think when I find out who it is at this station is feeding *The Chronicle* information I'm going to cut their balls off and shove them down their throat. Ha-ha.' She rather fancied that she'd carried that off well: she hadn't felt forced and hadn't felt awkward.

'Yes – ha-ha – good idea - I'll help you, if I may, ha-ha.'

'This isn't funny…'

'Sorry. Yes, I know.'

'Greg…' she said, putting a tone of mateyness into her voice.

'I can get myself in if you'd like – if you need some help. I'm away at Seaby but I can get in if you need me.'

Simone made a decision; it was the laughter that did it.

'That's kind of you, Greg, but not necessary. What I'd like you to do though over the weekend is to make a list of possible candidates - on paper – and bring it in on Monday and we'll discuss it straight away.'

'You don't want to meet tomorrow? I can come round…'

'No, no, not necessary. Things might have died down a bit by Monday anyway. I don't want to rush into things.' Not much, she thought and apologised to the Almighty for lying through her teeth, even though it was Greg.

'Okay, fine. Do you want me to be in early?'

'How about half-eight?'

'Fine, I can do that. Half-eight.'

'Half-eight.'

'You want a list of candidates...'

'A list of candidates. In case someone right here is causing all this mess.'

'Oh...' Greg sounded surprised. 'Really? Do you think so? Fine. Tell me, who do you have in mind?'

'I don't have anyone actually.'

'Hang on - I'm not sure I understand you - you think someone at TCR is behind everything?'

Simone, her antennae rigid, sat bolt upright. What was going on in that mind of his?

'Yes, Greg, I do.' She tried to tease him out. 'The article is terrible. And someone is definitely feeding them information. But it could have been worse.' She paused and thought, you better not be listening in to this, Daisy. Then she went for it. 'There's something I should tell you. In the strictest absolute confidence...'

'Go on...'

'Leah received some obscene drawings just before she left. These were why she left.'

'Obscene drawings? What do you mean?'

She described them to Greg McKenzie then waited for his reaction.

'Oh, God, that's terrible. She must be upset...'

'Terribly.'

'And where is she now?'

'I don't know.'

'And you must be upset...'

'I am.'

'I'll come in. I'll drop what I'm doing.'

'No.' She decided something else: she didn't want him anywhere near the place until Monday. Until she'd had time to think. 'No, I don't you spoiling your weekend for this. So, no, stay where you are. Okay?'

'Okay. If you're sure...'

That tone of voice, thought Simone. Is he being sincere? Or being guarded?

'I'm sure. You go on enjoy the seaside. The forecast isn't very good.'

'It's better tomorrow.'

'Good.'

'Look, Simone. It's trash, the article. Absolute trash. And I forgot to ask, how's Giles?'

'Didn't you know? He's been pulled.'

'Oh. I thought he might be. For how long?'

'About a week, and then there'll be a hearing of some description. I'll have to look it up in the Blue Book.'

'It'll be a 411. Serious misconduct hearing.'

Bloody typical, thought Simone, feeling thoroughly irritated, for him to know a detail like that. Is this the mind of someone who's a super artist, she thought?

'Oh. Okay. Well I'm going, Greg.'

'Just tell me, how is Giles holding up?'

Simone thought about it for a few seconds.

'Under the circumstances, he's doing very well indeed.'

'Oh, that's very good to hear.'

'Yes, isn't it. Well, I'm going now. 'Bye.'

''Bye, Simone. I'll see you Monday.'

'Yeh – 'bye.'

She put down the phone and went to the steel cabinet on which her coffee machine sat. She bent down and opened the bottom drawer, then skimmed through the file tabs for the relevant subject and found the one she wanted about three back. She pulled out the contents and took them to her desk. The contents constituted a box file filled with staff job applications in date order. Daisy Smith's stared up at her from the top of the pile. The one she was looking for, Greg McKenzie's, would be way down near the bottom. She thought of the year he joined. Six years he'd been at TCR. 2000. She put her hand deep into the pile and pulled a handful of papers out. She put them on the desk. Leon Dilkes' application sat on top, the date at the top of the page, 2001. The one underneath was that of 'Gregory Campbell McKenzie.' She put it in front of her on the desk in a clean space.

Each document had four pages. On the third the applicant had to write down the details of their education. She turned over Greg's front page and on the right hand page saw a line of school subjects under the heading, 'GCSE or equivalent qualifications'. She scanned down the list - English Language, English Literature, Mathematics and the rest. She got to the bottom. Art. It wasn't there. She looked at his A level subjects, noting that he hadn't gone to secondary school in Kent. English Lit, Biology and Economics. Damn, she said inside. Foiled. She thought she had him.

The obscene drawings, to her admittedly untrained eye, had been very skilfully done. She decided she wanted to see them again and moved her hand towards the desk drawer but then thought better of it. The less I handle them, the better, she thought. She could call them to

247

mind easily enough anyway. She thought about art again. It was hard to draw the male and female forms well, wasn't it? Therefore the artist had to have taken art to a good level at school.

If it wasn't Greg McKenzie, then, who did she have left? She had Big Dave. She considered the possibility that Greg might be working with an accomplice who'd produced these careful, semi-erotic drawings for him. No. This devious bastard had to be someone working alone. But then she realised that actually, the only resources she had at her disposal to process the clues was a penchant for television detective programmes from *Silent Witness* back to *Dixon of Dock Green* and about thirty paperbacks on her living room bookcase. She thought about getting the police involved. 'But where's the crime?' she thought, among other things. She felt she'd hit another brick wall. She put her head down and ran her fingers through her dry, scruffy hair.

Her mobile phone went again. She looked at it forgetting that she'd switched it back on. She thought of a film she'd seen where one of the characters flushed a phone down the loo as she opened up the bloody thing yet again.

'Simone Pound!' she said, her voice mid-way between a shout and a scream.

'Simone?'

'Oh, I'm sorry.'

'It's Giles.'

13

Two Bad Memories, One Good

'Oh, hi Giles.' She tried to make the greeting sound casual, but then she almost stopped breathing in case it was bad news.

'Simone, there are blokes with cameras outside.'

Oh, God - he was losing it. Or already had.

Are you still at home?'

'No, of course I'm not.'

'Where are you?'

'Just outside the station.'

'So the cameramen are outside here – outside the station?'

'Yes, they're in the street.'

'How many?'

'Two.'

In a way, she thought, it was an insult. They detonate a massive bomb in his life and he was only worth two paparazzi and one reporter?

'I don't like the look of them, Simone. What do you think I should do?'

'Are you in the Range Rover?'

'Yes.'

'Well, just drive past them.'

'Doesn't it matter if they see me?'

'No. Not really.' She thought about it and wasn't sure. 'Just drive through them and go round to the back door. Right to the back door. I'll be there to meet you.'

'Okay. What if they follow me?'

'They won't follow you.'

'Okay.'

'You okay with that?'

'Yeah. I'll see you in a minute. 'Bye.'

''Bye.'

She shut her phone and called the Newsroom from her office desk. It was picked up straight away.

'Newsroom…'

'Dave? Hi. Simone. Look – could you do me a big favour: could you go out front and stop the press following Giles into the car park. I'm sorry – I didn't call in any security for the day. I forgot.' She felt her face colouring.

'That's okay. Can I thump 'em if they cause any trouble?'

'No, I – '

'I'm joking, boss.'

'Oh…'

'I'm on to it, don't worry.'

'Thanks, David, you're a treasure.'

She made for the back door at pace checking things through. Did it matter that Giles was here? Greg wouldn't be in all day, nor would Damien and Sarah wouldn't mind. Bakerson only said he was off the air; he didn't say Giles was officially suspended. Not yet anyway.

When she got to the back door, Giles was already across the threshold.

'Come in, come in.'

'Thanks.'

'Is Dave with you?'

'He's talking to the photographers.'

'Is everything alright?'

'Yeah, I think so.'

Giles didn't look too bad, considering. She appraised him quickly hoping he wouldn't notice her examining him as if he were an institution inmate. His face was anxious and pale, but he was dressed normally: clothes immaculately ironed and new looking, stylish by comparison with her.

'Giles, I don't know how you do it – you're under all this pressure yet you still make me look like an absolute rag-bag.'

His hair looked okay too, though at that length it didn't need much tending.

'Did anyone see you?'

'They took a picture or two of me as I drove through.'

'Was it the same one that was here yesterday? Shaved head, low jeans?'

'It might have been, yeah.'

'So. What are we going to do with you?' she said.

'I don't know. Am I going to be in the way?'

'No, of course not.'

But he was. She thought about the sick room and whether he might like a sleep a little later on; that would tuck him out of the way for a good spell. But she didn't know what to do with him right now.

'Oh, I know what you could do for me,' she said suddenly. 'If you feel you want to…I've got a hits show to select the music for – you could do it for me – I don't know where I'm going to find the time, the way things are going.'

'Really? Okay, I could do that for you.'

'Good. Right, well, we'll set that up in a bit.' She paused, pretended to get something she needed out of a drawer. Then keeping her voice as light as she could, said,

'Oh – have you seen the paper?'

'Which one?'

'Oh, blast. Well, have you seen any?'

'Not yet, no.'

Simone went to her bag and ferreted out her address book. She went to the back and skimmed her forefinger down a list of emergency numbers. She took out her own phone and thumbed in the number. It answered on the third ring.

'Hello? Simone?'

'Hi, Sarah. Everything okay?'

'Um, sort of. I'm on the way in. Lucie's with me. I hope that's alright.'

'Of course it is. Can you do me a favour?'

'What is it?'

'Get me all today's newspapers – except for the blasted Chronicle. I'll pay you when you get here.'

Sarah was on the dual carriageway. She tried to remember if there was a newsagent's on her way in. There wasn't but she could go into town.

'Okay. I can do it, no problem.'

'Thanks. Thank you ever so much.'

'Okay, 'bye.'

Simone closed her phone again.

'Sarah's bringing the papers. Have a sit down - I'll be back in a bit.'

Simone left her office and beat it along the corridors to the newsroom. She was taken aback slightly – it looked like a weekday almost, compared the number of people there when she'd left ten minutes earlier.

'Hi, Tom, Marcus, Leon.' She nodded to each one in turn. 'What are you doing here?' She realised she was pleased to see Marcus: she could use him this morning if he was hanging around for a bit. She turned around to see who else was in.

'Hi, Jane, how was the show? Sorry, I wasn't listening, I was a bit busy.'

'That's okay, I understand, don't worry. It was – y'know – okay.'

'Thanks. Excuse me, Jane - Marcus, could you come with me?' She beckoned him with her head as she turned to leave, trying not to show the manic sense of urgency she felt in her head. At the first corridor angle she carried straight on into the kitchen through the ever-open door. She looked behind to check that Marcus was still behind her. The room was empty.

'Cloak and dagger stuff, isn't it?' she said, going over and shutting the second kitchen door that led into the other corridor. Marcus smiled, but was worried in case he was about to be accused of something. Like ghoulishly stopping by the station on a Saturday morning when he wasn't on the work rota in case something was going on.

'Marcus, two things.'

Marcus nodded.

'First – I'm so glad you're in. I want to sit down with you and pick your brains. Are you staying for a while?'

'Um, yeah, can do,' he said, relieved.

'I'm going to bring Sarah Billings in too. The three of us. I need us to have a little summit meeting.'

'Sure,' said Marcus, now looking perky but inquisitive.

'It's about this situation. Giles and the article.'

'Okay. Sure.'

'Secondly...' She turned and closed the kitchen door they'd just come through. 'I've got Sarah bringing in all the newspapers, but I want to know straight away, apart from The Chronicle, is there anything in the others about us?'

'Not that I've seen, or heard,' said Marcus.

'Which ones have you seen?'

'Well, I've just seen The Times, but there's a few others knocking about in there.'

'Has anyone in there found anything? Are they talking about another article?'

Marcus thought about it.

'Um, not really. The Chronicle's blown it all up but Clegg put his foot in it again at Lincoln, didn't he. They're writing about that now.'

'He did what?'

''bout five o'clock last night he was in Lincoln to visit a hospital and knocked an old woman over. Didn't you-'

'No. Did we have it on the news this morning?'

'Yeah. You didn't hear it?'

'No. He did what?'

'Knocked an old woman over. It was an accident but she broke her hip in the fall. His people tried to hush it up. So it missed the TV last night but it got out in the press and a few of the papers have got it this morning. They're concentrating on that. It barely mentions us.'

'Did you check The Independent carefully?'

'Um, yeah. I think I did. There's only a line about us at the bottom of a page about Clegg being a general liability for Bliss.'

Simone's face made a crushed look and she banged her foot on the hard floor again.

'Damn.'

'Can I ask why?'

'Yes. I was hoping for one of them to print something nice about Giles to balance the stuff in The Chronicle.'

It clicked with Marcus suddenly.

'Oh, you mean "Giles the People's hero, embarrassing Clegg on Thursday".'

'Yes. Am I asking for too much?'

'I don't know, I'm not an expert.'

That feeling came upon her again, the one where her stomach turned into solid iron and thudded into her boots.

'Okay, Thanks. Could you come along to my office in about ten minutes? Hang on, no - we'll go into Meeting Room 1. Actually, meet me in there. You can go there now if you want to.'

'Okay.' He looked at the Boss. Simone was a bit like his mum only with more authority. But he felt he had to say something. 'Are you okay?'

'No, but I'll be fine in a minute. Thanks for asking. Ten minutes, then,' she said, looking at Marcus again, who nodded back. He realised he felt as pleased as anything that she wanted to know what he thought.

'Okay.'

'Good.'

Simone opened the kitchen door again and rushed down the corridor to her office. She stopped outside to compose herself.

In she went.

'Hi.'

'Hi,' said Giles.

'Phew, I'm getting hot.'

Giles's smile was more like a wince. He was reading her Chronicle. She sat down at her desk.

'Oh, you found it – what do you think?'

'Amazing. I mean – it's not us, is it? Unbelievable. I don't know…'

'Go on.' She opened the window.

'I just…don't know how to feel about it, really. And it's weird, isn't it? We spend all – well, I seem to spend all my working life turning people's lives into news, and now it's our turn.'

It was odd to hear Giles being philosophical.

'But we don't do *this*, Giles,' she said, flicking the edge of the paper. 'We don't do this to people.'

'No, we don't,' he said.

Simone looked at Giles.

'Are you thinking about Leah?'

'Yeah. Of course.'

'You're wondering where she is…'

'Yes, and whether she's seen this.'

'Me too.'

'I think you should phone her.'

'You don't want to?'

'No,' he said.

Simone looked at him and wondered whether it was really Giles in there. Something about him didn't look right.

'And Lucie – look what they've done to Lucie,' he said, gesturing with the paper. 'Is she okay, do you know?'

'I'm not sure.' Her brow furrowed deep on account of knowing she was coming into the station. She didn't want her staff embarrassed and awkward with each other but she could hardly keep Lucie out of his way. 'She's coming in.'

'Is she?'

'Yes, with Sarah.'

'Oh,' said Giles. He would have to see her – apologize. It was all his fault, her getting mixed up in this. His heart turned over at the thought of her being upset – the humiliation of her family. What did these bastards call her? *Sex tramp*? Christ, they shouldn't be allowed to get away with it. There should be a law against it.

There was a tap on the door. Giles began to rise out of his seat to go answer it.

'It's okay, I'll go,' said Simone.

Giles watched her open the door a few inches then step back to allow Sarah Billings to enter, her arms full of newspapers.

'Tell you what…' said Simone.

'Hello, Giles,' she said, smiling at him, as if it were a normal day.

'Hi, Sarah.' He'd known her for two years, but they weren't firm friends. But she was very professional which he'd always liked a lot. And she always showed him respect. He smiled back at her as pleasantly as he could.

'…don't bring them in here. Take them – do you mind? – to MR 1. With a bit of luck Marcus should already be in there. I'll be along in a minute.'

'Oh. Okay.'

Sarah looked puzzled. Simone followed her out into the corridor.

'Lucie's here?' she whispered.

'Yes,' replied Sarah in a low voice, copying.

'Where is she?'

'In the newsroom.'

'Do you mind leaving her for a bit while you, me and Marcus have a talk? I need us to put our heads together.'

'Yeah – she'll be okay. I'll pop in and make sure, then I'll come along to - MR1?'

'Yep. Thanks.'

That's some girl, thought Simone for the hundredth time. She went back to Giles.

'Okay, my lad – I'm off to have a meeting with Marcus and Sarah. We're going to try to work out who's behind it all.'

'I don't suppose I could sit in?'

'Not this time. If you've been pulled, it wouldn't look right if...'

'Yeah, it's okay, I get it. You're right – it wouldn't.'

She was lying – she wondered whether Giles was too. Officially, the meeting that was about to take place in MR1 didn't and wouldn't ever exist.

When she arrived, within the minute, Marcus and Sarah had already spread a mass of papers across the large conference table and were turning the pages over, their faces full of concentration.

'We're just starting,' said Sarah.

'Any luck?'

'Not so far.'

Simone saw The Times sitting there still folded in half and picked it up. Under the famous banner and the headline, on the right hand side of the page was a picture of Clegg. She scowled at it at first, then had her attention pulled towards it.

"Clegg in New Gaffe" it said underneath a snap of the suited Deputy Prime Minister who was about to get into an official car. She opened the paper up and leaned over the table to read.

'Hey, have you seen this?' she said.

'What?'

'Huh?'

'Clegg.'

'Oh, yeah – he's dropped another bol – oh, um...'

'Exactly. Perfectly put.' Simone started reading. 'Oh, no,' she said after two paragraphs.

'What's the matter?' said Sarah. 'Didn't you know? It's been running on our bulletins this morning.'

'No, I didn't! Oh, he would go and spoil it all, wouldn't he.' She slumped into a chair and reached over for The Guardian. There was a similar picture of a rough-looking John Clegg and an almost identical headline on the bottom half of the page below another pair of bombs in Baghdad. She read aloud.

' *"Beleaguered Deputy Prime Minister John Clegg walked himself further into trouble yesterday in a Norwich City Centre hospital. His visit to the new neurological unit at the St Ann's Hospital Trust was proceeding well until he inadvertently trod on the bare toes of Mary Sneddon, a 72 year old patient, causing her to fall."* I don't bloody believe it.' She tossed the paper aside. Sarah picked it up.

'Read it, Sarah,' said Marcus, quietly.

' *"The impact with the ground resulted in her new hip being severely displaced. Mrs Sneddon of Catton, Norfolk was immediately rushed into surgery. Observers had difficulty in discerning who groaned the loudest: Clegg or the poor Mrs Sneddon. It is widely thought that the Deputy Prime Minister could be found groaning even more loudly later in the day as he considered this latest gaffe. Mr Clegg's job, if not whole political career, is now thought to be in serious jeopardy as a result of his latest misdemeanour."* '

'If he came anywhere near me, more than his career would be in jeopardy.' I'd tread on his other bollock for a start, she thought.

'Oh – here we are,' said Sarah, folding and placing a copy of The Independent on the desk in front of her. 'Hang on…um… Yeah - *"This was the accident-prone Mr Clegg's second PR disaster in two days. On Thursday, appearing on Two Counties Radio's Breakfast Show in Barton Townes, Bartonshire, he dramatically walked out on an interview with presenter Giles McAndrew after being insulted on air."* Oh - that's it.'

'That just about sums it up,' said Simone. She could hold herself up no longer for her youngsters. She sat back in the chair with a slump and stared out of the window. That was that. No room for heroic Giles. It was poor Mrs Sneddon now.

Sarah was going to say something encouraging, but wasn't sure whether it was the right thing to do so carried on scanning the papers in the hope of finding more on the Giles and the station.

'Anything else, yet, Marc?' said Simone after about a minute.

'Nothing in the Mail really, nor the Telegraph, just a brief mention about Thursday, same as The Times. It's all about Clegg and the hospital and the mess his career's in. You?' he said, looking at Sarah.

'I've done The Star – that took about five seconds –and now I'm on The Express.'

The two workers read in silence.

'Either of you two want coffee?'

'Me please,' said Sarah.

'Mmm, yes please,' said Marcus.

She exited MR1 closing the door quietly behind her. All I seem to do is walk up and down corridors, she thought. She felt for her calves aching but they weren't. Back in MR1, the workers worked.

'Well, that's it - nothing worth talking about,' said Sarah. 'Just mentions of our name. You?'

Marcus was flicking rapidly through The Sun.

'Same. He's a tit, isn't he, that Clegg…'

'Yep. Still – could you imagine our Giles McAndrew being written up as some kind of people's hero?' said Sarah.

'You tell me – you probably read the papers more than I do.'

Sarah thought about it.

'I suppose they could have done when you think of how many listeners rang in to support him. I just can't imagine…y'know, someone we work with being written about in the papers.'

'Well, you've got it today. Look in The Chronicle. There he is, and you…'

'Alright, Marcus, don't go on.'

'Oh, yeah, I'm sorry. Whoops. Sorry, Sarah. I didn't think…'

'Its okay.'

The conversation ended abruptly as they heard the door opening. Simone was back. She had everything on a tray. She put it down then noticed an atmosphere in the room.

'What's up?' she said.

Sarah told her.

Simone smiled a small smile of consolation for Marcus.

'Don't worry, Marc. If I had a tenner for every mistake I've made in the past few days…'

'Nice coffee, thanks,' said Sarah.

'Thanks, boss,' said Marcus.

Simone put some sugar in her coffee, for a change, and felt her mood levelling out. As much as she could easily be roused to incandescent anger at the maelstrom they were still trapped in, she knew it wouldn't do anyone much good. They'd had another blow with the papers having completely deserted Giles McAndrew but they'd just have to take it and move on. She knew that if they could only find out who was behind it all and nail him, or her, they could turn this around for Giles – that it would change everything. That would make a story.

Simone felt her mood improve before she was hit with another thought. *If the perpetrator works for the station, that really will make us look good. They'll crucify me for not being able to control my staff.* She looked out of the window again and felt the gloom descending again. *It's like going out to play a football match knowing you've already lost,* she thought. Because the more she thought about it, the more the thought that the guilty one was from TCR closed in on her. And if it wasn't obvious in her head, she felt it also in her bones. She had no choice but to battle on though. *You couldn't just give up.*

Sarah and Marcus waited for her to stop staring.

'Okay,' she said eventually, 'now I'm going to tell you what you're here for.' She looked each of them in the eye in turn. Both expressions said, 'this wasn't it?'

'First, I need you to promise me that what I'm going to tell you stays in this office. This is top secret.' She looked at them, already knowing she could trust Sarah to tell Lucie but no one else. She didn't mind that.

'Okay,' said the two reporters in turn.

'Sarah. Can I trust Marcus?'

Sarah looked at him.

'I don't know,' she said, slightly playfully. 'No,' she said, and put a serious expression on her face.

'What?' said Marcus. 'Oh, thanks.'

'You know what you men are like,' said Sarah. She thought of Marcus and Big Dave in the newsroom. Always in cahoots, those two; secretive.

Simone stepped in.

'Marcus.'

Marcus raised his expression at her.

'I need your help. What I want to tell you both is very personal – not about me, but other people you know. I *need* you to promise me you won't go straight to Big Dave or anyone else, blabbing.'

Marcus started to show the women that he was affronted, but decided that actually they were right to question him. He made his decision in seconds though.

'Look. I promise. Boss, you can do anything you like to me, give me any crappy jobs you want to come up with if you find that I've broken it. But you won't. I'll – '

'Okay, Marcus, I get the picture. Just look me in the eye and say, "I promise you, Simone, that I will not tell a soul what you're about to tell me."'

Simone fixed her gaze on him and didn't blink. Marcus looked at her, thinking, 'Is she serious?' But her expression left him in no doubt. He turning very serious himself.

'"I promise you, Simone, that I will not tell a soul what you're about to tell me."'

'Okay. That'll do for me.' Simone shuffled her bottom in her seat and began.

'You know what The Chronicle's printed this morning, alright? Have you been wondering how much of it is true?'

'It's the talk of the newsroom this morning, obviously, and we're all there guessing…and I've been asking Sarah about it but she says it's all rubbish.'

'And do you believe her?'

'I…No. There's no smoke without fire. So some of it must be true or pretty near the mark.'

'Okay,' said Simone. 'Here's the truth…' Simone told them the facts as she saw and knew them. She sketched out Giles and Leah's troubles briefly, including the painting and the visit from Catherine, and went into detail about the drawings. She finished by revealing the press mole theory. 'And it's likely that the one behind it all works here at the station.'

She watched and let them take it in. Sarah looked stunned even though she was hearing it all for the second time. Marcus's face was a picture of concentration. After a further pause for thought it was he who re-booted the conversation.

'Whoever did it followed Leah to Lichester, then.'

'Yes.' Blimey, thought Simone: Marcus was sharp.

'And you think this is all the work of one and the same person?' said Sarah carefully.

'I think so,' said Simone, 'but this is one of the reasons you're here. This is one of the things I want you both to think about. It might not be.'

'Has to be,' said Marcus.

'Remind me who opened the envelope?' Sarah asked.

'Leah did. She came straight to me to ask if she could be let go. She decided she had to get away.'

'I don't blame her,' said Sarah, sitting back in her chair, looking as if she'd taken part of the blow herself. Marcus nodded, his eyes wide.

'Me neither,' said Simone. 'So – what do you think this all means?' Silence.

'I can give you one theory…' said Marcus.

'Yes?' said Simone.

'This is about Leah Caighton. He's obsessed with her. Unhealthily obsessed, obviously. The drawings – that's a nutter at work. Obviously. All the drawings of her being, you know…'

'We know,' said Simone, quietly.

'That's jealousy, I reckon.'

'It's not Giles who's the key?' said Simone.

'He has to be a part of it, surely,' said Sarah. 'We all know what most people think of him. I don't see how you can leave Giles out of it…' She was looking at Marcus. But he was deep in thought, staring at the desk in front of him.

Simone and Sarah had a conversation of their own.

'Don't you think the drawings aimed to hurt Giles?' said Simone.

'Who were they sent to?'

'Leah's name was on the front of the envelope.'

'Oh – what about the writing? Or was it typed?'

'Handwritten.'

'Hmm. One word. And he would have written it with his other hand…'

'Yes.' Simone had already thought about that.

'The fourth drawing is the important one,' said Marcus suddenly. He sat up in his chair and leaned forward. 'That's the key. Like I say, whoever did it had to follow Leah to Lichester to spy on her. He didn't follow her because he knew she was going out looking for a bloke. It's obsession.' He leaned back again and folded his arms. 'He wants her for himself. Perhaps he follows her a lot. Or did.'

'Crikey – I got you together with me because I knew you were bright. I didn't think you'd crack it in two minutes.'

Marcus laughed. 'Isn't it obvious?' he said, looking at Simone, then at Sarah. 'Come on - it's the drawings – when you think about it they're a dead giveaway. It's sexual obsession. And I don't think he was especially bothered about whether Giles got hurt. He was bound to, wasn't he, if he felt a lot for Leah. But this is about splitting them up so he can have her.'

'But can't it just be someone playing games?' said Simone.

'Practical joke? No. Me and Dave – we like playing jokes on people-'

'But you wouldn't do this…'

'No. Not in a million years. This isn't pissing about. This is different level.'

'Takes a man, Simone – to understand a man,' said Sarah. She smiled at her boss. Simone smiled back, wondering how she was feeling. Then she said to Marcus,

'Okay. But if you're right, he's failed, hasn't he? Leah got the drawings and was so upset she felt she had to leave. His plan backfired.'

'True,' said Marcus.

'You don't think she'll come back?' said Sarah.

'No, I don't think so. I don't think she ever will,' said Simone.

'Hmm, then he just went too far with the drawings,' said Marcus. 'He was unlucky.'

'And what do you think he'll be doing now?' asked Sarah.

'Perhaps he's following her.'

'It depends who it is, doesn't it,' said Simone.

'He may have to work…' chipped in Sarah.

'Whoever it is,' said Marcus. 'has to know the two of them well. Very well. He had to know a lot about their relationship.'

'You think?' said Simone.

'Yeah, I do. And the obvious place to look first is here. It's probably someone at the station.'

'Not necessarily – they could have had friends, couldn't they, Giles and Leah?' said Sarah. 'Perhaps it's someone from Leah's past.' She looked to Simone for information.

'They were always a bit of a solitary couple. They kept themselves to themselves.' They're both loners, thought Simone for the first time.

'Hmm,' said Marcus. Something had been tickling his brain for a minute or so – something from his memory. It wouldn't come.

'I want to ask something else,' said Simone, her anger now gradually being displaced by adrenalin. 'Is this a man working on his own? Or with someone?'

Sarah thought about it. She thought of a pair of perverted blokes drooling over drawings of Giles with her Lucie and shivered with acute displeasure. She looked at Simone and shrugged her shoulders. Then she looked at Marcus and saw his face change from an expression of a troubled Mathematician to a comedian who'd just thought up a good joke.

'He's on his own,' he said, almost smiling. 'And what's more, I can tell you exactly who it is.'

To his immense pleasure, both women stared at him goggle eyed.

'It's Greg McKenzie.'

Two 'How do you knows?' overlapped in the air.

'Because they used to go out together.'

'Huh?'

'*Whattt!*'

'Blimey – am I the only one around here who remembers?'

261

14

The Music Library

Giles tried reading the rest of the paper but had neither the interest nor the concentration for it. He wondered why he wasn't more upset. He didn't really understand it but couldn't be bothered to explore the feeling. It was so. End of story. He swallowed and was distracted again by the taste of the saliva sliding down: it was still bad. It tasted of coffee and metal. He hated it. It had been like that for days now.

After a couple of minutes spent thinking about the article and being off the air, he decided to go to the music library to pick out some songs and CDs for Simone's show. He got up and left the office and turned left in the direction of the newsroom. On the way, it occurred to him that he wasn't angry about the article because he was at a low ebb already: he either didn't have the energy left or any anger left. And as for the contents, well, the accusations weren't exactly news to him.

The music library was two offices along from Simone. The door was open as usual and he walked in to find it empty. Empty of people anyway. The room was small, perhaps half the size of the managing editor's office, but crammed wall to wall with around five thousand CDs, a couple of hundred albums on vinyl, a shelf of vinyl singles and another one two-thirds full with music books.

Giles didn't know exactly what music Simone was looking for, but the word 'hits' in the context of local BRBC radio didn't load up the job with complications. He started thinking about what she might want. He wondered what the show was and whether it was themed. Was it a party song show or did she want love songs? Did she want just number 1's? And then there was the issue of time. Was it tied to a particular decade? He was wasting his time really, because he needed to ask her exactly what she wanted, but he had nothing else to do to divert his mind. I might as well just pull out twenty songs or so, he thought, and maybe after that she'd be around to ask for more specific instruction. He couldn't go back to her office and just sit there; he had to do something or he'd go mad.

Where shall I start? he said to himself. His favourites. What were his favourite singles? He tried to think of his very favourite, but he wasn't good at rank ordering records and songs, or films or anything. He knew that a lot of blokes enjoyed doing that sort of thing but he couldn't understand why – it had never interested him. He closed his eyes and thought, and music rushed in and ought of the chaos was Marvin Gaye. Yeah, that'll do, that song. 'I Heard It Through The Grapevine'. He loved that. That would do for a start. He started to look for the CD and realised he hadn't been in here for a long time. The music in his shows was all programmed from the national corporation computer, as it was for all the presenters of the daytime shows.

He had trouble working out what system they were using to store the CDs. He tried approaching the problem alphabetically but that didn't work. God, this was a stupid way of running things. And it was tiring. It must be genres, then. Then he finally noticed the labels on the shelf frontings, hand-written in black on white paper, and stuck on with clear sticky tape. There was "Disco" right in front of him. Right, genres. His eyes roamed past "Indie", "Jazz", "Metal", "New Wave", "Pop", "Punk/New Wave", "Reggae" and "Rock". By the time he found "Soul" he was over on the opposite side of the room. Giles soon dug out a Marvin Gaye greatest hits package. He checked that the song was on there and placed it on the little table behind him. He had to pick up a copy of *Kylie – the biography* and place it on top of the "Guinness Book of Hit Singles" to make some space.

He racked his brains for other songs he really liked. It was hard, the mood he was in. He couldn't summon up any enthusiasm for the job really. Be obvious, Giles, think obviously. He didn't much like The Beatles but he really liked David Bowie. He'd liked Bowie for as long as he could remember. He drifted back to "Pop" and found that the station had a line of Bowie albums. He looked for a hits package again and found *Changes*. And I ought to have 'Let's Dance,' he decided. He started to hum the chorus quietly then stopped. He was barely aware of his thought processes. Not 'Let's Dance', said an inner voice: too cheerful. Something moodier. But it's a hits show, came an answering phantom somewhere in his head. 'Sound and Vision.' He sang a snatch of that silently, testing it for a show like Simone's. Of course it would be fine, it had been a hit. But there was something moody about it too. Something dark. Good, his master voice decided. That's two in the bag then. He placed the *Changes* CD on the table on top of the Marvin Gaye.

O fuck, what next? Okay, what about The Eagles? He liked The Eagles, but wasn't sure they'd ever had a big hit. Oh - what was he thinking about? 'Hotel California' was a huge hit and had come up on his show about a month earlier. He hardly had to move to find it. It was about one step away to the right and down a shelf. Another greatest hits CD. The table now had something resembling a small pile on it. It's pointless doing this, he thought. He didn't know when Simone's show was. Someone else might need one of the CDs before she had time to programme them into the machine. Or does she want me to do it today? Giles thought about that. Could he see himself whiling the afternoon away preparing her show? He didn't know. He didn't know that he had that much concentration or that much energy. He thought about Simone doing a music show. Was she actually going to go behind the mike? To do a music show? That was odd. He tried to remember if she'd ever told him she'd presented when she was younger. Ah, well, what did he care? He decided to carry on. For the time being anyway. Until there was something better to do. And here, anyway, he was safe.

'*What?*'

'Sarah, you weren't here. But boss, you were. It was two thousand and...hold on a minute...three.'

'Well I can't remember.'

'It didn't last long, I remember that too. Only maybe a week or two. But it was all round the newsroom at the time.'

Marcus looked at the managing editor's look of bafflement and wondered at how little she probably knew about her staff. He thought about his liking for weed and hoped she had no idea about that. Or that Big Dave had once taken some office equipment, CDs and half the station's rubbishy collection of books home and sold it at a boot fair near Lincoln.

'Bloody hell!' said Sarah, revolted at the thought of Greg nakedly engaged with Leah, who was absolutely gorgeous.

'Well, I haven't a clue what you lot get up to, you must know that,' said a defensive Simone. Normally it didn't matter a jot to her that the staff had their liaisons and what-not with each other without her knowing. She thought it was good hands-off management, actually, but now she wondered if it wasn't time that she made a change of policy.

'Anyway, there's your motive,' said Marcus.

'Well, I'll be blowed,' said Simone. '"Bloody hell!" hardly does it justice.'

'So what now?' said Marcus, as pleased as punch at his performance.

Simone shook her head, thinking.

'Where's Greg today?' asked Sarah.

'Up the coast at Seaby with the bus.'

They heard the rush of feet outside before they heard the urgent knock on the door.

He was suddenly distracted by a noise behind him.

'Oh. Hi, Giles.'

It was Big Dave Plymouth.

'Hi,' said Giles.

'Have you seen Sarah - Sarah Billings, mate?'

'Er, no. Sorry, I haven't.'

'Oh. Right, okay. See you,' he said patting the doorframe with his huge right hand.

Giles was on his own again. He wondered whether Big Dave had displayed awkwardness or embarrassment at running into him. He wasn't sure. It didn't much matter anyway. Not really. He had much more to worry about than that.

What did he want next? After The Eagles and 'Hotel California' what would be a good song to follow? He didn't know. What would Simone choose, he wondered? Elton John, probably, he supposed. She was a mad Elton fan. What song would she choose, he thought, thinking "J" was only a short way along from "E" in "Pop"? 'Your Song' came into his head. He stopped. 'Your Song.' He stared at the shelf of CDs in front of him but didn't see them. He saw himself and Leah on his sofa watching a DVD. Musicals weren't his thing normally but he liked that one, *Moulin Rouge*, with Ewan McGregor who was great in *Trainspotting* and Nicole Kidman, who was beautiful, really stunning. Leah had been jealous, but only in a playful way. She'd cried when they sang 'Your Song' together. It wasn't that bad, he'd said and she'd punched him on the thigh and said, "Shut up, I'm enjoying this." He'd said, "how can you be enjoying this if you're crying," and she'd said, "you don't understand women then." Then, "If this is what you're all like, I don't care," he'd said, caring really. And they both laughed out loud again. Then they watched the rest of the film lying as close as they could without actually getting on top of each other and he was very, very happy that she was his girlfriend.

And the following Saturday after his show they'd driven up to Lincoln. They'd walked up by the cathedral and had a really nice late lunch in a swish sort of café. Then strolled down the steep hill into the shopping centre after buying some posh chocolate, and then some teacake sweets from the shop a little further along. They meandered along not caring about time. He bought her an Elton John album that had 'Your Song' on it - surprised her with it while she was leafing through the racks for a Madonna's greatest hits. Told her it wasn't the film version, obviously, but that it was Simone Pound's favourite song

266

of all time so she'd still like it. The look on her face said, "it doesn't matter." She had a look of real – well, he knew what the look on her face meant though she didn't put it into so many words.

They stopped in the bookshop halfway up the hill on the way back to the car where he bought a book by Lance Armstrong and she bought a cookery book by someone or other. He remembered them laughing in there together and stifling more giggles because they thought they might be making too much noise - the guy who ran the shop was such a misery. No, she was never one to want to put her feelings into words, never mind him.

Giles found himself looking at the spine of a Billy Joel CD and watched the writing blur and swell in front of him as both his eyes filled up. He turned his back on the shelving and slid slowly down until his bottom touched down on the dusty floor, his legs bent up under him like a whacked spider. The descent would have hurt his back but the part of his brain that registered physical pain was overridden by another type. He was crying and trying to pull himself back from tears at one and the same time. It was a battle he began to lose as soon as entered it. The box-square real world dissolved right in front of him. In the back of his mind a distant voice told him he was making a noise like a sobbing girl. He knew this was a mistake but he was helpless to stop it. He was conscious of the fact that he was being overwhelmed by forces beyond his control but that did not give him the power to make an intervention. He knew too that if he didn't shut up, someone would come and find him, thereby completing his humiliation. But that didn't empower him either. Then he found it was all he could do to keep himself breathing properly, never mind worry about who might hear him. It was weird. Everything was changing while everything was staying the same. The room was whirling around him but there he still was, arse on the floor bawling his eyes out. His mind and his emotions seemed to be disintegrating but he was still clearly the same person he'd been two minutes ago.

Someone did hear him; someone on their way to Simone's office. Giles was aware vaguely of looking down at his be-jeaned thighs and the tears dripping on to them when he saw another pair of legs arrive next to his. He registered the end of a skirt or dress, then knees and dark stockinged or tightened legs below the hem. A voice seemed to call for him from far away.

'Giles, hey, hey now, what's the matter?'

He heard his name fairly clearly but was unable to respond by looking up at the speaker's head where they face might be.

'Sshh,' went the voice.

It was soft and remained so as it came closer to his left ear. 'Hey, come on, sshh, come on now,' it went, in the way a voice does when all it wants to do is soothe you - it didn't want you or need you to talk back to it. Then he felt a hand on his hair rubbing the part at the back of the neck. It felt very good. The hand too was trying to soothe him. It *was* soothing, the voice too. His eyes closed firmly and he let himself relax while hand and voice did their work. Soothing: lovely. Despite everything he could feel himself being scooped up, being washed clean. In his mind's eye he saw fresh, clean waves washing a sunny shore of perfect sand. Sea waves in sunshine. He felt that if he could just let himself surrender to this person, this wonderful person, whoever she was, he would begin to heal. It might take time for the job to be complete, but to make a start would be heaven. In this person's care, he felt that anything might be possible. He let himself surrender.

The voice had a face and that face came close to his. It was the face of Lucie Bastable. Lucie's face was close to his. He was aware of the smell she brought with her and how fresh and lovely that was. He managed to look at her for a brief second and saw that she had beautiful, lovely eyes. Yes, that word again, *lovely*. The word itself was *lovely* just as Lucie, he could see now, was lovely. He saw the light in their coal dark circles that was made to shine even from the support of the dingy music library strip light.

The eyes were only eyes to their owner. They belonged to a woman who had heard heart rending sobs echoing down the corridor and who went to them with compassion without a second thought. She turned into the open doorway and immediately saw the figure of Giles McAndrew lying on the floor with his back propped up on the shelving, head bent forward dribbling tears onto his legs. She saw the two dark circular patches they were making on the material and found herself startled: they were somehow shocking. To see Giles McAndrew - the supremely confident presenter, the one she admired and tried to model herself on - reduced to these shreds of a man, split her into pieces. To see him like this, hopeless and bereft, powerless to cover the potential embarrassment of being found in such a state, was sad beyond words. She went down to the floor to be with him, said, 'Sshh, come on now - hey, it's okay, it'll be alright, Giles,' and stroked his hair. Her face came down close enough to his for the tip of her nose to be touching his cheek.

After twenty, maybe thirty ticks of the cruel clock above their heads, Giles turned his head slowly round and placed his lips gently on hers. But as he did so, sweet and tender Lucie pulled her head back deftly and whispered, 'Hey, no, Giles,' but not horribly, or coldly, not as if he'd made a terrible mistake that he would have to wear as a badge of shame for a week, a month or a year. She let him down in the gentlest way imaginable. But there was a note of finality in her voice that was unmistakable, and because he knew he had been completely rejected he died a thousand times on the spot and thought he would never rise from it again.

'Don't get me wrong,' she said in the same soft and lovely whisper, happily stroking his head again, 'I think you're a lovely guy - a brilliant guy - I really do. But I like girls, Giles, not men. Sarah and I live together. Hasn't anybody told you?'

And though she'd tried to break it to him in such a consoling way, with a tenderness that could have put Humpty Dumpty back together again, but not Giles McAndrew, he heard her words and died a thousand times more.

15

Old Maid

Monday 8th May

Simone studied the email on her screen:

Page 1 of 1

----- Original Message -----
From: Ian Bakerson
To: Simone Pound
Sent: Monday, May 7, 2006 09:23 AM
Subject: Re: Giles McAndrew Meeting

Simone

Following our telephone conversation of last night, I can now tell you that a discussion of Giles McAndrew's incident with John Clegg and the subsequent article in The Chronicle (and, as we discussed, the possibility of disciplinary action) has been brought forward to our regular Tuesday morning management meeting. I shall contact you later that afternoon to inform you of the outcome. As I have already outlined, the most likely result of that meeting is that he receives a brief suspension from his duties at the station and a severe warning as to his future conduct. However, and I mention this to you in the strictest confidence, in the light of Mr McAndrew's conduct, it is possible that the management team may recommend that you carefully consider the possibility of withdrawing the offer of contract renewal.

Best wishes,

Ian Bakerson
Assistant-head
BRBC LOCAL RADIO NATIONAL MANAGEMENT
Broadcasting Lane, The Bush, London W1A 4VV

"Mr McAndrew." She didn't like the sound of that at all. And she had to laugh at "may recommend"; she knew what their "recommend" meant: she would have no choice but to do their bidding. They didn't have the right to do it technically but she knew what they were like: if you ignored their recommendations you would effectively be at war with them. You didn't fight England, let alone go to war with them.

She rolled everything around her mind for the thousandth time. With every revolution there were difficulties, stresses and worries. Weighed down and wearied by the state of Giles' health she found the thought of Greg and Leah difficult to avoid considering, pathologically. How could she? How drunk would she have been to put herself in his bed? She hoped he hadn't drugged her. For all she knew, that might be exactly what happened. Just because Leah hadn't told her as much…Simone shuddered, and yet thought, how can we say we really know people? That line from an old song came into her mind: how no one knows what goes on behind closed doors. When was that – 1974? She started to count the years that had passed since then but stopped and said, oh, I'm not going to start playing that silly bloody game, to herself – I've got enough to worry about already.

And then there was the issue of the target. From the moment Leah showed her the drawings she'd been convinced the plot had been aimed pretty much solely at Giles: that the motivation was hatred or jealousy of him. But the more she re-visited Marcus' theory the more she felt he was right: this was centrally a Leah issue. I need another three-way meeting, she thought – as soon as I can organise it. I need their help if I'm going to sort this out, she told herself.

There was a knock at the door. Greg was ten minutes late. She'd changed the time to 9.30 and hoped he'd forgotten about the list of suspects. She'd changed her mind about that.

'Come in,' she called and clicked the mouse to minimise her inbox.

'Hi, Simone.'

'Oh, hi, Greg, come in.' She was going to make her best effort to be a great actress. Vanessa Redgrave. Kate Winslet.

'Thanks.'

'Take a seat.'

Greg McKenzie sat down. He was not unlike Giles physically, she thought this morning. Tall, almost as tall as Giles, but better built, though not by much.

'How're things?'

'Okay, but dreadful, if you see what I mean.'

'Ha-ha, I think I do, yeah.' He pushed his glasses up to the top of his nose as he finished his sentence. Why do I find everything he does annoying at the moment, thought Simone? Actually he wasn't better built than Giles – he just had more flesh on him.

'First, I should brief you. Management England are having – is having? "Is having" is correct isn't it?' You're nervous, Simone – stop it, she told herself, or he'll suspect you. 'A meeting – they're meeting on Friday to make their decision. Do you want a coffee?'

'Yeah, that'd be great.'

'Fine. I want one too. Need one.' I do like that shirt, though, she said to herself. It was navy blue and worn outside the trousers like that it wasn't far from making him look sexy. She shuddered at such a thought occurring at this time of all times, and concentrated on thinking that the shirt would look even better on Giles.

'What do you think the outcome will be, Simone?'

'I don't know, Greg. They're not at all happy with the situation, with him, to put it mildly.'

'Are they out for blood, do you think?'

'I think they'll keep him off the air for another couple of weeks and slap him very hard on the wrists. That's what I think.'

'Where does that leave us with Giles?'

'What do you mean?'

'Well, his contract is up for renewal - do we want to keep him on?'

'What? Of course we do? Don't you?'

'I don't know – I'm not sure.'

Oh, I bet you are, she thought.

'Take me through your thinking.'

'Well.' He stopped to cough. 'On the one hand he's the most popular presenter we've ever had. Does a great job. I've always loved his work…'

Had he? She started to trawl her memory for what he'd said about him in the past.

'…but - is he getting bigger than the station? That's one of the questions I ask myself.'

He leaned forward in his chair. He looks young, Simone thought. For thirty-six, he looked boyish, still, even though he tried to come on like the elder statesman all the time.

'I think, you know, this has been coming for a long time. I mean, he's very, very good, don't get me wrong – excellent. But as he's got better, he's got more – how shall I put it? – too confident. I think the Clegg thing was bound to happen sooner or later.'

What has he got to gain from Giles McAndrew leaving, she thought as he talked? Will Leah come back if Giles goes? It's possible, though not likely. She still thought Leah had gone for good. Then again, if she found out that Giles had been sacked, she might want to come back; people could do odd things. In the end, though, she didn't think it was likely. Dozy old Barton Townes wasn't much of a place for someone with her talents. If she ever decided she wanted to use them, that is.

'...and I wonder whether all the attention surrounding him isn't rather too disruptive for the station as a whole.'

Then again, she thought, she might come back if I can give her a big opportunity. She wondered how long it would take before she could get her behind a microphone if she came back. And then, she thought coming back to the point, Greg would be able to work at getting his teeth back into her.

'...Do you see what I mean?'

'Yes, I do - Go on,' she said getting the coffee organised, but listening more closely.

'Well, I don't want to be unkind, Simone, but Giles never has been popular here. I think the staff would be more than ready to accept a new breakfast presenter.'

'See the back of him, you mean?' She passed his mug of coffee across.

'Thanks. Well, I wouldn't quite put it quite like that,' he said, sitting back and crossing his legs. She had to admit she liked his navy blue trainers too.

'Try and put it differently to me again, then, would you?' She smiled as helpfully as she could, when really she hoped he would take it with all the insincerity with which it was offered.

'Well – to be brutally honest with you, I think Giles *is* very bad for team morale, and I think if we schooled Lucie for Giles's job it would bring a nice breath of fresh air to the station.'

'Lucie?'

'Yes - I think she'd be someone we could all kind of use as a fulcrum, for, um, our further, um – or, to put it another way...' He stopped to take a sip of coffee.

Lucie, thought Simone? What now – was he switching his attentions? Did he want Giles out of the way so he could now fixate on Lucie? That was a laugh. That genuinely was funny. Was he that dim?

'...someone we could all rally round as we try to sort of...renew ourselves...in the light of what Giles did. You know, the trouble he's caused.'

'Did to us, do you mean? To all of us?'

'Well, to the station. He's ruined our reputation, I think.'

Oh, you do think, do you?

'So – hmm, that's interesting, Gregory.' She got up and walked to the window. It wasn't a bad day and the sun was trying to break through. 'It really is. So what's in your plan? Giles to work out his contract? While we give Lucie some intensive training?'

'Yes, we could do that. Noona has a week's holiday coming up. And so has Jane Landings. We could give her those spots.'

'Hmm. Yes, I can see how that could work. We can get her to do some dummy shows in the spare studio. She could work off some old running orders of Giles's actually. We keep a few, don't we?'

'Yes,' said Greg leaning forward enthusiastically. 'And I'm sure Sonia and Ian would help out as dummy interviewees.'

'Okay, great. Look. I'll give it some thought through the rest of the day and I'll tell you what I think tomorrow morning. Does that work for you?'

'Yuh, that works fine,' said Greg, surprised that he'd got through to his boss so quickly. She seemed to be taking him seriously for once, he thought. He sipped at his coffee again. It was always good, Simone's coffee.

'How's Giles doing?' he said.

'Oh, okay. He's holding up very well, considering. It's interesting what you say, actually, about him moving on. It's something he's looking to do anyway.'

'Really?'

'Yes. He thinks a fresh start somewhere else might be a good thing for him. So, should England actually, you know...' I can't say it, she thought. '...it might be a blessing in disguise. You know, make his mind up for him.'

'Oh. Really. That's interesting.'

Simone watched him digest this. She didn't know how he had the nerve to sit there in her office drinking her coffee after what he'd done to Giles. And Leah. And her. It was like being in the same room as an axe murderer. She felt a shiver go right through her insides. And was it now going to be Lucie? Or was it a blind – was he about to resign and go chasing after Leah? No. She could see another truth. Was it just not him?

When he'd gone, Simone picked up the phone, desperate to call someone to tell them about Greg's brazen cheek and how eerie it had been, then how horrible it now was to deal with him, but she had to put the receiver back in its cradle: she had no one. Not since her new relationship had fallen through. She thought of Sarah, but she was out on a job and wouldn't be back for hours. She could tell Marcus but she couldn't *really* tell Marcus and talk to him properly about it, she hardly knew him really. She couldn't talk to Giles any more. A shadow fell over her thoughts. She was glad her latest sally into the romance game had ended in failure – apart from the sex there was nothing good in the relationship. She was well to be done with it. But look at me: I'm fifty-one. Fifty-bloody-one and fifty-two already waiting for me just round the corner. If it wasn't for computer dating, she said aloud in a quiet voice, you'd be an old maid.

She finished her coffee and switched up the studio feed. Noona was banging on about how good Thursday was because it was nearly the end of the week. She might have to have a word about presenters encouraging the people of Bart and Bilt to spend their lives living for the weekend; especially when about half the listeners were collecting their old-age pension. Noona went into a record so she turned the volume down low again.

She thought about Giles. How *was* he holding up? It was time she went round there to actually see for herself. His word wasn't to be trusted any more than hers was. She started to muse at the lack of honesty everywhere in the modern world, but decided that was another burden she wasn't going to shoulder on this particular morning.

She moved her thinking back to Greg McKenzie and tried to have a useful time conversing with herself about his brazen cheek. She thought back to their conversation and had the creepiest thought of all: that actually, he seemed totally normal. It was close to being very worrying. He was a pompous, ambitious, self-inflating workplace prat, certainly. A bullshitter, definitely. But devious schemer? Evil puppet master hell full of warped plans that destroyed careers, lives? Simone really wasn't sure, though she was ready to admit to Sarah and Marcus that she had no previous experience of dealing with psychos. All evidence roads led to Greg McKenzie but then again, no, she thought, her favourite song lyric leaking into her mind again. If it's him, how in hell have I not noticed something strange about him? Why only now is he giving me the creeps? Yes, and why do I nearly find him attractive? Maybe that's how it is with these people. They move around for years appearing to be as ordinary as Joe Bloggs and then bang - they're arrested for six murders. Then she was thinking about art again and whether she had ever seen him so much as doodle an idle drawing on a notepad? Never. The absence of the art qualification in his record nagged away at her again.

Well then, she thought as she got up to go to the newsroom and see who she could distract from their work for ten or fifteen minutes:

maybe it's not Greg McKenzie after all. The thought that it might be someone else, though, was the most frightening thing of all, though. She put that thought to the back of her mind.

She went to leave the room but remembered she'd forgotten something. 'Oh!' she went out loud. 'I forgot.' She leaned over her desk and picked up the tiny new recording gizmo England had sent her a couple of weeks ago from under a cardboard file. She looked at the control buttons, pressed 'off' and inspected it for 'rewind'. She whizzed it back for a few seconds, stopped it, and then clicked play.

'-wonder whether all the attention surrounding him isn't rather too disruptive for the station as a whole.'

Greg's voice was nice and clear. At least I haven't buggered that up, she thought. She slipped it into her pocket and left.

16

The Destruction of Giles McAndrew

Tuesday May 9th

Giles was sitting on the garden bench eating toast and drinking another cup of coffee when Simone arrived at The Barn House again at around four. Giles found half a smile for her as she came into view round the side of the house. He didn't jump in surprise because he'd heard the crunch of approaching footsteps on the gravel.

'Got the afternoon munchies?'

'I'm eating my breakfast,' said Giles, not looking up from his gaze out at the lane. She peeped in through open kitchen door. Oh, my God, she thought in horror. It was a wreck. There were cups, plates and dishes spread all over the normally immaculate counter, competing for space with empty pizza packets, dirty tea towels, pools of cold coffee and a half-destroyed plant pot, its contents spilling over an open packet of white sliced bread. For the first time since she'd known him Giles looked scruffy all over and hadn't shaved.

'All things considered, Giles, you look absolutely ghastly. I don't know whether you smack you hard or kiss you on the head.'

'As long as you don't ring for an ambulance.'

'Why should I do that?'

Giles grunted.

'No, I said, "Why should I do that?" Answer me.'

'Because I'm falling apart.'

'I was going to say, "I won't let you," but I know you well enough now – you'll do what you bloody well please.'

'What if I can't help it?'

She didn't know what to say. She wanted to say, "You're Giles McAndrew – 'course you won't have a bloody breakdown", but she was on shaky ground: she'd never been close to anyone who'd had one.

'How the hell are you going to have a nervous breakdown? – you're Giles McAndrew.'

She said it anyway because she had nothing better up her sleeve.

'I suppose you're an expert.'

'Yes, I am, actually. My mother had one and so did two of my aunties, it runs in the family.'

'When are you having yours, then?'

'Tomorrow when I come round here and find you haven't cleaned up the kitchen.'

That at least got the reaction of a halt to that line of conversation.

'I thought you were the one who gave me sympathy. The only one.'

'No. I'm not falling for that. I'm not going to indulge your ego.' She was doing that already but it was beside the point. 'I'll give you some facts - everyone's asking after you, wondering how you're taking it and wanting to know if you're okay.'

Taking what, he thought? Being taken off the air? The impending decision about suspension? Or making a pass at Lucie? He didn't have the energy to ask which of these she was talking about.

'I don't think I can go back now anyway, it'd be humiliating.'

'No, it wouldn't.'

'What - when everyone knows about me lying on the floor crying after making a pass at Lucie that she rebuffed?'

'Later on when this is all over and you can look back on it and laugh, you'll remember making a pass at Lucie Bastable and say, "despite it all I still proved my intelligence and good taste in women."'

'What are you talking about?' "you daft bat," he wanted to say. He felt such a ball of anger inside him.

'Lucie is only going to tell Sarah, no one else. I didn't even have to ask her, she told me so herself. Lucky you made your pass at just about the nicest, sweetest girl in the entire world.'

Giles looked out across the garden again.

'Yes, that spoils it for you in a way, doesn't it. You can't wallow in self-pity about that one. I'm sorry. The trouble with you, Giles, is that when the going gets tough in your life you fall apart like a wet paper bag.'

God, forgive me for saying that, she said inside her head.

'You should be Leah. You understand me.'

'Yes, but I'm not built like a goddess.'

'Neither is Lucie, actually.'

'Well, no, but what I mean is, my chest's sagging and my face is turning into a road map of London.'

'Anyway, you're right. I'm not caving in.'

'No, you're too bloody-minded. And vain. You couldn't bear being carted off in an ambulance and have them find your kitchen in that state.'

She went over and pulled his head into her midriff.

'And I'm getting a gut as well,' she said.

Giles let himself fall into her and she was glad he wasn't so revolted by her middle-age spread that he had to pull away.

278

As far as Giles was concerned he didn't deserve Simone, but she would have argued with him about that. He was arrogant and he could be guilty of loving himself too much, but there was something in him Simone could see that was pure loveliness. She wondered whether Leah had been able to see it - and bring it out. She was still so young. Or maybe it was just a case of Giles not being able to switch off the self-love when he got home.

Simone stroked his head and thought, Giles, come on now, fight back, don't go under. She tried to send the message through her fingertips to him but stopped when she realised she was practically washing his hair without either shampoo or water.

Giles hadn't noticed; he could easily have gone right back to sleep again. He felt tired all the time, and weak. He had no energy, no concentration, not even enough to go online and read up about nervous breakdowns. That was what really worried him: if he couldn't be bothered to do that, maybe it was a sign that he was sinking for real. Neither could he find the energy to tell Simone that arguing with her here like this was the only time he'd felt human in the past five days.

'Simone.'

'Yes?'

'When does it start? A breakdown? How do you know you're having one?'

Oh, Christ, here we go, she thought. This is where I get found out. She tried to bluff her way through it. Come on, she said to herself, you've seen enough episodes of *ER*, girl.

'You don't. The fact that you just asked me that question proves your miles away from having one. You're just depressed.'

'Am I?'

'Well, if you're not, I should hate to see you when you are.'

Giles tried to smile and Simone drew in a large lungful of air.

'And you've every right to be, that's the point. When this stuff happens to us, we're supposed to get depressed. It's nature's way.'

'Nature's way of what?'

'Of...of...of telling you how you need to protect yourself from harm.'

While Simone wandered where she'd plucked that idea from, Giles thought he could see her point but it didn't make him feel any better. Okay, so he felt depressed but wasn't having a nervous breakdown. Great, that was going to change everything. A tiny light appeared in his darkness however, like the first pale rim on the edge of dawn and he felt a signal of relief go off somewhere deep inside him.

The phone in Simone's bag started ringing.

'I'd better get it,' she said, breaking away. She dug it out and opened it, saw the caller's name and went white hot in the stomach.

'Hello?' she said, walking at swift retreating speed back towards her car.

'Simone? Ian. I have news for you.'

'Fire away.' She got in the driver's side and sat behind the wheel.

'Okay,' he said, heaving a sigh. 'the committee have decided not to renew his contract.'

'What? You can't do that!'

'I know how you feel, Simone, and I'm sorry.'

'Are you? Are you?' She was shouting.

'Calm down, Simone.'

'On what grounds are you doing this?' She could hear herself shrieking like a mad woman and thought, come on, Simone, you can do better than this.

'On the grounds that we can have who we damned well like presenting our radio programmes and that as a freelancer, as I'm sure you're aware, we can get rid of them at the end of a contract!'

She was lost for words.

'Look, Simone, I am sorry. I know what you think of this bloke and we know he's good. In time he'll get work somewhere else, I'm sure.'

'That's not the point.'

'Well, with the best will in the world, what is the point?'

That you're all heartless fuckers and bastards, she thought.

'The point is that you shouldn't have sacked him. You know what I think, Ian.'

'Well, you have to understand that it's the way of the world these days. There are no jobs for life anymore. We're in a competitive market place, and, you know, Giles gets paid a lot of money for the size of the station.'

'Oh, you're not saying this has something to do with money?' Cutbacks were all she needed: local radio, as everyone in it knew, had run itself on the loose change that dropped out of the pockets of the BRBC executives for years.

'That's not the main reason, but it's part of it, yes. We can get someone to replace him on a lot less. But more to the point, we really can't have our presenters getting themselves in this sort of mess. He's in a bad way, I understand...'

'How the hell do you know *that?*' she said, her voice rising to a shout again.

'It's common knowledge.'

Simone was confused. How the hell can it be common knowledge? She checked things through in her mind: I'm the only one I know who's visited him in the past week. And only Lucie, Sarah and I know about the Music Library. It didn't make sense.

'Well, I'm sorry, Simone, do call me again if there's anything else, but I have another meeting to go to in five minutes...'

'Okay, Ian.' Like hell you have, she thought.

'You've got my number...'

'Yes, I have...Oh, can I just check - is this official? I can break the news to Giles?'

'Um, a letter will be in the post this afternoon, but, um, yes, you can tell him if you think it's the right thing to do.'

'Thank you,' said Simone – thank you, you pompous, jumped up twerp. She closed the phone. She looked out the windscreen at Giles's lovely house. Skydays the cat came into view, walking along the path. She suddenly sat down in a curling motion and began licking herself. Simone wondered whether Giles would be able to take this. She decided not to think, just to get on with it. Better she tell it than he open a letter in the morning.

Giles heard the *thunk* of the car door and saw his boss come into view again, crunching the gravel more slowly this time. It's bad news, he thought. Simone turned the corner to see Giles' face looking up at her in such a way that she almost broke down herself there and then. She straightened out her throat and took a deep breath and went to his side again.

'Giles, it's bad news, I'm afraid,' she said in nothing more than a raised whisper.

He kept looking at her.

'They're letting you go.'

His face was a question mark. God, I watch too much bloody television, she thought. She searched her mind for a kind way of plunging the knife in his stomach.

'You have to leave.'

'The sack?'

'Yes.'

'You said "suspension". You said suspension was the worst it was going to be.'

'I know I did.'

'And you were wrong.'

'I know. They lied to me.' She couldn't believe it herself – and wanted to cry now from her own personal humiliation. 'They've made an idiot out of me too.'

Giles was looking away, into a vacant distance. Simone joined him. After a minute, she spoke.

'You should come and live with me for a bit.' No reaction. 'Until...until the worst is over.'

She felt a rubbing against her legs. She looked down to see Skydays. She looked up at Giles and miaowed at him.

'Does she want some food?' she said.

Giles nodded.

Simone went into the wreck of a kitchen. She thought for a few seconds, then went to the fridge. There wasn't much in there so she easily spotted the half-finished tin of cat food. She took it out and looked on the floor for the dish while Skydays mewled nearby and followed her with pleading eyes. She saw it just behind the kitchen door. She groaned as she bent to pick it up. Her mind made a new thought: I have to go to a fitness class. It jostled for attention alongside her feeling of utter betrayal and the terrible worry she now felt for Giles. Then her mind made another thought: Where does he keep the bloody cutlery? She found the drawer after two misses and took out a spoon, then dug the remaining brown sludge out of the upturned tin with it. She watched it slither into the dish that she'd put on the counter. She smell hit her: it was pretty disgusting. Skydays mewled again.

'Don't worry, puss, it's coming,' she said.

Skydays followed her as she crossed the kitchen and put the dish back down behind the door. She watched the cat dip its head into the food and then drop its rear end to the floor as it settled in for another hearty meal. She went out to Giles again, but he wasn't there.

She walked round to the back garden but he wasn't there either. Don't panic, she thought, he'll be okay. She headed for the front, clipping the handle of Giles' coffee mug as she passed the bench. She stopped to check it didn't topple on to the ground. It wobbled, then went back to an upright position. The first thing she saw when she reached the front of the house was the open garage door. She still didn't see Giles. Then he appeared from the garage opening carrying a bicycle. She stopped walking. He raised it over his head and threw it at his Range Rover. It skidded off the top of the windscreen and skimmed along the roof a little way then slid down onto the drive. He disappeared into the garage again. She started running.

'No, Giles!' she shouted.

He re-emerged with a hammer. Simone pulled up sharp still six feet from the car as Giles brought the thing down on the glass with a smash. But there was no break: the thing bounced off the surface and flew out of his hands. It sailed through the air and fell to earth on the grass. Christ, thought Simone, what are those things made of?

As Giles stood staring at the windscreen he'd failed to destroy, Simone heard his breathing. It creaked and moaned like nothing she had ever heard before. Her feet were cemented into the path as Giles turned and headed back inside the garage once more. As soon as he disappeared, she felt her feet suddenly unstuck. She went after him.

'No, Giles, stop it. It won't do any good!'

But as she reached the garage threshold he stormed past her knocking her sideway. As she reached out and grabbed the garage architrave to stop herself from falling she saw the huge sledgehammer in his hands. Then she watched him move to the side of the vehicle, raise the tool high above his head and bring it back down again.

Simone braced herself for the crash, shutting her eyes and covering her head with her arms. But there came instead a dull *thunk,* with a thin splintery sound following on immediately behind it, a grunt and cry of 'ugggh-aarggh' that could only have come from Giles, then a *bomp* and clatter that, opening her eyes, she saw and heard was the hammer ricocheting off the bonnet and then bouncing onto the gravel.

Giles had failed again.

'One more!' he shouted, 'one more!'

She tried to say, 'what do you mean, what do you mean?' but the sound wouldn't come out. In shock, she was totally lost for a course of action. She wasn't strong enough to physically prevent him from doing whatever he wanted to do, and had no faith in pleading with him to desist. In the whirling rush of her mind's energy, the thought of ringing the police skittered by with the return message that it was obvious that whatever was going to happen would be over long before they could arrive. Then she felt her legs move and the rest of her moving with them. She was following Giles to the house without knowing what purpose she could possibly serve. But her movement became irrelevant in the whirling spiral of events as Giles came rushing past her again before she could make the kitchen door. He was carrying again, but it wasn't a weapon this time. She clearly saw his eyes this time as he swept past, ignoring her. He wasn't Giles, he was someone else. He wore a look of complete madness. Simone turned on her heels and followed him once again. She tried to grasp what it was he was carrying. When she turned the corner of the house again, she saw the shape and knew.

It was the painting.

Giles stopped in front of his car again and tore at the wrapping with a demented fury, making roaring noises. The wrapping began to come away. Simone was at first frozen in horror for what seemed like an age, but then ran towards him screaming,

'No, Giles, no!' and waving her arms at him to stop.

He didn't see her anyway. He was already bringing the centre of the painting down on the wing mirror of the Range Rover. Once, twice, three times he did it then he stopped because he wasn't breaking through. He held the painting steady to inspect the damage: only a dent. Then he walked into the space of the front lawn, held the thing away from him, then kicked his leg into the middle of the canvas, heel pointing forward. The surface tore like a heartbreak, but it was wasn't enough. His heart pumping, his breath short and loud, Giles kicked through again and this time his leg went right through and held up at the knee. Then he pulled it back out of the frame and inspected his work. Apparently satisfied, he threw the remains onto the grass, then sank to the ground grunting and mumbling incoherently.

Simone Pound stood on the path behind him having watched it all, having sucked in the terror of every moment. Then she went to him with one single thought excluding all others at that moment in time: that the destruction of Catherine's beautiful painting was also the destruction of Giles McAndrew.

Part 3 – The Angel of Barton Townes

1

Goodnight Simone

Tuesday May 9th

Simone was knocked completely off her moorings. She stood above him, her legs shaking. Get a grip, woman, she said to herself, her mind reaching for itself in the midst of disaster. Her thoughts slid. *I have to get help. No, I won't. Are you going to deal with this yourself, then? – because you can't.*

She tried. She left Giles where he was. She swept up the glass with the broom she found standing at the back of the garage as if someone had put it there specifically for her. Then she efficiently swept the glittering fragments together into a small pile and steered it out of harm's way against the house wall. That would have to do for the time being. She leant the broom up against the garage wall just where she found it and went outside to tidy up the tools. She couldn't lift the dead weight of the sledgehammer so she tried dragging it. As if cowed by a loud grunt of effort, it began to follow her towards the garage opening.

Beside the entrance she noticed that the extra brick between the architrave and the house made a nice little corner into which to tuck the monstrous weapon. When you stood it up it hardly took up any space. But she had to use her foot to help push it into place and in her enthusiasm bashed her toes on the iron head. '*Bollocks!*' she said, then '*ouch!*'

She carried on.

She had no problem in dealing with the smaller hammer; there was plenty of space on one of the shelves in the back corner and she left it there. She turned round and rested for a second, and, hand on hips, found her breath coming back and the strength returning to her legs. Her arms ached though, and her toes hurt like buggery.

She went outside again and checked on Giles: he was still lying on the grass on his side. She looked for the rise and fall of his chest and saw it, bending her knees and using her hand to sight a line to his diaphragm like a civil engineer. Well, she thought: he's not dead and that's a start.

Feeling calmer, she went back into the house and searched hopefully for Giles's car keys. They weren't in the kitchen, or didn't seem to be amid the mucky debris on the counters, but she found them on the stairs, fourth step up. 'Luck, hold please,' she said aloud. She went outside again and parked Giles's Range Rover in the garage, listening for the crunch of tyre on glass.

She carefully opened and closed the car door without scratching it on the inner garage wall and felt pleased with herself. I'm calming down, she thought, pleased again, feeling a well of determination inside also. She stood behind the vehicle and clicked it all shut. The garage door was a reach, but on tiptoe she got enough hand on the handle to force it down. Once assisted, gravity swung it quickly into place with a squeak and a *clack*. Stay calm, Simone, she said. In her mind the road ahead seemed easier now. She went onto the grass and picked up what was left of the painting. She took it back to the house, hoisting the frame onto her shoulders with her arm right through the huge hole in the canvas, and after thinking about the matter for a good few moments, decided to put it out of sight behind the kitchen sofa. Then she went back to the kitchen and stood by the door as she flipped through Giles's car key ring looking for a house key. Sure enough, there it was. She tested it on the side door from the inside and it turned easily in the lock. Satisfied, she unlocked it again and re-locked it this time from the outside of the house. She marched now, round to the front of the barn house again, her jaw firmly set.

Giles was still on the grass where she last saw him. She strode across to his prostrate body and kneeled down. She tugged gently at his arm, and said, 'Come on, you're coming with me.'

As she spoke, she tugged gently at his arm to get him up. He wouldn't budge. He was moaning and muttering to himself, but almost inaudibly. She was alarmed, but carried on, with a bravado that wasn't yet ready to desert her. She tried to hear what he was saying but it seemed like a stream of nonsense so she ignored it.

'Come on, you can't stay here.' Still no movement. She tugged at him again. No response. He was quiet now.

'You better know this, McAndrew: I'm even more stubborn than you. I'm staying here until you agree to come home with me. I don't care if I sit her for a week.'

Once a minute she said more or less the same thing, but with no success. She looked up, saw the road and then the lane, but there was no one and nothing there. She tried another tack. 'Giles, if you don't come with me, I'm going to ring social services. They'll bring an ambulance and cart you off to a mental hospital.'

'I don't care,' says Giles. But within two minutes he'd changed his mind, at last moving then rising when Simone pulled again at his arm. As she walked him to the car she looked at his eyes to gauge his state of mind but they were looking down at the ground, the lower lids holding back a swelling bag of tears. The rest of his face was red and brown with teardrop stains and dirt. She opened the door for him and he got in without saying a word. Simone wasn't sure whether he was lost in some distant place or just embarrassed. As she drove homeward she asked him if he was okay but he didn't answer. She didn't bother again. When she glanced across at him at red traffic lights his eyes were fixed on the road ahead. She told him she'd go back to his house later to get him some clothes but there was no indication that the words registered.

Inside her house she made him drink some water. She took him up to the spare bedroom and told him to get in under the covers and sleep. 'I'm going downstairs,' she said, trying to keep her voice light. 'Get undressed or don't, it doesn't matter, but take your shoes off. The toilet's down the hall, the door facing you.' Simone went downstairs and left him, exhausted with distress but feeling more alive than she'd felt in a long time. She slumped on the sofa and sat there for a long time.

After she'd showered and changed, Simone Pound sat drinking whisky and watching Emmerdale with the sound on low. As she listened for Giles she kept thinking about the radio station feeling that things there were falling apart. She thought she ought to phone Sarah or Damien to make sure everything was okay but couldn't summon up the mental energy to get her backside off the couch; she'd left her mobile in the kitchen. I'll do it in a bit, she kept saying to herself. But it was evening now; TCR's output would have switched to the shared programming - broadcast from Norwich - at seven. At midnight BRMB National would kick in, and Lucie, she knew fully, would be at her post at five. Then Bob would be there. At nine Noona would take over, then Lynda, and before you knew it, Jane Landings, stepping in for Bob, would hand over to Jim and soon it would be evening again. No one would let her or the station down. The unease passed. TCR ran on tramlines. She spent some minutes wondering if it meant that her job wasn't really all that important, then said to herself, come on, Simone, you're just being a silly old fool now. She went back to thinking about Giles and listening for movement upstairs.

In the quiet of her living room, minutes passed into hours. Giles seemed settled. After the news, where no one was talking about John Clegg's hospital gaffe any more, never mind his TCR walkout, she crept upstairs to his room to check: he was fast asleep. She looked down at his face lit only by the hall light, and was amazed that it showed not a single sign of the day's holocaust. His features looked smooth and relaxed. She came downstairs again and fell asleep herself on the sofa. It was well past eleven when a stiff neck nagged her awake.

She lay in bed that night, her charge still safely tucked up in the spare bedroom, unable to fall away into sleep. She'd slept on the sofa way too long. She felt okay, only a little scared. She tried to think about what she should do in the morning but gave up within a minute. As soon as she started to process things, a kind of electrical interference cut into her mind. She couldn't form a clear picture of anything. Tomorrow she would turn her mind towards plans, schemes and secret meetings, but not now. She closed her eyes again and thought about the day just passed, though she emphatically didn't want to. She found herself dwelling on the fact that she was a sucker for waifs and strays, and how she could never pass a beggar in the street or ignore a phone call from Oxfam. As she went back past Tuesday into Monday, then further backwards into the weekend, Wednesday arrived with the silent click of 11.59 to 12.00 on her bedside clock. She was dimly aware of a change in her body. She sensed a relaxation there, something that had happened without her trying. She thought maybe it was her mind saying, Simone: enough; it's okay to let go – you can start again in the morning.

There were still many things to do and to worry about; myriad problems to solve and jobs to attend to, connected to Giles, surrounding the station, concerning her life. They would all have to wait. She turned over so she wasn't facing the luminous red light of the clock and by the time BRBC National was playing an interview Dolmo Okobole had conducted earlier that evening with a Scottish professor about his book on the philosophy of prostitution, Simone was in a deep and distant land, away with her fairies, her dreams and her garden.

2

The Excitement in the Newsroom

Wednesday May 10th

At ten-past-seven, as Lucie Bastable settled into the reporting side of her job in the newsroom having done her hour in the graveyard slot, Busy Ian Borage came through the door and said, 'Have you seen this?'

Lucie and Sonia Van Huisten both looked up instantly because of the unusual tone of his voice. Ian looked at both women.

'Giles has been sacked.'

Lucie and Sonia both got up in a hurry to read the contents of the single sheet of paper in Busy Ian's hand. It was a fax.

"Press Release," it said under the BRBC's corporate logo and London office address and began,

"Owing to these most unusual and critical circumstances, the British Radio Broadcasting Corporation yesterday terminated the contract of Two Counties presenter Giles McAndrew."

At the bottom of the page the line read,

"Elaine Wharton, Chief Press Officer, BRBC."

'Bloody hell,' said Sonia. 'We never thought for a minute they'd do that, did we? For Christ's sake…'

Busy Ian had already let his colleagues take possession of the document and was at his desk beginning to get the next part of his day organised. Lucie read the release through a third time wondering whether she'd missed something.

'It's a bit short, isn't it?' she said, wondering. 'Is it in your paper, Ian?'

'What? Oh, dunno. Take a look,' he said, handing Lucie his fresh copy of The Times. In less than two minutes she found it.

'It's in here,' she said. Sonia came over to her desk to take a look.

'It isn't much, is it?' she said; 'Two paragraphs...'

'Hmm,' said Lucie, thinking.

'…on the bottom of page…' She looked up at Lucie. '…thirteen.'

'At least we know the fax is real,' said Lucie.

'What do you mean?' said Sonia. She glanced at Busy Ian but he wasn't listening.

'Well, it's such a short press release, I wondered whether it was might be a fake or something.'

'What? Do you think someone would play games like that?' Sonia's big, nice- looking face registered a lack of belief.

'I don't know. Maybe. I don't know.'

Sonia was distracted by the arrival of Diana Clark, arriving to produce Lynda's lunchtime show.

'You're early,' she said.

'I know, I want to go into town when Next opens. They've got a sale starting. So I've got in early to get the show ready. Ooh, I am excited.'

Sonia didn't feel able to share Diana's passion for shopping but she was ready to pass on the big news.

'Giles has been sacked.'

'No!' said Diana, her voice almost a shriek. Lucie and Ian both looked up wincing. It wasn't that Diana was ditzy; she just seemed to believe that she was still five years old.

'Sorry,' said Diana, who noticed.

'It is only ten-past-seven, Diana.'

'Sorry. But blimey: Giles sacked? Where?'

Sonia handed over the press release.

'Where did you get this from?' she said. Sonia looked across at Busy Ian, who'd caught up with her in the corridor to show her a few minutes ago.

'Ian!'

'Huh?'

'Where did you find the press release?'

'It was on Jackie's desk when I came in,' he said, not looking up from his computer screen.

Lucie frowned.

For the next hour as the morning staff trickled in - Sarah; Big Dave Plymouth; Chris and Sam, the website guys; reporters Marcus, Reg and Sophie - the news was shared and the air crackled and hummed with excitement and tension. Then by the 8.30 news and sport, the room had settled again. It was sufficiently quiet for the station output to be clearly heard by any of the workers who wanted to listen. Marcus was already listening with one ear, but a jingle that he had himself written and recorded for the show last Saturday lunchtime caused him to prick up both.

"Have Bob Constable for breakfast, every day this week on Two Counties Radio."

"And, having me for breakfast at this very moment in time is Andy Hutchings, the new cricket director for Bartonshire County Cricket club. Morning, Andy..."

291

"Morning, Bob."

"Now, my spies tell me that the ECB are going to be bringing Bartonshire and Bilt into the county championship this very week, are they not?"

"Well, not exactly, Bob, and not this week." ["Oh, come on, Bob, read your script…"]

"Ah, so…"

"They're voting next week, actually, on first, whether to extend the county championship by bringing in two of the minor counties, and we're on a list of seven."

"Ah, so we've got a chance then…"

"Most certainly, Bob. But it's going to be very difficult, obviously."

"I played cricket once."

"Oh, yes?"

"Yes, I bowled a maiden over, you know."

"Oh, really?"

"Yes, we got married two months later, ha-ha."

"Ha-ha…"

"Not many people know that."

["Bloody hell, Bob, knock it off."]

Leon Dilkes was not alone in his exasperation. Bob's attempt to maintain the high standard of the breakfast show was so grimly, fascinatingly bad, Marcus had not only started to tune in on his way to the station, but was carrying on when he got to his desk. Even this morning's Giles McAndrew bombshell hadn't put a wrinkle in his new routine of switching the studio feed up when he came through the door so he could hear it clearly. Suddenly, however, he felt irritated beyond belief.

'Has anyone seen Simone? Bob Constable, this morning, Jesus!'

'She was in a while ago but I think she's gone out again,' said Lucie.

'You're right, Marcus,' said Sophie, 'somebody has to do something – what about Greg? Is he around?'

Listening intently, Sarah Billings decided that it was time to find Simone. She was aghast at the sacking of Giles but more immediately she needed to talk to her about the effect his temporary replacement was having on staff. It wasn't her place to suggest changes or even give advice without being asked first, but Bob was driving her bloody crazy too. As she exited, she had to squeeze in to let a new arrival pass through the door.

'Ah, Greg,' said Big Dave Plymouth loudly to the station number two as he ambled calmly into the room on silent shoes. 'Have you heard

292

Bob this morning? Naturally, as his afternoon producer I'm as loyal as you'd want me to be, but Marcus here seems to think that doing the breakfast show has caused his brain to spontaneously re-wire itself.'

'Really? What do you mean?'

'Well put it this way.' Big Dave took a time-out to work out exactly what he did mean. Then found the words. 'Imagine a male version of the Women's Institute in 1947 - that's who he seems to think he's broadcasting to; according to Marcus.'

Thanks, mate, thought Marcus, trying not to hide behind his monitor like a coward.

Criticizing a colleague - a non-senior management colleague, anyway - in the station hub like this was a no-no (though private conversation in pairs or small groups was a different matter altogether) but Big Dave couldn't help himself when he could use Marcus as a shield and wind him up at the same time.

'Marcus, do come and see me in my office if you've something to say in public about a presenter, but please, not here.'

There was a sudden change in the temperature of the room though no one actually said anything. Marcus went back to researching local bed and breakfasts for a package he was putting together for the drive-time show later on, but looked carefully at Greg McKenzie with a beady eye. He ducked down when he thought he might return his gaze, interesting himself in the special weekend rates at Mrs Callodyne's in Lichester Barton. Actually it was quite interesting: thirty-four quid a night? I wouldn't pay that, he thought. He swivelled his eyes towards Greg again, but he'd gone.

'Bastard,' said Marcus to Big Dave.

'Me or him?'

'Both,' said the two friends in chorus, and they both laughed.

In the Ops Room of studio 1, Leon Dilkes manfully continued the struggle with the quality of TCR morning broadcasting.

'Okay, Bob, we can't do the coastal erosion feature, we haven't enough time. I'm bringing Noona in early for a chat about last night's TV.'

'I didn't see any TV last night – I was in my shed all night.'

'Just make it up! Noona will see you through.'

'Okay.'

Bloody hell fire, thought Leon, how the hell does Bob get through his show every afternoon if he's like this? When he switched his concentration back on, a jingle was halfway through.

"– every weekday from two, stationed right here, for the people of Bart n Bilt."

"It's coming up to five-to-nine. Just time for one more item, then, ladies and gentle people of Bart n' Bilt: the erosion of our coastline. Tony Dimmock from an organisation called – "

["No, Bob - the bloke's gone, he's gone! He's not here!"]

"Bart and Bilt Coastwatch, speaking to us now from – Oh, it seems we won't be speaking to Tony Dimmock – we seem to have a technical hitch here…hang on…"

["I'm bringing in Noona, Bob. I've got her right here. Introduce her, Bob!"]

"So…I don't have a Tony but I do have a Noona. I wanted to say 'Afternoona' but I can't as it's still morning, ha-ha."

"Ha-ha, no you can't, Bob. Hi, it's me again."

"Hi, Noona, the tall, elegant Noona. I could talk to you morning, Noona and night, ha-ha."

["For goodness sake, Bob…"]

"Ha-ha. What about The Street last night Bob? Did you see it? Kevin getting barred from The Rovers…"

"I didn't see it, Noona, I was in me garden shed all night, calling a spade, a shovel."

"Oh, well then, you missed a treat."

"Something about Tranmere Rovers, was it?"

"No, The Rovers Return! Bob, where have you been all yer life?"

"Or are we talking Bristol Rovers?"

["Bob, just dry up and let Noona pilot the thing…"]

"Ha-ha, don't start talking to me about Bristols, Bob…ha-ha"

["Noona! Christ, what's got into everybody today, for crying out loud!"]

"Sounds like we need to move on, Noona, Leon – that's our producer everyone – seems to be getting his knickers in a twist."

"Sounds to me more like panties in a bunch, Bob."

"Ooh, you are awful, Noona, but I like you!"

["Fucking hell, you two! Oh, I bloody give up…"]

Marcus looked up at Big Dave who was some distance across the room. He could see from the pained sneer on his pudgy, bearded face he'd heard it too. Marcus beckoned him over with a flick of the head. Big Dave pulled up a chair and moved in close for a quiet pow-pow.

'I've got a feeling…' said Marcus.

'So have I, and it's not doing me much good,' said BD.

Marcus had to choose his words carefully. He had made his promise to Simone and was going to keep it.

294

'We've got to get a hold of Simone Pound and see if we can get her to shift Bob. He's doing my head in.'

'I know,' said BD, 'is it me or is he putting everyone in a funny mood? The place doesn't feel right.'

'Giles has been sacked - what do you expect?'

'No, it's more than that. Giles didn't have many fans in here.'

Marcus agreed. The station seemed to be completely out of sync, essentially because of one change: Bob for Marcus, Jane for Bob. He'd never thought of the day's programming having a rhythm before, one that worked, enabling the station to run with machine-like smoothness.

'It would help,' said Marcus, 'if we could start the day not listening to Bob, but everyone seems to be hooked.'

Their heads parted briefly as they paused their conversation to listen to the offending show.

'Yeah, listen,' said Big Dave, 'It's never usually turned up this high.'

Marcus didn't want to admit to being the culprit. He wasn't proud of his new obsession. He listened along with his mate.

I think, when it comes down to it, that things were never the same in Noreham after the old Empire theatre closed,' Bob was saying to the Mayor of the town. They were supposed to be having an enthusiastic discussion about the decision to build a new Arts Centre in the town. But he was steadily building a case for the fall of civilisation caused by the end of the 1950s and the rise of Cliff Richard.

'I think you may be exaggerating there,' said Mayor Jenkins, *'I think Noreham has come a long way since those days. We've - '*

'I used to go there when I was a lad. I saw Bruce Forsyth there in 1959 when he was an up and coming comedian...'

Big Dave could take no more.

'Bloody 'ell fire,' said Big Dave, leaning over Marc's monitor to switch the volume right down to nothing. 'What's got into him? He's never as bad as this on his own show.'

'He's embarrassing you, isn't he...'

'Shut up.'

'Oy, I was listening to that,' said Allan Ruzinski.

'I'm sorry, Al, but if I don't shut him off my headache's going to explode.'

'You should consider other people. It's not only me that wants to hear the programme.'

Allan looked around for support but received none. No one was ever keen to run up against Big Dave Plymouth when his temper was anywhere the wrong side of sweet, so Lynda, Busy Ian, Sophie and

Website Chris kept their heads down and their mouths closed. Allan took their apparent deafness in with disappointment but no real surprise.

'Bloody hairy-arsed biker,' he muttered, sufficiently quietly for Big Dave to miss out on the detailed contents, but he got the gist.

'Go boil your screwdriver,' he replied only loud enough for Marcus to hear. His pal laughed appreciatively, sensing that this might not be one of those days that swept by without you realizing it.

'I'm going to the loo,' said Marcus. 'Mind big Al doesn't pump up the volume while I'm gone.'

Big Dave Plymouth was bored and looked again for distraction.

'You're very quiet, Lucie,' he said, studying the fraction of her immaculate petite features not hidden by a computer screen, a pile of folders and someone else's assorted junk. She looked up and smiled.

'Are you okay?' he asked.

'Yeah – I'm okay. Y'know…'

She went back to her work. Big Dave scanned his eyes across all sides of the room like a lighthouse beam, but his colleagues were intent for now to get on with researching, writing and preparing local radio output.

Marcus didn't need to go, he just needed a break. In the corridor he met Sarah Billings for the second time that morning. They both checked behind them before they spoke.

'I'm looking for Simone – have you seen her?'

'No.'

'I'm worried, Marcus.'

'Me too.'

'What about?'

'Bob, for a start: he's a disaster. And he's making everyone jumpy.'

'Let's go to the kitchen. There was no one there a minute ago.'

They went to the kitchen and shut both doors.

Back in the newsroom, the arrival of Damien Read not long before ten aroused the quietly beavering workers' appetite for conversation again.

'Damien,' said Big Dave, still bored, waiting for Jane Landings to show. 'As one of our esteemed SBJs, what do you think of the sacking of one Giles McAndrew? Only I want him back after listening to me old friend Bob for three days. I love him and all that but he's just not a morning person.'

'It's too late for that, I think,' said Damien putting some papers down on Sarah's desk. 'Once they've made up their mind at England, that'll be it.'

'Couldn't we at least call for his reinstatement?' said Website Chris.

'Hang on,' said BD, 'I thought you hated Giles?'

'No – I never said "hate".'

'You as good as!'

'Maybe, but we've got to be professional about it. Giles is a first-rate presenter,' said the TCR webdrone, suddenly itching to get back to uploading some new material on Noreham's new Youth Hostel.

'Was,' said the normally quiet Busy Ian.

'Ian – tell us what you think for a change.' Big Dave could feel something nasty inside him incubating.

'Dave...' said Lucie Bastable, sensing the danger to the working atmosphere. She looked at him and saw him looking back; saw his eyes change. She put her head down again and wondered what it was about her that men liked so much.

'I don't think we need presenters like Giles. He got above his station-'

'Oh, very good, Ian,' said Website Chris, wheeling his chair back towards the centre of the room and the conversation.

'Above himself, I mean, and *ideas* above his station.'

'Hang on.' Lynda Parvis had finished typing an important line into her script and now looked up animatedly. 'Without freedom of speech, what is the point of radio? And whatever you say about Giles McAndrew - '

'Don't tell me: "he was popular",' said BD.

'There's no need to be cynical, darling,' said Lynda. 'Without good ratings, we'd all be out of a job.'

Big Dave wanted to tell her how thick she was, knowing that local radio was more than holding its own in 2006 and that BRBC moved so slowly anyway, they'd all be past retirement age if they ever decided to abandon the regions.

'I don't think things will ever come to that,' said Website Chris.

'Don't you bank on it,' said Lynda. 'This digital thing means thousands of stations, potentially. If people don't listen to us, we've had it.'

'I'll just go and work for one of the new ones, don't worry,' said Big Dave, annoyed.

'They won't want reporters, and even if you can get a producer's job, they won't let the likes of you on the radio in the evenings, honey. No offence.'

'Steady, Lynda,' said Damien. 'And anyway, we're more than doing alright. We've got a very decent audience share at the moment, so none of us has any cause to worry.'

'So what are you saying, then, Damien, that we don't need Giles back?' said Chris.

'Whether we do or we don't is not the issue. He's had his contract terminated, so...'

'He couldn't come back anyway from what I hear,' said Sophie, who'd just come back two minutes before from reading the news.

Busy Ian and Lynda, who'd started to look at their screens again, and Big Dave, who was cleaning out one of his ears, looked interested again.

'Well, go on then,' said Lynda, as Greg McKenzie ambled into their midst.

'No, it's okay.'

'Have you clammed up because of me, Sophie?' said Greg. 'Whatever it is, I don't mind.'

Her uncertain eyes returned to a look of neutral concern.

'I just heard that he wasn't doing too well, that's all.'

'Have you heard how he's doing, Greg?' said Big Dave.

'It wouldn't be right of me to say anything,' said Greg, addressing the whole room.

'Oh, come on now, Greg, don't be a spoil sport,' said an interested Lynda.

'Okay. I suppose I can let you know that he hasn't taken the news of his being released very well.'

'Funny that: I was expecting him to come bursting through the door with a crate of Champagne any moment,' said BD.

Several people laughed really quite loudly in response, even though none of them much liked the joke-maker. Greg McKenzie, holding his folder closely to his chest, looked less than amused.

'We were talking just now about whether it would be a good idea to try to get Giles back,' said Lynda, swinging her chair right round to face the station number two. 'What do you think? Hypothetically – we know we won't get him back, but in a perfect world...'

'We're already looking at possible replacements.'

There was almost a team response to that in the form of a loud groan.

'How are you looking at replacements? He only got the push yesterday afternoon.'

'I've just taken a phone call from England: we've been told we've to find a replacement, and find one from within.'

There was an almost audible gasp that went 'ooh' and swept across the whole newsroom.

'The excitement,' said Sophie, to no one in particular, 'it's almost too much.'

3

Do Not Forsake Me, O My Elton

Simone awoke at ten-to-six because she needed the loo. On her way back to bed she touched the button on top of her radio alarm with a fingernail that triggered the sound of a song petering out and Lucie Bastable's voice kicking in:

'Todd Rundgren there with 'I Saw The Light.' *It's nine minutes to six at Two Counties Radio... You probably haven't got your morning paper yet, but I tell you what: I was wondering the other day about our papers after reading about journalists going through Gwyneth Paltrow's dustbin; and I thought, "what gives them the right? What sort of country are we living in when grown men are paid by newspapers to stick their hands in chicken bones, used tissues and wet nappies? Have you got any thoughts on that? Give me a call, Lucy Bastable, on 0299 454545..."'*

Simone smiled. She'd do alright in the business would that girl. But she wasn't in any shape yet to listen to any more so she hit the off button and lay right down again in the hope of falling asleep again. The next thing she knew the seven o'clock alarm was thrusting boy band pop music like a man's fist through a hole in her consciousness. It was fine, though: she was pleased to know she'd managed to give her body almost an hour's more rest. If she was any judge of how the day in front of her was going to unfold she would need it.

She checked on Giles again. He was still sleeping soundly. Great, she thought, but she dreaded his waking up and having to face the unknown of his mood. What was she going to do with him? He had no family to go to or call up to come and look after him and no close friends either as far as she knew. He'd have to stay cooped up in the house all day, with perhaps a walk into town if he felt up to it for variety. But one thing was certain: she'd have to make sure he stayed away from the station this time.

She slipped downstairs on deliberately light feet and put on the kettle for a cup of tea, then she leant on the counter deep in thought about Giles. Was his act of vandalism just his mind's healthy response to appalling stress? Or was it the beginning of complete mental disintegration? She didn't know the answer and didn't want to guess. She took a single mug of tea upstairs and went to her bedroom again, creeping softly as if trying not to wake a fractious baby. She lay on the bed, switched TCR on again and got Bob running down the list of wonderful Wednesday events across the two counties. She thought of Lucie again and smiled. She was proud of her. Then she turned Bob right down low so she could think.

She finished her tea and lay her head down on the pillow. Where do I stand in all this, she mused? Where is my place? She didn't mind taking responsibility for Giles, she really didn't, but still, she had to keep some sort of focus on herself lest she lose her grip on the station. Life could be so hard, even when you knew that you were so well off compared to most human beings on the planet, you deserved a smack in the chops if you ever moaned about anything.

Oh, Elton, she said as if he could hear her, what would you say to me now if you were here? What song would you play for me? Her thoughts became hazy as her horizontal rest made her slightly drowsy again.

Within moments she was away back in her teenage Elton John daydreams - she still used them in times of stress even after all this time. She was back in the days of '72 and '73. She and her friends, Mary Hynes, Ann Norris and Susanne Chanter taking the train up to town for big concert nights: Rod Stewart and The Faces at the Sundown; Bowie at The Rainbow; Elton at Hammersmith; Roxy at the Rainbow too. Coming home on the last train to be taxied home by Dad, going to bed late on school nights drunk with pleasure and fantasizing about the next time. In a year's time, a single but important year older, she'd be in the limo with Elt as they slipped away from the stage door after the second sell-out night at the Odeon, screaming, delirious fans pressing their made up faces and feather cut hair at the windows, shouting *'Elton, we love you'*. The adrenalin from another fantastic concert would launch them all the way back to their West End hotel: Rod – in his tartan scarf - and his latest flame would be there. Wrapped up in Elton and glasses of champagne she would hear him saying,

'I'm looking for a personal assistant, Simone; you're young but you're just what I need. Come and work for me.'

She came out of the dream. Oh, Elton, where did it all go wrong for you and me? You with your wild spending, your confused sexuality and your cocaine habit: me with my boring face and dodgy degree from Leeds Poly? Deep inside her head, Simone laughed at herself. She was ridiculous, she knew that. I didn't do so bad with my career, she thought. Radio has been good to me, said a voice somewhere in the swirl of the dream's dissolving fragments, and she heard a chuckle come out of her mouth even though she would have sworn she hadn't intended one to.

Her idol was still there. Don't forsake me, will you, Elton, she said to him. Don't let go of me. Help me get Giles out of this mess. And when you've done that, please help me to get out of mine.

In her mind's music room she was humming *Your Song*, then *Rocket Man*, then the chorus of *Daniel*. She felt herself becoming more cheerful. Ah, Elton, you never let me down, she thought, and in a few more seconds had fallen off a ledge into the soft morning clouds of extra sleep.

She knew even before she opened her eyes that she'd really messed up and overslept. She twisted her body round so she could see the clock: 8.40. Twenty-to-bloody-nine! Her first decision was to get into the shower double quick, but she quickly reversed that to go check on Giles. She left her bedroom with a bit of a bang but opened his door with exaggerated care so as not to wake him. When her head reached the gap and her eyes met the room the duvet was pulled back to reveal a rumpled bed sheet, and the chair in the corner was shockingly empty of the clothes she'd put out for him last night. She turned around and checked the bathroom but she knew before she saw the wide open door and the empty space beyond that he was gone.

4

He's Leaving Home

Giles McAndrew woke as soon as he saw light filtering in between the bedroom curtains. Within two minutes his mind was gathering itself up into a state of readiness for movement. He was getting out. He found his clothes where Simone had neatly stacked them on a small armchair and pulled them on being careful to keep his noise to an absolute minimum. He by-passed the bathroom on tiptoes with a certain amount of regret and found his way downstairs. Full bladder or no, he was not going to risk waking her. He thought her intentions fine and noble but he wasn't going to be anyone's patient or prisoner.

He thought he could make a quieter exit from the back door and he was right. Once he'd closed the hall door to the kitchen Simone's unconscious mind failed to pick up the click of the turning lock and the creaking of the door as Giles pulled it to, even as it surged on full alert in the world of sleep.

The escapee trod as lightly as he could with trainer footsteps on Simone's front drive. No sound emanated from each collision of shoe with ground. He stopped as the drive gave way to pavement and looked up at the front upstairs windows. Nothing moved behind the glass. The state of the day gave him cause to pause further like some animal sniffing the wind: this was almost the early morning he was used to getting up to, only the light of dawn was later and less blue. He looked up to get a sense of where he was. Parsons Avenue. He knew it. Going left would take him towards town, easily the shortest way to Corumby. He started off and began to calculate how many miles it was on foot. Five-ish was the reckoning, so not all that far. And he wouldn't need to go right into town; he could cut through the road that went past the train station and then turn right into John Street. That would cut a mile off his normal route home from TCR.

Giles started to run, jogging quite slowly, trying to pace himself. The bland suburbs of Barton Townes lay on dead flat ground so he made good progress. He was surprised at how many windows were lit and how many cars and vans went past him; how early people went to work. It was only twenty-to-six. On a normal working weekday, he would have been at the station for more than an hour already, getting ready for his show, oblivious to the rest of the town.

After about five minutes he began to slow down to a fast walk and decided to hold it there. The railway station came within sight on the left and quickly grew in size. People in smart office garb were already making their way to the trains from taxis and cars that dropped them off before moving smartly away again, their exhausts puffing out little tufts of white smoke. Giles could feel the dawn urgency of the London-bound traveller as he and she marched past the red station sign as if already late for an important meeting.

He felt like he was steaming with sweat. In John Street he slowed to look in the huge glass frontages of Sweet Suites and Co, the place where he bought his sofa and easy chairs, new coffee table and matching CD storage unit. It was six months ago now. He suddenly saw an image of Leah standing in the store hands on hips looking down at the creamy material covering a gorgeous sofa. He could hear her saying, 'Giles, if you don't buy this right now, you're an idiot,' in the days when she said such things in jest. He wondered where she was and whether she missed him. He pictured her in bed still asleep, looking like an angel. He felt himself missing her, pining for her, somewhere in the morass of the churning hurt inside him. He started to jog again, thinking that it might help the feeling to pass away. He realised within a few strides however, that he didn't really want it to.

He'd tried to bury the loss of her in the past few days but he realised it had been a mistake. The pain of missing her wasn't as bad as trying to blot her out. And it wasn't as bad as the one that had overwhelmed him straight after Simone told him in the studio that she'd left - the one that made him feel like his whole life was sliding down a chute towards oblivion. This pain wasn't like a slow fall into the abyss, but one with a burning sweetness to it. And instead of coming at him like a knife in the head, this one hit him in the stomach and chest. This one left him smouldering in romantic betrayal and loss, like a thousand burned love letters.

He tried to hold on to the new and better pain as he reached the end of John Street and turned right where the road became a lane that opened up rural Bartonshire again. He was still three miles from home. He stopped before crossing the road and realised he was out of breath. He felt tired and uncomfortable. The heroic chest pain began to feel more like an oncoming heart attack. He looked down at his left arm as his mind felt there for a real stabbing or shooting discomfort but there was nothing there. Still. He was a fit guy of forty and he'd had a lot of good sleep overnight. He should have had more energy than this.

He walked out on to the left hand side of the road and started thumbing for a lift. He didn't fancy his chances, a man alone at this time of the morning, but in less than a minute and not much progress along the grass verge, a small yellow car pulled up ten yards in front of him. When Giles reached the passenger door the driver, a woman had already lowered the window and was leaning over towards him.

'Hello. Do you need a lift?'

'Yes. Please.'

'Where are you going?'

'Corumby.'

'I can take you. Get in.'

He thought he could have walked the rest of the way but when he put his bottom on the seat and felt the backrest against his spine he realised that the only thing that had kept him moving was adrenalin. He felt exhausted. He wanted to go back to sleep.

'Are you okay?'

Giles was busy wondering whether she'd say anything about the state he was in. He looked down at his trousers and realised that he'd put on clean clothes that Simone had put out for him without realizing. They looked terrible. I must look like a madman to a woman like this, he thought to himself. His face had to be grubby because he hadn't washed and he was still sweating.

He didn't know what to say.

'You're puffing and blowing – have you been running?'

The woman had a sort of knowing look on her face that started up his thinking again. Did he know her? He took a quick sidelong look at her but didn't recognize her. At least he didn't think he did.

'Yes. I've been working all night.'

It came out before he realised it must have made him sound like some kind of idiot. He tried to think of a way to explain his unwashed face and his dirt smeared hands, thinking of a sensible way to answer the inevitable question,

'So what have you been doing to get so dirty?'

But it never came. At least her silence told him that she didn't recognize Giles McAndrew of Two Counties Radio fame. That was a relief. He looked at his dirty hands again and was thankful it wasn't blood. He turned his head a fraction so he could see her from the corner of his eye while he waited for another question. She was younger than him, with blonde hair cut straight, neat and clean to her shoulders. She wore a deep pink sweater over a white t-shirt and black cords. Casual black shoes. She also wore a facial expression that didn't change through the next mile and beyond, a half-smile, as if she saw right through him.

'Whereabouts in Corumby?'

Smart woman, he thought. We're not there yet but she's already getting prepared to drop him. Her smile is a front. She's a little scared. I don't blame her, he decided. On the other hand, he couldn't feel any fear on her.

'Do you know the Farmer's Arms?'

'Yes.'

She nodded her head. Giles saw the Corumby road sign coming into view about a hundred metres ahead.

'It's the next right down the lane there, signposted to Newton Stone, but you can drop me at the pub.'

'Okay,' she said brightly.

She reminded him of an actress he'd seen on television. Or in a film. Maybe it was both. He knew in the circumstances that his mind might be playing him tricks but he didn't think so. He didn't know her name, but he knew she was good looking. Giles found himself looking at the woman's hand for a wedding or engagement ring before he realised what he was doing. Her fingers were completely clean.

When he looked out the window again she was pulling up right next to the pub.

'There we go. Is that okay?'

'Yeah, fine, I can walk from here, it's not far.'

'Right,' she said, smiling at him full in the face.

'Well,' he said, opening the door. He looked back as he went to close it. 'Thanks very much, I really appreciate it.' He tried to smile brightly back.

'That's okay,' she said, and as soon as he closed the door she drove off. He watched the car disappear into the morning. Then he looked at his watch. It was a touch past six-twenty. She was bright and awake for this time of the morning, he thought. He crossed the road and started walking down the lane, not feeling quite so bad. He was still alive after all. And the pain in his chest seemed to be drifting away.

5

Simone's Station Nightmares

Simone swept back to her room where she wrenched off her pyjamas and threw them at the bed. She stood there in a rage cursing her luck then stomped along the landing to the bathroom and got in the shower. It was all getting messier and messier and it was hard to see a way out. She kept the shower head down at shoulder height to keep her hair from getting wet then struggled to wash her face without splashing water upwards. She more of less succeeded but the effort this fussing cost her made her half-scream, half-shout in frustration.

'Bloody bastard,' she muttered under her breath, meaning the situation, not Giles. It was fine playing the good Samaritan but it was tiring and it was irritating and she would just be so pleased for things to return to some sort of normality; to the problems she was used to: of being plain, flat-chested and fifty-one.

Mess, mess, mess, it was all a *fucking* mess. She turned up the temperature of the water and tried to picture the morning ahead of her in terms of planned events, but she couldn't do it. When she thought of Giles she saw a massive distraction from her job. When she thought of Greg McKenzie, a fog descended on her mind. Fixing him was also part of her job but in the end it was another additional extra. She didn't even know for sure that he was the one. Further, she'd done nothing yet to trap him so his guilt might be revealed. She felt bad about her inaction. Terrible. No excuses, Simone. Come on, wise up; get smart. Get moving, get working. Get thinking, for Christ's sake.

She stepped out and grabbed a big towel down from the heated rail. Drying off the edges of her hair where the water splashed, she examined the Giles situation again. I have tried, she said to herself, but I can't keep him prisoner. If something terrible is happening to him right now then at least I was the one who tried to save him. Even if I'd locked the doors and hidden the keys he would still have climbed out the window.

Now bloody Greg McKenzie flooded her mind. I have to get help on this, she said to herself. I need to get Sarah and Marcus together at the station as soon as I can. But the time wasn't there to think clearly about anything yet - she was appallingly late. When she'd dressed, fixed her face and done the best she could with her hair she went down to the kitchen and switched on her phone. There were seven messages. Three were from Sarah, all sent this morning, saying 'Where are you?' No detail. She scooted from the house and drove off with her engine burning petrol hard, deciding now to forget the Giles disaster for a bit, and focus properly on the Greg problem.

She looked to Elton again to keep her going. She sang the one about being in a bad patch to herself unaccompanied with a despondent look in her eyes as she turned onto the main road into town. She hummed the line about not being able to get much sleep. The lyrics were too near the mark. She might start to cry if she wasn't careful, if she wasn't determined. She concentrated on accurately keeping the tune to tamp down her emotion. Her singing wasn't that bad, but it was suited to a church choir, not pop. She hummed on as her car flew past the entry sign into Barton Townes by the old brewery ten miles an hour over the legal limit. When she reached the chorus of 'Too Low For Zero' she was a little calmer, considering now how well the title fit the day. No, it wasn't that good a match really. In the songs, Elton's glitzy rock and roll world seemed a much simpler place than the one she inhabited on a daily basis. Here in Barton Townes, poetically simplifying life's grim reality was nothing short of an unearned luxury.

Then she was back to thinking about Giles. She felt herself beginning to lose patience with him and this made her feel guilty. No, Simone, went the sound of her own mind in her head, that's a luxury now. You must focus on the station – you've so much to do. It was twenty-past nine and she hadn't shown her face yet, today of all days, the one when she'd have to begin by telling everyone that Giles had been sacked. She wouldn't go further than that. His mere dismissal would be more than enough juice for them to be going on with. Then straight after she'd have to negotiate her way through a meeting with Greg McKenzie, which might prove to be very interesting but was still a total pain in the mind. She desperately needed a coffee. She felt for the taste in her mouth but there was nothing but staleness. She wondered if her breath smelt.

When she turned into the station she noticed the absence of press – 'that's something at least,' she muttered aloud, and was about to curse the lack of a car space when she saw Sarah on her way out in a TCR Peugeot daubed with town and village names from both counties. God, it looked horrendous, she thought; we must do something about it when this is over. She wound her window down as the cars met. Sarah was doing the same.

'I've noted the mileage, don't worry,' she called across.

'Bugger the mileage,' said Simone, 'I wanted to see you.'

307

Sarah pulled up the handbrake, got out of the car and started round towards Simone's open window.

'It's okay, you didn't have to-'

'Marcus and I were wondering – I hope this isn't going to sound rude – but we thought you might have got in touch to warn us that Giles had got the sack.'

Horror leaked from some place deep inside Simone and spread like burning butter down her stomach lining.

'What are you talking about? I'm the only one who knows!'

Sarah looked puzzled.

'There's a press release at the station.'

'What?'

'Saying that Giles has had his contract terminated.'

'Who gave it to you?'

'No one – it wasn't given to any of us, I don't think. I think someone just found it on the front desk when they came in this morning.'

This was completely wrong.

'Who is it addressed to?'

'Um, don't know,' said Sarah.

'Where is it?'

'I got it from Damien, and put it on your desk. Under your mouse mat.'

Simone grunted her approval.

'Fine. Where are you off to?'

'Barchester.'

'For?'

'Report on school dinners.'

'Why are you going out to do it?' said Simone. As a rule, SBJs didn't go do much bog standard reporting.

'Oh, I felt like I needed a break from the station. And Lucie's got a bad stomach. I'm doing her a favour.'

'Is she at home?'

'No. She's in.'

'You're not meeting Jamie Oliver are you?' said Simone.

'I wish.' They both knew that if Sarah was meeting Jamie Oliver, Simone would have known about it, but it didn't matter. 'No. Just something on price rises.'

'Come and see me as soon as you get back, I want to meet with you and Marcus.'

'Okay. I'll be as quick as I can.'

' When you get back, if I'm not in, phone me straight away.'

'Okay. Good luck.'

'Good luck? What do you mean?'

'Oh. People are going fairly crazy inside.'

'About Giles?'

'No, about Bob.'

Sarah saw her reaction.

'Actually, it isn't that bad... Well, not really.'

'Is Greg in?'

He had to be. She wanted to nail him. Otherwise the day was going to be the worst of all time.

'Oh, yes.'

'Okay.   See   you.'

'You too.'

Simone parked her Golf in the space Marcus had left behind spraying 'f' words under her breath as she got out. Then she stopped herself. Simone, get a grip, she told herself. She stood still and took in deep breaths. One, two, three, four, five. Come on, you're going to get nowhere if you don't calm down. Another favourite song came into her head, the David Gray one about the madness all around. She started walking at a deliberately steady pace towards the back door. Then she changed her mind; she would attack the problem from the front. She began to pick up speed as she walked around the side of the building towards the front entrance. When she reached the threshold she fairly burst through it. Jackie Husband immediately came out from behind her desk to meet her.

'Simone, thank God – they're going a bit doo-lally in there this morning.'

'So I hear...'

'Oh,' Jackie replied, a touch disappointed, but carried on. She nodded over Simone's shoulder. 'Bob Constable's went through that door in a huff a minute ago and people keep coming through here to me moaning and complaining.'

'What about?'

'Oh, you know, everything, really.'

Simone felt the finger of pressure pressing harder inside her head.

'No, I don't know, Jackie.'

'Oh, hello, can I help?'

Jackie was now smiling over her shoulder. Simone turned to see a smartly dressed, pretty east Asian woman smiling back.

'I'm Fung-Lee Cho – I'm on Noona's show just after ten?'

'I'll catch you later, Jackie,' said Simone smiling politely but briefly at a successful local restauranteur.

'No, hang on.'

Simone hung on while Jackie made Fung-Lee welcome and asked her to take a seat.

'Come behind my desk,' said Jackie. 'I need to tell you something.'

'What?' The look on Jackie's face caused Simone to feel the finger now hovering over the panic button ready to press.

'You had a phone call from England. From Her Majesty herself…'

Oh, my God, thought Simone.

'…Andrea Potter-Symons.'

'Fine,' she said, glumly nodding.

'Not that it was her in person; it was her PA.'

'She wants to come here to see you.'

'Oh, sh-ugar, you are joking?'

'No. You've got to ring the PA.'

'Okay, give me the number.'

Jackie Husband tore off the page from her notebook and gave it to Simone.

'Shall I wear my best dress when she comes?' said Jackie.

'Of course. And we'll do cucumber sandwiches for her,' said Simone.

She went into the station proper via the security-coded door. The corridor was empty, which was a relief, failing as it did to reveal any panicking employees. She peeked through the small circular window into the studios corridor but there was no sign of life there either. She stood stock-still and turned up her hearing, and heard Noona introducing a record from a speaker in the ceiling. She felt her stomach relax. For a second of madness she'd been struck by the irrational fear that everyone had deserted the building leaving TCR broadcasting silence to the two counties.

Through the fire door ahead of her she saw the closed Newsroom door shut. It was never closed. As she reached it, she heard raised, muffled voices. She opened the door and immediately found herself on the edge of a volcanic argument.

6

The Tower on Tower Hill

'...and that's the Two Counties travel news from me, Sheila Davidson!'

[Jingle] "Two Counties Tra-vel."

'Thank you, Sheila. That's not too depressing then for a Thursday morning.'

'No, Bob, everything's going pretty well out there on the roads of the two counties this morning.'

'I've always said, "I like our roads."'

'Really?'

'Yes. Despite what everyone says these days, they're still one of the best things about living in the Untied Kingdom.'

'You mean, "United",' said Sheila.

'What did I say?'

'"Untied".'

'That reminds me.'

'What?'

' I need to buy some new shoelaces on the way home.'

'Ha-ha.'

'No, I'm serious; I snapped one doing them up this morning and I had to tie one of those funny little knots that my wife says make me look like a tramp. Shame you're in Birmingham and I'm here otherwise you could see it.'

'Bob, you're not supposed to tell the listeners we're in separate studios, ha-ha.'

'Well, actually, you're not in a studio at all, are you, Sheila, more a cell with an old desk and a microphone.'

['There goes the magic of radio; thanks, Bob' said Big Dave]

Skydays was outside the back door curled up in a discontented sleep. When she heard Giles's feet on the gravel she immediately sprang up and started making a noise. Giles heard it before he turned the corner.

Giles went to the rockery surrounding his barbeque, got the spare back door key from under the stone and let himself in. He saw the mess in the kitchen and was surprised - he didn't remember it being that bad yesterday. It looked like a wave of terror had been inflicted on the place. Skydays had followed him in yowling for food. He bent down to a cupboard and got hold of a tin of Felix. He ripped the top off and placed the can on the floor. The cat pounced on it and started biting into the top layer of meat.

He went up to the top of the house to get changed, then came straight down again. Skydays had tipped her tin of Felix over in the struggle to fill her belly. Giles picked her up and dropped her outside the door. She yowled at him again. He went back inside and put on the trainers he used for biking, then went to the utility room to get out his machine. He pushed it outside and left it against the wall while he locked up the house. He placed the single key into the small pocket of his biking top and cycled off.

As he turned off the path into the lane, he checked the sky for weather as a matter of routine. It was a hazy blue, the sun still rising. It was ten to seven.

Giles didn't know if he was tired. He just wanted to get where he'd decided where he was going: Tower Hill. A mile from the house the familiar sign came into view: 'Tower Hill 3'. It was a road he often took: at the end of it was the best view in the east of England.

The miles passed quickly as Giles's £900 racer ate up the ground. He had to slow down while a guy, on the phone in a silver Audi, flashed by going the other way. The road gradually sloped upwards, but Giles didn't need to change gear. He was fitter and stronger than most men of forty and his speed barely slowed. Despite everything, even now he enjoyed the comforting feel of the way his feet slotted into the toe clips on the pedals. His body was grooved to the process of forward movement today as it always was, which seemed rather marvellous in the circumstances.

Five minutes further on the road swerved sedately around a copse and like a scene from a fairy tale a tower appeared in the distance at the top of the hill. It was tall and rounded, made of two hundred year-old stone and its crusty castellated top, an oddity of the Bartonshire landscape, attracted visitors of all sorts at all times of the year. The last mile of road that led right up to it was dead straight; Giles cruised along it, watching the grey tarmac ahead, occasionally raising his eyes to the tower as it got larger and larger.

Then he was there. At the t-junction that almost collided with the foot of the building, he pulled up gently, though there wasn't a single piece of traffic within sight and sound. He looked all around him; it was a lonely spot, almost deathly quiet. Then he looked up at the top of the tower, shielding his eyes from the rising sun, half-expecting someone to look out over the edge at him. There was no one up there. Looking down again, just across the road the white street sign with its special, stylish black lettering stared at him: 'Tower Hill' it pronounced.

Without knowing why, he dismounted and walked his bike across the junction to the narrow tower gate that was painted in dark blue. On the grass just behind it was a blue sign with a gold border. 'Barton's Tower' it said; built in 1817 by the fourth Earl of Barton to celebrate the defeat of Napoleon a couple of years previously it said underneath. Beside it was a smaller newer sign telling the visitor about the Trudby windmill that was knocked down to make way for the landmark. Giles read, but couldn't have cared less, even though Daisy Smith had done her first ever live report from here almost a year earlier that had gone out on his show. It had been Windmill Week on Two Counties Radio.

Giles picked up his bike and swung it over the gate and, tensing his biceps, was able to hold it steady as it completed its journey to ground again. He walked himself and his machine along the short path to the splendid edifice. He patted the stone with his right hand and rubbed it a little. It was reddy-coloured, actually, the stone. Then he continued along the path as it curved around and behind the tower. The wheels of the bike made a gentle clicking sound beside him as he went. Beyond the far side of the tower the path pushed out another twenty metres to an edge, Barton's Edge. A fence stopped him, neatly made of cast iron, consisting of two horizontal lengths at calf and groin height and a vertical post every four metres. Giles went to the edge, parked his bike carefully and looked out.

A broad plain of fields lay before him in gold, green and brown, stretching out almost biblically in the morning sunshine to a new horizon ten or twenty miles away. He had no idea about distance really. Giles shielded his eyes again and concentrated on the farthest point at the edge of sight, looking for the sea. He felt his body pushing at the metal bars of the fence. The meeting point of land and sky was lost in a haze of mist, but the dark end of land could have been the sludgy seabed left by a receded tide; he wanted it to be but it was too far away to be certain. Then he pulled back a foot and looked down right below him. His eyes were pulled towards a grey tarmac road that seemed to come out from under the hill he was standing on. It made off towards the horizon in an arrow-straight line, accompanied all the way by a blue-water dyke. They two lines didn't so much split the coloured fields as balance them in a stunning harmony through perfect arterial correctness. Giles travelled along them with his eyes, mesmerised, until the road made a crossroads about a mile away. There was a building there, a pub. You could see the sign. Its walls were painted yellow. Then he was drawn to a car coming to the crossroads from the north. He followed it as it slowed, turned right, then begin to come towards him. He watched it close in on the foot of Tower Hill, then stop at a junction almost directly below his feet. He recognized the make of car: a blue sports car, a Toyota. The top was down so he had a good view of the couple in the front. They wore casual clothes, and both had sunglasses on already. It was going to be some day; a day for a road trip, to somewhere special perhaps. Flying across the land they'd go, the wind in their hair, landing at an idyllic country pub for lunch in a coloured garden. They'd probably taken the day off work.

If I were to just walk off the edge, Giles thought, it would all be over.

Five minutes later, though he had no idea how long, Giles McAndrew was still looking out over the Bilt plain. He was leaning on the railing again but it was higher here, out on a curved parapet built specially for a tourist telescope.

'Wise move.'

He turned around to his left. A woman was standing there.

'What?'

'Wise move – I wouldn't have done that either.'

It was the woman who'd given him a lift home an hour ago.

'What do you mean?'

'Well, if you'd jumped, you'd have just become a pile of bones, mush and tomato sauce down there. Not good.'

'I had no intention of jumping.'

'Good.'

Giles hadn't meant to say that. That he had had no intention of jumping.

He tried to take a good look at her. She seemed to be about thirty, and she was tallish and slim standing up. She was blonder than he remembered from the car, though it may have been the sun.

'Yes?' she said.

'Are…whe…Nothing.'

'Can we go and sit down over there?' There was a bench further along the path overlooking the view. Giles said nothing but started walking with her.

'It also leaves a lot of other mess behind.'

'What does?' said Giles.

'Dying.' She looked towards the edge.

'I'm sorry?'

'It's not just the one who comes to identify what's left of you, it's the people who care about you, who'll miss you.'

'Just a minute.'

'You're always saying you're Giles McAndrew – it's time you started to think a lot harder about what that means.'

What?

'How the hell do you know I'm always saying that?'

'You can admit it to me. Come on.'

Giles just looked at the view.

'You're a doer; so stay here and do.'

'I wasn't going to do it. I told you!'

'Not this time.'

He thought about that. He thought about why he'd come to Tower Hill.

'Alright, not this time, no…'

'I thought you weren't a quitter.'

'I'm not. You know my radio show, don't you?'

'Of course.'

Ah, there it was.

'So I'm not a quitter; I'm not cowardly.'

'That's not what your friends think.'

'What friends?' The thought that he hardly had any friends flashed across his mind again like electricity. 'Who have you been talking to?'

'That's a private matter. Sorry.'

Secrets and confidences; he hated them. Then Giles had an inspiration.

'Do you know Leah? Are you a friend of Leah?'

'I have to go.' But she didn't get up, she looked at him. She was better than nice looking. She was very pretty, with a strong, yet womanly face.

'I just came to tell you not to quit.'

'Quit?'

'You know: give up. Don't give up.'

Easier said than done, he thought; he didn't say it.

'Well, I have to go.'

She looked at him. He was looking across at the view.

''Bye, Giles.'

He was miles away, mulling over the quitting issue, but the voice, as if working off some time-delay device, eventually reached him. He looked at her again.

'Oh. Okay. 'Bye.'

There was something he wanted to say, something to do with Leah, but he lost it. He decided to let her go. If Leah did send this woman, she'd be back. Or – his hopes rose – Leah herself would return. He watched the woman walk to her car that she'd parked by the gate in front of the tower; then he followed it with his eyes as it sped off down the road that went north to Noreham, the sun glinting off the roof. Giles decided to get back on his bike. He started to follow the woman's trail but really it was only a coincidence. After a hundred yards or so he turned left onto a lane that would soon link up with the road on which he'd pedalled up to the tower not half an hour before.

As he smoothly powered his wheels round he felt better, but he didn't know why. He thought it might be the knowledge that Leah hadn't gone for good, that she hadn't forsaken him. But the idea didn't catch hold. His mind went back to the woman's words about quitting; something inside was agreeing with her: that maybe there were times in life where the burden you carried just got too much for you and left you with no choice but to buckle at the knees. But this moment wasn't such a one for Giles. Rhythmically progressing along the lane, the sun still warming his back and making the fields shine before the blue sky, he suddenly felt stronger, as if his feet were planted on solid ground again. That's an odd thought, he said to himself, seeing as I'm pedalling my bike. He laughed ruefully out loud. He did feel better, he really did. He looked up and noticed how clear the sky was, how gorgeous and sort of milky it was. He had a feeling that it had been up there shining for the last few days. He realised he couldn't remember the last time he'd noticed the weather.

'I *am* Giles McAndrew,' he said aloud, knowing there was no one around to hear him as he gathered speed on the downward slope of the escarpment. He lifted his backside above the saddle and looked into the sunny fields that seemed to be sharing his journey. There was a scarecrow over the low hedge to his left, but not a living soul within earshot.

Maybe there is a way out of this, he thought. He could see more clearly now what a daze he'd been in since Leah left him. Worse, he'd been in some deep dark place, in some sort of cave. He increased the pressure on the pedals and picked up more speed. The air felt good as it rushed past his face. That's a start at least, he said inside: just to feel things again. He rode along further, not rushing and thought, but I'm not out of the woods yet, not by a long chalk.

Giles pulled over to the verge and stopped. There was still no sign of any traffic. He closed his eyes and looked deeply inside his mind. He felt something like an ache and his eyelids felt heavy, sore. He imagined this conscious part of his mind probing down, down, deeper down into the centre of his being. He was looking for something.

He found it. He kept his eyes closed and his mind fully concentrated on what he was doing. And there it was, a something he had little idea

316

how to put properly into words. He felt that something deep inside his soul had shifted - just maybe; he wasn't quite sure he was imagining it because he wanted it to be so. He wondered about the woman on the hill. Maybe it's false hope to think that Leah sent her, nothing more than that.

He reached inside for his state of mind, waiting for the feeling to come again, feeling scared in case it didn't. He thought he felt it lingering, but wasn't sure. He opened his eyes. The light hit him with such a jolt of brightness he had to squint deeply. He looked to the left into a small stands of trees to soothe his eyes. The green shade was cool and soothing to look into. Eyes open this time he sent his sensors out to take another reading of his state of mind. He felt the air breathing on him from the wide-open space around him and heard the birdsong above him, then he looked ahead at the tarmac black of the empty road that stretched away into the distance. He had to give his head a slight shake, side to side, to take in where he was. He pushed his left foot in its waiting toe grip and forced down the pressure from his calf muscles to propel himself forward again. But after just a few seconds he let himself freewheel and slow right down again, lifting his head up towards the sky to take another sounding of his mental state. He had to stop again. He closed his eyes again, ignoring the fear.

When he burrowed right in again, there it was, unmistakably: the sense of a sick, terrible, darkness being pushed back for a feeling, or a sense, of light to come through. He held on, wanting to make sure he wasn't being tricked by some fatal enemy, and after a space of time that might as well have been a semblance of eternity but that he knew was only seconds, a previously un-met instinct registered the fact that the oppressive feeling of pure, dark hellish night wasn't there. It didn't seem to be receding at any sort of speed, but it had begun to shift. Still holding on to the probing, probing, probing, he could sense the darkness still lying in wait for him if he should fall back in any way; but at this moment it wasn't clutching at him; it had let go. It suddenly occurred to him to actually attack it for the first time.

'I'm *fucking* Giles McAndrew!' he shouted at it. It was not a shout for joy; it was an act of sheer bravado. And when the echo died away on the crisp spring air across the fields, the feeling of dread was still absent. He pushed on again.

He came to a copse that had been split in two by the road a long, long time ago when it was only a cart track, and slowed again. He found himself looking at the trees: saw the new, fresh leaves sprouting from the branches and was rather taken by their colour. They were not just green but bright green, no – deep green – no, that wasn't it either; they were like the limes he cut in his kitchen for beers and gin, only much more – what was the word? *Vivid*, yes, and intense. Wow, he thought and realised this was something he'd never noticed before. It's amazing, incredible: *green*, so *green*. He didn't have any better words than those, and didn't care. He was crawling along now, almost at a standstill again as he approached the copse end, the gate way to the return of wide, flat vistas of ploughed fields, save for a village spire in the distance to the north-west, standing defiantly against the bright blue horizon. He felt the light in the head but at the same time felt something splitting inside him; a feeling like a nut cracking. Almost without thinking he checked the empty road ahead then raised his head to the sun, eyes closed.

'I really am Giles McAndrew, and I'm really coming back,' he said, speaking low. Then he laughed. Of course, I'm not, he thought; not really. 'I'm Gilles Andrews,' he said aloud again, and laughed softly again too at the absurdity of the whole thing, of everything.

'I'm Gilles Andrews!' he shouted to the air and the birds and the sky and anything listening that wasn't human, hearing the oddness of the soft, French 'G'. He winked at the sunlight and laughed again.

No one heard Giles shouting and talking aloud on the road from Tower Hill that would eventually lead him back to The Barn House in Corumby. When he got there he felt hungry for the first time since Simone Pound had walked into Studio 1 on the morning after his reunion with Leah.

7

Troubleshooting

The coffee drinking party in Simone's office had quickly broken up. Reg and Marcus went back to their desks, apparently friends. Greg remained and now leant on the window frame with his arms folded, waiting for her to return from doing a job.

She came in with the speed of an old-fashioned matron and made straight for the coffee jug.

'Greg. Thanks for getting me that milk just now.'

'Oh, you know, only too pleased.'

You lying little shit-bag, thought Simone as she sat back down. She'd been wrong to ask him really, but still. Okay, liar, she went on - have some lies.

'There was a reason - I wanted you out of the room for a few minutes.'

'Oh, really?' Greg languidly came away from the window and took a seat across the desk from the boss.

'Yes, ha-ha. Don't worry. I wanted to do some informal surveying.'

She smiled her best winning smile at him.

'Oh?'

'Yes, I'm casually asking staff what their feelings are about you and me and the SBJs. In view of the last week, I think it's time we really took stock in a serious way.'

I can't possibly be getting away with this, she thought – I'm such a bad liar.

'Oh. Erm, it's not the usual way...'

'No, it's not, but official interviews and questionnaires make people so guarded.'

'True.'

Yes, that wasn't a lie - she'd done some sociology at University.

'So when you went out of the room I asked Marcus and Reg what they thought about you. The way you do your job.'

Thinking about it, it wasn't such a bad idea. She'd had a lot worse.

'Oh.'

'I also did it because I thought it might be useful just to take their mind off their row for a minute. Y'know, I thought it might help them to calm down.'

Simone watched Greg pause for thought before speaking. She had seen him do this many times. It had always given her the impression that he was either a bit slow or rather over-thoughtful. Now she suspected him of scheming menacingly behind Himmler spectacles. She got up and brought one of her two Wandering Jews over to the desk to fuss with.

'Should you not have informed me about this before you went ahead?'

'Yes, of course – it was just an off the cuff thing to start just now.'

'Oh.'

'When are you and I next meeting?'

'Friday. I think,' said Greg. That was unfair: his spectacles were much squarer than Himmler's.

'Well, I was going to bring it up then, but I found myself asking Jane the other day for a brief, um, appraisal of Damien and the websiters about the four of us. Then I thought, well, I've started...'

So I'll finish. Shut up, Simone.

'So you'd carry on, I see.'

'Exactly, ha-ha. So, I've made my usual mess of things. I hope you can forgive me.'

He hates me; I can see it in his eyes, she said to herself. She got up again and got the spray bottle.

'Well, actually, it's an interesting idea. And I'm a little fed up too with the official appraisal ideas England are sending us.'

'Oh, are you?' That'll be the day, she thought. 'That's great, but again – I'm sorry I just sort of floated into it. We should have had a meeting first.'

'No, I think you're being hard on yourself, Simone. A little spontaneity is probably what we need.'

There. There it was: that look of fake sincerity. Or am I imagining it because of what I think he's been up to? She thought about it while letting him continue.

'There's too much management of staff creeping in,' said Greg, fiddling with his empty coffee cup on the edge of the desk as he spoke. 'We have to be careful that we don't start imposing it so that people begin to lose their sense of creativity.'

I've always kept you at arms length, Greg, haven't I, she thought. I've been such a bad boss for him – never trusted him. The question is, whether I've always done that because something in me spotted the fact that he's a bad 'un.

'What music do you like?'

'I'm sorry?'

'Music. I've never asked you who you like, Greg, and we've worked together for years now. And you probably know that I love my music. So who do you like?'

'Me? Oh. I've always liked a lot of people.'

'Well, who? – out of interest…'

Um, Queen…Pink Floyd, and I've always liked The Beatles. Hang on – we've talked about music before haven't we? We have that discussion about music every year…'

'About the music we play, yes. But I've never bothered to ask you about what you like.'

'Okay. Oh, I like the Kaiser Chiefs. And this new lot, The Arctic Monkeys.'

There was a knock on the door. Thank God, thought Simone; I can't go on with this for much longer.

'Come in!' she shouted. The door opened fairly tentatively.

'Hi. Can I see you?'

'Sure, come in, Lucie.'

'Shall I go?'

'No, stay.'

'Do you have a minute?'

'I'm in an important meeting, Lucie. Could you come back in fifteen?'

'Sure.'

'Great.'

The door closed again. I've got to show I'm not frightened of him and that I don't suspect him, she thought. She battled on, trying once again to size him up. She still had a little time.

'So how are you, Greg?'

'Oh - fine. How are you? I suppose–'

'Exactly, it's madness round here at the moment. I like them. Well, used to.'

'Who?'

'Madness. I always thought the singer was very interesting.'

'Oh.'

She fussed with some papers in front of her thinking that Greg's inability to deal with her going off at a tangent was a sign that he was strange. And he had no idea who Madness were. What was he, 31? He clearly had no idea about music. Arctic Monkeys, my drooping arse. They probably weren't even a real band.

'So what did he say?' said Greg.

321

'What?'

'Reg – what did he say about me?'

'What? Oh, good. Good. You know people think highly of you,' she said. 'But I'm noting down all the comments, don't worry. And I'll present them officially at some stage.'

She stopped herself taking time out to make a massive sigh. This was killing her.

'How are you coping?' said Greg.

'Oh, I'm managing.' Just about, she thought. 'Sort of.'

'Just let me know what I can do to help you, won't you.'

'Thanks. Well, let me answer that. The first thing is that I want you to keep doing your job, Greg. That's the most important thing. Keep running the review meetings, keep up the input you're putting into the Community Bus, keep coming up with ideas.'

'That's no problem, Simone, you know I'm happy doing all that.'

'Great. That's good to hear.' She had a sudden idea. 'Now, I'd like to hear – know, what you think about the row this morning. Were you not around when it all happened?'

'No, I was in my office making calls. It was a pity no one came and got me.'

'Yes.'

'We need to get a grip on things, don't we?'

'Yes, we do. Do you have any thoughts?'

The phone went. Damn. But this was probably the call she wanted.

'Hello, Simone Pound?'

'Oh, hi, Bob. *It's Bob Constable,*' she whispered with her hand over the mouthpiece. She gave Greg a meaningful look as she listened.

'Hi, Simone. Did I do it at the right time?'

'Bob, I'm really sorry but your voice is very loud. Could you just take it down a little bit?'

She made a wincing face and looked pointedly at Greg.

'Simone. What are you talking about? You told me to ring you in exactly ten minutes – have I done it at the right time?'

'Yes, I see. Uh-huh. '

'Simone? Are you…do you know who this is? It's Jackie.'

'Uh-huh. I see. Look – don't fret. I'll be straight round.'

'I'm not fretting. Oh…'

'Yes, straight away. And we'll get this sorted, Bob, I promise you. Bob, I need you to keep doing the morning show.'

'Oh, I get it. You want whoever you've got there to think you're talking to Bob Constable. Ha-ha.'

'No, it's not funny at all, I completely agree with you. Okay, then. How long does it take you in the morning? Uh-huh.'

'Oh, sorry…Do you want me to hang on?'

'I'll see you in half an hour.'

'Oh, you're finishing.'

''Bye.'

''Bye, Boss.'

'That was Bob.'

'Yes.'

'He's in a bit of a state so I'm going to go round there.'

She got up from her chair and pulled her jacket away from the chair back.

'I see.'

'…right now.'

'Do you want me to come?'

'Yes. Good idea.'

'Great.'

'Hang on. I need you here. In the circumstances we can't have numbers one and two off the premises. I need you to hold the fort.'

'Okay. You're probably right.'

'And if you feel you could, pull Marcus and Reg in for a chat. Do the pastoral care bit. You're good at that.'

'Yeah, sure.'

'Great. Right, I'm off.'

Simone grabbed her bag and keys and politely shepherded Greg from the room. They both started down the corridor that led to the front of the building but Greg detoured off to the small corridor where his and Damien Read's offices were situated.

'See you later.'

'Yes, 'bye,' said Greg McKenzie.

I'm sweating again, she thought, and wasn't surprised. She was quickly in Jackie Husband's domain. There was nothing going on in reception. She stood there and let out the sigh.

'Ooh, you're like a hot air balloon. What were you up to just now?'

'Preparing you for your office intrigue exam.'

'What? Oh, he-he. Did I pass?'

'With flying colours.'

'Where are you off to now?'

Simone gave her a look without being able to help herself.

'Oh, sorry.'

'No, it's okay. I'm going round to see Bob Constable.'

'What?'

'No?'

'Oh. I think I get it.'

'I'll leave you to think about it. Meanwhile, not a word about the phone call we just had, right?'

'Right. Don't worry.'

'And by the way, what do you think of Damien?'

'Not my type.'

'I thought not.'

'Why do you ask?'

'I'll tell you later.'

The trip to Bob Constable's charming house out in East Vale was non-eventful. He just needed his back stroking.

'They're right,' he'd said. 'I'm not cut out for the morning show. I'm a disaster.'

'No, you're not. We should have given you more support. It's not easy switching shows. What works fantastically at three o'clock just doesn't at seven – that's all it is. That's not your fault.'

'I suppose you're right...'

'I know I'm right.'

Bob ended up being happy to carry on for at least a week after this one to give Simone time to appoint someone permanently, as far as permanent went in the radio business, to Giles's job. Meanwhile, Sarah and Leon, when he got back, would give him plenty of feedback each morning for as long as he needed it. Which reminded her of something.

'Haven't you had a review meeting this week?'

The breakfast show had a meeting Monday, Wednesday and Friday to review what they'd done and to generate ideas for upcoming shows.

'Yes, on Monday.'

'How was it?'

'Short.'

'And today?'

'Yes, and that was fine, except for Greg.'

'Oh?'

'He wasn't there. He sent his apologies. Dentist.'

Simone scribbled a short note down in front of her to check.

'And how did it go?'

'I think everyone's a bit, er, pre-occupied at the moment, what with everything.'

And a bit embarrassed about giving you some honest advice, she thought. Bob was double the age of some of his colleagues.

'Right, well, we'll have another one tomorrow as well. I'll make sure Damien's there and I'll get along myself if I can. We have to give you all the support you need.

'Oh, right. Well, that'll be a help.'

'Good.'

'I like Sarah. She's very supportive.'

'Me too.'

'She's such a smart dresser.'

'She is.'

'I must ask her where she buys her shirts,' he said.

Simone had looked at him and wondered if he was a lot smarter than she let on. Or a lot dimmer. The important thing anyway was that he would be back in the studio tomorrow morning at six, which still gave her ample time to talk to Damien, Sarah and Leon and get them to rally round him. She could have done with Giles on hand to give him some first-hand advice too.

She drove about a hundred yards down the road from the house and parked beside a small row of village shops. She got out her phone and checked her calls. Nothing. She called Sarah. She answered straight away.

'Simone, hi.'

'I haven't interrupted anything crucial have I?'

'No, I've just finished. I'm about to set off back to the station.'

'Great. Are you in a place so that we can talk?'

'Hang on - I'm just walking to my car.'

'Okay.'

Simone heard the sound of keys jangling, traffic noise, and then a *thunk*-ing noise as a car door was unlocked by signal.

'Okay. I'm in the car – fire away.'

'Right. I've got to talk to someone about Greg, Sarah, before I burst.'

'Okay.'

'Secrecy remember.'

'Of course. Go on.' Sarah could barely contain her excitement, but tried to restrain it to show that she was a true professional.

'I think we should do something to prove categorically that he's a liar. Then see if we can take it from there.'

'What?'

'I want to know what's in his record collection.'

'CD collection, you mean?'

'Yes.'

'What for?'

'I asked him about the music he likes.'

325

'Uh-huh?'

'And he says he likes the Arctic thingammies. Are they a real band?'

'Yes,' said Sarah, her face breaking into a smile. Simone looked back at her with a raised eyebrow. Which made Sarah laugh.

'Oh. And the ones that did – what was it? – oh...' Simone racked her brains for the name of the band but she'd forgotten it if she ever knew it. She'd watched them do it on the telly all the way to the end because she thought the singer was dishy. '...the one about the riot.'

'Kaiser Chiefs.'

'Bingo. And he says he likes Queen.'

'I'm sorry, Simone, but he may have any number of reasons for lying to you about what music he likes.'

'Name one.'

The silence was long enough for Simone to start thinking about how much money she was spending to make the call.

'I can't. Why would he try and impress you? I can't think of a reason.'

'Exactly. Unless he's...'

'Is this a test, Simone? Unless he's just weird.'

'Exactly.'

'And a bit of a bullshitter.'

'A man who enjoys covering his real self.'

'Hmm, that's not going to get us very far.'

'Unless we do something really daft.'

'Like what?'

'Break into his house...'

'What?'

'...and find other evidence.'

'No, we can't! What if we get caught?'

'Let's meet and talk about it. Think about it while you're driving in. And round up Marcus – tell you what, Sarah, how about you two come round tonight...to my place...at about half-six or something?'

'Um...Okay, I'll tell Marcus, I'm sure he'll come. But I think the answer's going to be the same from both of us: "you're mad, boss."'

'You're right. That's what Andrea Potter-Symons is going to think too when she comes.'

Sarah knew the name. It was the sort you didn't forget.

'She coming here? What for?'

'To give me a good duffing over, I should think.'

'She can't-'

'Fire me?'

'She's not coming here to do that. It was really an official thing I'd be summoned to headquarters. She's nearby next week and wants to drop in. I could get moved sideways though when this is all over.'

'Excuse if I'm saying the wrong thing. But who looks after you? You're busy all the time looking after everyone's needs. You need to look out for yourself.'

'I had a boyfriend until about three weeks ago. But it was just sex.'

Sarah burst out laughing.

'I'm sorry, I didn't mean it to sound...'

'It's okay,' said Simone. Oh, how she liked Sarah. Whenever they got together they ended up laughing. She could see what Lucie saw in her.

'You deserve someone...really, you know – someone really nice.'

'Sarah, if we don't sort things out here, no one will have me. But if we do, I'm going to go out and get me a man, don't worry. And anyone under sixty with a decent stiffy will keep me happy for a bloody long while.'

'Ha-ha-ha - you do make me laugh,' said Sarah, giggling. And she did. She really did.

8

Hubby

Simone chewed the break-in idea over as she drove along quiet lunchtime roads. The sun was out and the land around the Bart and Bilt border looked very fine, the dyke waters glinting blue along the side of the road. It kept her going, but she was very, very tired. She felt the aching of it behind her eyes.

It's illegal, of course, was her first thought but if they could find a foolproof way of doing the job she would consider persuading someone to execute it.

The first part would be easy. We steal Greg's keys at work, whip them down town and get a duplicate made. Then, while we know he's at work, we go to his house and look around. The CD collection issue would become minor, though still useful, now they'd be looking for evidence of wrong-doing: some rude drawings; the original fax of the press release containing the news of Giles's sacking; general signs of - what, Simone - weirdness? What I really need, she thought, is his mobile phone, and his computer - could they hack into that? Probably not. But his phone; if he accidentally lost it and it fell into their hands then maybe she could work some magic. Or more to the point get someone she knew to work it for them.

Woah! Her thoughts had led her to a blinding idea. At last, she thought, and blew out a sigh, at last you've come up with a good idea.

She drove for another mile or so, excited but deep in thought, chewing her lower lip, then pulled the car over into the next lay-by. She drove well past the hot food van, stopped and took out her phone again. She knew the number by heart. It wasn't pleasant to know she could still get it to spill out of her head as easy as anything but this wasn't the time to sit around worrying about it.

Three rings and then a voice.

'Hello?'

'Bartonshire and Bilt Constabulary, how can I help you?'

'Could I speak to DI Collins, please?'

'Who's calling, please?'

'Simone Pound from Two Counties Radio.'

'One moment please.'

She didn't have to wait long but the on-hold music put her teeth on edge, and they were that way inclined already.

'Hello? Simone?'

'Barrie. Hi, it's me.'

'Oh. Hi. Hello. How are you - okay?'

'Yes, I'm fine. Well, no, I'm not fine. Well, I am in general terms but work is going crazy. I'm right up to the neck in it and I need a bloody big favour. Can we meet?'

Luck was flowing in her direction. The Detective Inspector told her he could meet her in an hour if she could get out to Noreham for one o'clock. They met at the same café-restaurant where Catherine and Giles met for dinner some two weeks previously, though Simone didn't know it. It was the only one Simone liked in the main street there. She sipped a glass of water and waited, sending a text and making a couple of calls to use up the time. Things seemed to be calm at the station. She'd just push-buttoned Jackie away when he finally arrived, twenty minutes late. A detective's day was even more unpredictable than a radio station managing editor's in the midst of a crisis, apparently. They kissed cheeks, but awkwardly. Simone had decided resolutely that she wasn't going to but when she saw him she couldn't not.

'I was surprised when you called - to put it mildly.'

'I thought you would be.'

'You must be desperate.' The man laughed in the most tentative way.

'I am. First I've got to be humble and ask you if you mind even considering helping me. Not just me - others, the station, a good friend of mine.'

'Of course. Oh. Yes. What are you having?' The waitress had arrived. She was unusually young and keen.

'What would you like?'

'Do you do mocha?' said the man.

'Yes, sir, we do.'

'I'll have a large one.'

'Cappuccino for me – same, large.'

'Would you like something to eat?'

'Not just yet, thanks,' said Simone, who quite fancied a sandwich.

'Nothing for me.'

'Okay, the drinks won't be long.' She smiled again, all smart hair and clean face. Simone couldn't help being impressed enough by the girl's confidence to start sizing her up for a career in radio.

'Where were we?' said Simone. It was going well so far considering that this was the man with whom she'd just ended eighteen years of marriage, finishing it with an attempt to screw every penny she could from the divorce.

'A favour,' said Barrie.

'The thing is, I want you to forget about me. I just want you to consider the plight of someone I respect very much, and to know that you'll be helping to do down someone I think is an evil, well, bastard, to put a finer point on it.'

'Has he done something illegal?'

'I don't really know.'

She should have rung him sooner. Or the other contact she had in the police, Alan Dowling, the only male friend she had who offered her sympathy when Barrie had brought everything crashing down.

'Well, tell me what he's done.'

'The only thing I can think of that might be illegal is, he maybe drew some sexual drawings and sent them to a girl.'

Barrie was immediately nodding back.

'It could be harassment if the girl's in the drawings.'

'She is.'

'Any message with the drawings? Anything threatening?'

'No.'

'Hmm. Have you still got the drawings?'

'Yes. DNA?' she said, thinking of countless detective programmes.

'Yes, if what you want me to do is prove he's the culprit - unless he handled the paper with gloves on and managed to keep his saliva off it.'

'He might well have been that careful.'

'What else has he been doing?'

'Hard to be sure. I think he's been feeding information to the press about one of my workers that helped get him the sack - and to his employers.'

'Telling tales?'

'Uh-huh,' she said, nodding and watching his expression carefully.

'How bad?'

Simone shrugged.

'You don't know – okay. Could be libel, but bloody hard to prove, unless it led to something put into the public domain.'

'No. That didn't happen. And the other thing is sending a false fax releasing information that he shouldn't have had to my workers.'

'Not illegal. But it'll get him the sack easily enough if you can prove it.'

She thought about that. Was getting the boot enough of a punishment for Greg McKenzie? No, she didn't think it was. She had chewed this over for days and had already decided that obsessives who went about smashing other people's lives up deserved some sort of jail sentence. After a public flogging. And having all his pubic hair removed straight afterwards. But getting him out of Two Counties would count as a start.

'Well, that's it. That's what I wanted to see you about,' she said. She looked at the table feeling very uncomfortable. She was about to ask a question that might get her a ticking off – and the man across the table was very good at administering those – but these were special circumstances.

'What, is that it? That was the favour?'

'Oh – hah – no. I haven't come to the question yet. Look, I know this is a massive favour; and perhaps, Barrie, barefaced cheek - and that I'm guilty of naivety for just asking. So please don't be hard on me or put me down when I ask it.'

Barrie looked at her square between the eyes, which forced hers up to his.

'Simone. If I can help you, I will.'

'Why?'

'Therapy.'

'Blood and sand, you've become honest all of a sudden.'

'Therapy.'

His ruddy, blotchy face made a smile that began to break Simone's heart until she remembered some of the things he'd done to her. But she smiled back.

'How long?'

'What's your favour?'

'I want you to get the paper records off a mobile phone and give them to me.'

She waited for the answer with her stomach in a state. They were still waiting for their coffee. Finally, heaving a heavy sigh, Barrie answered.

'Is that all?'

'You bastard.' But she laughed.

'Here, where has all this bad language come from?'

'You don't want to know.' Simone looked sheepishly at her lap then pushed her luck further. 'How about DNA – could you find out whether his DNA is on the drawings?'

'In theory, of course, but look – I can help you with the phone if you can get it to me, but it'll be strictly hush-hush. I can't do any more than that unless we go into an official investigation. I just can't spare the time or the resources.'

'Not even for me?' she said, trying to make doleful eyes.

'I'm only doing the phone because it's you.'

'Okay. I understand. Thanks. I do appreciate it.' The man she'd been unable to provide with children looked back at her and smiled briefly.

'It's okay. I'm only too glad to do something. Let's hope I can get a result for you.'

'Here we are,' said the waitress, carefully putting down a tray containing two big, steaming cupfuls of coffee between them. They both thanked the girl as if she'd brought the certain answers to life's fundamental questions.

'Nice,' said Simone.

'Mmm,' said Barrie, lathering his top lip.

The atmosphere was suddenly twenty degrees warmer between them.

'So what do you want the records for? Dirty phone calls, is it?'

'No, I would have told you that: I want to see whether he's phoned the papers and the bigwigs at the BRCB to do the dirty on my guy.'

'Who is it, your guy?'

'Giles McAndrew.'

'Oh, Giles, right. I read about that.'

'Good, I won't have to bore you with the whole story in a minute then.'

'I'd like to hear it.'

'Barrie. First – you're being very good, to put it mildly. You do realise...'

'That you've got to nick the phone? Was I ever that stupid?'

'You don't care?'

'No. Did you think I would?'

'I wasn't sure.'

'You should have known me better. We were married for eighteen years.'

'You don't need to tell me,' Simone looking into the distance. She tried to smile so Barrie didn't think she was trying to start something.

'Can I ask you one thing though?'

A hitch, thought Simone.

'Did you have to revert to your maiden name so bloody quickly?'

'Yes. It was part of the cure.'

'I see.'

'Do you?'

'I'll ask my therapist if she sees, then I'll get back to you.'

'How long will it take?'

'I see her every Friday, so–'

'No, to get the phone records.'

'Oh, right. Once I've got the phone? Maybe three days, two and a half.'

'Can't you do it any quicker?'

He laughed.

'Is it a race against time?'

She thought about it.

'No, not really.'

'When I say three, I mean no more than three. Could be less than two if I pull one or two strings. So...'

'Good.' She sipped contentedly at the coffee that was almost strong enough. 'Great, Barrie.'

'When are you going to take the man's phone?'

'As soon as I can.'

'Would you like some help?'

'How do you mean?'

'I can pull him in about the drawings. Has he ever been in a police station before?'

'I doubt it.'

That made her think. If Greg was a bad 'un, then of course, he could easily have lied on his job application. He might have done time - he might have done anything.

'Well then - we'll get him in, ask him some questions. He'll be shitting himself most probably. So he won't notice one of my team liberating his phone for a few hours.'

'Crikey, Barrie.'

'I know. Handy, eh?'

'How come you weren't so open about your work with me when we were still together?'

He looked at her in a hard, pained sort of way. Then the look softened to something else.

'It just changes things, doesn't it – not being married to the person any more. I've no reason to keep anything from you any more.'

The words were well meant, she thought, but took her to places she didn't want to go to.

'Shall we come in for him tomorrow?' he said, supping his hot drink.

'That'd be brilliant. Come in the back way, won't you.'

'Yeah, yeah, yeah, don't worry, we'll be discreet.'

'But hang on – this might be complicated. He's in early in the morning, 'til eleven, and then he's out with our community bus.'

'Ring me in the morning. About half-eight. By then I'll know what time we can get him.' Barrie took out a card and put it on the table next to her hand. 'That's got my new mobile number on it. If you need me, use that, it'll be quicker.'

'Great.'

'Where's he going to be with this bus?'

'Barton. At County High.'

'What time?'

'Between midday and half-one. Then at a junior school 'til three.' She couldn't remember which one. 'I'll let you know which one in the morning.'

'Okay.' Barrie made a note.

'But look: I might not be there in person. I don't know where I'm due to be tomorrow. But don't worry if I'm not - I've got someone in mind who does this sort of thing much better than I do. He can be a bit of a bastard sometimes, but he's a really good copper.'

Simone looked worried.

'Don't fret – he's not going to beat him up.'

'No?'

'No,' said Barrie, laughing. 'So. Write his name down on this piece of paper. And address if you know it. And his DOB if you know it. And we'll see if there's anything on him.'

She'd come prepared in case Barrie came through. She took a piece of paper out of her bag and pushed it across the table. Can you get copies of these drawings to me this afternoon?'

She thought about it for a second.

'Yeah. I can do that, no problem.'

'Good. Fine. Don't worry - we'll sort this character out for you.'

'Do you think?'

'Yeah, I think.'

'Unless he's a pro. Most people just collapse like a pack of cards in ten seconds once we've got them behind four police walls. I must have told you that.'

'Yes, you told me.'

Then they went back to their coffee and talked a little more about nothing terribly important. She looked over at him a couple of times and thought, that used to be my husband, the copper who still looks more like a branch manager of a Sainbury's.

On the way back to BT, Simone felt as though the car was floating above the road. The investigation had taken a quantum leap forward. I was just pissing about like an amateur before, she told herself, but this is taking things on to a different scale.

9

What would Giles McAndrew Do?

The strength that had returned lasted for a couple of hours but began to ebb away again after he cleaned up the house. The kitchen was almost back to its immaculate self, the work surfaces empty and shining, the windows and door wide open letting in the unmistakable smell of spring from outside.

Maybe I'm just tired, Giles advised himself, and suddenly realised he was absolutely knackered and needed more sleep. When he woke up a few hours later it was nearly midday on his bedroom clock. He came to, sat on the edge of the bed, and as the fog cleared he felt for his state of mind. He didn't want to go back to Tower Hill but he still felt low. He normally had so much energy – in his head if not in his body - but it had been smashed by everything that had happened. Riding home he'd felt it gushing back into him, but had left him again. Leah seemed to be the cloud. She's not really going to come back to me. I'm kidding myself to think otherwise. He felt it somewhere deep inside him, right inside his bones, maybe. It was over. He looked for the energy that had seemed to come back but it just wasn't there.

He went back to the source, to the woman on Tower Hill – who was she? Her appearances made no sense. But then, when did life ever? What, even before he fell out with Leah really badly, had he achieved in his life? He had no children, he had no wife. He'd left nothing behind but a load of words that had just floated away and gone. No one remembered them and no one ever would. Well, maybe his efforts to raise money for charity might mean something, but it hadn't been that much of a big deal – anyone in his position could have done it. The woman had said that people would feel bad when I'm gone but how many? How many would come to his funeral to really mourn him? He had one parent, no brothers or sisters. Simone would be there. Leon, he supposed, but Leon wouldn't mourn him. Would some of his old girlfriends go? Friends from school? I built my life on my shows. I built my life on being a minor celebrity – no, a mini-celebrity in a couple of small towns, an E-list celebrity. I wanted the glamour of being on the radio. Fuck, what kind of idiot am I?

He took a shower and got dressed and then, he had to admit, he did feel a bit better. He rubbed his face, felt the roughness of stubble and remembered what the woman had said about not quitting and leading.

He went back to the bathroom and carefully removed the growth of several days. He felt like putting on a little aftershave, so he did. Depression, he thought? I don't feel depressed. Not really. Leah came into his mind again and he felt a welling up from his chest to his eyes. It was sadness, intense sadness at loss; not depression. He wiped away his tears. And remembered something else that wasn't nice, something that made him feel bad, feel guilty. If it wasn't time to quit, and if it was time he went back to being a leader, then he would stick his chin out and try to make amends with Catherine. He felt the need there to make a fresh start. Then he thought something that made him laugh a little out loud.

'What would Giles McAndrew do now?' he asked himself. He found an answer straight away.

'He'd phone Catherine, or go to see her, to own up to what he did, and ask for her forgiveness.'

Giles went to find his mobile. She didn't answer but he left her a message. He felt that he'd done a huge thing. He also felt pressure inside him being released. Thank God, he thought. The relief was almost overwhelming. He went to his kitchen window and looked out. It was so sunny outside. He decided he would venture out into civilisation for the first time since he was taken off the radio. Why not? I'll just take a walk down the high street in Barton Townes, he suggested to himself. If I change my mind on the way I can always turn the car around and come back. He thought that actually he might buy a CD or something, or a book, and get a cup of coffee somewhere. He thought about his wallet. He hadn't seen it or thought about it for days. He found it up in his bedroom in the draw of his bedside table where he usually put it at night for safekeeping. 'Right then', he said aloud, and went down the stairs on quick legs. As he reversed the car from the garage into the light he barely noticed the huge crack he'd made on the windshield with the sledgehammer except to consider the possibility of getting it fixed that afternoon. Maybe he would.

Giles kept away from TCR. He parked in the spacious car park behind the town hall for the first time since he didn't know when and walked to the high street.

He bought a ticket from the pay machine and felt okay. He was too warm in the jacket he'd put on, so he took it off and left it in the front passenger seat of the car.

The high streets and the side streets were busy. Giles looked up at the church tower clock. It was the lunchtime hour. That explained all the people, and the fact that the sun was shining brilliantly. There was a good feeling about the town, he thought. Even though he didn't exactly feel close to his fellow man right now he could sense it: the country completely through the winter now with the promise of the summer months ahead. All sorts of shop windows were full of the World Cup to come, not just the sports shops. One was even displaying the blue and gold of the Barton Townes Hardware, but Giles noticed this only marginally, not being much of a football fan. People were shedding clothes now: he noticed the t-shirts on the mums with prams, and the shorts on the men that showed their white legs. Giles looked down at his jeans to check that they were clean. They'd do. He went inside Her Majesty's Vinyl to have a scout around for a good CD he could buy.

His phone buzzed in his pocket as he was thinking about getting a Rolling Stones hits album, that big one.

'Hi, Catherine.' He started for the door of the shop. He needed somewhere more appropriate.

'Gilles, hey, how are you?'

'I'm okay.'

'I've been trying to get you for days and days. I tried to come up but I couldn't get away. What's up?'

'Hang on, Cath – I'm trying to get to somewhere quieter – I'm in the high street in Barton and it's chokka-block. Keep talking.'

'Can you hear me okay?'

'Yeah. Talk to me – tell me where you are.'

'I'm in Paris.'

'Paris! Wow, what are you doing there?' Giles was sidestepping shoppers like a slalom skier. He was making for the church and he was nearly there.

'Selling paintings. Or trying to.'

'How's it going?'

'Not good, I'm struggling, but I've done really well in London.'

'Right...'

He was through the lych-gate and inside the churchyard. The noise level had fallen right away.

'...Okay, that's better. It's quieter now.'

Giles walked past the east door towards the gravestones. It was much quieter.

'So, what's been happening? Your mom rang me about the newspaper articles. She's been going crazy! You haven't rung and you obviously haven't been answering your phone.'

'Steady on.'

'If you're okay, you should have been more thoughtful, you know.'

Giles felt his nerves tightening, but he knew he had to get this thing done with.

'I know. I'm sorry. I'll ring her.'

'You'd better...I'm sorry – I'm interfering...'

'No, no, you're right. Look, is she that bad?'

'G, she doesn't drive as you well know - so she couldn't come to see for herself. She's been worried sick, come on!'

Damn it. It was going to sound like excuse-making now.

'Look, Catherine, I've got some things to tell you.'

He told her the outline of the story – about being taken off the air and getting the sack.

'Oh no, you're kidding...okay, you're not kidding.'

'There's worse – which is why I'm phoning.'

At the other end, it was Catherine's turn to feel tension squeeze her. What was worse than the sack: cancer?

'I smashed up your painting.'

'You did *what*?'

'Your painting, *Who Shot the Prairie Dog?*'

'*Who Shot the Prairie Dog? 2.*'

'What?'

'"*2*" – it's the second version you've got, remember?'

'Oh, yeah,' said Giles. He'd forgotten.

'You smashed it up?'

He told her how, and then why.

'Thank God,' said Catherine.

Giles waited for the explanation.

'I wanted to do that myself several times after I finished it.'

'You mean...you...?' At the other end of the phone she was laughing - it was too good an outbreak of good fortune to grasp properly. He wanted to cry again.

'Ha-ha. I don't care – that's right, I don't care. Well...' She interrupted herself, and chuckled '...I was going to say, "I'm sorry that the painting didn't work out for you and Leah" and I am. But I have to confess, I'm quite glad no one's going to get their hands on the piece of crap now.'

Giles laughed with her.

'It's not a piece of crap,' he said.

'Okay, whatever you say. Look, get straight with your mom. It's okay about the painting, forget it. I just want you to be well. I'm coming back there as soon as I finish here. And I'll come straight up to see you. Is that okay?'

Giles felt his insides take another leap for joy. Catherine would come to his funeral.

'When will that be?'

'In a couple of days, I think.'

'Really?'

'So I may see you Saturday if you're not doing anything.'

'Yeah, come over, it'll be great.'

She felt she might be guilty of being insensitive, saying the next thing that was in her mind but she decided to risk it seeing as she'd just given Gilles some good news.

'I've got something to tell you. Some news.'

'Oh, what's that?'

'I've got a new man.'

'You have?' Giles tried to keep his voice very light, but he felt, despite his better judgement, disappointed. 'That's great. Who is he?'

'I'll tell you when I see you.'

'Are you bringing him?'

'No, he's had to go Barcelona to buy paintings. Or look at some anyway. He's a dealer.'

'Oh, well, that sounds great, Catherine, I'm really pleased for you.'

'Thanks – it's time I caught a break, ha-ha.'

'Well, you deserve it,' he said and meant it. He had no doubts at all about how good a person the grown-up Catherine was.

He said goodbye to his cousin, flipped his phone shut and set off for the main street shops again. The station, TCR, was close by, just a short walk away across the road and down Bridges Lane, and as he passed through the lych-gate again he couldn't help looking down the road where his workplace was. He expected that crushed feeling to come on him again but it didn't. The negative thought had a weight, but something in his head seemed to be supporting it this time. He thought about his Stones CD and yes, he still wanted it. So he marched down the road back to the Townes Centre shopping mall to Her Majesty's.

He had the compilation CD in his right hand and was browsing the Elton John section, almost without thinking about what he was doing, when he saw a box set of the great man's stuff. He picked it up. Simone would like this, it occurred to him, but he wondered whether she might already have it. She was a fanatic. He thought she might not be a box set sort of a person, but decided to buy it for her anyway. She could always change it if she already had it. A promotional card next to it said 'New Release' so he decided to chance his arm.

Giles walked out of the shop and stood on the pavement. Coffee time. He made what he thought was good stuff at home, but he did like a cappuccino if it was properly done, and at Di Mario's down the bottom of the high street they did a really good one. He headed off.

The street was even more crowded now with office workers buying lunch and shopping for stuff. Giles didn't mind. It felt good to be out and about again. He found himself sighing with relief as he walked, over and over. It's not me to be depressed, he said to himself. It just isn't. He had a very strong sense of coming back from the brink. I'm not going to collapse, he realised, passing a throng outside a popular sandwich shop. He felt a mad urge to kiss someone, anyone. He thought about how he'd tried to kiss Lucie. Ah, sod it, you can't get it right all the time, he told no one in particular silently.

He pushed open the door of Di Mario's, the Italian restaurant that had been in Barton Townes for much longer than Giles knew, and found a table in the window. The place was busy, but not too busy. Most people were eating, some in twos and fours, and some alone.

'Is it okay just to have a coffee?' he said to the waiter who came up pretty promptly.

'No problem, sir, what would you like, cappuccino, a latte?' He had an authentic accent.

'Cappuccino, please.'

'Large or small?'

'Large, please.'

'Okay.'

To pass the time, Giles picked his purple HMV bag off the spare chair seat and took out his wares. He looked at the track listing of the Rolling Stones CD and looked for songs he recognised. He knew most of them. He'd played a good few on his Saturday morning programme and indeed, on other shows down the years before he'd found his way to TCR. 'Wild Horses,' his favourite, was there.

He realised with a sudden mental shift of gear that he was absorbed in trivia for the first time in days and days. He looked out of the window into the street and saw the sun come out shining brightly, then go in again. Then he stopped seeing the street. His eyes glazed over and turned inward. He was in the vast, terrifying cave. It closed in on him, trying to devour him. But the picture was clear: the cave had a mouth. It was there in the distance, a vague, dimmed brightness. Towards it, away from Giles, walked a man, a figure in dark shadow. He was fifty yards in the distance and moving further away all the time. Then he was sixty yards away, seventy yards, a hundred yards away, getting smaller and smaller all the time as the light came to meet him.

Giles' eyes were closed but suddenly the cave was behind him now – he was out. He knew because he felt the light all around him. He could see sunshine, hear birds singing. He was in his garden. He was sitting in his garden looking at his lawn and his tulips and the light was the strong light of summer. And the blackbird - the song of the blackbird came into his head again, and he felt safe. The cave and the massive threat was gone.

Giles opened his eyes. Suddenly all he could hear was the chatter of customers and staff. It seemed incredibly loud. He realised he had been away and looked at the peoples at the tables nearby to see if they were looking at him. No one was looking at him. Could I go back to it though, he thought? Could I sink back down again, go back to the cave, or is this it; have I broken through it? He didn't know. What would Giles McAndrew think, he asked.

'I've broken through - I'm on the road to recovery,' came the answer. His coffee came.

Before he sipped it he suddenly found himself tasting his mouth - it felt neutral, clean even, which made him realise that for days his breath had tasted like the bottom of a hamster cage. Giles began to sip his coffee and couldn't stop a feeling of elation coming over him because at last things seemed to be moving in his direction. I was in a cave, his inner self was saying, but I'm out again - I got out of it. But there was more to it than that. He felt clean, clean inside. He felt lighter. He felt different, as if he'd shed a skin, a tough, old skin. The skin felt old, but the rest of him felt younger – young, even. I'm only forty. That's all. And not an old forty: a young forty. He carried on the team talk: And I don't work in a bank, I work in radio. I'm a presenter. I'm still young and I'm out there doing an interesting, cool thing. It's still there for me, life. Come on, Giles!

He felt so much better it wasn't true. But it was.

He went home via the supermarket and sat down with the feeling of just wanting to get off life's merry go round and be still. The energy he'd felt in De Mario's had subsided but he still felt good. He wanted to ring Simone, but he put it off. Her messages showed she was worried about him. He ought to tell her he was okay, but he *was* okay, that was the important thing. She'd find out soon enough. Sorry, Simone, he said to her as if she could hear him or transfer his thoughts directly to her. I'm switching myself off, but I'm coming back.

He closed his phone wondering whether Leah was about to contact him again, then switched off that type of thinking too. It could wait, all of it. It was two-twenty in the afternoon. He felt sleepy again so he put aside the idea of playing his new CD. He locked the back door and went upstairs again, slow now with fatigue. He stripped off to his underpants, got under the duvet and went to sleep. He didn't wake again until another bright May morning came calling at his bedroom windows.

10

Tanya and the Prevailing Madness

4.33 said the clock on the TCR wall to the right of Jackie Husband as she picked up the ringing reception phone.

'Two Counties Radio, how may I help you?'

'Hi. Could I speak to Simone Pound, please?'

'Who's calling please?'

'Tanya Howe.'

'Just one moment please Tanya, I'll see if she's available.'

'Thank you.'

Whoever was doing the tap dance inside Tanya's stomach started banging their feet down even harder.

'Hello?'

'Hi, my name's Tanya Howe...'

'Yes?' Simone had finally, after getting back from Noreham and then from delivering photocopies of the drawings to the police station in town, got back to her list of 'Things Accomplished' and 'Things Still to Accomplish.' She was still only halfway down the first column.

'I'm sorry...'

Tanya giggled very slightly at the end of her 'sorry', though nothing was funny. It was sheer nerves.

'...this may be quite unusual for you – it's certainly unusual for me...'

There was something in the woman's - a young woman – voice that didn't make Simone want to say 'stop wasting my bloody time whoever you are.'

'It's okay, you can take your time,' she said instead.

'Thank you. My name is Tanya Howe, I live in London and I've been following the story of Giles McAndrew and your radio station.'

'Oh, yes?'

Oh, no. Simone felt her guard going up. She'd had enough of people in London over the past two weeks to last her the rest of her life.

'I'm going to admit something too: I've been working on your case...'

In the pause, Tanya heard Simone listening hard. The silence told her to start digging herself out of the hole she just made.

'...I work at 10 Downing Street...in the Media Intelligence Unit.'

Simone had long been in the habit at work of fastening on very quickly to what a phone caller wanted from her, how much and why. But she couldn't this time.

'Oh yes?' she said.

'And the thing is, I'm disgusted with what's been going on – what the press have been doing to you, and, though I shouldn't say it, what my unit has been doing to you. To put it very simply, I want to come and work for you.'

Simone was nonplussed.

'Oh...I really don't know what to say.' She really didn't know what to say.

Tanya wasn't sure she did either, at least not how to express it elegantly, though she'd rehearsed her pitch, so the rest of it just came out in a blurt.

'I know it sounds ridiculous, but I just want to ask you now - can I come and see you? Can I come and talk to you? I want to work in radio and I want to come and work for you.'

The fog in Simone's mind began to clear. She heard sincerity in the girl's voice, but with all that had happened she'd be a fool to trust her. It had to be some kind of trick. She thought of Greg McKenzie and whether she could fit this into his planning and scheming. She only gave herself about six seconds, but she couldn't and she was thinking very hard.

'Why, Tanya? Why here?'

'I know. I must sound like I'm round the twist.'

'Well, yes.'

Suddenly a light came on for Simone.

'Tanya, give me your number.'

'What?'

'At the Intelligence Unit. I need to know who you are.'

'I can't Mizz Pound. If I make a call at work it might be recorded and listened to. I work at 10 Downing Street.'

'Where are you calling from?'

'I'm on my mobile – in the street.'

'You can understand why I'm wary.'

'Yes, of course.' Stupid Tanya, she told herself. Considering the job you do you should have seen this coming. She decided to bear the risk.

'Okay. If you ring me in five minutes I'll be back in the office. The number is – have you got a pen there?'

'Yup.'

'Great. Ready?'

'Yup.'

'0--- -------. Ask for me and they'll put you through.'

'Okay, I'll do that.'

'Would you? That'll be fantastic. But look – I'll have to put the phone down on you. But I'll ring you a few minutes later on my mobile again from outside.'

'Won't your people at work think that's a bit strange?'

'It doesn't matter. I don't care – I'm quitting.'

There was some restrained laughter at both ends. I must be mad, said Tan in her head. The sun that had been out all day suddenly went behind a cloud and Tanya felt her face relax and realized she'd been squinting. It was a lovely warm London May day. I've got to first base, she thought. Simone Pound is listening to me.

'Okay. I'll ring this number in five minutes then?'

'Thanks so much, Mizz Pound.'

Simone went out and did a wee. When she came back she sat in one of her guest chairs for a minute and closed her eyes. She could easily have gone to sleep. She got up after a minute though, went to her desk, and dialled the number on the pad in front of her.

'Hello, 10 Downing Street?'

Blood and sand, she thought. Is it really this easy?

'Tanya Howe, please, Media Intelligence Unit.'

'One moment…'

'Tanya Howe?'

'It's Simone.'

'Yeah. Okay. I'll do that. Right away.'

Five minutes later, the phone went.

'Hello?'

'Call for you, boss.'

'Will you stop calling me boss, Jackie? Everyone seems to have started doing it and I hate it.'

'Okay. I'm putting Tanya Howe on the line…'

'Hello? Simone?'

'Speaking.'

'Thank you so, so much for doing this.'

'It's okay. Just tell me about what the hell you're doing.' Simone put her hand over the mouthpiece and produced a huge yawn.

'Well, part of the reason is that I've spoken to a couple of people who you've had to deal with in the past week from the press. They've been telling me about you.'

'Really?' Simone was wracking her brains to recall who she might be thinking of. As far as she could remember, the man from the Chronicle was a sod who she'd given short shrift to and the rest were a blur of names, though she had them written down somewhere.

'And someone I know at Radio 4 sent a tape of your interview across to me. The man at the Star is a bloke called Matt Stone. I speak to him regularly as part of my job. He said you gave him a real hammering on the phone. Said he didn't like it but respected you for it.'

'Well, I'm blowed.' She sounded like she could organize things, this girl.

'And basically, anyone who thinks Matt deserves a hammering is someone I want to work for. There's more to it than that though. I bet this all sounds ridiculous...'

'Not completely.'

'But a bit?'

'Yes, but listen - do you have any radio experience?' Simone supposed not.

'No, but I've got a degree in History from Exeter, I can write and I can speak French. Basically my job is about reporting. Talking to people, winkling things out of them and writing reports. Briefing people...'

'So is it a reporter's job you're looking for?'

'God, yes. But I'll take anything you can give me.'

'Have you ever been to Barton Townes?'

'No...'

'Oh...well, I should tell you-'

'...but I'm desperate to get out of London.'

Oh, what the hell, thought Simone. What do I have to lose?

'Why don't you come and see me then. I can't promise anything...'

'Of course not.'

'...because I can't just appoint people willy-nilly...'

'I see...of course.'

'...but I can recommend.'

'And I know you probably don't have anything just now. But I'm prepared to wait for an opening. Just let me come and talk to you.'

'I'm letting you, ha-ha.'

'Okay then, when?' Tanya wanted to jump up and down but she was in the street.

'God, I'm not sure – it's absolutely monkey houses in the zoo here at the moment...'

'How about this - I'm coming up tomorrow. I'm going to stay for a few nights at a hotel or a bed and breakfast, and you call me whenever you can see me. I'll wait by the phone.'

My, my, the girl was desperate.

'Look, if you come tomorrow, I'll see you tomorrow - we'll call it a preliminary interview. And then we'll take it from there.'

'Fantastic.'

'I think you're mad, you know.'

'It's quite okay - I expected you to.'

'Okay then: you've obviously got my number.'

'Yes, I've got it.'

'And there are loads of trains.'

'I'm driving.'

'You might as well come straight here – on the off chance. There's a map on the website, we're right near the town centre.'

'Okay. Fantastic. I'll see you tomorrow.'

'Okay, 'bye then.'

''Bye – and thanks.'

Well, thought Simone, whatever bloody next? The world around me has gone stark, staring bonkers in the past ten days. A kid from London seeing me as some kind of heroine just about caps things off. If she turned out to be somebody's spy, she'd know. And if she was she'd shut the girl's head in the filing cabinet and spray diluted plant feed in her ear until she screamed for mercy.

11

Sleuthing at Simone's

Just after six-thirty, the doorbell rang while Simone Pound was trying to salvage a jasmine plant in the conservatory. The company was arriving and she felt good about that.

'Hi, come in! Oh, you're together.'

'No,' said Sarah Billings, 'We just got here at the same time.'

'Hi, boss,' said Marcus.

'I'd prefer "Simone", Marcus.'

'Oh, sorry.'

'It's okay - I won't be a moment.' She went off towards the kitchen. 'Go through,' she said, pointing to the open door to the living room.

'I love this room,' said Sarah, calling to Simone. Her old man must have had some money, she thought. It was the size that impressed her really. It was as big as the whole downstairs of her and Lucie's new place. Marcus didn't really notice anything. It looked a lot like his parents' lounge, only bigger.

'I've been meaning to make changes,' said Simone, joining her, 'but I haven't got round to it.' When this is all over I will, she thought.

Sarah walked over to the open doors that led into the back garden.

'Crikey!'

The 'back yard', as she liked to call it, sang with colour even in the evening light. Simone stood in the doorway and was pleased with what she saw too, but now wasn't the time for peonies and violas.

'And the smell!'

'Honeysuckle,' said Simone. The huge plant by the kitchen door, loving the onset of dusk, poured its luscious, heavy odour across the air towards them. Simone smiled.

'I'm jealous,' said Sarah, who dreamed of one day soon finding the time to start building up something like this. They turned to go back inside where Marcus flicked through a Sunday magazine without interest.

'Finally, here we are,' said Simone. It seemed as though an age had passed since their meeting at the station on Saturday morning. 'Let's make a start.' She led them to the dining table and sat down next to a note pad and pen. Her colleagues took their cue, pulled out a chair and followed suit.

'Oh! I forgot the beer!' Simone, and got up again and rushed to the kitchen. She felt so exhausted, but the adrenalin of the whole, huge business was keeping her going. She came back to the table with three cold bottles of Czech beer; the opener and the glasses were already there.

'I've made a list of things we should talk about...' she said, as she removed the bottle tops.

'Don't look like that, Marc,' said Sarah, sitting directly across from table from him. 'He hates agendas and stuff like that.'

'I know.' Simone leaned over and patted his hand. 'Don't worry, you'll survive, luvvie,' she said. Marcus frowned and took a swig of beer. It was surprisingly cold.

'...and I've got something big to tell you both.'

'Good or bad?' said Sarah.

'Good.'

'What is it?' said Sarah, eager.

'I'll tell you in a minute. Sorry to be a pain, but it's worth waiting for.'

'Ttsuh,' went Sarah, disappointed. Marcus didn't protest.

'Ah – before I forget,' said Simone. 'Before we start, phones off.'

The ritual of the taking out and switching off of the mobile phones resembled a trio of gunfighters taking off their gun belts. After all three had been re-pocketed, Simone began the proceedings.

'"Item 1." Greg and Leah. I just want to tie this up completely.'

'What do you mean?' said Sarah.

'Have you remembered any details, found anyone else who remembers seeing them together?'

'Yes, we have,' said Sarah. 'We had a talk with Dave and he remembers when it started.'

'It was a staff do,' said Marcus. 'Basically, we all went out drinking round town. You probably weren't there...'

'Don't rub it in.'

'...and then we went on to a club. Right, so, we'd all had a lot to drink, but Leah was new and I don't know what the reason was, but she got absolutely rat-arsed drunk. I remember it because – well, as I say, she was new and...'

'And you all bloody fancied her, you blokes,' said Sarah.

'Whatever. The things is – *Sarah*,' said Marcus, admonishing her, 'it that she was seen at the end of the night disappearing into a taxi with Greg McKenzie.'

Simone shuddered, feeling for Leah.

'*Seen* getting into a taxi with her?'

'I saw her,' replied Marcus.

'And then, nothing.' Sarah made a chopping motion with her right hand.

'What do you mean?'

'That was it. She dumped him.'

How come I never knew any of this, Simone was going to say. Memo to myself, she said inside her head: spend a part of every week getting the latest gossip out of Jackie and Sarah.

'I thought you said they went out for two weeks?' said Simone.

'That's what we thought, but our memories have been playing tricks on us, haven't they, Marcus? We remembered it wrong. But we're certain now we've got it right.'

'Leah ended it very quickly,' said Marcus. 'And as we said, there's your motive. And getting rid of him straight away probably did him more damage than if she'd done it after a few weeks.'

'I don't get it,' said Simone.

'It mystifies her in his eyes.'

Both women didn't get it.

'I mean it gives her a mystique.'

'Oh, yes,' said Simone, shuffling her bottom in her seat. 'I know what you mean.'

'So he obsesses…' said Simone.

'It's only a guess.' Marcus didn't want to make himself out to be a genius. 'We've found a problem with the theory, though,' he added.

'What?' Simone wanted no problems tonight.

'There's a long time-lag between the first event and May 2006.'

'That's true,' said Sarah, holding the cold bottle against her cheek for a few seconds. 'The first event was at least three years ago.'

'Hmm, that is weird,' Simone admitted. She yawned again. The stretching of her jaw made her head ache. 'Sorry,' she said. 'Okay, so we've got that straight, his motive. Are we ready to move on?'

The other two nodded.

'Okay – Item 2 on my list. This is for you, Sarah…'

'Right…'

'Did you tell Greg about the drawings?'

'What do you mean?'

'Do you remember, after I told you about the drawings on Friday morning, telling Greg about them?'

'No.' Sarah was shaking her head, sure she was right. She hadn't told anyone apart from Lucie. 'Definitely not. I wouldn't break a confidence like that, and certainly if I opened my mouth by mistake, it wouldn't be to him.'

349

'Fine, I know you wouldn't but I just thought I'd ask to make sure.'

'Why are you asking?'

'Greg told me on that Saturday morning that you'd told him about the drawings.'

'No!' said Sarah; 'No way!'

Simone nodded. Sarah's thoughtful eyes gazed unseeing at a kitchen cupboard. Marcus watched her, keeping silent counsel.

'So,' said Simone. 'are we saying that this is a slip that gives his game away?'

Marcus spoke.

'It's an inconsistency. Is there another way he could have found out about the pictures?' he said to Simone.

'No. None.'

'You sure?' asked Sarah. 'Who knows about them? Who knows they exist?'

'You two. Me. Giles. Leah. Greg McKenzie...and someone else if the artist was someone else.'

'I'm afraid I told Dave about them. Sorry, but I had to.'

Sarah looked hard into Marcus's face while Simone did the same, trying not to smile.

'Do you trust him, Marcus, totally?' asked Sarah.

'Do you?' asked Simone.

'Totally.'

'I think we should believe him,' said Sarah to the managing editor. 'They're like the mafia inside the newsroom.'

'What?' said Marcus innocently, who had the Godfather films on DVD, Goodfellas and more besides.

'You know what I mean. You're as thick as thieves, a club of two.'

'You can trust BD, I promise you.'

Simone checked her thinking about who she might have told about the drawings. Who did she talk to about it on the phone? Did Jackie listen in to a call? Did she pass the information on? If she did, it would be all over the station like cheap paint.

'There's just one thing.' Marcus again. 'Greg McKenzie is the sort of bloke who always has to be the first to know everything. It's possible he claimed he knew about them to sort of, preserve his image.'

Simone had two thoughts. One: that finding out who produced the drawings was going to be harder than she thought. Two: that Marcus had a mind like a razor.

They each sat quietly for a minute drinking, trying to absorb the discussion so far, especially this impasse. Then Simone popped another question.

'Do either of you know whether Jackie Husband listens into people's calls in the station.'

She didn't get a quick answer. The other two pondered.

'No idea,' said Marcus. 'What do you think?' he asked Sarah.

'She doesn't like Greg McKenzie, I know that.'

'Doesn't she?'

'No. Take my word for it. But apart from that...'

Simone wished she hadn't raised the issue. She decided she'd try to find a way of asking Jackie whether she knew about the drawings as soon as was feasible.

'Okay. Let's move on. Item 3 – Breaking into Greg's flat.'

'What?' said Marcus, nearly choking. He looked across at Sarah.

'She already told me this afternoon,' said Sarah, 'and I told her - I think she's mad.'

'Dead right. Boss, you're not serious?'

'Relax. I was, but I've changed my mind.'

'Meaning?' said Sarah.

'I had a meeting with my ex-husband this afternoon.' She looked up at the other two. 'He's a policeman...'

Sarah nodded. She knew. Marcus didn't.

'...a detective. Works out of Noreham. Now. This is my good news.' Simone had expected to be able to present this information as a triumph, but the meeting wasn't going as smoothly as she'd hoped. 'Barrie is going to take Greg in for questioning in tomorrow.'

This had the desired effect. The two young faces were agog. Simone rolled out the details.

'He's going to take his mobile phone while he's not looking and they're going to process it for the records so we can see who he's been phoning in the past week or two.'

Nice work, thought Marcus.

'Brilliant,' said Sarah.

'I know – The idea is mostly Barrie's, not mine. I only thought we should steal it...'

Sarah's mouth made the shape of a shocked goldfish.

'...but he offered to bring Greg in for questioning about a harassment case when I told him what we think he's done and I bit his hand off.'

'You're kidding!' said Sarah.

'Nice,' said Marcus. Those devious fuckers, the police - you can't trust them, he thought. But he didn't much care. You dark horse, he wanted to tell his boss. I never imagined in a million years you could be like this. He couldn't wait to tell Big Dave.

'It's awful in a way,' said Simone.

'Very much so,' said Sarah. 'But this once…'

'Yes, this once, morality has to go out of the window.'

'All in the name of a larger morality,' said Marcus.

'Well, exactly,' agreed his superior.

'When will you get the results?' said Sarah to Simone.

'Friday afternoon, I would think. Or Saturday.'

'I can't wait that long,' replied Sarah, grimacing.

'You'll have to.' Simone went and fetched some more beer from the fridge.

'Help yourselves,' she said, putting three more bottles on the table.

'Not for me – I'm driving,' said Sarah.

Marcus decided to take one. He only lived five minutes away. As he reached for the opener, he said to Simone,

'But have you still got the envelope the drawings came in? If he licked it down, it'll have his DNA on it.'

'Oh, crikey, I never thought of that either…hang on…' She thought about it. 'I can't remember. I'll have to look at work. It's all still locked up in a cabinet.'

Not a clever place to leave it with McKenzie around, thought Marcus.

'I'll get it tomorrow and take it in to Barrie,' said Simone. She wrote down another note to herself so she didn't forget.

'And there'll be fingerprints on the drawings and the envelope, unless he was deliberately wearing gloves,' said Marcus, focusing again.

'Problem there,' said Simone. 'Barrie says he's no time and no resources to do any more than he's doing. I'll ask him about a fingerprint test, but from what he told me, we've no chance with DNA.'

Another unscheduled cessation of business occurred for the letting out of breath, sighs and exclamations of surprise and disbelief. Then Marcus got up to go to the loo, so Sarah and Simone started chatting. Marcus idly walked over to Simone's CD collection, and, not liking what he saw, meandered out into the backyard. He wondered around, not having the remotest interest in gardens, but picking up on the ambience of warm dusk and heaven scented flowers. I like my job, he found himself thinking. He wasn't entirely sure how long he wanted to stay in local radio, but for the time being, he realized, he would hang around at TCR and be quite happy about it. His reverie was interrupted by both women calling him back to continue the discussion. It's nice to be wanted, he thought.

'Okay. Item 4 - The fax this morning that was supposed to be from England. I've rung London and checked on the matter and it's a fake. I knew it was, because they wouldn't fax me information like that, but I checked to be sure.'

'What's the point of it - if you're Greg McKenzie?' said Sarah.

'It makes me look a fool,' said Simone.

'Yeah,' said Marcus, 'like you're not in control of things. Sorry.'

'Marcus, it's okay,' said Simone, and made a point of patting his hand again as she added, 'I'm not the Queen.'

He blushed and didn't reply, but wasn't annoyed. More than ever this evening he was inclined to the view that she was alright, the boss. Sarah Billings was giggling at him. He'd pay her back with some practical joke or other. Big Dave would help him think of something. The subject of the fax brought to mind the possibility of a phoney letter from someone landing on her desk one morning.

'He's right, though,' said Sarah. 'It gets everyone wondering what's going on and speculating about things before you've had a chance to do your job. Marcus?'

'Yeah, it unsettles people,' he agreed.

'It explains why you and Reg totally lost it this morning in the newsroom for a start,' said Sarah.

'He's clever, isn't he...' said Marcus, quickly changing the subject.

'Who?' asked Simone.

'McKenzie.'

So he was 'McKenzie' now, thought Simone.

'What time does the post come on a weekday?' Marcus again.

'Early – about a quarter-to-six,' said Sarah.

'So if England sent the official letter yesterday afternoon, McKenzie could have slipped into the station really early this morning, taken it, steamed it open at home and worked up a fax there. Then come back to the station and casually place it on the reception desk.' Marcus folded his arms again, as if to say, 'QED.'

'How long would all that take him, do you think?'

They spent a few minutes trying to figure it out. Given that he lived in Barton Townes, they agreed it could all be done in around twenty minutes.

'What time was the fax found?' said Marcus.

'Just after seven,' said Sarah.

'So he had more than an hour to play with,' said Marcus again.

'He could have taken longer,' said Simone, 'there's no one on the desk until half-past-eight.'

'He's an operator alright,' said Marcus. 'Or thinks he is.'

'It's like something off the telly,' said Sarah, 'or a film.'

No, thought Simone, it isn't at all. At the end, you walk out to your car and drive home, or turn over and watch something else, or go up to bed thinking about next day's work. Bad things in life are a hundred times worse than television.

'What are we going to do then, just wait, yes?' said Sarah.

'I think,' said Simone, opening herself a second bottle, 'that if he's made those phone calls, I can get him sacked. As for the law, whether he's done enough to get himself arrested, I'll have to leave that to Barrie.'

'The key is the drawings,' said Marcus.

'Why do you say that?' asked Simone.

'Well, the phone calls. If you find he's been ringing the press and making calls to this bloke Bakerson, it doesn't prove anything. He could have been returning their calls...'

'Come on...' said Sarah.

'I know, but I'm just thinking, can anyone prove he was the instigator?'

'Thanks, Marcus,' said his friend.

'I'm just being honest.'

Quiet settled on the room. The women looked at Marcus, then at each other, then took a drink. Marcus watched them, looked into Simone's kitchen, what he could see of it, and had a think.

'But the drawings are a different matter,' he said.

No one answered him.

Simone was thinking about Barrie. I never thought when I woke up this morning I'd end the day waiting him to bail me out of a problem.

Sarah was thinking about Lucie. I wonder if I can persuade Simone to give her Giles's job if he doesn't come back?

And I wonder what Lucie and Sarah get up to in bed, pondered Marcus?

'What are you thinking about, Marcus?' said Sarah.

'The drawings. The drawings are the key.'

'And if we can't prove that he did them?'

Both Simone and Sarah knew the answer before Marcus produced it.

'We're in the shit.'

Next, Simone played them the tape recording of her conversation with Greg. Afterwards, she wondered what she'd been thinking.

'You can't tell anything from that,' Sarah had said immediately afterwards, and Marcus had agreed.

'He doesn't sound any shiftier than he normally does.'

After the young ones left Simone walked up and down the lounge then up and down the back yard chewing everything over, itching to do something more but able to do absolutely nothing. Or so she believed for twenty minutes. Then she decided to call Jackie to check one of Greg's stories.

'Hello, Husband Central?...Yeah, I'll get her for you.'

'Jackie – Simone. Sorry to ring you at home in the evening.'

'It's okay, I'm only pottering.'

'Good. Thanks. Look, Greg McKenzie. Did he come in late this morning?'

'Um, hang on, let me think...no, don't think so. He wasn't in when I got in.'

'What time did you get in?'

'Um, hang on – just after twenty-five past because I had to go and pick up a prescription and there was a queue...'

Simone took the phone outside and sat on the seat. It was a cool evening, but she didn't notice.

'...hang on...yes, of course, he came through the front door at about ten-past nine.'

'How do you know?'

'Because I looked at the clock. He was holding an appointment card from his dentist, which meant I looked to see how late he was for work – it's instinct.'

'You mean you're a scandal monger...'

'And I'm nosy.'

'Fair enough. He was at the dentist?' said Simone.

'Yes - and he asked me to write down the date of the next appointment.'

'What do you mean?'

'He had a check up this morning and he needs a filling.'

Oh, did he.

'Who was the dentist, Jackie?'

'What? Um...Reeves and Darling. In the High Street. They're very good. Why?'

'I can't tell you why, Jackie, you'll just have to guess until I can tell you.'

'When's that going to be?'

'Soon, I hope.'

'I wonder what he's been up to?'

'Nothing, Jackie, nothing.'

'If I didn't know you better, Simone, I might have to accuse you of lying to me, ha-ha.'

'Jackie?'

'Yes, Simone?'

'I haven't called you, okay?'

There was a pause on the other end of the line, then.

'Okay. Got it.'

'I really do mean it – this is of the very greatest importance – okay?'

'Okay.'

'Great. Right, you go back to your boozing and your telly.'

'You, too. 'Bye, ha-ha.'

''Bye, Jackie.'

'He asked me to write down the date of the next one.' That's someone being too bloody careful to be real, figured Simone. And of course, how difficult would it be to fake an appointment card? To steal one and fill it in yourself? Not remotely if you had the mentality of…Simone didn't want to finish the sentence. She thought again of the drawings; of how Giles's place was so isolated you had to know exactly where it was to be able to time the posting perfectly; and that you had to know what time Giles and Leah started work. It was almost physically painful to hear each part of the puzzle slotting together. The pieces seemed huge and kept going *thunk!* into place in the back of her head. She should have seen this coming. She should have been more awake and aware. She'd thought him odd for a long time but – it was just such a mess and reflected so badly on her.

She went to the sofa and lay down and tried to think positively. There was nothing more she could do now - just wait for the police results and then, if they gave her what she needed, make one phone call to Andrea Potter-Symons, the head of England, and McKenzie would be gone. She wouldn't need DNA evidence for that to happen. Then, they would just need a new breakfast presenter for everything to go back to normal. Yes, it you were positive in your thinking, this scenario was just about believable. If it turned out from the phone records that Greg wasn't the mole, then she would be like Sisyphus, rolling with the boulder to the bottom of the hill to start all over again.

Simone closed her eyes and tried to relax her mind. It had been such a day. She needed a little nap and then she'd get something to eat. Bugger, I should have offered those two something. She felt bad about that. It was almost rude.

Shit! shouted a voice inside her head. Her eyes sprang open again. She had forgotten Giles! She rang him again every ten minutes for the next hour. No answer. She decided then that she'd had enough of the fight for one day. A phrase came into her head from a long time ago.

The morning and the evening were the fifth day. It was the evening of the third day of the week and the seventh since Giles's Clegg interview, but it didn't matter. She liked the sound the sentence made. '*And the morning and the evening...*' Yes, she liked that. Tomorrow had better not be like today, she thought. If it turns out that it is, I might go and find Giles and jump off a bridge with him. She was scared of growing old and dying alone. It wouldn't be such a bad way to go.

12

A Refugee in Barton Townes

Thursday May 11th

Thursday began to roll itself out for Simone before six a.m. She was woken up by her bladder and realized even while she was sitting on the loo that she wouldn't be able to get back to sleep if she tried. She laid her head down again on the pillow but the birdsong coming in through the small open window and the light behind the curtains distracted her attempt to rest her mind again. She gave up and got up.

The air was cool and nice at the back door when she opened it to fetch in the milk but the fact and the feeling disappeared in an instant. She was already too engrossed in her Two Counties nightmare to truly notice summer's swift advance upon Barton Townes.

She got showered and dressed in a tearing hurry. She put on only the barest minimum of make up. She was careful to drive to the speed limit on the way across town to the station where there were cameras, but pushed it like hell where there weren't. From the car park she practically ran to her office. It was a quarter to seven. She had her drawer key ready well before she got to her desk. Her stomach was hot and nervy with the fear that when she opened the drawer, the drawings would be gone. She'd stuffed them in a padded enveloped marked 'Holiday Photos'. That would have delayed Greg McKenzie for all of ten seconds, she thought as she sat on her chair and put the key in the little lock. She took a moment to look at the metal to see if someone had tried to force it. No one had. The thought occurred again: It isn't him.

She began to reach down to open the relevant drawer, the third one down from the bottom of four, but stopped suddenly, her hand in mid-air. She eyed the door. She didn't think Greg would be in for at least another hour but the way things were, she decided she couldn't be sure. She got up and walked around her desk and picked up a visitors' chair. She took it to the door and leaned it over so the handle wouldn't push down from outside. Then she went back to the desk, leant down and opened the drawer. The envelope was there, her writing in blue permanent marker ink staring up at her. Thank God, she said to herself, but she still admonished herself. You're so stupid - he could have had them away easily. Then that thought prodded her again: it's not him. If it was him - or anyone else at the station come to that - the drawings would be gone.

Please, no, she found herself asking her maker. And realized that she needed it to be Greg, now – the thought of it being someone else would just make everything impossible.

She opened the big envelope and carefully pulled out the pieces of paper that held the marks of the obscene drawings and the envelope they'd come in. She placed them carefully on the desk in front of her, cleared her throat, and began the inspection.

Using her forefinger, she turned the smaller envelope around so the sealing end was closest to her. It was clear in a second that the flap had been tucked under, not stuck down. Damn! The bastard wasn't stupid. Or was he? Had he really not touched the drawings with bare fingers? Not left a hair behind? Some skin? A bead or two of sweat?

With exaggerated care she put the drawings back in the small envelope, then that envelope inside the big one touching all the edges as minimally as she could and took them with her back to the car. She was headed for the police station. Barrie had told her he couldn't get the drawings tested but she didn't care – she would try to persuade him to change his mind.

When she got there he hadn't arrived, indeed, wasn't expected for another hour, so she stood at the reception counter and wrote him a note. She took great care that the important part of it was legible because she thought she had scruffy handwriting.

"If you really can't wangle a DNA test at least try to find some fingerprints for me? I wouldn't ask only it's a matter of life and death. You don't have to match any fingerprints you find. We just need to know how many sets there are, two or three? We know mine and the girl who received it are on it but any extra ones must be from the sender. Suspect won't have a crim record, but try the database in case. If it's three, try to match it but I'm pretty sure our suspect doesn't have a record."

She left it with the member of staff on duty and went into town. It was twenty-five to eight and there was space to park on the high street near a paper shop. She bought an Independent and some chocolate and went back to TCR. She made some coffee, read the paper and listened to Bob for a minute or two.

'...I've been just three times this season and they won each time, Alan.'

'Make sure you're at the second leg then Bob - they need every bit of help they can get.'

'What do you think the key was last night?'

'Well, Bob...'

He was fine. He's on top of it, she thought. Simone struggled with sport but she knew they were talking about the football. BT Hardware were on the verge of making it into the big league or whatever they called it for the first time in their history. They must have played last night. She'd try to make a point of finding out what the score was later.

No one bothered her until the clock hit two minutes to eight and she was ready to go into action. She went looking for Greg. Simone found him in his office talking to Lucie Bastable. She went cold when she realized who he was with, but as his door was more or less wide open, she felt she needn't worry. Despite the conversation of the previous evening at her house, she was sure Greg was suddenly going to turn into a kidnapper or a murderer.

'Morning, you two,' she said going in, trying hard to be bright and breezy.

'Hi, come in...So, I'd just relax a little more. You've earned the right to, you really have.' He smiled at Lucie who smiled back winningly, making Simone think hard about both of them. She assumed Sarah told her everything.

'Thanks, Greg. Hi, Simone, just leaving,' said Lucie. She's a tough little nut, thought the managing editor of Two Counties Radio.

'Now, what can I do for you,' said Greg. 'How are you? And how's Giles?'

'I'm fine. Giles is doing okay.'

She still didn't know but was damned if she was going to let on.

'Good.'

'So. Where's the bus today? You're here in town, aren't you?'

'No, that's tomorrow...'

Fuck, cursed Simone. *How could I have read the dates wrong?*

'...Today we're in the main square at Noreham at eleven. Should be very busy.'

Shit, she'd have to ring Barrie to sort a time out.

'That's fine,' she said, getting a grip, 'but I want to pin you down to a meeting before the week's end. We haven't had a strategy meeting, just the two of us, for about a month. I've been checking. We should have met a week ago.'

'Yes, I know. Still, what with everything, it's not your fault you forgot. And I did too, actually.' Simone could have thumped him.

'I've brought my diary,' said Simone.

Within three minutes Simone was back in her office having kept the chat to a minimum. She'd had the time to look him over though. She'd looked at his clothes to see that they were clean and ironed, and she

360

surreptitiously studied his face for whiskers missed whilst shaving but he was immaculate. How can he iron at a time like this, she thought?

She was frantic with worry that between them she and Barrie could mess this up. She had told Barrie that Greg would be in Barton Townes and now he was going to be in bloody Noreham.

She got to her office and flipped open her phone. It wasn't too early now to get him on his mobile.

'Hi, Barrie. Everything okay?'

'Shit, sorry,' said DI Barrie Jones. 'I haven't fully organized everything…'

How bloody typical. *Bloody* Barrie.

'…but it's in hand. Don't say anything, please. We're incredibly busy.'

'No, no, no, I wasn't going to, don't worry.'

'What time do you want us to go and get him?'

'There might be a problem - he's going out to Noreham at half-past ten.'

'That's okay. I'll get someone to pick him up there.'

'Don't you want to do it in town here?'

'No, I can't do it, anyway. The bloke I've set on to it is over at Noreham all day today anyway, so it's perfect. He'll do an excellent job for you. Don't worry.'

'I shouldn't worry?'

'No. He's really good. I'll brief him, I promise.'

'You've not forgotten the details?'

'I've got notes here, don't fret. Though Iain might like to ring you though, if you wouldn't mind.'

God, thought Simone, this was falling apart.

'He likes to do a thorough job.' he said.

'Tell him to make it subtle, Barrie, won't you.'

'You'll probably be able to tell him yourself. Look, Simone, stop worrying. It won't be a problem. Give me some credit.'

'Okay. I trust you.'

'Dozens wouldn't, ha-ha,' said Barrie. And I'd be one of them she thought with a sigh.

'Did you get the envelope?'

'What envelope?'

Oh, for God's sake. She wanted to scream at him.

'I'm just kidding - of course I got it. I thought I told you I couldn't do it for you?'

'Please, Barrie. Please. Just dust it for the number of people who've had their prints on it. You don't even have to match any of them. I just want to know for now if it's more than two.'

'We should do this properly at the proper time – and I'll tell you flat, there's no way we can do a DNA. This isn't a murder, you know.'

'Okay, I understand, so just do the prints then...Please...?'

She could hear herself whining at her ex-husband, hated herself but knew it had to be done. There was a long pause at the other end. When after three seconds she heard him sigh Simone knew she'd won.

'Oh, alright, I'll see what I can do. But I want to tell you, on paper we haven't got the time even to do the prints.'

'Thank you, thank you, thank you, you won't regret it.'

'Won't I?'

'No, this bloke's either very nasty or very sick. Either way-'

'Yes, I know, you think we need to nail him. Look. Leave it with me. I'll phone you as soon as I know.'

'You haven't lost my mobile number?'

'No, I've got it. Actually you'd better give it me.'

'Okay, got a pen...'

She felt better. So they might have this thing wrapped up in another day. That would do. Persistence, she thought, that was something else to work on. She still wasn't good at getting men to do things for her. She usually backed down way too easily.

Simone was thinking about how she might ring the dentist to check that Greg had actually been there yesterday when the phone rang.

'Yep.'

'Hi, Simone.'

'You're in early, Jackie.'

'It's the tension: I'm addicted to it. I've been here since twenty-to-eight.'

'As long as you don't want paying overtime...'

'Ha-ha-ha. You are funny sometimes, boss.'

'Stop calling me "Boss"!'

'Ha-ha. Tanya Howe is in reception.'

'Oh!' She paused and looked at her watch. There was nothing urgent to attend to for the next half an hour or so. At 9.15 she had the review meeting for Bob's show, before that, nothing pressing.

'Is anyone on hand to bring her through?'

'I'll do it.'

'Thanks, Jack.'

Simone went out with the empty coffee jug to the kitchen. She soon heard two voices going past the open door.

'Jackie? I'm in here.'

She swung round from the sink to see a very neatly dressed, slightly overweight girl in her twenties, holding a slightly nervous smile for her underneath very straight blonde hair. She looks Swedish, Simone thought, or Danish.

'Hello, I'm Tanya Wood.'

Simone had never seen anyone so pleased to see her in her entire life. She looked like a lottery winner.

'Thank you so much for seeing me,' she said. I'm having her, thought Simone. Let them try and stop me.

'Are you Swedish?' said Simone.

A surprised 'Oh!' popped out of her wide mouth followed by a short laugh. 'No!' she said, and she laughed again. 'But my mum's family's from America. And they were Norwegian immigrants originally.'

'And your Dad's not Greek...' said Simone.

'No, ha-ha.' It was an odd way to kick off, but otherwise, Simone Pound was just as she imagined her. Don't try too hard to impress her otherwise you'll blow it, she told herself.

'Don't mind me,' said Simone, taking the girl's hand and touching her sleeve above the elbow. 'I'm just having one of those days – no! Weeks!'

They both laughed and Tanya couldn't help but keep smiling. This is exactly why she'd come. 'Oh – right, well,' she said, 'if there's anything I can do right now to help, just tell me.'

'To start with, just don't tell me you don't drink coffee, or you can go straight back to London right now.'

'I'm green tea only, I'm afraid.'

Typical modern southerner, thought Simone. She wished she hadn't made the joke.

'Just kidding. Milk, three sugars,' said Tanya, with a glint in her one ever-so-slightly crooked eye.

'Three!' said Simone.

'Kidding again, sorry - one and a half.' And they both laughed again. I'm definitely having her, thought Simone.

They'd just sat down in the office when the phone rang again. Simone looked at her watch: ten-fifteen.

'Yep?'

'Are you going to be like this all day?'

'Like what?'

'"Yep!"'

'No. Sorry.'

'That's alright, then! Chap called Iain Blame on the line for you.'

'Put him through.'

'He won't say what it's about.'

'Doesn't matter, Jack, I know who this is.'

'Okay.'

'Hello?'

'Simone? DS Blame from Bart Constabulary. Colleague of Barrie's.'

I bet he's told him I'm a cow, she thought.

'Hi.'

'This feller you want bringing in.'

She recognized a Scottish accent. She loved Scottish accents.

'Yes.'

'Can I get this absolutely clear? He's sent some obscene drawings to a woman colleague of yours.'

Bloody Barrie. He can't have told him the story properly.

'Yes. That's right.'

'Okay. I want to get things clear here. So, was it specific that the name of the woman who received the drawings was actually in them?'

'Yes, absolutely.' He sounded young and he had a funny way of saying things.

'She was labelled or something. Clearly, though.'

'Yes, that's right.'

'Can I just say...do you have someone with you? You can't really speak.'

'Yes, that's right.'

Simone was distracted. Tanya was getting up.

'I'll wait outside,' she mouthed slowly.

Good girl, thought Simone. Simone mouthed back her thanks. The door closed.

'It's okay. I can speak now, Iain.'

'Great. So the drawings had an effect on the girl – I take it the girl was very upset...'

'Yes, we're talking traumatic. She immediately quit her job - and the drawings were very explicit.'

'Any written obscenities?'

'No, the pictures were obscene enough.'

'Could you describe them for me?'

She could. And did.

'Okay. And can you tell me how strongly you suspect this feller of sending the drawings?'

'Convinced.'

'Why's that?'

'We think it had to be someone from this radio station. And he has a clear motive. We think he wanted to break up the girl's relationship so he could have another go at her or just out of revenge. They had a fling three years ago.'

'Right, that's great. Three years.'

He repeated the three years. Did this give him doubts? He was writing it down. Was it going to ruin everything?

'Oh!' said Simone, 'and we think we know he's been following the girl and following her boyfriend, Giles. Which is how he came by certain information.'

'Tough to prove unless somebody saw him. Still, not to worry, there's plenty there to work on. And the phone – when we've finished with it we'll need to drop it off. Shall I have it brought to your house?'

'Yes. Do you need the address?'

'Aye, that'd be great.'

She gave him the address, thinking, blimey, he's a cool one. He's dealing with this like a man from the Citizens Advice Bureau – even nicking the phone isn't fazing him in the slightest.

'We can slip it through the door if you're not in.'

'Yes, that'll be great.' What a service the police could put up for you these days!

'Okay. That's great, Mrs. Jones.'

'It's Mizz Pound, actually. But you can call me "Simone".'

Especially with that sexy voice, she thought. She put the phone down. Then she was cursing again. Bugger it, I should have asked him about the bloody fingerprints.

'Thanks for doing that,' said Simone when she'd fetched Tanya back. She'd been nosing around the Music Library with a polite, interested look on her face.

'No problem.'

'Right, let's get down to cases.'

'Okay.'

'Occasionally I get phone calls from people who want jobs here,' said Simone, 'but not from people ready to leave an amazing job like yours.'

Tanya wasn't sure whether or not to tell her about the unit's 'work' on Giles McAndrew. She decided to hold off for the time being.

'It's not – well, it is, I suppose, but I hate it. It's not what I thought it was going to be.'

'Tough world, I should imagine…'

'Very. I haven't been there long, but I need to get out. Before…' The girl coloured very slightly.

'…before I start to enjoy it.'

'Oh, yes…?' Simone wanted more.

'It's nasty, but there's something addictive about it. It's the adrenalin, I think.'

'But from where you are you must be able to move up, or across to something else, no?'

Simone looked again at Tanya's CV. Politics degree from York, a First, Masters in Politics from Manchester, specialising in voting behaviour.

'I suppose…' she said modestly.

'Your qualifications are amazing. You'd be out of your depth in reverse in a place like this.' Simone's hopes had begun sinking about five minutes ago. Tanya needed a fifty grand a year job by the time she was 30 to match what Simone had in front of her.

'I don't care.'

'Why?'

'I want to work in radio.'

'But you know, I think you could go straight into BRBC in London or BRBC TV. They'd snap you up in a second.'

'I want to work here.'

'I think you'd be bored here, love. It's mostly broken bus stops, seed prices and outsized marrows. What's been going on here with Giles McAndrew – it's completely abnormal.'

'Why are you trying to put me off? You don't have anything for me?'

'On the contrary: I may have something for you very, very soon the way things are going here. I just don't want you to be disappointed after two weeks and come and tell me you want to leave.'

'So you think I'd be good enough for you?'

'Of course.'

'That's all I wanted to hear. Please give me a job.'

'Why? Why are you so desperate?'

Tanya stopped and thought about it.

'I don't know why…I was reading the paper last Saturday - about Giles and John Clegg. And I'd heard you on the radio defending the station - what day would that have been…' She looked to Simone for guidance.

'Don't look at me - it's been a complete blur, the past week.'

Tanya found herself laughing. She couldn't remember the last time she'd found anything in the unit funny, or anyone.

'Okay, well – I was reading the paper and thinking again about your interview and I thought, I've got to go there.' Tanya knew what she wanted to say next but wasn't sure it wouldn't sink her.

'I thought, I've got to and work for this woman.' She continued to look at Simone Pound right smack in the eye. 'There, I've said it.'

Simone had nothing to say in reply, though she thought, 'Really? You must be completely off your head.'

'I've blown it now, haven't I...' God, thought Tanya - she thinks I'm bullshitting. 'You don't believe me, do you...'

'No, no it's not that.'

'Then I started listening to you on the Internet. To the station, I mean.'

She had to be kidding.

'And you weren't put off?'

They both giggled, Simone's squeak sticking out above Tanya's soft gurgle at the back of the throat.

'No! It was Bob Constable.'

Bloody hell, she knew the names.

'I was listening to him last Saturday morning. I was lying in bed...I've got my computer in my bedroom...'

It must have been the way Simone was looking at her.

'...Anyway, there was something about him - and the stuff he was talking about.'

'The broken bus stops and the seed prices...'

'Exactly,' said Tanya laughing. 'He conjured up a completely different world to the one I'm in - and he was so funny. I knew then I had to contact you.'

'If only you knew,' said Simone, quietly.

'Pardon?'

'Nothing, it doesn't matter – I'll tell you another time.'

Tanya's heart rose. 'Another time,' she just said. This is working, she thought – I'm getting through to her.

'Well, that's it,' said Tanya.

'And now you've seen Barton Townes...and you've seen the station...and you're not put off?'

'I love it. It's just how I imagined it.'

'You're mad,' said Simone.

'No. I'm not.' said Tanya emphatically.

'No?' said Simone.

'No – there's nothing I'd like better than an outsized marrow.'

They both giggled again.

'Don't tell anyone I said that,' said Tanya.

'Don't worry, your secret's safe with me, dear.'

Simone laughed again, her squeak a little lower this time, and Tanya thought, 'I'm in.' It was one of the best feelings she'd had in a long, long time.

13

Station to Station

The door of the interrogation room opened at last and two people entered: a policewoman in uniform and a man in a business suit. The man had ID clipped on to his belt. A detective, though Greg McKenzie had never seen one in the flesh before.

'Sorry to keep you waiting Mr. McKenzie.'

'It's okay.'

'And I'm sorry to drag you in today; only there's a matter we're looking into and we think you can help. Oh, sorry,' said the detective offering his hand, 'Iain Blame.'

Greg returned the gesture and wondered tensely how this was going to go while DS Blame considered the handshake.

'You're Greg, right?'

'Yes, that's right.'

'You look a little nervous,' said Blame, smiling broadly and sitting down.

Crikey, what a bastard, thought Greg, and a confident bastard too. You're on home territory; you think you hold all the cards here.

'No - well, a little. I'm just wondering what all this is about.'

'Well. We're investigating a simple case of harassment. Someone's produced some very nice drawings that, unfortunately, have caused some people a lot of...' Blame paused, stood up, and ostentatiously took off his jacket without his eyes leaving the listener's.

'...distress,' he said, finishing the sentence like the slamming of a door. The eyes were now menacing and Greg wondered whether in real life people really did get beaten up in police stations.

'You work at Two Counties Radio, I understand...'

Greg nodded solemnly.

'...and very good at your job, I hear.'

'Oh?'

'Yes. Your boss rates you highly. Very highly. She's very upset that you're here.'

'Oh?'

Blame nodded back.

'So you'll have heard all about the drawings, yes? Seen them perhaps.'

'I...no, I don't know what you're talking about, basically.'

'You don't.'

'No. Who were they sent to?'

'A girl.'

'Which girl? Oh, Leah Caighton.'

Greg's expression lifted to form an innocent question that wasn't in his intonation. Iain Blame nodded.

'That's right, Leah Caighton. Very upset, that girl. Wants to press charges against whoever we find was responsible. Comes from a very rich family, did you know that? She tries to hide it from people. They're ready to pile into a civil prosecution if we don't do the business, do you know what I mean?'

Greg wasn't very keen on Scottish people, even though he came from the same stock himself, originally. He was a short-arse for a copper too; was he the product of some drive towards a more democratic police force in terms of height that had escaped his news net in the past ten years? He didn't know. But he wasn't stupid, this bloke; he might be one of the new breed that come in with a degree; he had an unmistakably intelligent face. And something in the eyes that made the fellow very hard to dislike. Greg nodded at him again.

'Do you mind if I take my jacket off?' He was beginning to settle down.

'Be my guest, Mr. McKenzie. It is warm.'

Greg thought they were mad having the heating on this high in May when it was a nice day outside. That's the police for you, he thought. As he took it off he stood up and noticed the policewoman near the door look at him with concern, as if he might be about to make a run for it. He carefully placed his jacket on the back of the chair, just as the detective had, and sat down again.

'Don't sit down. I want you to come with me.'

Greg looked mystified, and his nervous tension increased again. He started to get up.

'That's it. Don't worry, it's okay. I just want to show you something.'

He was shown through the door again and out into the corridor, but instead of going right down to the end door which went to the front desk, he was shown a left turn into a room very much like the newsroom at TCR. It was untidy, full of the same sort of desks with computers on, but instead of reporters, presenters and producers, it had police in it. The door was open just like the TCR newsroom, and just like TCR, hardly anyone noticed him when he walked into the room.

'This is my desk. Take a seat.'

Greg McKenzie did as he was told and sat down.

370

'That's it. Thanks.'

DS Blame momentarily turned to the desk behind him and picked up a buff-coloured envelope. Greg looked over his shoulder as Blame came back and stood next to him on his right-hand side. He watched him shake a sheaf of papers out of the envelope on to the desk in front of them. They split apart slightly.

'Here, let me make them easier for you to see.'

Blame set the four photographs out with exaggerated care so they both could see them very clearly.

'There. Do you recognize them?'

Greg was distracted by a man staring in at him through a facing window, with folded arms and a very serious face. He wondered whether there was a camera on him above his head but he didn't look up. He looked down at the pictures.

'No.'

He kept looking, and felt Blame scrutinizing him, even though he couldn't see his whole face. He waited for Blame to speak again: to put pressure on him; ask him the question again; produce at least one of the tricks he'd seen on television and in films, but he didn't. Greg decided he wasn't going to say any more.

'Okay.'

The expression in his voice made Greg relax. He let out a quiet sigh of relief. Then he tensed very quickly. Was this the moment when they hit him?

'Okay. Look. Go back and get your jacket and you can go. I'll come with you.'

Greg wanted to say "Thank you" but no words came out. He just pushed of from the swivel chair and followed Blame back to the interview room. The detective said nothing while they both plucked their jackets off the backs of their respective chairs. They started walking back towards the squad room door, the detective leading. H stopped at the door and turned.

'Thanks for coming in, Mr. McKenzie.'

Greg stopped too.

'No, it's okay, keep coming.'

Blame stood by the open door pointing down the corridor.

'It's okay.' Greg didn't know what else to say. He could the heat of his neck.

'We'll let you know if we need you again, okay?' He looked down the corridor again where a colleague had opened the door from the reception area.

'Constable Barnes, could you show Mr. McKenzie out?'

'Yeah, 'course,' said a slightly plump-looking uniform.

'Thanks.' Iain Blame turned again to look at Greg.

'Goodbye, Mr. McKenzie.'

'G'bye,' said Greg and began walking to the reception door. In a few seconds he stood in the afternoon Noreham sunlight feeling very strange. He realized that he wasn't going to get a lift back to the market square so he started to walk. It wasn't far.

Back in the squad room, DS Blame was thinking about his next job but looked across the room to Constable Jenks.

'Did you get it, Teri?'

Teri Jenkins swung round and held up a mobile phone. 'Yep,' she said with a short, matter of fact smile.

'God, is this country not full of mugs or what, Teri?'

'I hate to say it, but you're right, boss.'

'I despair of us sometimes, I really do.'

'Shall I run it over to Pete?'

'Thanks, do that. And tell him it's for DI Jones, will you. It'll get done in half the time.'

'Okay.'

'Hang on, Teri - what do you think?'

'You mean, "is he guilty?"'

'Aye.'

'I'm not sure.'

'But if there was a tenner riding on it...'

She thought about it hard for some seconds.

'I think it was probably him. Am I right?'

'He's as guilty as hell.'

'You think?' said Teri, feeling fairly pleased but wishing she'd expressed her opinion more confidently.

'He thinks he's smart, but he's nothing but a bloody amateur.'

14

Simone Frets At Phone Calls

Simone looked again at her watch: 11.30. With any luck Iain would have Greg McKenzie there at the station right now. She tried to imagine the scene but couldn't. She was more nervous, she thought, than she'd been since her finals. No, her wedding day. She'd been to the toilet twice already this morning.

She thought Greg would be out all day now and would have enough on his plate when he returned but she got her story ready concerning Tanya. He might still want to know what she was doing there: she was just observing because she was interested in a career in local radio. It was no big deal - people were dropping for stuff like that all the time. Simone had put Tanya with Sarah for the rest of the morning; she could learn a hell of a lot from just shadowing a news editor. After a meeting here and a discussion or two there, Tanya would begin to understand how they did things, what their values were.

But doubts still gnawed at Simone's bones. Tanya's desire to work at Two Counties seemed to be absolutely genuine but she was outrageously over-qualified. She had fantastic qualifications and her job in London had clearly given her reporting skills by the bucket load already. If she could deal with politicos and hacks in the capital, she'd be able to do local radio standing on her head in about a week. The thing was, why on earth did someone like her want to come to Barton Townes? Was she, Simone, really being had again? Was this another bloody Downing Street trick? Surely not. Or had she left Downing Street - was that true? - and gone to work for a tabloid paper? Didn't they trap people with dirty tricks like this? She thought they did.

Tanya Howe turning up was just typical of the madness. A tonic for the spirit or devious actress intent of doing them more damage? Trust your instincts, Simone, she told herself. What did they tell her? They told her to put the girl to good use and see where that got the both of them. She mulled something over while she chewed on a Brunch Bar that she got from a box in her drawer and sipped at her third cup of coffee.

When, after dealing with some paperwork and studying the latest listening figures which as usual made very interesting reading she looked up and saw that it was past midday, she realised she hadn't fretted about Greg for nearly an hour. By now DS Blame should have done his work. She got her phone out and rang Barrie, her tummy all molten metal again.

'Yes?' said a man with obviously a lot on his plate and no time to talk.

'It's me.'

'Oh, hi. Right - I've had a call from my colleague, Iain, and it's all gone to plan. Hasn't he rung you yet?'

'No.'

'He will – he's meticulous.'

'Really? You've done it?' She was excited.

'Yeah. When he says he's going to do something, he does it, and I'll tell you this, it stays done.'

'Wonderful.'

'I didn't want to tell you this until I knew he'd delivered though.'

'It's not like you to avoid an idle boast, dear,'

'Now, now, I thought we'd agreed to leave all of that behind.'

'Sorry. Can I have his number? I can't wait for him to call. I'm too on edge. I need to know exactly how it went.'

'Okay – look, I'll get a girl to text you the number in a minute.'

'What? You'll get a–'

'Go easy on me – I've only just got used to a text not being writing in a book.'

'Okay. I'll just knee you in the groin if I ever see you again.'

'What do you mean 'if'? 'Course you'll see me again.'

Something in his voice made her smile – a boyishness. 'That would be good, you know. Just a coffee or something once in a while.'

'Sure. We'll do that. Look – I'm really up to here at the mo – I'll call you sometime.'

'Do that.'

He wasn't completely bad, her ex-husband.

Simone paced up and down her office for about a minute then went to find Sarah and Tanya. They were in one of the meeting rooms where, alone, Sarah was telling the newcomer about the community bus project.

'Sorry to interrupt. Can you come and see me when you're done in here?'

'Who me?' said Tanya, looking slightly worried.

'Yes, you,' she said breezily.

She looked at Sarah and smiled. She was worried about her feeling pushed out by the newcomer. But Sarah Billings smiled back, apparently her normal, wonderful self.

Simone had held her phone in her hand on the trip round the station to find the girls. In the toilet on the way back to her office, it buzzed into life. The phone number had arrived. Simone did a wee in a hurry and went back to her office. She rang the Detective with the sexy voice.

'Hello?'

'Hello. Simone Pound. It's Iain, isn't it?'

'Aye, that'll do. You're wanting to know about the interview we carried out this morning, I understand.'

'Yes, how did it go?' Her heart fluttered.

'It went well.'

'Oh, good.'

'For a start we got his phone.'

'Great. I'm going to send someone over to get it. Shall I sent them tomorrow or is that too soon?'

'We can do better than that. If you come at about four this afternoon it'll be ready. That ex-husband of yours has some clout round here, I'm telling you.'

'Really?'

'Aye. They're backed up solid in there, really.'

'I was going to say if only had that sort of magic when he was my husband but I won't, ha-ha,'

'Ha-ha, that's fine, Simone, you can tell me any dark secrets about the DI you like, I don't mind.'

'Ha-ha. Wait until you're having a really bad day then call me, I'll give you something to cheer you up, don't worry.'

'Okay. I'll do that.'

'I'll send someone over to you at about four then. Have you seen the results?'

'No, they're not ready yet. But a kind lady in the lab has promised me not later than four o'clock. We don't get sneak previews. But I can tell you something else about our friend Mr McKenzie.'

'Oh, yes?'

'Are you coming this afternoon?'

'Probably not, no.'

'Okay, I'll tell you now, then. The man, for me, is as guilty as anything.'

'What, he admitted it?'

'No, no. I'm not that good - but if I'd had another half an hour he would have done.'

'Wh- Well, how do you know then?' Simone suddenly found herself standing up and her heart was thudding. She wished she'd been there for the interview.

'Experience, Simone. In most cases, you know in sixty seconds whether they're innocent or guilty – it's in the body language. This fellow of yours had the words "I'm Matisse" practically tattooed on his forehead.'

'Oh, my Lord.'

'Is that not what you wanted?'

'Yes, oh yes. It's just that, well, it's just amazing. Something going right for a change.'

'Well, it's nice to hear someone saying something nice about us for a change. For that, I'll tell you something else - if it ever gets to pressing charges for harassment, which I'm happy to do if Barrie ever agrees, you're Greg fall apart in about ten minutes.'

'Why didn't you, um…' She didn't want to sound ungrateful.

'Why didn't I extract a full confession this morning, is that what you want to know?'

'Yes. If I might ask you that.'

'Time. We didn't really have the time to do what we did, and Barrie said that all you really wanted was the phone, and that was against the regs anyway, so…'

'I understand.'

'I'm glad.'

'No, that's brilliant. Thanks, I'm so grateful.'

'No problem.'

'And not just me, a lot of people are going to be very pleased when all this gets sorted out.'

'I'm glad to hear it. Anything else you want doing, just ask.'

'I will.'

'Take care, then.'

'I will, you too. 'Bye.'

''Bye.'

Simone was pulsating with excitement when she closed the phone. She got up and paced the space in front of her desk working out what to do next, though she'd tried to think it through dozens of times already. So, do I phone Andrea Potter-Symons or do I phone Ian Bakerson? Do I phone now or do I phone when I get the results? You phone when you get the results, idiot! He said he was guilty of the drawings not that he'd seen the phone records! She was a bundle of nerves. She went on pacing and went on troubling herself. That's right, Simone, give yourself varicose veins. She looked at the clock. Twenty-past-twelve, nearly.

Now she needed the fingerprint results. She rang Barrie again on her mobile but couldn't get him. She kept trying, pacing the floor. Then between attempts the office phone went and she nearly jumped out of her skin.

'Barrie for you, Simone.'

'Thanks.'

'Oh – Greg McKenzie just rang. He's lost his phone and wants us to have a look for it. He wanted me to tell you.'

'Oh, did he now, Jackie?' She had expected this but it didn't stop the news ratcheting up her stress level.

'Oh, yes, he did.'

'Okay, find someone to take a look around, could you?'

'Sure. Putting Barrie through.'

'Thanks, Jack.'

God forgive my deceiving tongue, she said aloud.

'Simone?'

'Barrie?'

'Yes. I've got the results.'

'Yes?'

'There are two sets of prints on the drawings...'

'Yes?'

'And two sets of prints on the envelope.'

Bollocks, she said inside.

'You're sure?'

'Of course – I know the girl who did the test - she doesn't make simple mistakes. He's not stupid, this fellow of yours.'

'I know.'

'Okay, I've got to dash.'

'Okay, thanks.'

It was too much. A detective believed in Greg's guilt but even if the phone records did go on to prove that he was the mole, they would have no fingerprint evidence and no DNA evidence either. Simone tried to think the thing through. What would the evidence look like in a court of law? With what they had, would they be laughed out into the street? Marcus Shifley's words from the meeting the previous night echoed again in her head: 'The key to this is the drawings...this is where we'll get him.' He was probably right: without evidence that he actually did the drawings, the best they could do was to get him kicked him out of TCR.

It all seemed to be falling apart again. What if the phone records didn't show he made the calls to the press and to England? What if he was smart enough to use another phone? Which he'd since thrown away. Maybe he used a landline at home; and maybe Barrie could get those records looked at. But she was clutching at straws, she knew.

377

She'd used up her ration of favours there for a long while. So, she thought. If he really was a serious operator, he was going to get off scot-free and she would have to carry on working with him. She'd done it for six years but now it was unthinkable that she could start again. She was coming to the end of the road, or *a* road, that was clear. But what was beyond it?

For the first time in months, Simone sat down, dropped her guard and let the floodgates of a good cry open wide.

15

Giles and the Third Meeting

As she was drying her eyes and feeling lucky that no one had knocked on her door while she was having her wet emotional outburst, Giles Wilkinson was thinking how odd it was that sleeping past the hour of 4 am was beginning to feel quite natural. And that it didn't feel all that strange not going to work considering all the years of radio graft he'd put in. When it comes down to it, he thought, I don't understand life. I'm forty but I don't understand it at all. He asked Giles McAndrew whether he understood life but he didn't either. Just as well I'm leaving him, he said to his new self. He belted up and set off to Simone at TCR.

Her box set sat on the front seat still in an HMV bag. He looked at it and thought, I should have wrapped it in nice paper. He still could. He would. What hurry was he in? He wasn't in any hurry. He didn't turn left into Bridges Lane when he got to the church but went straight on to the town centre and parked again behind the high street. He put money into the machine again for his ticket and felt fine about it.

In the stationary shop where he bought some pretty green paper, the girl at the counter was happy to wrap the box for him.

'No problem, sir.'

He signed a gift tag too, 'love from Giles.' He didn't think he'd ever told her his real name. He walked out of the shop feeling ready to begin thinking everything through - to think out what he really wanted to do next. No, more than that, to decide what he wanted to do with the rest of his life. He felt strong and he felt like a cup of coffee. Di Mario's was just along the street.

He'd only just sat down and ordered when he looked up from the magazine he'd taken off the rack in the direction of the voice.

'Hello,' it went a second time.

Giles looked up.

'Me again.'

Giles was at something of a loss.

'Fancy seeing you here!' she said. It was the woman again.

'I've never seen you here before.'

'Well, that's what's odd, you see. I've never been here before – and the first time I come in, you're here!' She was very bright and cheerful.

Giles instinctively looked across the room to spot the table she might have vacated.

'No, I'm on my own,' she said.

He was confused.

'I'm really glad to see you,' said the woman, 'there's something I forget to tell you.'

Oh, yes? said Giles's face.

'Can I sit down?'

'Be my guest,' said Giles, gesturing with an open palm.

'Thanks. It's just that there's a programme on the TV you should see tonight.'

'Really?'

'Yes, really.'

'Tonight?'

'Yes, Thursday night. That's tonight, right?'

Giles had to think about it. Then he nodded.

'Yes, I thought it was,' she said. 'Sorry, I can be a bit scatterbrained.'

'So I see.'

'Don't.'

'I'm sorry?'

'Don't be like that.' She smiled at him. He studied her face, trying desperately to place her from somewhere.

'Sorry.' He hadn't meant to be snotty with her.

'That's okay. Don't worry about it.'

Giles made a point of putting on a smile himself and then said, 'So, the programme-' He interrupted himself suddenly. 'Hang on. Sorry, but you haven't told me your name.'

'My name? Oh, you don't want to know, it's a silly name.'

'Doesn't matter, tell me.'

'People just call me "Mally". Now, the programme is on BBC 2, at nine o'clock. And it's called, "Intervention".'

The title didn't mean anything to Giles.

'You won't have seen it,' she said, 'it's the first one tonight, first series.'

'Why should I watch it?'

'Trust me. You need to watch it. Well, I've got to shoot again. Sorry. I'll let you get on with your coffee.'

'It doesn't matter, it hasn't arrived yet.'

'Oh, no, it hasn't. I have to go anyway. I'll see you around.'

'Soon, I suppose.'

'Hmm?'

'This is the third time in two days.' Giles could feel his thinking coming right back. He felt himself smile again.

'Oh, right, ha-ha.'

Mally began to move towards the door.

'Well, see ya,' she said. At the door she stopped, turned and came back within speaking distance.

'I nearly forgot...'

'Yes?'

'You must tell Simone. Make sure she watches it too. 'Bye.'

She was gone before Giles began to think properly about what she'd said.

'Here you are.'

His coffee had arrived. He looked up at the young girl serving him. He smiled at her too.

'Thanks a lot,' he said.

The girl looked and smiled back, said, 'you're welcome' and coloured. I'm coming right back, he thought. He felt his face and its smoothness. He'd shaved when he got up. I must be looking much better too, he thought. He looked down into his cup after noticing the rather nice shape it made on the table and the neat chocolate-brown pattern in the glaze, and admired the creamy thick beige surface of froth speckled with chocolate. That looks pretty great, he said to himself. It smelt pretty good too. He opened the wrapper on the biscuit that came with the drink. This smelt good too, even before he bit into it. He bit it in half. It was nice and crunchy. He added a sip of coffee to the malty taste in his mouth, using the liquid to wash some of the masticated biscuit off his back teeth. It was, he decided, the best thing he'd tasted in ages.

Then he went back to thinking about the three-time woman. Simone had to watch the programme? Then she knew Simone. So Leah was the key, she had to be. He almost leaped out of the chair to run after her but in the next instant knew that she'd be way down the street by now.

Giles tried to grasp what was going on here, tried hard. Yesterday morning his life was in pieces. A day later he seemed to have put a lot of them back together, some in a very different position. One day he was on the verge of drowning, the next he was swimming for the shore knowing he would survive. In the middle of this was a strange woman who kept appearing out of the blue. Who seemed to know him. Each time he wondered whether he should be concerned about this he was conscious that his internal system refused to send out stress hormones or whatever it was that made you feel worried. It was a puzzle. The woman didn't seem to want anything from him so what was to worry about? She couldn't be a stalker. She was too happy for a start , and she kept leaving him almost as soon as she turned up. What would Giles

381

McAndrew do, he started to ask again but decided he was done with that. It was now a matter of what Giles Wilkinson was going to do.

He decided it was all a part of life's rich tapestry and confirmed that he should just take the next step in front of him and see where it took him. For the time being he would do no more than that.

Giles looked through the café's plate glass window into the street, watching the people going by, noticing their many sizes shapes and ages, their clothes and hairstyles, their facial expressions. All these people trying to make a life out here in Barton Townes, Bartonshire, England, Europe, the world; it lifted his spirits just to see them all, happy or sad, just making their way through another day.

He sipped his coffee and let the minutes of the afternoon tick by. Leaning on the table, chin in hand, his thoughts idling by, watching the people.

The mystery woman came back into his mind with the question, who was she? Was she Leah's messenger? He would, he supposed, have to try to find out. But no, actually, he wouldn't. She kept coming to him, so she would come again, and he would probably find a little more about her each time. Or not. Whatever happens will be…whatever happens, he decided.

He missed Leah, but he was beginning to feel more philosophical about the situation. If I can get her back I will, he thought. Oh, yes, I will. But if I can't, well, I'll just have to move on. He pulled out his phone and checked his messages, as if Leah might magically have just sent him a text, but she hadn't.

16

The Return to TCR

When his coffee cup was empty he went back to his Range Rover and pootered along to TCR listening to his new CD. He found the one remaining space in the car park, got out and started for the front, not the back door. He stopped. He'd forgotten Simone's present. He went back to the car and fetched it. Re-tracing his steps along the side of the building he realised he was feeling a visitor already. He'd only been gone, what, five days, six?

'Hello, stranger, is that for me?' said Jackie Husband when she looked up from her desk diary and saw him. 'You shouldn't have.'

Giles suddenly liked her a lot for being so nice.

'Hi, Jackie. Unfortunately it's not for you. Next time.'

'Bottle of Champagne'll do,' she said smiling at him broadly again. She went up to him and pinched his cheek. He felt surprisingly bashful. Then he remembered he had to be Giles McAndrew again in here.

'Done, but it comes with a weekend in Tenerife.'

'Ooh, I'm up for that,' she said, delighted to be having this much fun with a Giles McAndrew she normally saw very little of.

'Is Simone in?'

'She should be, yes.'

Giles punched in the code and went through to the main station corridor. He walked past the door to the studio where Lynda Parvis was now well into her lunchtime show.

'Give me a candlelit bath at the end of the day with lots of bubbles and I'm anybody's,' he heard her cooing from the corridor speakers above his head. She could hear a listener laughing along. *'Trouble with that, Lynda is you can't see what he's got if you've got loads of bubble bath in there, ha-ha!'*

The two women started giggling like schoolgirls. They're getting along perfectly fine without me, he thought. And why wouldn't they?

He didn't much want to go into the newsroom but decided that Giles McAndrew wouldn't have minded in the slightest if he met someone going in or coming out. As he passed the open door without looking in, Lucie Bastable was coming towards him from the kitchen. He saw her and his stomach rolled over.

'Hi, Giles!' she said with amazing warmth. It almost knocked him over.

383

'Hi, Lucie, how's things, how was she show this morning?'

Lucie, surprised at how present he immediately was in the conversation told him about the mess she'd made of an interview with the curator of the town museum, embarrassing Mr Barstead by suggesting that he had an unfortunate name.

'...and there was dead air for about ten seconds after I said it.'

'Ha-ha, don't worry, it always feels like ten when that happens but it's always only about a second and a half. Simone know?'

'Not yet, no.'

'Don't worry - she'll probably wet herself laughing when you tell her.'

Lucie took in the face of the man looking at her. He seemed to have aged two years in a week and his mouth looked down and troubled, but his eyes were bright and sincere.

'Ha-ha, I hope you're right,' she said. 'But maybe this experiment with interviewing people at the crack of dawn just isn't a good idea.'

'It'll sort itself out, Luce. Don't worry about it, will you...'

'Giles, I hope you get your job back, I really do.'

'Oh - thanks.' The thing he really liked about Lucie Bastable was the way she made you feel good about yourself about three seconds into every occasion.

'And I think you will.'

'Oh, really?' She was looking at him in a slightly peculiar way.

'Yes – you wait and see what we've got on the go for you.'

'Really?'

'Simone hasn't told you?'

'No.'

'You'd better ask her about it, then. Are you on your way in to see her?'

'Yeah, is she in?'

'I think so.'

'I'll maybe catch you later.'

'Hope so.'

Giles felt even better. Lucie obviously held no grudge against him for his idiocy in the music room. He moved on down the corridor and knocked on Simone's door.

'Come in,' he heard from the other side. She didn't sound as if she was in a good mood. Still, he had to go in.

'Giles!' she said when she saw it was him. He wasn't the last person she'd expected to walk through the door that morning but he wasn't in the top 20 runners either. She took a good look at him then practically threw herself at him, clasping him tightly and almost choking him with the power of her relief.

'Cr-rikey, are you a sight for sore eyes!' she said into his right armpit.

'It's a good job I've had a shower,' he said.

She stood back and appraised him again.

'Blimey, you're actually laughing! And you look half-decent! What's happened to you! I've been trying to get you since you ran out on me – where have you been?'

'I'm going to tell you about that. Sorry. But – you know – the last few days have been…y'know…'

'I know - difficult, tell me about it, ha-ha!' she said and felt a pool of worry form again in her stomach.

'Yes,' said Giles, 'how are you? How-'

'Tell me first. You look so much better. What did you do?'

'Well…I don't know, really. I suppose…I'll tell you in a bit. Um…' He held out his package. 'I got you this - as a thank you present.'

'What for? You shouldn't have! I didn't do anything!' A warm feeling began to cover the worry inside her.

'Oh, shut up, of course you did. If it wasn't for you I don't know what I would have done.'

But you did go completely to pieces, she thought, producing a laugh that she didn't think was too false. She slapped him on the chest playfully.

'You shouldn't have. Still, I do like presents, I have to admit, ha-ha. I don't get many at my age.'

Giles smiled and chuckled along with her. He was beginning to feel pretty good.

'Open it if you like.'

Simone was already ripping the paper off.

'Nice paper,' she said. 'I'd better be careful.' She stopped ripping and pulled the wrapping off at the joins. The face of Elton John was soon revealed.

'Oh, Giles, you shouldn't have!'

'Have you got it already?' he said, but he saw she look as curious as she looked thrilled and she was no Meryl Streep.

'No! I didn't know it was out yet!'

'Oh, you knew about it?'

''Course! I get emails from his website with all the news!'

I should have known, thought Giles. He was delighted more than he could say that she was so pleased with the thing.

'Lucie says you've got something to tell me.'

'Oh, have I,' she said, coming down hard on the first person usage. 'You've got to swear not to tell anyone though. I've been a very bad girl,' she said and cackled with laughter. She looked at the door to make sure it was closed and dropped her voice.

'You remember I told you that I thought Greg was making calls to the press?'

Giles nodded. 'Yes, I remember,' he said. 'Just about.'

'Well, I rang Barrie and he offered to take Greg in for questioning so he could take his phone "by accident" and get the call record from it to see if I was right about him being the mole.'

'Right,' said Giles, trying to take it in.

'Do you remember, at your place the other day I told you someone here was phoning the press?'

'Um...no. Not really. Did you?'

'Yes! About the fight, you know...' Simone had started tiptoeing around the word, 'Leah'. '...so I'm waiting for the results from Noreham. If Greg is the mole, then I'm going to phone England and finally sort this out. Got it?'

'Yes. What do you think I am, stupid?'

'Ha-ha, you are on good form this morning, aren't you...'

'I'm okay, yeah.'

'And this brings the drawings into play.'

'How?' said Giles, still trying to take in the fact of Greg McKenzie being questioned by the police. It wasn't exactly news he'd expected to hear.

'I'll be able to convince the bosses that Greg's done those as well as part of a...' She was still finding it hard to know how to sum up what he'd done. '...well, a big conspiracy.'

Giles leaned his backside on the edge of Simone's desk.

'You're probably going to have to prove it, though, no?'

'Iain Blame - the detective - says he could extract a confession easily enough if he was to get him in again.'

'But what if that doesn't work?'

Simone glared at him. She couldn't help it.

'Sorry,' said Giles.

'It's okay.' She was about to say, 'I suppose you're right,' but she couldn't let her optimism level drop that low. She told Giles about the desultory meeting she'd had with Marcus and Sarah, but returned quickly to the results from the Greg McKenzie mobile.

'They'll show that he's the one, I promise you. Then they'll have to sack him. And then I'll be able to get you your job back.'

'Just like that...'

'Yes!'

'What about the finance issue? They want rid of me, don't they?'

'Come on,' said Simone, beginning to get slightly annoyed. 'You just wave one solicitor's letter at England if they stall over this and they'll cave in. You know that.'

Simone thought that this time, Giles was guilty of holding wildly optimistic hopes, but she decided not to tell him so. Then Giles was smiling at her.

'I'm so grateful for what you're doing for me, I really am.'

'Don't be silly,' Simone said

'Come here.'

Giles opened his arms and Simone let him enfold her. Giles held her close. It was much better to do this, he thought, that try to use words to tell how he felt.

The hug only stopped when they heard a polite knock at the door.

'Ah,' said Simone, breaking away from Giles's lovely gesture, 'I think this is someone I want you to meet.'

She went to the door to open it while Giles's stomach continued to drop towards the centre of the earth. This will be Leah, he thought.

'Ah, Tanya, come in...Giles, I want you to meet Tanya Wood. Tanya...Giles McAndrew.'

Giles, a whirl of disappointment and relief, did his best to present his politest self.

'Hi, Giles, I'm really pleased to meet you. Really pleased.'

They shook hands. Simone stepped in to explain.

'Tanya's been following your story from London. In fact, not just from London, but 10 Downing Street. She works in a media unit that, um, worked on your case.' She passed Tanya a knowing look.

Giles passed his own looks in the direction of the two women.

'I know, and I'm ashamed to admit it. I *did* work in the Media Intelligence Unit at Number 10, but I'm about to quit. We discussed you last week and I'll come clean – I rang some of the papers to try to smear your good name. I don't know what to say except that I'm so, so sorry.'

Simone, observing the girl's contrition, half-expected her to drop to her knees at any moment to beg Giles for forgiveness. The way he was looking daggers at her she thought it might be a good idea. He looked ready to bang her one.

There was another knock at the door.

'Come in!' called Simone, grateful but still tense.

It was Damien Read.

'Hi – can I have your advice about a website content matter?' he said.

'Sure. It is urgent?'

'It is rather, yes.'

'Okay. You two, stay here, I won't be long. Won't take long, will it, Day?'

'Shouldn't do – we just want your say-so about something presenter info.'

When Simone had gone, Tanya took control of the situation.

'Look. I know this must be difficult for you…'

'Well-'

'But – oh, sorry - I really am sorry about what I've been involved in. I'd like to buy you lunch if you'll let me – to help make up for it. If you're not busy.'

Giles didn't understand what she was doing here. He felt knocked back by this, but he gathered himself in and said, looking out through the window, 'I suppose you were only doing your job.'

'Yes, but it's not much of an excuse. But that's why I'm leaving. It's not exactly what I left university to do.'

'It's a tough old world,' said Giles, looking at the floor.

'No one put a gun to my head and said "you've got to go and work for Tony Bliss."'

'Still, it sounds like a great job.' He decided he was ready to look at the girl now. 'What did you say about me?'

Simone burst into the room again.

'I've got a job for you, Tanya, if you wouldn't mind. I was going to ask Sarah but she's got an important planning meeting in the middle of the afternoon that might take a couple of hours.'

'No, go on, I'd love to do something…'

'It needs doing later on – and it's pretty boring, really. I want you to go over to Noreham police station to collect something for me.'

'Sure. I can do that. I've got my car. What time?'

'Um…It'll take you about forty minutes…You need to get there by four. So you need to leave here at about 3.10, 3.15, something like that.'

'Fine. That's great.' Tanya was shining like car headlights on full beam.

'Tell you what, you can take Giles with you if you like. If you're not doing anything this afternoon that is…'

Giles wasn't exactly backed up with appointments and didn't mind letting them know.

'What am *I* doing? Crikey, nothing. Fine, I'd like to go.'

'Great!' said Simone, crossing fingers in her mind Giles wouldn't use the opportunity to murder one of his recent enemies and leave her headless in a wet ditch somewhere.

388

'In the meantime, though,' said Giles, 'there's something I want to talk to you about.'

'Do you want me to leave?' said Tanya pointing at the door.

'If you wouldn't mind,' said Giles.

'I'll go and find Sarah or something.'

'Nice girl, isn't she?' said Simone after Tanya had closed the door.

'For sure, yeah.'

'Well, you know,' said Simone, wanting to clarify, 'nice perhaps isn't the right word.'

'No,' said Giles, 'but I think I know what you mean. She's not a bad person or anything.'

'No, she's not.'

'What's she doing here?' said Giles.

'She wants a job.'

'She what?' Giles tried to process that - from Downing Street to Barton Townes?

'I know. Don't even think about it now – I'll explain it in full later.'

'Okay,' said Giles.

'I will, I...'

Giles interrupted her.

'Look – there's something I need to talk to you about.'

'Sure, sit down. Would you like a mug of coffee? It's still hot.'

'Yeah, that'd be good.'

Simone went to her coffee-making area and began rattling mugs around.

'So what is it?'

'Um, it's a bit of a strange one.'

'Of course, what else would I expect, my whole life's become a complete soap opera,' she said, smiling.

'It's very strange, actually - I keep bumping into someone.'

'Oh?' said Simone trying to turn to look at Giles and do the coffee at the same time.

'Or rather, she keeps bumping into me.'

Simone put the full cups down on the desk. Giles had put himself down in a visitor's chair.

'Well go on,' she said. 'Give me some details.' He told about being picked up on the road by a woman he didn't know in a car. Simone listened. At first she was going to say that there was nothing strange about a good looking man being picked up by a young woman in a car these days but she could still see in her mind's eye the wild-looking, deranged person who put his foot through a painting of that day. Still, people were odd.

389

'Then, I went for a bike ride up to Tower Hill – you know Tower Hill?'

''Course I do, yes,' said Simone, listening and inspecting her nails. 'Uh-oh,' went a voice in her brain.

'I was standing there doing, y'know, a bit of thinking...'

'I hope that's all you were doing, thinking.'

'...when this woman spoke to me - the same woman from the car.'

'Okay, so she followed you. That is a bit weird. What did she say?'

'Oh, just what a nice spot it was and fancy seeing you again up here.' Giles hoped Simone didn't see through the lie. He wasn't in the mood to discuss the state of his soul.

'Well, seems reasonable.'

'But it's an odd coincidence, don't you think?'

'I suppose. What was her name?'

'I don't know, I didn't ask.'

'You didn't ask! Giles!'

'I know – but, y'know.' Giles didn't want to reveal his weakness. He felt another light in his mind being switched back on.

'Mmm,' went Simone, reaching into a desk drawer for a nail file. She considered the possibility that Giles, though apparently returned to mental health, was imagining things; specifically being carried off in cars and met on hilltops by a mystery woman. She looked carefully into his eyes.

'Then, just now, just now, Simone, she came up to me in Di Mario's.'

'I'm not sure I understand you.' She looked again, trying to see right into the centre of his mind. Come on, Giles, she thought, *please* prove to me you're sane.

'I'm not surprised. It's ridiculous. I don't understand me – or it, either.'

His eyes were fine. It was definitely Giles McAndrew in there, not some mental case. She was at least ninety per cent certain.

'So what did you think?' she said, filing an end that didn't really need attention.

'I know you're going to think I'm a fool, but I wondered whether it was Leah who sent her.'

'Did you ask her?'

'Who, the girl? No.'

'What made you think of Leah?'

He started feeling like a prat. It was obvious from her voice that she'd already dismissed the Leah's Messenger idea. He was flummoxed. The idea came to him again, 'What would Giles McAndrew do?'

He leaned forward in his chair and looked Simone in the eye.

'Well, she could be checking me out, don't you think?' She might still care about me, was what he wanted to say. She might want him back.

'Who, this woman?'

'Yes, doing it for Leah.'

Simone didn't want to crush Giles but decided it wouldn't do him much good if she pussyfooted around too much.

'She could just ring you if she wanted to know how you are.'

'She had a lot of pride,' said Giles. '*Has* a lot of pride.'

That was a fair point, she had to give him that. 'True,' she said.

'So the last thing she'd do is ring me.'

'Oh, Giles, don't get your hopes up, love, please.' So the poor man was sane, thankfully, but still capable of romantically deluding himself. She didn't agree with his argument: if Leah did want to know how Giles was she'd hardly send an envoy charging around the county following him all day long.

'Yeah, okay, probably I'm just kidding myself.'

She looked at him carefully but there was no sign that he was going to cry. Well done, Giles, she wanted to say.

'The strangest thing, though-'

'You said you didn't get her name...' said Simone.

'What? Oh, "Mally." Sorry.'

'O'Mally?' said Simone. Did she go around using her surname?

'No, *Mally.*'

She'd never heard it before but there were so many newfangled names knocking about these days that seemed to come from outer space, none surprised her any more.

'...but the strangest thing,' he said, reasserting his hold on the conversation, 'is what she said when she left me a while ago in the cafe. She said I had to watch a programme on TV that's on tonight, on BBC 2.'

Simone stopped mid-buff.

'It's called "Intervention".'

She'd never heard of it.

'But here's the thing. She says you've got to watch it as well.'

'She said what?'

'Says you've got to watch it. I swear to God. As sure as you're sitting here in front of me.' Giles was practically giving her the deadeye.

'She used my name?'

'Simone. She said "Simone."'

She had to re-think the Leah situation, she decided.

'What did this woman look like?' she asked.

'What did she look like?' Giles stared at the wall and thought about it.

'Fair hair, light hair. Straight.' He described the length with his hands.

'Like Tanya's you mean?'

'Shorter. Not so blonde. Nice face.'

'Oh, you would notice that.'

'No, I wasn't thinking about that. Not at any time. She…she's pretty. I suppose. Very pleasant looking.' He tried to recall her in his mind but he was losing the memory already.

'And very clean.'

Simone laughed, 'Very clean?'

Giles laughed with her.

'Big nose?' she said.

'No.'

'Big breasts?'

'Stop it.' They were both smiling. Then Giles stopped smiling. 'Come on, this is serious.'

'Is she from Barton Townes, do you think?'

'She didn't say.'

'And you didn't recognise her?'

'Well, that's another odd thing. When she picked me up in the car, her face looked oddly familiar.'

'Fan of the show?' said Simone. 'Another stalker?'

Giles made a face. 'I don't think so, no. But she obviously knows you.'

'Or more to the point, perhaps, Leah knows me.'

'Thank you.'

A fire was lit up now inside Giles.

'Did she say what the programme was about?'

'No. She said she was in a hurry. The bit about you was the last thing she said.'

'Well…' said Simone.

Giles was nodding at her.

'…we'd better watch it, hadn't we?'

'Yes, I think we should,' said Giles.

17

Letter from Father Christmas

They were on the way to Noreham, Giles and Tanya Wood. Tanya drove. 'I don't mind,' she'd said in the car park, which Giles took as her wanting to do the honours, and for once in his life he let the woman take the wheel in good grace. Leah and he used to fight about it.

'I'm really glad to get the chance to talk to you,' said Tanya just after she saw a nice clear sign saying, 'A 567 Noreham and Coast' on the edge of town.

Giles said nothing in reply. He knew there was another speech coming.

'I still feel I owe you an apology. But I wanted to tell you as well...' she paused as she came to the by-pass roundabout. '...that the Chronicle stitch up wasn't me. When I rang my contact there he told me they'd already written the article.' She paused to see what sort of reaction she was getting.

Anger stirred in Giles's gut as soon as she'd said the word 'article.' It was hard for him to believe that she'd had nothing to do with it. He tried to be Giles McAndrew on the show – neutral, enquiring, stern with the potentially disreputable, but fair.

'Look, it's over and done with. It doesn't matter.'

'It does matter to me,' said Tanya. 'It matters to me a lot.' But how do you undo something you'd already done, she thought? Giles still quiet, she carried on.

'Can I get some more off my chest? Can I tell you what I was going to say to them?'

Giles instinctively looked at Tanya's chest. A sly glance at the extent of her bosom, he figured, was a fair inclusion in the payback deal.

'Okay, tell me.'

'One of my colleagues had made up lies about you, based on the inquiries I'd made. We knew you were something of a sex symbol up here and...'

'No, that's not true. And anyway, where could you possibly get such information from down there? You can't possibly know anyone up at the station.'

'I got it from the station website. There were several references.'

'I'll have to look at that bloody thing,' he said, but feeling quite pleased with what he was hearing.

'And there are a few pictures of you up on it too…'

Enough, thought Giles. He liked compliments from women, but hadn't any time for bullshit.

'…but we take lessons from the press on stuff like this. The Chronicle was already miles ahead of us. It probably took them about five minutes to knock out an article about you as the "radio station wrecking Romeo", if that.'

'Hmmp,' grunted Giles.

'They were way ahead of us in terms of rumours too.'

'None of what they wrote was true, you know,' he said.

'That – hang on.' She came to another roundabout. 'Thanks a lot, mate!' she said as someone cut in front of her. 'I can believe that.'

'No, really. None of it. Listen: my girlfriend and I did fight, but I was no more to blame than she was. Well, I may have been guilty of taking her for granted sometimes, and patronising her a bit.'

'But apart from that…'

'Okay, then, I could have been a nicer person. I get a bit caught up with Giles McAndrew sometimes, I guess. That's the problem.'

'I thought you were Giles McAndrew.'

'It's a complicated story.'

'You can tell me if you like,' said Tanya.

'Another time.'

Rain started splattering on the windscreen. Giles looked up at the sky. A big black cloud had spread out across the sky fat with rain. Tanya put on the wipers.

'So what else wasn't true?' said Tanya, probing again.

'All of it was rubbish, apart from Leah and me fighting sometimes.'

'All couples fight.'

'I gather they do, yes. Anyway, the rest was invented. Leah did threaten a colleague one morning but I stood there horrified not laughing "gleefully" or however they put it. And my cousin and I are just cousins. We'd only just met up for the first time in twenty-five years. It was ridiculous what they were suggesting.'

Giles sounded convincing to Tanya Wood. It hadn't taken her long working at the unit to realise that the people at the papers who did these hatchet jobs made any old stuff up when they felt like it. With someone like Giles, a hick from the Styx as far as they'd be concerned, they'd take liberties without so much as a glance at the libel laws.

Yes, it's scandalous, she would have said but she was part of it. The presence of one of the victims beside her suddenly made her feel very uncomfortable.

'I would say "I'm sorry" again but I'd probably just sound a hypocrite.' She buttoned her lip and watched the road ahead, straight as a die and heading into the broad, flat horizon.

The man beside her had taken it well as far as she could tell. He was bitter, of course, but so would anyone be. She liked him. He wasn't all that bright, but he clearly had something about him. He was a world away from the bloody prats she worked with in the unit and most of the blokes she'd known at university. She would like to work with people like this, she was certain. She was bored with pretension, fed up with pompous and sick to death of ambitious tossers in suits. She knew now after just half a day in Barton Townes that she wasn't going back to all that. Even if it turned out that there was no job for her at the station.

'You don't believe me...' said Giles.

'What? I do.'

'You don't sound convinced.'

How could she change the subject? She couldn't. She wanted to make a complete breast of things, be completely honest, but thought this wasn't the time or place. But, ah, well, she thought, here we go. If he hates me afterwards, I deserve it.

'You know how it is with the papers. Once you see the headlines screaming at you and you read the salacious details, they get into your head. You think it's rubbish but something in your mind goes, "well, what if it's not?" And there are people out there who do do the thing you were accused of. Plus, there are some people who do things that even the red tops won't print – unbelievable things. You must know that doing the job you do. Don't tell me people up here are different.'

Giles laughed ironically.

'You must be kidding. Some of the worst people live up here, though I'd like to be wrong. I know, you're right. And I'm the same. They have the same effect on me, the tabloids.'

'They do on everyone,' said Tanya. 'Sorry, I sound like I'm being patronising, don't I. First I'm being hypocritical slamming the tabloids and now I'm patronising you.' She wasn't going to say 'Sorry' again and risk sounding pathetic on top. That's it, she decided. That's all I'm saying about newspapers and media units. She glanced across at Giles. He was looking out of his window.

Christ, it's flat up here, she thought, glancing at the fields either side of the road stretching away into the sky.

'Flat up here, isn't it,' she said.

'I was wondering when you were going to say that.'

'I quite like it though.'

Giles didn't believe her. 'It's good for cycling, though.'

'Oh, do you cycle?'

'Yeah.'

'I do too.'

He didn't believe that either. He wanted to but he had no idea whether she could trust a girl like this or not. Not, probably. She comes up here from London and says she wants to work in old Bart and Bilt? This flat, lonely place, seventy miles from the nearest city? Who was she kidding?

'So,' said Giles, 'what exactly were you going to say to the papers about me?'

Tanya paused.

'Honestly?'

'Honestly.'

Despite her wanting to move on, she felt she owed it to the guy. And if it cost her, then it cost her. Perhaps she still needed to purify herself.

'I was going to tell them that you shagged anything that moved and had left a few pregnant teenagers around the place.'

'Classy.'

'Isn't it, though. I also phoned a lot of newspapers to spread the Chronicle stories about.'

The conversation died down to nothing. The tall church spire of Noreham spiked the sky five miles ahead. It was as if an unspoken agreement had been made between them. Enough of the tabloid nonsense. Enough of the bad. Because even talking about it put a poison in the air. But Tanya thought, well, if he hates me, he hates me. It's up to him.

'Do you know where the police station is?' she said when they passed the 'Welcome to Noreham, County Town of Bilt,' sign.

'No, sorry.'

'Do you know where the police station is?' said Tanya some minutes later to a man walking along a Noreham street with the word, 'please?' attached to the end of the question.

'You'll need to turn your car around,' said a jovial man in a shirt and tie. It had stopped raining.

They found a place to park just across the road from the front door. Giles had tinkered with the idea of joining the force when he was in the sixth form so he liked police stations. He watched a marked car with the light, the Bart and Bilt insignia and all the trimmings pull out of the 'official vehicles only' car park and felt he wouldn't mind a late change of career. He wondered if he could cut it as a copper at his age but knew he was only playing around. He was too old now, and too long a radio man to change careers, unless he absolutely had to.

396

He walked up the concrete slope for wheelchairs rather than the steps and went through the door to the reception. The smell was peculiar, institutional. He looked at Tanya and couldn't guess what she was thinking. Apart from the smell, it was much like TCR. The receptionist however was a bald man in a short-sleeved police shirt who would never see twelve stone again.

'Afternoon and what can I do for you two?' he said.

Giles looked at Tanya and motioned her forward. He couldn't remember the name of the man they had to ask for.

'Hi. We're here to see DS Blame,' said Tanya smiling brightly. 'He's expecting us - we're from Two Counties Radio.'

'I'll tell him you're here. Take a seat.'

Five minutes later, by which time the posters about home security and drugs had become very boring, a shortish man in a suit with very dark hair appeared behind the counter. He had his hands on his hips and was looking over waiting to be spotted.

'Hello,' he said. 'You want me, I think. Iain,' he said coming out to meet them. 'Come through.'

He walked them out of the reception area and halfway down a corridor to an interview room and sat them down. He picked up a brown envelope from the desk in his left hand and looked up fairly cheerfully.

'Now. Here's the phone,' he said, taking slipped the small, shiny black object from his jacket. 'Who am I giving it to?'

Giles let Tanya put her right hand forward across the table to take it.

'What does he think has happened to it?'

'Don't know – he just knows he's lost it.'

'Oh. Well, he'll have it back soon enough. Now...' Blame's cheeriness disappeared momentarily. '...So,' he said bringing the envelope to centre stage, 'here's the bit that'll really interest you.'

Tanya thought this was pretty exciting stuff for a local radio station, but Giles's heart was practically leaping out of his throat.

'In case you don't know, Simone rang me just now and told me it was okay for me to tell you about the contents. Is that how you have it?'

'Yes,' said Giles. 'What's the story?'

'Inside the envelope is a list of the calls made from the phone in the last month. On the list are the names of people I believe your boss was hoping to find.'

Giles right hand made a fist under the table and he clenched his teeth. He nodded, trying to convey a sense of seriousness and calm. He looked at Tanya – she had a modest sized grin on her face. So Simone briefed you, he said to himself. Her smile revealed a very white, straight upper set of teeth.

'Yes,' the DS carried on, 'she got very, very excited when I read down the list, I can tell you.'

'Did she really?' asked Giles.

'I would say so, yes.' His face a controlled smile, Blame handed the envelope to Giles.

'Thanks a lot, sir, for doing this,' said Tanya. Giles had pulled out the sheaf of A4 paper from the envelope and was now studying the top page.

'Oh, well – it's nice to get the chance, just occasionally, to make somebody's day.'

He began to stand up, then looked at Giles and Tanya in turn.

'One more thing. I'm sure Simone's told you this already, but as far as all this is concerned, the envelope and its contents don't exist, okay?'

'Fine,' said Tanya.

'Understood,' said Giles, putting the papers back in the envelope and getting up.

The drive back to Barton Townes was a happy one, though the rain lashed against the windows again in two separate bursts on the way.

When they arrived at TCR, they went straight to Simone's office. Simone immediately locked the door. Her initial excitement had given way to grim determination tinged with clench-jawed optimism. She studied the phone records for ages, as if she couldn't believe them. She looked up.

'It's like getting a letter from Father Christmas,' she said to Giles and Tanya.

'Sorry – can I see them for a moment?' said Tanya.

'Yes, of course,' said Simone, pushing the sheaf of paper across the desk. 'Can I ask why?' Then it clicked. 'Of course - you'll know a lot of these names, won't you?'

'Some of them on this page, yes. About four. And this one, the one who he's rung the most. I know him.' She was looking in her bag for something. 'Hang on – sorry, I don't mean to be rude – I'm looking...for my phone. Ah...Excuse me – this is to do with...'

She hit a couple of buttons then put the phone to her ear.

'I'll explain in a minute...Derek?'

'Tanya. To what do I owe it?'

'The pleasure? Coming straight to the point, you know that local radio guy who insulted Clegg last week? Giles McAndrew of Two Counties Radio?'

'My memory's not going yet, Tan.'

She shuddered. She only approved of people she liked shortening her name.

'You told me you got your information from someone in your family at the radio station, didn't you?'

'Did I?'

'You know you did.' It was obvious from his tone of voice.

'Can't remember.'

'You did. You definitely told me that you'd got all the information about his lovers – they were lies, of course, don't worry, I'm not stupid...' She looked at Giles. '...from someone in your family.'

'Come again?'

'Don't come the old innocent, Derek.'

'I don't think you're understanding me, Tanya, dear, ha-ha.'

But she did.

'He's not telling me,' she said softly to Simone, her mouth away from the mouthpiece, though she knew she didn't know who she was talking to and why.

'And I'm not stupid either, Derek.' She played the game one more time. 'Do you mean to say you still won't tell me when I'm about to tell your wife who you're screwing?'

'I'm divorced, Tanya.'

'You won't tell me even when I'm about to tell your girlfriend you like little boys?'

'I'm currently unattached.'

'Okay, so when I'm about to prove to your next girlfriend that you pay for paedophile porn?'

'She'll know me well enough to know that I would never do such a thing.'

'Your faith in human nature is very touching, Derek.'

'This is all a waste of time, dear girl.'

'Then don't be surprised if you see your mug shot with the word "Paedophile" across it on the fifty lamp posts nearest your house, Derek.'

'Ha-ha, that's very good.'

'And the toilets of all the pubs you drink in.'

'Ha-ha, I love it, Tanya. I haven't been in a pub in two and a half years.'

'Ha-ha, I know you wouldn't do that, Tanya. And you can try telling my boss, my mum and all my friends anything you like: they won't believe you.'

'You know Greg McKenzie, don't you, Derek?'

'Who, ha-ha?'

'You do. He's your connection at the radio station, isn't he – Greg McKenzie.'

'I don't like Scotsmen, Tanya, ha-ha. And my surname's Tyler, as you well know. I could make it "McTyler" for you if it makes you any happier, ha-ha.'

'You know that lunch, Derek?'

'Name the day. My treat.'

'No, my treat – go and buy yourself a big, rubber cock and fuck yourself up the arse with it.'

She clicked her phone shut.

'I'm really sorry about the language.'

'What was all that about?' said Simone.

She told them both.

'I'm sorry,' said Tanya, 'I thought there was a slim chance that I could...no actually, I thought there was next to no chance of Derek giving away his source, but I still thought it was worth giving it a go.'

'When can you start?' said Simone. 'I'll get your pay back-dated to March the first.'

'What?'

'When can you start work here - as a reporter?'

'Are you joking?' said Tanya.

'No, of course not.'

While a part of Simone's mind started dreaming about more awards, Giles looked at Tanya and smiled.

'Tanya?' he said.

'Yeah?'

'I forgive you and believe you.'

'What do you believe?'

'That you are who say you are.'

'Thanks. Giles?'

'Yes?'

'I know now for sure you weren't having sex with your cousin.'

'Or Lucie Bastable.'

'Or Lucie Bastable.'

'Or gleefully watching a cat-fight involving my girlfriend.'

'Or gleefully watching a cat-fight involving your girlfriend.'

'And wasn't mistreating my girlfriend.'

'And weren't mistreating your girlfriend.'

'Thank you,' he said.

18

The Showdown with Bakerson

It was fourteen minutes past five when Simone Pound picked up her office telephone to ring Ian Bakerson at BRBC England with Greg's phone records in her hand. The mobile phone itself sat in reception awaiting the owner's return from the seaside. A kind Jackie Husband had already rung him to give him the good news that Marcus Shifley had found it by the Community bus's car park berth.

She was too nervous to sit down. She stood round at the visitor's side of her desk fiddling with one of her slip-on shoes with her foot. On, off, on, off, on off it went, making a constant *thuck* on the cheap carpet as she waited for him to come on the line.

'Hello. Simone – what can I do for you?'

'Hi, Ian. I've got some pretty big news for you. This is about Giles, of course, and the run up to his suspension.'

'His contract's been effectively cancelled, remember.'

'I stand corrected – contract cancelled. Well, this is about the fall out from his interview with Clegg, then.'

'Okay-' Simone could hear his reluctance to deal with this and was immediately irritated. Why, she thought? I haven't even started yet! Are you in on this too?

'I've been able to see Greg McKenzie's phone records for the period covering the interview and the days following. I have them here in front of me, in fact.' Simone looked down at them as if Bakerson could see her. She enunciated her words slowly, like a courtier announcing a royal birth.

'We now know – definitely – that he was the one who phoned the press to pass on details of events that took place here that should have remained private.' She paused to gauge the reaction at the other end. Silence. Then Bakerson spoke.

'Okay...'

Simone's heart was moving from fluttering to sinking. He seemed to want more, but this was enough, surely.

'Well, isn't that enough? He's the mole!'

'Alright, Simone, phn-hah –' He made a pseudo-laugh sound. '- fine. So tell me, what is it you'd like me to do?'

It wasn't an offer to help, just a grudging acceptance of minimal responsibility. She pressed for all she was worth.

'I want rid of Greg McKenzie. And I want you to give Giles McAndrew his job back.'

A pause at the other end. Simone wanted to scream.

'Okay. On what basis?'

'What - McKenzie to be sacked or Giles to be reinstated?'

'Well, both – but start with Giles.'

Simone was reeling backwards, but she had imagined this call for days so was ready to answer him. She'd rehearsed her case over and over.

'Simple. Without Greg McKenzie sending his drawings to Leah Caighton, Giles would not have insulted John Clegg on air. Plus, without McKenzie acting as a mole, there would have been no press articles full of scandalous lies that embarrassed the station and BRBC. The contact with the press represents a complete lack of respect for the station and for the staff if not an actual breach of contract.'

'Well, hang on, you're now getting the two confused. Let's stick with McAndrew for the time being.'

I'm ballsing this up, she thought; but I didn't expect to be put on trial here.

'Look, Ian...' His name came out through gritted teeth. '...why don't you – why aren't you prepared to cut Giles McAndrew some slack? This is a man who messed up on air because of intense personal pressure, brought on by a fellow BRBC worker. And because of that he's lost his job. It's not fair, Ian, it's just not fair. And it's not professional either.' He was letting her have her say but she was struggling to find the right words.

'I see your point, but with the best will in the world, we acted within our rights in not keeping Giles McAndrew on. And – uh-hah – that decision has been taken and I really think that it's in the interest of all concerned to accept it and move on.'

'Oh, it's in the best interests of Giles McAndrew to accept it, is it? It's in the best interest of Two Counties radio to accept it, is it?'

'I think you should calm down, Simone.'

'No, with respect I don't think I should calm down. You mean it might make you and Andrea Potter-Symons look stupid or feel awkward if you reinstate him. You mean that you'll actually have to get off your backsides and do some work if you have to reinstate him.'

'I hardly think that's called for.'

'Or perhaps there is some connection between you and Greg McKenzie that you're not telling me. Or between Greg McKenzie and your boss, Andrea. Or some other BRBC big wig.'

Even as she was losing control, a voice in her head was saying loudly and clearly, 'That's your BRBC career up the Swanee, Simone Pound, you bloody stupid woman.' And all she heard at the other end was a loud, exasperating sigh as if that was exactly what she'd done and now he was going to have to deal with it.

'Wait, Ian - I haven't finished. You also mean that to reinstate Giles McAndrew would muck up your budget. Well, he'll sue you for wrongful dismissal and he'll win, and then there'll be a hole in your budget bigger than the one that sunk the Titanic!'

Silence. It was a ludicrous analogy, she could see that. And not only have I screwed myself, she thought, I've just finished off Giles's chances of reinstatement.

'How did you get McKenzie's phone records, Simone?'

'I'm sorry?'

'How did you get McKenzie's phone records?'

The penny dropped, landing on a bomb that went off in her head making a very large black hole in her thinking.

'I – my, er, ex-husband is a detective inspector in the Bartonshire Constabulary.'

'Was it a part of official enquiries into the committing of a crime?'

The bastard. The fucking bastard.

'No, but-'

'Then there is no way we could look at the evidence as acceptable, I'm afraid.'

'What?' she said, but she knew she was beaten. He was a clever bastard, Bakerson. No wonder he had a better job than hers. He went on pulling her case apart.

'It'll get out in the press that we've got rid of McKenzie because of illegally gained documents and we'd be a laughing stock.'

'So you're telling me that I have to keep on an employee who is psychotic, who has harassed a worker with obscene drawings and been a mole for the press, thus bringing Two Counties Radio and BRBC into shocking disrepute? Is that what you're saying?' There was no answer. That was a good recovery, actually, Simone, she thought.

She was waiting for it. "Sorry, but we have to do this by the book"; but it didn't come.

'I'll see him. And I'll see if I can persuade him to move stations. I'm prepared to do that for you.'

'That's it, is it?'

'And I have to tell you, any more of these police shenanigans and you'll be putting yourself in a very difficult position.'

Simone was virtually speechless with rage. She tried to hang on in the conversation, to keep herself thinking properly.

'When are you going to see him?'

'I can't tell you now.'

'I want him suspended.'

'No. I couldn't possibly do that.'

'Why not?'

'On paper he's done nothing wrong.'

Paper. Shit, went Simone inside her head. The fax!

'We also think he's sent a false fax to us, purporting to be from your office, telling us that you'd sacked Giles.'

'Okay, I'll look into it.'

Simone's response got stuck on her realization of what was going on here. He'd 'look into it'?

'Don't you want to know the details?' she said.

'Email them to me. Or send me a fax.'

There was a sulk at both ends. Simone then felt another surge of anger well up inside her but didn't know how to express it.

'Can I ask you, Simone, what you've said to Greg?'

'Nothing.'

'You haven't-'

'Nothing. As far as he knows, we know nothing untoward about his behaviour. He knows we think there's a mole here, but I haven't said a thing to suggest we think it's him.'

'Well, it's up to you how you deal with it. However, I think it might be in your best interests to let him know something in advance of our speaking to him at this end. Otherwise your relationship with him is going to be compromised.'

She wanted to burst into hysterical laughter. What sort of relationship did he think she had with him now? But she didn't want to argue the toss; she just wanted to get off the phone now.

'Okay, I'll think about that,' she said.

'Look, I'm sure you're very busy…'

'Yes, and I'm sure you are too. Thanks for your time.' You bastard.

'That's no problem. I'll be in touch.'

'Okay, 'bye.'

Simone didn't bother to hear the reply, she slammed the phone down. It jumped back out of the cradle. It took her three goes to put it back in place. Her hands, when she looked at them, were shaking. To hell with him. The prick. The cock. Her mind became a slew of curse words. Cocksucker. That's what he is. Motherfucker. Fucking prick. Bakerson. You fucking bastard. Then the image of mess take over her mind. Mess,

mess, mess, it's all a bloody, fucking mess, and just when light was appearing at the end of the tunnel. But it was worse than that: she'd thought that the one phone call to Bakerson would be enough. She thought that the phone record information would change everything and they'd be having a piss up and a firework display five minutes later. What a fool she'd been.

She went round the desk and slumped into the chair feeling a mixture of embarrassment and febrile righteous anger. How could BRBC possibly employ such a man? How could they possibly be so lacking in morality and basic ethics? How could they be so cowardly? And how can you, Simone Pound, be so bloody naïve as to think you could make that phone call and expect them so say, "It's Greg McKenzie? Oh, really? Thank you much, Simone, we're sacking him right this second and please, can you tell us which police station you'd like us to drag him by the ear to? And by the way, we were thinking of recommending you to the Palace to become Dame Simone." Christ, fifty-one years of age and you still get given the runaround by management.

The phone rang – it was a call about nothing much but she had to deal with it. Then another of the same came straight afterwards. Then she was free to stew again. She hated above all to have to break the bad news to the people around her she trusted: Sarah; Giles; Marcus; Lucie and now, even, Tanya. Oh, my aching arse, she said to herself. That was one of Barrie's favourite expressions. And now they won't let me take on Tanya. Not when they see she's got no radio experience and no postgraduate diploma in Broadcast Journalism. Simone looked at her watch. Tanya would still be on her way back to London. She would have to ring her tomorrow and warn her that she'd probably wasted her day.

She decided to phone Barrie to tell him that his help had all been in vain straight away. She felt she had to thank him again profusely even so. It's getting easier to talk to him, she thought, and was surprised.

'I'm sorry it didn't work out,' he said when she broke the news and he seemed genuinely disappointed.

'I don't suppose you would consider another favour?'

'What's that?'

'Iain said he could crack him if he had longer with him, and is there any chance you could do a DNA test on the drawings?'

'I don't know about that, to be honest. I might have to let you down over that.'

'Oh, okay.'

'Don't get me wrong – I'd like to do more, but one is the question of time and the other's a question of money. And you know, if he was careful enough not to leave any prints on them, he won't have left anything else on them either. And I have to be honest, in terms of the law it's only a case of harassment we're talking about and really, though it's very upsetting for the victim, a minor one.'

'Okay.' She made sure to be ever so polite - she knew how hard Barrie worked and how nice he was trying to be. 'Barrie, I'm going to whine, but I promise it'll be the only one – isn't a crime a crime? You should see the heartache this man's caused.'

'Technically, yes, of course, but the bottom line is, unless he confesses, you have no evidence. And I'll have to ask you again - is the victim in distress? Does she want to press charges? Has she even been in touch with you?'

'You know the answer – "No, she hasn't."'

'So, realistically, never mind the Director of Public Prosecutions laughing if we stick this one on the list, if I even mention this to my boss here I'd be a laughing stock. Do you see what I mean?'

The day was ending in complete disaster. Simone went home - rang Giles.

'It's okay, Simone, don't get too down about it.'

'But your job, Giles…' she said.

'I'll get another one, don't worry. With you as my referee, and all the tapes I've got, I'll get something. And I'll build myself back up again.'

'Oh, Giles.' Tears formed in her eyes.

'And you have to admit, I'm hardly Nicky Campbell or Noel Edmonds – I haven't got far to climb to get back to where I was last week.'

In her concern for her best ever breakfast guy, she didn't even hear the implied insult.

'But you're so good, Giles.'

'But I got good too late. I'm nearly forty. I need to be thirty to have any chance of making it to BRBC London or Radio 5.'

He was being so magnificent, the tears rained onto her top. He'd gone through so much but he'd come bouncing right back. She was so proud of him.

'Come on now, Simone, you're going to make me cry in a minute and I bet you don't want that.'

'Is this for real, Giles, your getting better?'

'Stop worrying, my darling. I'm not deranged and I don't think I'm even depressed any more.'

'I'm worried now that you've got that thing – what is it – bi-polar disorder.'

406

'Oh, stop it – you sound like my mum, now. Of course I'm not! I'm okay, don't worry. I'm just very hurt and very upset. But I'm dealing with it, you've seen me today, you know I am. Relax.'

'Okay. I'm sorry – I don't usually do this, you know.'

'Don't forget the programme tonight,' said Giles.

'Is it actually on?' She was on her feet now, fetching a tissue.

'Yeah, I checked in the paper.'

'What time was it?' said Simone wiping her eyes.

'Nine o'clock, BBC 2.'

'What's it called?'

'"Intervention."'

'Okay. I might watch it.'

'You have to watch it. You must – okay?'

Simone put the phone down doubting whether she'd be in any shape to watch the TV later on. She wasn't going to cry any more, though, she'd already made up her mind about that. She ran a bath and went back downstairs to open a bottle of wine. Halfway down the second glass, she closed her eyes, still thinking about Bakerson down there in London and how he'd stitched her up. She fell asleep wanting to float a barge down the Thames with him tied up inside and personally set alight to it.

19

Intervention Andy

Simone was awake again now, watching the programme and sipping a mug of raspberry tea. If Giles hadn't phoned her at five-to-nine to remind her she would probably be missing it.

Twenty minutes later, the show was reaching its climax. She was totally absorbed in it. It was following the story of a young man from Yorkshire, somewhere near Barnsley. He had problems that the TV programme itself was doing its best to solve. It had a method and for twenty-two minutes Simone had watched it being rolled out. Now it was crunch time.

Centre frame was the woman who held the show together, a highly confident professional, fresh from the American war on drugs. Alana. In the front room of a family house. She began to speak.

"Andy – I guess you don't quite understand yet why we've all gathered here at your mom's house this morning?"

The camera switched to Andy, 23 years old but worn out like an ancient piece of human machinery. His wary, tragic eyes scanned the crowded room, then settled on the carpet. Constantly sniffing, he looked half-confused and fully terrified. The lens stayed on him, determined to seek out every possible horror. Simone watched it capturing his milk white face beginning to droop, first at the eyes, then the cheeks, then the jaw finally giving up the struggle to remain resolute. Andy brought his left hand up to cover his face. Between two rough knuckles a cigarette burned down to the half-way point apparently forgotten. He sniffed again. Then he shook his head once, twice, perhaps because he didn't want to be there, maybe because he didn't know what to do. He certainly didn't know what to say. He started to cry.

The perfectly manicured and coiffed woman somewhere still the right side of forty, continued in a perfectly calm, well-rehearsed manner. "Okay, Andy, that's okay," she said, her accent calling out to him softly and sympathetically from the mid-west of the United States, "because we're gonna tell you exactly why we're all here today."

Andy looked as though he fully expected to be taken out on to the back lawn and executed by firing squad.

Simone watched the frame change. The camera moved panned away from Andy to reveal Alana's bottom half and five significant others in the room, all of them seated. The room seemed to overflow with them.

The house was only a semi, and semis in this part of this town weren't exactly spacious. Their faces were weighed down with emotion and almost twitching with nervous anticipation. Apart from one: that which belonged to a child. Andy, surrounded, was being pulled so hard in so many directions Simone thought he might split in two right before her eyes. Cornered like some clueless murderer, he seemed desperate to tear out of the house and run back to heroin, crack-cocaine or whatever other concoction was eating him alive from the inside out. At the same time he also looked desperate to stay, just in case the woman with the accent and the beautiful long hair was going to offer him a ticket out of hell.

The moment of reckoning approaching, Alana, with great deliberation, spelled things out for him.

"Andy, we're here this morning with your mom and your dad, your brother Anthony..." The camera panned around. "...your sister Amy and your grandpa Lewis to tell you something very important. They are all going to tell how they feel about you and what you're doing to your life, and what you're doing to their lives. Okay?" She left no pause for Andy's reaction. "Mom, would you like to start?"

'Mom', a forty-three year old office worker, dressed in her very best outfit, nodded solemnly from the sofa as if she was on trial for her life. A piece of white writing paper trembled in her hands as she began to read aloud.

"Andrew, I want to tell you today how much I love you and how I feel inside about the way you have let yourself fall into the hands of the drug, he-heroin."

Mum's voice was very shaky.

"I want to tell you how much you have hurt us: me; your dad; Anthony; Amy and your grandpa along the way; how much your stealing and your lying has disappointed and upset us. But most of all, how we are all broken hearted from watching your...your decline."

Mum paused again to take a huge breath.

"Please accept this offer of help this morning from Alana, because if you do not, I will have to cast you out of my life for good because I cannot take it any more, watching you kill yourself. Please do this Andy. Not just for us, but for yourself. I love you so very much."

She put the paper back in her lap, looking at Andy, desperately trying to hold her face together. She just about succeeded.

"Dad?" said Alana, her face still smiling, her voice still warm and cosy.

Dad, totally unaccustomed to public speaking but prepared to bear the weight of at least some family leadership looked at the addict with total uncertainty from behind a pair of black-rimmed reading glasses. Then he looked down at his piece of paper and started to read his piece.

"Andrew, you are my son and I love you very much. I hate what you have done with your life since you started taking heroin and it breaks my heart to watch you go down and down."

He read in a wooden, child-like way and his voice wavered as he spoke.

"Andrew. Please take this opportunity being offered to you. If you do not I am afraid to say I will no longer be able to call you 'son' any more." His voice wobbled badly on the word "son". His speech was over. He looked at Andy once again as he folded his page into four.

The camera found Andy who looked at his Dad quickly then looked away again. He closed his eyes, sniffed hard, twitched his head towards the clock on the mantelpiece and looked down again at the carpet.

"Okay, Dad..." Alana's voice was slow, careful and momentous. "...that was great. Now Amy, do you want to say a few words?"

Amy, a confident looking young woman of twenty-one, dressed in the latest happy-go-lucky girl fashions, sat in her armchair with her legs underneath her and smiled back at Alana as she began.

"Andy. Hi – this is your sister Amy." She stopped to look at her brother. She smiled at him. In the pause, Andy looked up at his sister with tortured eyes. The camera went back to Amy.

"I want to tell you this morning how much you mean to me and how much I care about you - how much I love you and want you to get better. But Andy since you became addicted to heroin our family has been in - in ruins, our life one long torment. Please take this opportunity of help being so generously offered here this mornin'. Please, Andy. We cannot carry on if you don't." She smiled again at her brother, her eyes shiny with light and moisture.

"Thank you so much for that, Amy. Anthony?"

Anthony, just twelve, avoided looking at his older brother and looked down instead at his school jotter with much seriousness, and began to read his effort.

"Andy. You're my brother and I love you a lot even though you used to hit me when you were younger."

Anthony paused as if he knew someone would laugh. But no one did.

"I want you to stop taking heroin before you kill yourself. Please take the...the help being offered to you here to-day, Andy."

On the settee beside him, Mrs Rowcliffe made a herculean effort to keep from crying and just about succeeded. The camera failed to notice her squeezing the skin on her calf with all her might. Andy was faring less well in the self-control stakes: he wiped tears from his cheeks with his left sleeve his ghostly face grotesque with distress.

"Thank you, Anthony. Finally, grandpa Lewis?"

Grandpa, with hair thinning and slicked tight to his head, coughed himself and the room to attention and opened out his piece of paper with steady hands. Andy looked across the room at his grandpa, the man who used to hold his soft, tiny hand when he was small as he began to read.

"Andy. I have watched you destroying yourself for the last two years on that dreadful stuff, heroin, and it has been very, very upsetting for me as it has been for all of us. I have watched your mother go down and down, breaking her heart over you. She loves you very much, your Dad and your brother and sister love you very much. I..." He looked up from his page to his grandson, "...love you very much. But if you do not accept this wonderful offer of help here today, I fear that your family will say 'goodbye' to you for good, myself included." He folded his page back into half on the last word, his hands still steady.

"Thank you, Grandpa Lewis," said Alana, still smiling, her voice still a massive slab of unflappable comfort and gentle purpose. "So, Andy, it's time for you to make up your mind." Her voice was gentle, light. "Do you want to take the offer of help, to spend six weeks separated from all your friends and family, but in one of the top drug rehabilitation centres in the country, or do you want to refuse and lose your family, these people who love you and care about you so very much, for ever?"

Simone watched her television screen with tears sliding down her face like rain on a window.

The camera came back to ghostyhead Andy, writhing and sniffing in his armchair, still wearing a look that constantly alternated between bland incomprehension and impending doom. He wasn't yet answering. He sniffed again. Then, unable to stop himself, he wiped the end of his nose on his sweatshirt sleeve.

Alana repeated the ultimatum.

He wouldn't answer - wouldn't answer or couldn't answer. Or a cynical director had told him to delay answering for as long as was possible so as to torture the programme's audience to an excruciating maximum of time. No, thought Simone. That's not the way it is. This is the genuine article.

Back on screen, Alana was beginning to sound as though she was running out of patience for real. She repeated the ultimatum a third time. Alan's face wandered all around the room like a lost bird looking for home while his family waited, while Alana waited, while three

411

million viewers waited – for Andy to finish fighting his demons, wrestling his past, trying to grip the present, all while trying to box clever with his future. Simone felt like her whole house was going to explode.

Andy covered his face again as he finally said,

"Yeah. I do."

"You do what, Andy?"

Andy's eyes make an effort to make contact with Alana but gave up halfway round. 'I do want it."

"You're accepting the offer of help, Andy, is that what you're saying?"

"Yeah. That's what I'm saying. Yeah."

A shower of noise broke out in the room as the camera stepped back to capture the family coming towards Andy, still sniffing but beginning to look more cheerful. He stood and allowed his mum to gather him up in a huge hug. Dad and Grandpa looked at each other and smiled in happiness and relief. Sister Amy hugged Andy and mum together while Anthony stood to one side appearing to be studying the soundman's huge boom but smiling like mad too.

A few minutes later the programme ended with Andy again hugging his mother but six weeks later, having progressed beautifully through the rehabilitation programme. This new Andy had a face that glowed with colour, eyes as clear as mountain water and a nose that didn't run. In her living room, Simone continued to wipe up her messy face with tissues and marvelled at television's ability, despite all the odds, to still be a wondrous thing.

At nine-thirty five as she wondered whether she could steal the idea for Two Counties radio, the house phone started ringing. She reached across for the cordless handset.

'Hi, it's Giles.'

'Hi. Okay?'

'Yeah, fine. Did you see it?'

'Yes. You?'

'Yeah. Any ideas?'

'I'm still balling my eyes out.'

'Ha-ha. Typical.'

'Didn't you find it moving? Upsetting, even?'

'Yeah, I did,' he said, but sounding cheerful. 'It was moving, certainly. I don't know about upsetting. Uplifting. It was uplifting.'

'Yes, it was. It was like seeing someone come back from the dead.'

'It was a bit manipulative though, didn't you think?'

'No, I did not think,' said Simone tutting. Men. Then she realised how healthy Giles's response was. This was the old Giles, the one who thought that emotional reactions to events were true signs of weakness.

'So why were we told to watch it?' said Giles.

'Is this a test?'

'No. I don't know why we were told to watch it. What do you think?'

Simone gave the matter a brief pondering. She'd wondered quite hard about it during the programme's first ten minutes before she got completely sucked up by the story.

'I need to think about it some more. You any ideas?'

'No.' He sounded emphatic.

'No?'

'I don't know any addicts. Do you?'

'No,' said Simone. 'Why don't we think about it overnight? Will you ring me if you think of anything?'

'Yeah, of course I will.'

'Okay, then.'

Giles said goodbye and turned on his garden spotlight and went to get some food and drink to put out for his hedgehog. He'd been neglecting it badly for over a week and wondered if it had given up on him. He thought about Andy and, like Simone had said, how he seemed to have come back from the dead. He thought of himself; how he'd come back from the dead. Was that the message he was supposed to see in the programme? That you should never give up hope, however far down your face was in the dirt? Is this what Leah was trying to say?

He stood in the bright light of his back lawn and put down the bowls on the top of the hump next to the apple tree and kept thinking. Leah was trying to tell him not to give up? He didn't buy it. He thought about the mystery woman again. Somehow she was obviously the key. If it was the first show in the first series, how did she know it would be relevant to Giles McAndrew? Did she have a relation or a friend who was in on the production and who sent her a tape in advance? Was she asked to participate or something? Had she been an addict herself? No, he was going in too deep. More likely she'd seen a trailer for the series a week ago.

No, the recommendation to watch the programme really didn't make sense at all as far as he could see. Except that it was good. It was a good programme. A very good programme. Manipulative, of course, but still, very good stuff, very entertaining. Giles walked back to the house and yawned hugely as he turned out the garden light. He was still so very tired.

20

Tanya and Giles

Brrrrnnngg. Brrrrnnngg.Clrrk!

'Hello?'

'Giles?'

'Speaking...'

'It's Tanya.'

'Oh, hi, Tanya.' This was a surprise. They'd exchanged phone numbers but he hadn't expected her to be in touch so soon.

'Hi, is it too late to ring you? I'll go-'

'No, it's okay – I haven't any work in the morning.'

'Oh, yeah, I'm sorry about that.'

'Stop it. Don't be. What can I do for you?'

'Well, that's the funny thing. I don't know. I just had this urge to ring you, only I don't know why.'

'Oh,' said Giles.

'You must think I'm crazy, ha-ha.'

'No, I know you're not crazy, ha-ha.'

'Ha-ha. Um, I just watched a good TV programme. Did you see it? It was called "Intervention."'

Simone can't have told her about the mystery woman's command, surely...

'Yes, I did, actually.'

'What did you think?'

'It was okay. I always wonder about shows like that.'

'What do you mean? I liked it.'

'Well, these things can look real, but they can be as staged as anything.'

'I thought it was amazing. And I'm a bit of a cynic.'

'Maybe I'm being harsh then.'

'I think you are. The addict looked real enough to me. His addiction looked real.'

'Yeah, you're right about that – I'll give you that,' said Giles.

'Oh, there was something I wanted to ask you today, but I forgot...'

'Go on.'

'What are you going to do next if you can't get your job back?'

'I don't know. Another radio job, I think. Someone'll have me.'

'But you may have to move, no?'

'Yeah, I'll have to do that.'

'And you don't mind...'

'No, not really.' Now Leah had gone – if Leah had gone, really gone, he wouldn't be sad to see the back of The Barn House.

'Where will you go, do you know?'

'I've one or two places in mind – I've maybe reached a time in my life where it's time for me to go and live where I really want to be – and to hell with my career.'

'You still have to eat...'

'There are radio stations everywhere, Tanya. Everyone needs radio.'

'Hmm, and you've got the digital explosion.'

'There you go. What about you? You're definitely quitting your job, yeah?'

'Yep. I'm going to tell them tomorrow. And they probably won't want me to work out my notice, especially if Derek Bastard from the Chronicle rings my boss to complain about the phone call this afternoon. They'll stick me on gardening leave.'

'Is his name really "Bastard"?'

'No, he just is one.'

'Ha-ha. Did Simone say anything more to you about a job?'

'No. I spoke to her this evening, though. She told me about the bloke at BRBC England, that he wasn't helpful. That Greg might stay.'

Giles knew about the phone call.

'And if Greg stays...'

'There might not be any job at all for me to apply for.'

'I'd wait and see. You never know what's round the corner. Believe me, I speak from experience.'

'Ha-ha, I know, yes, you do.'

'If I leave, then there should be a hole for you; Simone's been told to find someone from inside. Has she told you?'

'No, she didn't tell me any details.'

'Oh. There's talk of Lucie going into my spot. So that opens a hole for a reporter. And if Greg goes, then okay, someone may come in from outside, but if they promote from within, there's another one – two holes.'

'I might not get the job, though.'

'You don't know Simone – if she wants you, she'll have you.'

'I hope you're right.'

'Unless she gets the sack or gets moved sideways. Then you're in big trouble.'

'Thanks.'

'Well, you might as well know the score.'

'I know. I know you're right.'

'Then again, my judgement's been a bit shaky recently, so you'd better not take my word for anything.'

'No, I'm sure you're right. Look. I have to go but, if you're thinking of coming down to London soon, do think about giving me a call.'

Giles was surprised but not surprised.

'Okay, I will.'

'Have you got any plans to come down?'

'N-no, not immediately, but I might have to look to the south to get a job.'

'Oh.'

'But knowing my luck, by then you'll already be back in Barton Townes.'

'Hey, you can stay in my flat while you're looking, ha-ha.'

'And you could have The Barn House, ha-ha.'

21

Ideas Machine

Friday May 12th

'It's eighteen minutes to nine and time to finally talk to Alan Barker our sports expert about the Hardware's play off triumph last night – Alan, I hear you had problems getting into the station this morning...'

'Yes, morning Bob – yes I did. The kitchen flooded again.'

'You're not going to go into another tirade about plastic piping this morning are you?'

'I may do, I may do.'

'Oh, dear. I hope it didn't do any damage.'

'The cat almost drowned.'

'Now. Listeners: I've known Alan for the best part of twenty years and he is not the type to joke about such things, are you, Alan.'

'No, Bob.'

'So tell us how your cat almost drowned.'

'Are you sure our listeners want to hear this?'

'Of course they do!'

'Okay, well, Sootie is a very old cat and yesterday he had an operation at the vet. So this morning he was still sleeping off the anaesthetic. And, um, I came downstairs this morning to find the kitchen under a foot of water and rising, and eventually, when I found Sootie, the water was just coming up to the level of her chin.'

'Poor thing...'

'Yes.'

'And I suppose you thought you'd go over and sweep her out of harm's way.'

'Well, yes.'

'I bet you were Sue pleased.'

'Well, of course I was, yes.'

'You're just like a puppet master Alan, aren't you.'

'What?'

'Anyway, tell us about the Hardware.'

'Oh, they were great last night, Bob, they were like a pack of rabid dogs.'

'Yes?'

'Oh, yes. Last segment of the match they surged forward like a tsunami tide, ravishing the Torquay defence like so many dusky maidens.'

'Two-nil the final score…'

'The sea goddess was vanquished by the mighty Hardware.'

'Five-two on aggregate, wasn't it?'

'That's right, Bob.'

'Did you manage to get a plumber?'

'Eventually.'

'You want to sue the last one.'

'I may do.'

'You might want to consider getting a Polish one this time.'

'Really?'

'Yep. Mine's from Gdansk.'

'Really?'

'Yep. Hell of a call out charge but his work is spot-on.'

'Oh, yes?'

'Yes. Fifteen minutes-to-nine here on Two Counties Radio, coming to you all the way from the beautiful settlement that is Barton Townes. Now, NHS dentistry…'

In her office, Simone sprayed her plants and listened to big bad Bobby Constable. She thought about the review meeting she would lead later and what she might say to him, apart from thanking him for stepping into the breach. The issue of who to replace him with loomed ever closer. She was toying with the idea of trying Lucie for a spell, though the sensible approach was to move Jim Johnson to the morning show for a week and plug his gap with Jane who would be dull, but wouldn't make any cock ups. There was a knock at the door.

'Come in!' she shouted over Bob's interview with a local dentist about the travails of working within the NHS structure.

'Hello, boss, do you have a minute?'

A magazine flapped open as it passed by Marcus Shifley's left ear.

'My name is Simone and I am not in the mood to be trifled with this morning, you miserable little worm!' said Simone.

'Sorry,' said Marcus, taken aback. He picked up the magazine, the May copy of *BRBC Radio!* the in-house magazine.

'I'm sorry, love; I'm just practicing for Andrea Potter-Symonds.' She met him as he approached a visitor's chair and took the magazine. 'We had teachers who used to talk to us like that all the time.'

'Oh, did you?' said Marcus, wary, but underneath rather liking the idea of an eccentric radio station boss. 'Is she coming here? The Big Boss?'

'Hmm, I'll let you get away with that – just. Yes, she is. Don't worry, she's gunning for me, not you lot.'

'Oh.' That's good news, he thought.

'Now, what can I do for you, my young lad?'

'I've got an idea that I want to run past you.'

'Fire away.'

'It's about Greg.' Simone stopped spraying and turned full round to face him. 'What we need to do is to do one of those interventions you see on TV where they have a drug ad-'

'What? Where did you get that idea from?'

'Big Dave. There was one on the box last night and he told me just now that the thought one of those might just work to get that so and so – I won't tell you what he really said – to confess.'

'Was he approached by a strange young woman who told him to watch it?'

'What, the programme?'

'Yes.'

'I don't know.'

'Go and ask him.'

Marcus looked at Simone and waited, to make sure she was being serious.

'Go on: ask him! Shoo!'

'By a strange woman?'

'Yes. Trust me on this. If he thinks I've lost my mind, it doesn't matter. I'll explain it to him eventually, tell him.'

'Okay, then.'

'Good lad.'

Something funny was still going on with the Boss, thought Marcus: first she's throwing magazines and now this weird question. I'm going to lose that bet with Big Dave that the Boss would be gone by the first of June, he thought. He'd lain a tenner down on the prediction that she'd still be here.

Simone got on the phone to the newsroom while she waited for him to return.

'Hello, Sarah?'

'Yes, Simone.'

'Hi.'

'Could you do me a favour?'

'Sure, what is it?'

'Has Marcus come back yet?'

'Um, no.'

'Well, when he does, could you find an excuse to eavesdrop on the conversation he's about to have with Dave Plymouth?'

'Tee-hee, that's a bit naughty. But okay.'

'Good girl.'

Less than five minutes later there was a firm tap at the door followed by the reappearance of Marcus Shifley.

'Well?' said Simone.

'No.'

'Bugger,' said Simone. 'Sure?'

'Yes. He's sure.'

'You're not messing me about? Not playing a joke?'

'Would Dave tell you if a strange woman appeared to him out of the mist and told him to watch a programme about a drug addict?'

'Oh, yes.'

'And would you believe him?'

'Um, no.'

'Okay,' said Simone. 'Let's start from the beginning again. Come and sit down.'

Marcus wasn't sure now if he wanted to. Simone's mind really did appear to be fraying at the edges. It was bound to be considering all the stress she'd been under. The idea was so good though, he thought, that he had to give her another chance to grasp it.

'So tell me about the idea. Do you want a coffee?'

'No, thanks. This idea, anyway. It's based on the drug intervention idea, where you confront the addict with their loved ones at home and they get told by their family, that, um, they love them very much and that they're wrecking their lives completely...'

'I saw it! Last night – did you see it?'

'Yes. No! Dave saw it, like I said.'

'Right, carry on.'

'Well, no, if you saw it, you know what I mean.'

'You mean we all meet round Greg's house and tell him that we love him and he promises not to be a naughty boy any more?'

'No, not quite. What Dave thought was that we might get him in a Meeting Room and shame him into submission.'

Simone's first reaction was that it was too far-fetched.

'I don't see it, Marcus. I'd like to, obviously...'

'Hang on. I was thinking also that there's a link here to the thing where the criminal meets the victim to hear what the crime has done to them. So the perp sees the damage he's done to the vic. So we have Giles there, and Leah Caighton...'

Simone's face began to engage as her mind absorbed Marcus's explanation.

'We could have the drawings, present them to him, in front of the crowd – a crowded room. Lucie and Leah can tell him just how they made them feel. Giles too, if he's feeling, um, strong enough.'

As Marcus laid it out for the Boss, he realized for the first time that he really did like the idea. But Simone wasn't responding. She was thinking. Then she slapped her hands down on her thighs.

'Look – I'll tell you – part of me thinks that it'll never work in a hundred years. That he'll find a way of slipping out of it and we'll all be waiting in the room for hours on end and it'll be a total disaster. But the other part thinks it might be a fantastic idea. Could you write something down for me – discretely? Set it out in as much detail as you can? I want to take it home, study it and have a really good think about it.'

Half an hour later, Marcus came back with Sarah Billings.

'We've given it some more thought,' said Marcus, handing over two sheets of A4 in a smart coloured folder with the label, 'Wheat Farming' on the front.

'I think it's a great idea,' said Sarah. 'It's just getting the right balance between getting him to see how he's hurt people and proving to the police that he's guilty, with him still there watching them get it.'

'The police?'

'Yeah,' said Marcus, 'We thought if your Barrie could be there, or better still, the bloke who interrogated him, he might break down. He's a bit scared of them, hasn't he? Sarah tells me he didn't do very well at the police station.'

'What do you think?' said Sarah.

'I've had one idea.' Simone came right up to them. 'And I think it's a belter – the clincher. But we need to do some investigative work.'

'What is it?'

'I need to prove that Greg can draw. I believe he falsified his application form when he applied for the job.'

'What?'

'Just in a small way, but it's important. Those drawings weren't crude - they were stylish. Whoever did them can really draw. I mean, I've got Art O level but I couldn't have done those half as well as whoever did these. And I can't believe that a man with that much talent didn't get an art qualification at school.'

'You know what you're suggesting...' said Marcus.

'Go on...'

421

'That when he came to TCR, he'd done this before.'

'Am I?'

'He's sent drawings to people anonymously,' said Marcus.

Both women needed help.

'Unless he'd already done funny stuff with drawings, pictures, and got into trouble,' said Marcus, 'why would he need to cover up the fact that he had an art qualification?'

'Bloody hell, Marcus. So there are other victims, somewhere,' said Sarah.

'Right,' said Marcus.

They all looked at each other. Sarah was excited again and Marcus looked like Poirot after he'd made a 'I am now going to tell you all who committed the murder' speech.

'We couldn't possibly find people he's done this too before now though, can we?' said Marcus.

'You're a reporter,' said Simone. 'Go away and think about it how you're going to do it. Go for a walk round town.'

'Okay.'

'Get yourself a coffee and a bit of cake and send the bill to me.'

'Can Sarah come?'

'Yes, sure. Can you spare an hour?' said Simone.

'Yes. If you can excuse me from Bob's review meeting.'

'Of course. But hang on – Marcus, I want a word with Sarah alone; I just want to talk to her about you for five minutes.'

Marcus looked at Simone.

'Oh, right,' he said, confused, but knowing he had to leave.

As soon as the door closed, Simone sat down in Marcus's seat next to Sarah.

'I do want to talk to you about Marcus, actually – did you listen to his conversation with Dave?'

'Most of it, yeah.'

'What did they say?'

'Well, the intervention idea – it was all Marcus.' Sarah was very amused.

'What? Really? So...'

'Yeah, he was scared to tell you it was him.'

'But why?'

'Because you're turning into a monster, boss.'

They both laughed out loud.

'I think, actually, he was worried in case you didn't like it.'

'I don't understand,' said Simone.

'I think Marcus wants to please you. Impress you. Or just doesn't want to let you down.'

'Oh, don't be silly.'

'It's true. I'm going to give him such a hard time though, in town.'

'Good, do. He doesn't have to do anything more to impress me. I'm impressed enough already.'

'Have you told him?'

'No, I don't suppose I have.'

'You should, if you don't mind me saying so.'

As if I don't have enough to think about, Simone thought. Still, she liked the idea of being scary. It beat being thought of as being a soft touch by all the men in the newsroom. Some good might come of all this yet, she thought.

'I've just thought of something else,' said Sarah. 'You know you've got Andrea Potter-Symonds coming up.'

Simone nodded at her. 'Mmm...'

'She can be there too.'

'Can she?'

'Yes, because how could she not take serious action against Greg if she hears and sees the evidence right there in front of her eyes?'

'I see...'

'And how can Greg have the front to keep up the lie when the boss of the whole of the local radio network is staring right at him?'

'Sarah, I could kiss you.'

'You can, but not on the lips mind.'

She put her hand to her mouth like a naughty schoolgirl.

'You're fired,' said Simone, with a deadly serious look on her face.

Sarah's face actually began to fall.

'It's okay - I'm just doing an impersonation.'

'Oh,' Sarah giggled. 'Who?' she said, quickly recovering.

'Anthea Potty-Training - when she fires Greg McKenzie.'

When Sarah left, Simone began to calm down. It wasn't going to be as easy as that, she was sure of it. She went back to the newsroom to get Marcus.

22

Down In Herne Bay

After a review meeting with Bob that went very well, Simone cleared the decks for a meeting at twelve in her office with Marcus and Sarah nursing her big current worry: though she thought her idea of getting the facts about Greg's artistic career was great, she was almost out of time already: Andrea Potter-Symons was due on Monday.

Meanwhile she tried to get hold of Barrie but it was proving impossible. He wasn't at the station and he wasn't answering his mobile and he couldn't even get to his voicemail to leave a message. She was impatient. She needed to crack on. She decided to change tack and get hold of Tanya. She got her voicemail, but near eleven the office phone went and Jackie put her through.

'Hi, Tanya, how're things?'

'Okay – the work's driving me even more crazy, but apart from that, fine.'

'Any change of mind about radio?'

'None.'

'Have you quit yet?'

'I'm going to do it this afternoon. Any news for me?'

'Same. My hands are tied until I can sort things out at this end.'

'Okay – I see.'

'But there's something I want you to do for me.'

'Fire away- I'll do it, whatever it is.'

Simone had a file in front of her, which she looked up and down as she spoke and listened.

'I'd like you to go to Herne Bay.'

'Herne Bay? Where's that, exactly?'

'Kent – on the coast, not far from Canterbury. But the thing is, you have to go during the day.'

'I can already feel a cold coming on.'

'Ha-ha. Okay, well, do whatever you have to do – this is too important for me to worry about ethics.'

'What do you want me to do in Herne Bay?'

'I want you to go to a school. Where are you now?'

'On the street.'

'You need a pen and paper.'

'I've got it – I brought my notebook out with me.'

424

'Fantastic. Okay, I want you to go to Herne Bay Grammar School.'
Simone waited for Tanya to scribble at the other end.

'Okay.'

'Talk to whoever you need to, to find out about Greg McKenzie's
school record. I need to find out what he took at GCSE and A level.
You're looking for Art.'

'Hang on...okay – got that. You mean I have to find out whether he
did Art at GCSE or A level.'

'Bingo. Have a think about how you're going to do it. It'll be
confidential information.'

'Wouldn't it be easier to use your husband or someone else in the
police where you are to ring them?'

'I've thought of that but I can't get through to him and I'm running
out of time. This could be the key, Tanya – I want to know about Greg
and art today or I'll burst. It's almost the weekend – I have to have
everything in place for Monday by the end of today. Or almost
everything.'

'Couldn't I do this on the phone?'

'No, dear – I need the physical evidence and there isn't enough time
for the documents to go through the mail.'

'Fax?'

'I don't trust them at England. I want to be able to hand over the real
thing to Potty-Training. The real thing.'

'I understand – I'll go this afternoon.'

'Can you just do that?'

'I'll quit at about two. They'll probably chuck me out anyway. It'll
be okay, don't worry.'

'You're sure?'

'Yes. It's fine. Consider it done.'

'Fantastic. So have you an idea of your "in"?'

'Um, I'm thinking – yes, I've got one or two ideas.'

'What?'

'I'll tell you after I've tried them. I'm going to ring them before I go.
If I get a result I'll let you know as I'm setting off.'

'"Get a result"? You don't go out with a cop, do you?'

'I don't go out with anyone. The boys I work with say it all the time
– I think they'd all like to be coppers.'

'Boys will be boys.'

'Don't remind me. Okay, if there's nothing else, I'll get on with it.'

'Okay – I'll let you go. 'Bye, Tanya.'

''Bye. Talk to you later.'

Simone gritted her teeth with determination. Tanya. She was like Sarah for work like this only better. She had the experience. She tried Barrie again; there was no harm in having a back up if Tanya couldn't get the job done. She still couldn't get him.

Tanya pressed the '0' button on her phone. She got through quickly.

'Hello, may I speak to whoever deals with information about your school records, please?'

'Who's speaking, please?'

'This is Robina O'Donnell, head of Human Resources at 10 Downing Street.'

'Oh. One moment, please.'

'Hello? This is Emma Anderson, school secretary. How can I help you? '

'Oh, good afternoon. This is Robina O'Donnell, head of Human Resources at 10 Downing Street.'

'Oh!' The woman sounded like she was shitting herself; it happened all the time.

'We're carrying out a check on a potential employee – I wonder if you be able to provide me with a copy of the school qualification record of one of your ex-pupils if I sent someone down this afternoon to pick it up?'

'Um, yes, that shouldn't be a problem. What's the name of the pupil?'

'Gregory McKenzie.'

'And what year did he leave the school?'

'July 1989.'

'Right. Leave that with me. I'll get one of the office staff to locate that for you this afternoon.'

'Great.'

'Can we not fax it through to you? I can get it to you within the half-hour.'

'That's very kind of you, but a faxed copy doesn't comply with our very strict rules, I'm afraid.'

'And I can't post it to you?'

'We're in a bit of a hurry – the PM wants to appoint a special adviser before the weekend and we're all going mad at this end getting all the checks done – security and what have you.'

'I understand. What time can you get here? We close the office up at half-past four.'

Tanya looked at her watch, smiling.

'I – One of my employees will be with you by four. I'll be sending a young woman called "Tanya Howe."'

'Not a courier?'

'No, this is too important to be left to a courier. Security, you understand.'

'Oh, yes. Of course. Understood.'

'Great.'

'Someone will be here at four ready with the file for you.'

'Lovely. Thank you so much for your cooperation.'

'Pleasure. It's nice to be – um, to have contact with Number 10!'

The woman sounded tickled pink. She'd send Tony her regards.

She got straight on to Simone as soon as she disconnected from the school.

'Hi, Tanya.'

'Hi, Simone, good news. They'll have the record ready for me when I get down there.'

'Crikey, you're quick. I don't suppose you thought to ask them about it

over the phone.'

'Um, no, I was 10 Downing Street when I rang them – it wouldn't have been very professional.'

'No, right.'

'I'll phone you as soon as I get the information then.'

'Fine, I'll be here.'

Brilliant. So far, so bloody good. She still hadn't figured out one thing, though, and that was how to find out who Greg McKenzie had done this to before, if he had. The problem was solved when Tanya rang at half-two.

'Simone, listen.'

'I'm here.'

'I've just had a call from the headmaster of Herne Bay Grammar.'

'What is it?'

'He wants to see me when I get there.'

'Did he say why?'

'Not exactly. I asked him why and he just said he was pleasantly surprised that Greg had done so well for himself that we wanted to employ him.'

'What do you think he means?'

'Well, I suppose he can't have been much of a pupil. Either stupid or bad, I guess. Unless that's just wishful thinking. Maybe he just wants to see me in person because it'll be a big thing for the school.'

Simone had already settled on 'Bad'. My God. Has he taken us all in completely – were all his qualifications bogus?

'Sounds very interesting though, doesn't it.'

'You think?' Simone wanted to know she wasn't deluding herself.

'Yes – you get a nose for things in this job. I just hope the head doesn't smell a rat and have the police there when I turn up.'

'Tanya, don't say that or I'll be pacing up and down all afternoon.'

'It's okay – he sounded quite nice, actually. Friendly.'

'Oh, good – you had me worried.'

'Just keep your fingers crossed he hasn't got connections in MI6.'

'Tanya...'

'Kidding.'

Tanya Wood arrived at twenty-past three in her car. She parked in the road right next to the entrance. Herne Bay Grammar had swish blue gates and railings and an even swisher crest above the special wrought iron entrance gate. The core buildings were impressively old. She followed the sign to reception. She was attended to at the window, which was opened for her by a short woman of about fifty with a questionable perm but a sweet, friendly smile.

'Tanya Howe. I've come-'

'Ah,' said the woman. 'The head's expecting you.'

'Richard Hutchins - pleased to meet you,' he said at his open door a few moments later. He looked like a proper headmaster, Tanya thought: a tall man not far from retirement age; thinning brown hair and one in need of a better suit and haircut. He smiled warmly but looked tired at the end of the long school week.

'Tanya Howe – Human Resources, Number 10.'

'Hello, very pleased to meet you, come in. How's Tony, ha-ha?'

'Oh, bearing up, ha-ha.'

They went to their seats either side of a huge, old wooden desk.

'I don't suppose you know when he's leaving us?'

'Even if I did...ha-ha, I couldn't tell you.'

'Of course, of course, ha-ha. So, can I get you a cup of something?'

'No, thanks, but I'm fine.'

'Okay. Now, Gregory McKenzie.'

'Yes,' said Tanya smoothing down her skirt and making herself presentable.

'I'm very interested in this.'

'Oh, really?'

'Yes. I was here when Greg was. I knew him. I taught him.'

'Really?' Tanya's surprise was genuine. And this was cash; she knew immediately how she was going to proceed. 'What was he like?'

428

'Well – how can I put this?' Richard placed his hands together in prayer under his chin and looked slightly perturbed. 'Not the sort of lad you could imagine being taken on by 10 Downing Street.'

'People change.'

'Then again, the game you're in, ha-ha-ha.' Richard's expression changed to one of enjoyment in his own joke about the inferred twisted cynicism of the political world.

'Oh – don't believe everything you read in the press about the government.'

'I don't, don't worry. Can I ask you something ever-so-slightly personal?'

'Are you a supporter?'

'Of the government, you mean?'

She couldn't quite see where this was going. As she'd just quit, she didn't see how an honest answer would be a bad thing.

'Yes, I am, actually,' she said.

'May I let you into a guilty little secret? I am too.'

'Guilty?'

'Well, you know how much the Tories love grammar schools. And this is just about the most conservative county in the country. I practically feel like one of the Bader Meinhof gang every day I come into work, ha-ha.'

'Oh, right, I see,' said Tanya, actually laughing. He didn't look like a Labour voter. He looked like the president of the local Rotary Club. Which made what he said funny in a quiet, rather charming sort of way.

Then the penny dropped. Bugger, I've let my guard down, she thought. She saw where he was going.

'Don't worry, Mr Hutchins, we only want to take on Mr. McKenzie for a very short period, for something very specific.'

'Oh. But look, I still feel I ought to be very frank with you, in the circumstances.'

Tanya looked at him quizzically.

'Of me being of the persuasion, as it were.'

'Oh,' said Tanya, 'right, right. Do.'

'I know I might be a bit out of line here, but I just want to say, you mustn't take any short cuts with your checks on him. Unless he's had a change of personality, I wouldn't touch Gregory with a barge pole.'

'Oh?'

'He was a furtive boy. Bright, but unreliable. He got into a lot of trouble.'

'Really? What kind of trouble?'

'Let me tell you what I've done. I've personally photocopied his entire school record. I think you might find it very interesting.'

Tanya's mind reverberated to the sound of a massive *ker-ching!*

'Let me just give you a rough outline while you're here. Gregory was involved in one or two incidents that I can only describe as "unsavoury".'

The familiarity of Richard's old-school vocabulary was amusing to Tanya. He was just like a lot of the wankers in the Foreign Office.

'In what way?'

'We share a site with Herne Bay Girls Grammar. One day, when I was his house master, we received a call from the headmistress. She came over to our building later the same day and I was called in as Gregory's house master. She had some drawings. Obscene drawings.'

All manner of bells clanged in Tanya's head now, accompanied by huge bright flashing lights.

'Oh dear,' she said, holding herself in firmly. 'That must have been awful.' She couldn't wait to get out now and ring Simone.

As Richard continued the story in great detail, Tanya opened the fresh folder on her knee. Three documents down was a list of the academic achievements of Gregory Wilson McKenzie. She expertly flipped it to the top of the pile as she looked at Richard again and nodded. He may have enjoyed revealing the details of a scandalous episode in the life of one Kent schoolboy in the 1980s, but he wasn't showing it. He gazed at a glass-fronted bookcase on the wall near the desk as he spoke, making Tanya's job easy. She looked down the list of GCSE subjects attained by the student in the summer of 1987.

English Language Grade B, English Literature Grade A

'Oh, yes?' she said. Greg was in the middle of getting the cane. Richard was still looking at the bookcase.

Mathematics Grade C, Physics Grade C, Chemistry Grade C, Biology Grade B, French Grade C, History Grade A...

'Oh, no, that's awful,' said Tanya. She glanced down again.

Art, Grade A

'Uh-huh,' said Tanya. 'That must have been terrible for the school.'

'It was,' said Richard. 'Relations with the Girls Grammar were strained for quite a time. We had a devil of a job keeping the police out of it...'

'I see,' she said as her eyes scanned the bottom half of the page like an eagle-eyed counterfeiter for Gregory's A level results. Ah - there they were.

English Language Grade C, History Grade C, Art - Grade B

It was difficult now to keep concentrating. This is better than anything

I've done or seen in my job at the unit, she said to herself. She wanted to tell Richard what this information meant, but she had to stay in role.

'Of course, this will have little or no bearing on whether we take Gregory into the employ of Number 10,' she said gravely.

'Can I just ask you – what does Gregory do now that makes you want to take him on?'

'I'm sorry,' said Tanya. 'Official Secrets and all that.'

Richard, who was enjoying this diversion at the fag end of a Friday afternoon, not least in talking to a pretty young woman, began to feel disheartened. On the balance of his judgment, whatever the reason was behind Number 10 wanting him, it couldn't be an entirely clean one.

In a way it doesn't surprise me that someone has obviously recommended Gregory to you, you know. I suppose it's something to do with spin doctoring, isn't it. Yes, I'm sorry – of course – you can't tell me. I understand.'

Tanya felt a pang of guilt in having to deceive such a pleasant man as Richard Hutchins. Even after quitting it was better just to keep her mouth shut.

'Or is it something to do with Mandelberry? I thought he was working with the EU these days...'

Tanya just smiled politely back. At that second all she wanted was to be running back to the car shouting 'Yes! Yes! Yes!'

'...You can't tell me, can you. I do understand.'

'I am sorry. I can tell you you're cold on that one, though. I rather like Mandy. You don't want to believe everything you read about him in the papers.'

'Really? Oh, well, that's something. That's quite heartening.'

As she walked, calmly, back to her Mini, she said to herself, I have to get a job at Two Counties, and the thought was painful. I have to,

431

please, she said to whoever out there in the universe might have their hand on the tiller, as she took her phone and punched the buttons.

'Simone! It's Tanya!'

'Hi, what?' That was all Simone could force out over her tongue she was so nervous.

'I want to tell you something: something my big boss Tony said on election night in '97 – it's legend in Number 10 circles.'

'Go on.' She was dying. And she wanted to go to the toilet.

'He was at his constituency house drinking a mug of coffee at about one in the morning when the marginal constituency results started flooding in and it was obvious we – sorry – Labour was going to win. He stood there apparently, in the living room watching the telly with Rich Campbell and one or two others, Cerise, of course – and in a state of disbelief, said, "It's happening"…are you still there?'

'Yes!'

'Well it's happening, Simone. C at GCSE, B at A level and a whole lot of other stuff besides.'

'Tell me, tell me!' screamed Simone at the other end of the line.

So Tanya told her in detail how the interview with the headmaster had gone and at the end of it Simone had to agree: it seemed as though it was really happening.

23

Simone and Potty-Training

Simone's heart was pumping hard and she felt out of breath even though she was only pacing the floor. So it was him. She looked at her watch and thought about where he'd be now, this disturbed man she'd worked with for three years. Why now, she thought? Why has he done this now? Then she realised that actually she had no idea how often he might have done this sort of thing, messed with people in a criminal or almost criminal way. Perhaps there were others in her situation and in Giles' and Leah's, or among her family or friends. Friends! Pah! What sort of friends can a man like this have? A man who behaviour was... She shook her head and looked down at the desk. Sick. Sicko. I've been working with a sicko.

This prompted her to remember something Sarah had said to her the other night. 'It's unbelievable, isn't it, to think you could work with someone who would do all this. Harass a woman, stalk her, and be so cold blooded. Do you know what I mean?' And Marcus has said, 'It's like something off the telly, or a film.' No, thought Simone, it isn't at all. At the end, you walk out to your car and drive home, or turn over and watch something else, or go up to bed thinking about next day's work. Bad things in life are a hundred times worse than television.

And on the box, the directors marked out the sickos by casting men with evil or shifty looking faces wearing dark or scruffy clothes. They took you into their homes, filthy, or threateningly bland, showed you the shrines to their victims in bedrooms and backrooms. Did Greg McKenzie have something like that for Leah Caighton? A hundred photographs secretly taken? Was he now building one for Lucie Bastable?

The weight of everything seemed to be crushing her again. There was only one way to get out from under it: to make the intervention work. And if it does, she told herself, then you'll be able to get back to your normal life. Yes, she thought: fifty-one and alone. But maybe, when everything was back to normal, she could do something about that. She thought about all the TV makeover programmes she'd watched in recent years, especially where women over 50 were transformed and had their self-esteem retrieved for them. I could buy the DVDs, she thought. And I'll break open the bank account to buy a load of new clothes. Colour my hair too.

She felt a little better.

She looked at her watch. Greg would soon be back from his day with the Community bus, but they might not bump into each other. It seemed obvious to her now that he'd deliberately engineered a week away with the bus to avoid Simone and the rest of the station. Until she realised that he'd been down to do this weeks ago. Or did was he planning the drawings back then? Was he that clever? She managed to give this two seconds of consideration before her mind, choked with the weeds of stress, stopped her dead.

She focussed on the weekend ahead instead. She had tonight, Saturday and Sunday to prepare the ground for Monday.

The Intervention.

Her stomach went hot on her and she wanted to defecate. She had to go. Christ, I hope I don't meet anyone in there, she thought. She had to use the same facilities as the rest of the female staff. There were no management loos at Two Counties Radio.

She was in a cubicle setting herself right when someone came in alone and entered the one next to her. The smell she'd made was bad and she felt awful for inflicting it on one of her colleagues. She flushed and got out of the room before the other woman could finish, hardly washing her hands. She shut her office door and realised she was sweating.

Slow down, Simone, slow down, she coached herself. Get the last things organised from here you can before you go home. She sat at her desk, dialled '0' for an outside line and started making calls.

She'd already made a list. Most of the names had numbers written next to them. She added the name of Richard Hutchins to the list and typed 'Herne Bay Grammar School for Girls' into *Ask Jeeves* to get the number, even though she was still mulling this one over. He'd probably freak out if she told him that she'd sent Tanya down on false pretences. Why hadn't they come clean about the whole thing? I bet he'd have helped though, she thought, if he knew everything. Maybe, just maybe, he still would. Even if he went mad on her, what could he do? They had the information and Tanya was speeding back to London.

She took in a huge breath and dialled the third number down. There was a click of connection followed by the sound of the phone ringing at the other end. After four rings there was another click then a voice cut in. Simone spoke.

'Can I speak to Andrea Potter-Symons, please?'

'Can I say who's calling?' said a perky female at the other end.

'Er, Simone Pound from Two Counties Radio in Barton Townes.'

'Hold on – I'll see if she's available.' Click.

The hold music that played was tolerable: a string quartet. It played away while Simone tapped her pen on her pad and watched the dots it made to try to block out her nerves. Then *click!* – voice.

'She's on another line, would you like to hold?'

'Yes, please.'

The quartet came back. She went back to studying the pen but she got lost, quite by accident, wondering what her favourite Elton songs might sound like played by two violins, a viola and a cello. So she barely noticed the next click.

'Andrea Potter-Symons?'

Hadn't the secretary told her who was on the line?

'Hello, it's Simone Pound, here, managing editor Two Counties Radio.' Or was Andrea deliberately trying to intimidate her.

'Oh, hello Simone, what can I do for you?'

You might acknowledge the fact that you're coming to see me.

'I just want to pass one or two things on to you in advance of our meeting on Monday. Is that okay?'

'Oh, okay.' She sounded dubious. Suspicious even.

Simone knew that in the grand BRBC hierarchical scheme of things what she about to do was a managerial unorthodoxy to the point of madness, but she was past caring.

'I don't know if Ian Bakerson has informed you...' The gap was deliberate.

'He may have done, depends what it is exactly you're talking about.' The voice was not a friendly one. Simone heard an accent with no traces of origin, like a BRBC newsreader trying faintly to be posh. She didn't like it.

'Oh, okay. Well, I'll just – I'm having a lot of trouble with one of my employees, my deputy in fact, Greg McKenzie.' She left a silence. No reply. 'And because of that I've been carrying out a number of investigations.'

'I see,' came the reply. No, you don't see, thought Simone, you're weighing me up like someone who's just found themselves trapped in a room with a scorpion.

'Now, the thing is, I've completed my investigations,' said Simone with deliberation, 'and I just wanted you to know that when you come on Monday, I shall be laying the results before you.'

Simone wanted to know if she was definitely coming.

'Okay, fine,' said Andrea, suddenly all business. 'This connects up with Giles McAndrew does it?' The Big Boss voice was a little more interested now.

'Yes it does.'

'Okay. Did my PA say anything about the reasons why I wanted to come up and see you?' And her speed of delivery was increasing.

'Um, no.' You know she didn't, Potty-Training, stop playing bloody games with me.

'Well, I can tell you now that it is about Giles McAndrew and the way you've handled the situation there at TCR.'

These people, thought Simone – they always have to control the conversation when they're even vaguely threatened.

'That's great. That's exactly what I'm looking forward to discussing,' Simone said.

'I want to walk you through one or two things that could have been handled quite differently.'

See? She's doing it again, Simone said to herself. I'll have to let her win. There was no point in doing otherwise. She could feel mood beginning to sink again.

'Okay, fine. I'll look forward to that.' Simone tried to sound subservient. There was no point in doing otherwise in that respect either.

'Okay, Simone.' That was her cue to get lost.

'Okay. Thank you for your time.'

'No problem.'

''Bye.'

Andrea's ''bye' was clipped. She hates me, thought Simone. She was really sweating now. I'm going to have to take these tights off, she thought. She instinctively looked at the door as she stood up, hitched up her skirt and started pulling them down.

Management, Simone said to herself – it's all about knowing when to take your tights off. She thought about this piece of internal dialogue, gave a short laugh, and feeling better, and made the next call.

Later, at home, her phone was hot with phone calls as she tried to muster all her troops for the big day, and to work everything out down to the last detail. It may be happening for the others, she thought, but it doesn't feel like it's happening, to me. She couldn't assume for a moment that the job was done.

One of the people she called was Sarah. At the end of a second conversation, just after eight when she felt exhausted and was about to get into a hot bath, Sarah said,

'What are you doing tonight? Do you want to come over for a drink?'

'What are you and Lucie doing tonight – aren't you going clubbing or something?'

Sarah laughed.

'No, we're more like an old married couple – we like quiet nights in. Come over.'

'I was going to get into the bath.'

But Sarah could tell her boss was just playing hard to get.

'Come on, come over. If you get a taxi over here, one of us'll drive you back. Or you can sleep over. Bring your toothbrush and your nightie.' She said laughing.

'Don't be so cheeky – but okay. That sounds great.'

'Have you eaten? We haven't got around to it yet – we thought of ordering some Indian.'

'No - haven't eaten.'

'Shall I order you something? What do you like?'

'Anything. So long as there's chicken something or other and some naan bread – oh, and an onion bhaji – I'll be more than happy.'

'Right. It'll be about forty minutes. If you're any later we'll keep it warm.'

'Okay.'

Simone decided to walk up to the main road and get the bus instead of a taxi. She was glad she did. As she strolled up her long street in the lovely May dusk, she felt the madness in her head that passed for a life begin to slow down. I should walk much more than I do, she thought. I'm going to become an unfit old bag if I'm not careful. She stood and waited at the stop for over ten minutes but it was fine, it was nice. The drumming in her mind got slower and slower and so did the world around her. There was some Friday night traffic on the roads, but nothing that made her feel as though everything in Britain was going crazy, which she felt sometimes driving around in the car.

She was joined at the stop by a couple of girls going into town. They wore tops that showed a mass of cleavage and chunks of midriff. Their skirts came up to their arses, there was no other way off putting it. Simone saw it in town all the time but there she was never still; she was always rushing. Now, leaning against the shelter, it just amazed her. The girls laughed and joked about the things teenagers do and always did and Simone smiled at them, at their hair and at their clothes. She didn't have to worry about them looking her way. To them, Simone was invisible. They were so young, so naïve and so free. She felt some of her tiredness disappear just looking at them.

The bus came, then wended its way into town, picking up more youngsters going out 'on the razzle,' as the lads used to say in her day. The nights were getting lighter, the summer was coming, and the bus was buzzing with expectation and the sound of fun already being had. Sure, lots of them would have their anxieties and their problems, but tonight the only vibration they gave off was excitement about the evening and night ahead.

They got off at various points on the high street and the *Bart and Bilt Rider* number 491, now almost empty, went on to Sarah and Lucie's village as the last, soft, slanting rays of evening sunshine lolled over the fields. Simone began to feel really good. She was looking forward to seeing Sarah and Lucie, and when she thought of Two Counties Radio – and she did – the crisis surrounding Greg McKenzie seemed far away and hardly threatening at all.

24

Friday Night Running Man

The running man ran and ran. Out of the town he went, along the dyke and into the country where in the distance there was nothing but a wide sheet of land in front of the sky - until a windmill came into view on his right, closely followed by a red brick farmhouse.

As the miles accumulated, the sweat trickled down his temples, thence down his cheeks then fell on the ground in drips. It was the first properly warm evening of the year. Soon the broken airfield fence came into view then almost before he knew it he was through the gap and turning right onto the long expanse of cracked and broken tarmac that led eventually to the main road. He passed the derelict buildings: the control tower with its jagged broken windows and the remains of Nissan huts fallen into poignant decay. The running man knew his history. He thought of the pilots laying on the grass in the spring sunshine of 1940 waiting for the call to come, their machines at bay just yards away, itching to be cranked up and flown into the sky. He thought of those who never came back - who fell out of the sky.

He heard an aeroplane not that far above him and wondered whether it was about to swoop down, grab him by the back of the neck and whisk him up into the wild blue yonder and away, his legs dangling and kicking.

The failing sun was now behind him. He was running, not falling. Still erect, still on his feet, still running. The sound of traffic reached him, and then he was on the main road back into town.

The running man: never sure if he was running to, or running from, and which was the better way to go. If he could never stop running, he might achieve his dreams, or find peace of mind. The running man: racing away from the setting sun, racing nobody but himself. It was safer that way, never winning but never losing. But the pain of running alone was hard to take. And as he got older, the solitary run got harder and scarier to make. Yet still he ran.

Maybe I do it because I can't make connections, he thought, nearly home. But how do I change? Once you're grown to man's estate, how do you make yourself something and someone you're not? And the hardest thing was the thought that it was too late; that he'd had his chance somewhere along the line, and blown it. The thought grew into something sore, like a boil. I can't find her – why can't I find her? He thought for a second that he could feel the soreness of the boil under his armpit. And it was always about her, only her. Him, I didn't need to touch, except I couldn't resist it. And now I have to keep running.

He had to keep running. If he kept running and made himself stronger, maybe when the next test came he would come through unscathed. And then I can find her, he thought - I'm not giving up yet.

25

Saturday's Alright For Giles

Saturday May 13th

On Saturday afternoon, Giles knocked on Simone's front door.

'Hey, there! Come in,' she said.

'Thanks. I was on my bike and I was close by so I thought I'd pop round on the off chance.'

'What, you're out in this rain? Come in.'

'Can I wheel this round the back?'

'Yeah, sure, I'll see you in the kitchen.'

Giles propped his bike up against the garden shed nearest the back door, left his wet jacket and helmet in the porch and walked straight in.

'Cup of tea would be nice,' he said.

'I'll put the kettle on. How's things?'

'Fine.'

'How're things with you?'

'Oh – you know...'

'Well, no, I don't really. Don't be lazy – tell me.'

'Lazy? Huh! Okay, I'll try to put it into words. Apart from not being able to get out into the garden this afternoon - I'm – excuse me – absolutely shitting myself about Monday. I'm frantically making calls to get everything set up. And even if it goes well, I'm thinking, I can't see an end to any of this. I've still got to sort the whole station out – maybe – when it's all done.'

'The whole station?'

'Well, no – figure of speech – but it flippin' well feels like it. If I can get rid of Greg McKenzie I've got to get a new deputy and a replacement for Leah. And...and...'

'Go on, "if they still want to get rid of Giles McAndrew, I've got to replace him as well."'

Simone inspected Giles again, rather than looked at him.

'Yes. That's right.'

'And you'll be feeling as though things are all up in the air for a long time, won't you. Even if things go well and you get people in quickly. Even if one of them is Tanya.'

'Yes, okay, steady on, there's no need to be so aggressive.' But he was smiling. My God, I still don't believe it, she observed to herself, he really is going to be okay.

'I'm sorry to make things worse for you.'

'What do you mean?' said Simone.

'That's really why I've come round - to tell you now rather than after Monday. Y'know, the big event.'

The kettle came to the boil and clicked. Simone stood there holding the teapot.

'I'm leaving,' said Giles. Simone still stood there. She gawped at him. 'Go on, say something.'

'Explain,' she said, still not moving.

'I want them to reinstate me, don't get me wrong. I'm nervous about Monday too. I still want my moment. More than that. I want an apology from Potter-Symons herself, and one from that bastard Bakerson. And then I want to tell them where they can stick their job.'

You can't, she thought – not when I've done all this for you. Giles saw her face.

'I know, Simone, I feel bad – letting you down – after everything you've done for me. But it's time for me to leave. I've done my time in Barton Townes and it's time for me to move on.'

Simone felt like someone had already torn out her insides and thrown them onto a rubbish heap.

'No, Giles. You can't.'

She had to say it - she couldn't help it. He saw her downcast face and felt as if he was leaving a child.

'I've decided I have to.'

'I'm really going to get that bastard now.'

'Which one? Me or Bakerson? Or Greg?' said Giles, and they both laughed. Simone didn't really want to but couldn't stop herself. She thought it was the pleasure of seeing Giles McAndrew being the Giles McAndrew who made most of the listeners love him and his work colleagues want to see him get a comeuppance.

'Where are you – what are you going to do?' said Simone.

'I don't know yet,' he said, lying through his teeth. He thought it might soften the blow if his plans appeared not to have been cold-bloodedly worked out behind her back.

'Are you going to stay around here? No, you've already said, you've done your time here.'

'Yes, I have. I might go abroad.'

'Good idea – there'd be lots of opportunities for someone like you all over the place.' She was trying to be nice but her heart wasn't in it.

She poured the tea into two china mugs. Giles had the urge to tell her how much he hated them and Simone's chintzy taste. He made up his mind to try to shake her up a few times before he left.

Simone sipped her tea but she didn't taste it: the lights had gone out. She couldn't escape the feeling now that if Giles was going to leave, Monday's cause just wasn't worth fighting for in the same way. She got up and thought of the worst album she had in her collection, or at least, the one that Giles might hate most. She found Barry Manilow's Greatest Hits. Within thirty seconds, he was singing 'Mandy'.

'I love this one,' said Giles, looking at her with the straightest face he could.

'Well, if you're going to leave me, you can at least help me find your replacement. If we don't go for someone from outside, who do you think is worth shoving into your slot from what we've got?'

'If you can persuade him to leave drive time, Jim. If not, you're struggling.'

'What about Noona?'

'You're not serious.'

'No, I suppose I'm not.'

'Lynda's the same: too smooth. Jane hasn't got the personality.'

'Bob's a non-starter…'

'It was brave of you to even put him in as a substitute.'

'Thanks.'

'I didn't mean it as a compliment.'

A cushion went flying across the room in Giles' direction.

'Mind out! I might spill my tea on one of these nice cushions.'

'Shut up. I think I preferred you depressed.'

Giles threw back his head and laughed at the ceiling. But he said,

'Come on, Simone, let's not go there. I'm in recovery, I'm not recovered.'

'Sorry.'

'You'll come and visit it me, won't you, wherever I go?'

She thought that was a nice thing to say, but envisaged a case of her playing gooseberry with Giles and some beauty.

'If I can bring my Elton John albums with me,' she said.

'You can bring 'em all.'

She smiled again. The afternoon really did feel as though it was closing right in on her. She no longer wanted to put a brave face on her disappointment. It was pouring with rain outside, Giles was leaving her and she had the hardest and perhaps the worst day of her professional life looming less than 48 hours ahead.

'On one condition,' he said.

'What?'

'That you take this Barry Manilow crap off right now.'

'It's a deal,' she said, and cut the music with the remote control.

I just want you to go now, she thought. So she could spend the rest of the afternoon sulking in peace.

When the rain had almost stopped, Giles cycled back to The Barn House. The wet day had a richness that made him feel good. The smell of rain on the spring growth was irresistible. I'm only thirty-nine, he thought. There's plenty of time left yet to do things. His tyres made a *wheeshing* sound as he zipped along, regularly being overtaken on the main road by hordes of Saturday travellers until he turned off for Corumby, whence the busy roads became his lovely quiet lanes again.

His thoughts zig-zagged around. As usual, Leah was never far away from them. He thought of her and felt the wound inside him, a roughly stitched up thing still sore where the two folds of skin had been joined. Still, it beat crying and wondering whether he was on the verge of being taken away in an ambulance. He liked the idea of accepting that they just weren't meant for each other; that as much as they were attracted to each other, as much as he felt he was in love with her, or had been, they were too different to make a life together. Time to be a big boy, he sighed, as he saw his house come into view. Time to accept things as they are instead of how you'd like them to be.

It was definitely time to take off in another direction, he'd decided. Wherever you go, he thought, you'll always have women like you. It was, anyone had to admit, a fact of his life. It was just a question of finding one that was less volatile than Leah, and, it had to be said, of him starting to take a hard look at himself and the way he went about his relationships. Perhaps it was time for therapy. He mulled over that and in only a few seconds had made a decision he intended to stick to: if I can afford it after I get a new job, I will. Maybe he'd be lucky in love too and find someone whom he'd let take him in hand and bash him into shape. He was ready to do that too, if the person was right in other ways.

He slowed right down to take the front wheel on to his narrow path. He looked up at his house. He always wondered at this point in his journey home whether he'd go round to the side door to find it bashed in and the place turned over. But again today everything was fine. The next place I get, though, he told himself, would have to be among people.

He walked into the kitchen and was pleased about the improvement in its looks. He stood still and listened for intruders: no, nothing. He thought he might hear Leah padding about upstairs having come back, but there was no one there. Then he suddenly found himself staring at the mat in front of the front door, the one that received his mail, the place where the fateful drawings that took her away must have fallen. The moment was dark and scary as he felt the demons stir into activity deep inside him. But the moment passed. Now he thought of the woman on the hill, the woman he had met in the car. Somehow the image made him feel better; settled him down. He spent the rest of the afternoon watching TV and thinking about her. He thought about Tanya Howe too.

And he thought about his prayers, all the scattered thoughts he'd sent up towards the place he wanted God to be, and his whole battered, despairing heart, offered up without conditions or strings attached. Where do prayers go, Giles wondered. Do they just drift off into the distant universe and become nothing?

The rest of the day passed happily enough. No one phoned or sent him a text apart from Leon; no one knocked unexpectedly on the door or pushed any unwelcome envelopes through the letterbox. Before he went to bed he remembered to put some food out for his friend, the hedgehog.

What will he do after I've gone and someone else moves in, he thought? He felt quite concerned. Will I leave them a note when I go? Yes, he would. *Don't forget the nightcaller, Fred the Hedgehog - likes fibre bars crumbled into warm water*, he'd write.

I wonder if hedgehogs come out at night in Cornwall, he thought as he put out the light.

26

Unlovely Sunday

Sunday May 14th

"Radio –You can't mend a broken heart with music, but you can try. Alan and Lexi's Sunday Romance on Two Counties."

'Hi, and welcome to Alan and Lexi's Sunday Romance, here on Two Counties Radio.'

'Alan Schumann here with you until four o'clock...'

'...and Lexi Covington. How are you today, Alan?'

'I'm great, Lexi – as right as ninepence – ready to chill out all the way through two hours of romantic songs and heartfelt ditties. How about you?'

'I'm more an expensive bottle of wine than ninepence, Alan, ha-ha.'

'Well, if that all it takes, I might nip out to the off license during this one – this is 10 CC and I'm Not In Love.'

'Aren't you in love, Alan?'

'Apart from with you, Lex? That would be telling, wouldn't it?'

"I'm no-ot..."

Simone switched off the transistor radio in her greenhouse and went back to worrying about late frost and her whole bloody future. She normally loved Sundays, especially in the spring and summer, but today she was finding it hard to settle. She couldn't seem to concentrate at the moment.

At the start of the growing season she should have been on top of all her seedlings by now, clear about how long it would be before each one was ready to go in the ground, but she wasn't. She walked along the rows of petunia, Lobelia, French Marigolds and Cosmos trying to focus on how advanced each pot was for about the seventh time in an hour and a half but the bloody phone went again.

It hadn't stopped since eight in the morning and she'd already made she didn't know how many calls herself.

She stuck at it. She took all the pots outside to give them some warmth and air and said, 'for goodness sake now, Simone, don't bloody forget to put them back before you go to bed. Shit!' She hadn't checked the forecast for overnight frost and it was almost two in the afternoon. She went to her office and logged on to the BRBC website.

The whirling day flew quickly by which was something, but the tension and suspense involved in organizing everything and preparing the ground meant she was in a terrible state by seven o'clock. She dropped into a chair, trowel still in hand and thought, right, come on, get a grip. She ran everything through her head for the hundredth time. Not good enough. She went to the draw for some paper, and with a good pen, drew out a timeline of the morrow's intended order of events. It began neatly but by the time she'd finished there were notes all over the place, mostly starting, 'IF THIS HAPPENS…' and 'PLAN B'…

Then Sarah dropped in and she her mood immediately brightened but she could only stay for ten minutes. Her stomach dropped when Sarah told her. She was hoping for an hour worth of calm at least. After that there were just a few more calls to make which seemed to spring out of nowhere and waiting, waiting, waiting. Slowly the evening passed through dusk into darkness and on into midnight, at which point she thought she might try falling asleep. The pots! And slugs! The night air in the garden was fresh but no worse and she only found one fat slug trailing sick-looking slime across her paving stones. She put her gloves back on, picked it up and dropped it into large pot of stale beer at the back of the greenhouse. She traipsed in and out until everything was back in place. She closed the windows and switched out the light and locked the French doors.

All the while, thoughts of the woman she'd never met, Andrea Potter-Symons, seeped in and out of her mind like gas. She lacerated herself with the issue of what to wear for the leader of all-England local radio. She went up to her bedroom and tried on clothes in various permutations. She looked a rag-bag in everything. When she found a split down the seam of her best bra she flung it on the bed and jumped after it bursting into tears like a kid of fourteen. She went to the bathroom and looked in the mirror. She saw her mother in her reflection, which would have turned her face a ghostly white had it not resembled a bottle of milk already. It was nearly one o'clock in the morning.

She got undressed and got into bed cursing all her deficiencies and woes, but only after carefully laying out her best navy blue suit, a blue shirt she'd ironed with the precision of a brain surgeon, and her only pair of decent matching shoes. She thought she was in for a long, tortuous wait to drop off, but suddenly, while she'd accidentally placed her thoughts elsewhere, a couple of sleep's tireless angels dragged her off into the wide open spaces of dreams she would never remember.

Then she woke and in her room was the daylight of the day of the intervention.

27

The Second Intervention

Monday May 15th

Overnight, Simone didn't sleep much at all before two am. She was awake again shortly after four, but dozed off again a few minutes later. The light of dawn then separated her from rest at five and that was it. She admitted defeat with bad grace and opened the bedroom curtains wide at ten-past. This is it, she said. For better or worse. When I close these curtains again I'll know.

She switched on the radio to make sure Two Counties was still there and it was: Lucie was in the chair already going strong.

"Come on, you lot, it's nearly ten-past-five, what's the matter with you? It's Monday morning! No? Oh, well then: stay in bed. But don't say I didn't try. Here's The Beatles...
'Da-da-da-daaaa...G-...'
See? You can't argue with The Beatles! On Two Counties Radio..."

A bolt of electricity went through Simone. From this point on, she told herself, I am fear nothing and no one. She stripped right off and went to the bathroom for a shower.

At ten-oh-five when Simone went down to reception upon getting the call from Jackie, Simone knew it was Andrea Potter-Symons sitting there simply because of her clothes. She was late. Upon closer inspection, it was more than that: it was the deftly applied make-up and the perfume too. She liked very much the fact that Jackie had her waiting there on the blue reception chairs just like anyone else.

The boss of English local radio smiled as she unfolded a slim frame of average height and came forward to shake hands. It was a well-practiced social manoeuvre, Simone knew that. She probably still hates me, she thought, but I don't care. She took in the clothes again. They were expensively cut but didn't add up to the sort of look she imagined female bosses on a hundred grand a year wore to work. She looked like a ladies-who-lunched-in-rather-nice-places-in-Knightsbridge-type. She couldn't imagine her listening to Chris de Burgh and Tina Turner.

'I'm Simone Pound,' she said, helplessly striking a much more formal note than normal. 'Welcome.'

'Andrea Potter-Symons.' There was an even greater sense of formality in her voice than she'd heard down the phone, but the smile, to her surprise, wasn't cold. 'It's going to be a warm day.'

Simone smiled.

'Yes, probably,' she said. The Big Boss made her feel shabby. She'd put on her one really nice suit, a Laura Ashley. Three years ago it had cost her a hundred and fifty pounds; it was expensive. Now it just felt three years old.

Jackie was holding open the security door for them.

'How does the station get in the summer – hot?'

'No, not too bad; we've a lot of windows.'

'Good.'

Private school, thought Simone. It wasn't just the voice, it was the manners. I bet that helped her get to the top. They started up the main corridor. Half way along there was a rise of two steps. Simone waited politely so Potter-Symons could go first; as The Big Boss said, 'thanks' Simone got a surprise. As APS went up she watched a pair of plump buttocks pushing the trouser material to a resolute tightness. She's got a really good bum on her, Simone thought, and giggled inside. Suddenly she belonged to BRBC, not Bond Street or the Royal Academy and Simone felt herself relax. She thought of Elton again, but Elton said,

'You're okay now, Simone: you don't need me for this' and disappeared singing *Amoreena*.

When they got to the newsroom Simone led them inside and began to introduce the England boss to her crew. She was even more proud of them the way they'd come through the past two weeks. They were on best behaviour and were immaculately polite, treating the woman like visiting royalty, coming forward to smile like dutiful sons and daughters. Simone looked at the wall clock twice as they went round. Nearly a quarter past ten. Then she was distracted by someone passing through the open door. It was Greg.

'Hi, Greg,' she said, striving to be natural.

'Morning,' he said, looking intently at the England boss's back. Then she turned round, assisted by Simone Pound.

'Andrea, I'd like you to meet my number two, Greg McKenzie.'

'Hello, very good to meet you, finally.' She flicked a sideways look at Simone.

'You too,' said Greg, smiling and looking pleased. 'So,' he began, 'you've come up to take a good look at us.'

'Well, it's always nice to go to a new station. I try to get round to three or four a year I haven't been to.'

'I suppose this is a special occasion,' said Greg.

'Ah-hah, yes, well, sort of,' said Andrea. 'You've been put through the mill in the last couple of weeks, haven't you?'

'Yes, you could certainly say that, Andrea,' he replied.

'I'm sure we'll run into each other later,' she said. She could see Simone waiting for her, hovering by the door.

'That would be good,' he said, nodding, as if he had business he wanted to bring up with her. Simone saw his expression and did not feel any better. She glanced at her watch. It was time to get on with this.

'Shall we...?' she said, pointing the way through the door. Andrea Potter-Symons smiled to anyone who might be still looking her way and followed.

'I thought we might chat in Meeting Room 1,' said Simone, turning left and looking over her shoulder.

'Fine, okay,' came the reply.

They had to sidestep both techs, Graham and Allan, on the way in the tight corridor, who both looked a bit miserable, but they were quickly at their destination. Ten-fifteen, said Simone's watch. Should be okay, she said to herself.

Simone closed the door.

'Some coffee will be along in a minute,' said Simone.

'Oh, that'll be lovely,' said Andrea Potter-Symons.

Simone felt an enormous shot of adrenalin surge down her, right through to the anus. She tightened the muscle there, gritted her teeth and concentrated on starting the conversation in the way she'd rehearsed it in her mind.

'Okay, shall we get down to cases?' she said.

'Yes, let's.'

'Do you want to say your piece, or shall I say mine?' Simone tried to disarm The Boss with a frank smile.

'I hope that's not a declaration of war.'

'No, not at all; I didn't mean it like that.'

'Oh, fine. Well, why don't you begin?'

'Okay.' Simone drew in a breath and hoped like hell that what she was about to say came out right. 'Well, first, I need to know whether what I told Ian Bakerson on Thursday came through to you.'

'You mean...'

'About Greg McKenzie's drawings, his harassment of a member of my staff; the police proof we have of his having made phone calls to the press, shopping us, basically; sending a fax here supposedly from your office informing us that you'd sacked Giles McAndrew-'

'I didn't know that...'

Shit, thought Simone. Did I not tell Bakerson?

450

'…that's very interesting.'

'But you did know about the other stuff?'

'The accusations? Yes, I did.' The Big Boss was playing a careful game of poker. Simone had feared as much.

'So that's what they are to you, is it, just "accusations"?'

'I think, um…'

'You don't believe me, is that it?'

'…I should tell you that Greg McKenzie has been in touch with our office regularly over the past few months.'

The meaning behind the words was like a punch to the side of the head. Simone couldn't respond straight away.

'He's had a number of concerns about some of the things going on here at Two Counties and he's, um, shared those with us.'

Simone still couldn't speak, but Andrea Potter-Symons absorbed her expression.

'Oh, don't worry - we didn't really take all that much notice of them. It's not at all uncommon for the odd disgruntled worker, presenters as well as management, to contact us for a good old moan…'

Simone's fear, like a tightly clenched fist inside her stomach, uncoiled just a little.

'…but I am concerned at what he calls harassment, and bullying. The police interview, which he thinks you fixed, and the stealing of the phone, well, I'm very concerned about that. Very.'

The fist tightened again and she had to squeeze her sphincter like a clam.

'So he rings you? Emails you…?'

'Both. And I should warn you, he keeps written records.'

Oh, he bloody does, does he, thought Simone. But she was still scared, her curtain bravado all gone: scared of what this interview would have been like if she hadn't organized the intervention. Scared by the knowledge now that if the intervention didn't work, she'd have to resign; she'd be through as a managing editor at BRBC. She looked at her watch: twenty-five-past-ten, just gone.

'What on earth am I supposed to have done? Bullying? It's ridiculous.'

'I haven't got a record of it with me. But from what I remember, deliberately shutting him out of meetings, not giving him enough responsibility-'

'That's not bullying-'

'Hang on,' said Potter-Symons, holding up a hand. She wasn't smiling now. 'A patronizing tone of voice, which he regards as tantamount to bullying; sidelining him on the community bus when he

451

should be doing things more, what shall we say…' She looked across the room, concentrating. '…integral to the management of the station.'

Simone was outraged, but thought, am I like that? And in her heart she knew that some of it was true; recently anyway. But she'd had good reason.

'But he's psychotic.'

'If you're right, or rather, if you could prove that he's done the things you say he's done, then you're probably right, but right now it's your word against his. I think he should come into the discussion – in person, I mean. Don't you?'

Oh, yes, she thought; that was a bloody great idea. She was momentarily lost for words. But there was a knock on the door.

'Come in!' called Simone.

A man in a navy suit, about thirty, dark, not tall, but quite good-looking, who Andrea Potter-Symons immediately spotted as someone in authority stepped into the room. He ignored Simone and offered his hand and a sight of his identification to Potter-Symons.

'Hello – Iain Blame, or rather, Detective Sergeant Blame of Bartonshire and Bilt Constabulary. You must be Andrea Potter-Symons; very pleased to meet you. Am I early, Mizz Pound?' he said with much respect, turning to Simone.

'Just a touch. But don't worry.'

Talk about the cavalry, thought Simone. She looked at Andrea, who looked ruffled by the entry of a policeman, not to say put out. She looked at Simone for some sort of explanation.

'I think you should have told me you were bringing a detective to see me,' said Andrea.

'I'm sorry,' said Simone. There was another knock at the door. A young woman entered and went straight across to The Big Boss.

'Hi, I'm Tanya Howe, Media and Communications Unit, 10 Downing Street; very pleased to meet you, Mrs. Potter-Symons.'

Mrs. Potter-Symons, looking nonplussed, shook Tanya's hand. There was immediately another knock. Before Simone could answer, Iain Blame opened the door to let in two more intruders. They both came over to the desk-bound women, but The Big Boss had decided to stand up.

'Hello,' said an extremely polite, smiling man. 'Derek Hutchins. I'm the Head of Herne Bay Grammar School for Boys,' he said, then stood aside to let through a young woman of around thirty, with, Andrea thought despite her utterly confused mind, rather striking features.

'Hello – I'm very pleased to meet you. Leah Caighton. I used to work here at Two Counties.'

In the reception area, Jackie Husband and Sarah Billings were having a frantic conversation.

'Where the bloody hell is he, Jackie?'

'He said he was just nipping out to get a new printer cartridge.'

'Well, why didn't he send one of the techs?'

'I don't know!'

'Oh, look, here he is, he's back.'

'Ah, Greg. You're back.'

'Yeah. What's the problem?'

'No problem - but Simone's been trying to find you – you're wanted. She's in Meeting Room 1.'

Finally, thought Greg. He went through the security door and strolled down the corridor towards the appointed room. Here we go, he thought. This is where I finally nail the bitch. He thought about best behaviour and lightly tapped the door. But he opened it immediately and went in. His mind opened with surprise at first, then when he spread his eyes around the packed room and saw who was there, it widened into an enormous chasm.

'Hello, Gregory,' said Simone, 'do come in.' She was so excited, the words came out like a mouse's squeak.

Greg made a half-turn as if he might be thinking of going out again, but Iain Blame was standing in front of the door. It clicked shut.

'Have a seat.'

He looked at the empty chair waiting for him, feeling the eyes and minds of the entire room bearing down on him. He daren't look to left and right, but the room felt full to capacity. He looked at Andrea Potter-Symons. She was looking at him with such a doubtful face. He moved forward and sat down.

'That's it, sit down,' Simone continued. You're among friends, she nearly said but realized it was patently untrue. Simone's legs felt like jelly even though she was sitting and she could hear her voice wavering.

'As you can see, there are some familiar faces here for you today; who've come to see you.' Steady, Simone, she said to herself. Go slowly. 'They've all got something to say to you.'

Greg's mind was a jumble of high speed noise. He didn't reply.

'I want to show you these first, because really, these are what this meeting is all about.' She was holding up the drawings that Leah had shown her, and given to her. 'Do you recognize them?'

Simone saw his jaw wobble, as if it was coming apart from the rest of his head, then he answered.

'No.'

'Okay,' said Simone. 'I want you to look across the room at somebody.' She looked to her right, and Greg's head turned to the left. 'Do you recognize him?'

'Hello Gregory,' said Derek Hutchins.

Greg McKenzie stared at the man but said nothing. Derek got out of his seat and came over to the desk. He was carrying a clean, bright green cardboard folder.

'I want to show you something, Greg.'

He opened the folder with his right hand and pulled the contents out with his left and spread them out on the desk in front of them. They were drawings on white paper.

'Do you remember these, Gregory? From when I used to be your house master?'

Derek's voice was kind, his eyes verging on the sad. His hands went to the drawings again and he turned them round and presented them to Andrea Potter-Symons. She looked at them with dark concentration as the room looked to Greg McKenzie for a response. The Big Boss leaned forward and placed the drawings back in front of him. He looked at the drawings briefly, then down at his knees.

Simone Pound spoke again.

'Now I want you to look at these, Greg.' She had produced an envelope of her own, a large white one, and pulled out the contents carefully. She looked at the two documents to make sure she hadn't made a mistake then placed them across the table, upside down to her, one beside the other, next to the drawings.

'Your school exam results, Greg, the ones we got from Mr. Hutchins, are on the left. On the right are the ones you wrote on your job application. On this one…' She pointed to the job application form. '…you left out Art at GCSE and Art at A level. You were very good at Art, weren't you, Greg. It was your best subject.'

Greg McKenzie didn't move his head, but he rolled his eyeballs down so his pupils could check that the documents put in front of him were the ones Pound said were in front of him.

Simone watched him. She thought she saw his body trembling but couldn't be sure.

'Have you anything to say?'

Her voice was getting quieter and quieter. The room waited. Greg McKenzie said nothing.

'Okay,' said Simone, calmly. 'I want you to hear, now, something one of us wants to say to you. Someone who until very recently, you used to work with.'

Leah was sitting almost behind the door so Greg hadn't yet seen her. She got up and walked up to the desk, bringing her chair with her, and sat down four feet away from him, well outside her personal space, but within grabbing reach.

'Greg.'

He was looking at his knees, his resolve crumbling, his inner toughness melting.

'Will you turn around to face me?'

Slowly, the head turned. His eyes looked into Leah Caighton's. Ignoring the emotion she thought she saw in them, she gripped herself very hard and began to speak.

'Do you remember the night we went out?' she said. 'It was over four years ago. I remember it.'

She waited for what seemed a long time for him to reply. He just carried on looking at her. 'Do you remember what happened after we...slept together.'

Giles McAndrew, in his seat in the far corner of the room winced, then closed and re-opened his eyes in a very long blink. He looked across at Greg McKenzie and saw him make a tiny nod in Leah's direction.

'I'm sorry if I offended you by leaving so suddenly that night...and ignoring you at work afterwards. Not explaining things properly.'

Simone looked at the subject and seemed to see his whole body contracting in embarrassment, or possibly shame, she couldn't be sure.

'I didn't mean to hurt you. Or insult you. It's just that I made a mistake in sleeping with you. Not because there was anything wrong with you – but because I had drunk far too much that night...and I don't like giving people the wrong impression...that I just go to bed with people at the drop of a hat.'

Leah grabbed hold of the truth in the statement and held on.

'Now – I'm sorry if you felt insulted, but that didn't give you the right to try to destroy what I had with Giles.' She paused, to see if he was taking it in what she was saying. 'It didn't give you the right to upset me by sending me these drawings.'

Simone Pound passed them over. Leah touched the edge of one of them with her fingers.

'Did you not realize how upsetting that was for me? How offended I was by the untruths in them?' She paused again to listen for her words reaching their target; to try to judge their effect. 'By your suggestion that Giles was sleeping with his cousin?'

She waited for a response, even though she knew that the chance of getting a response was next to none.

'And by your suggestion that Giles was sleeping with Lucie?'

Leah carried on waiting. And waiting. She felt her anger rise now. He should respond, no matter how disturbed he might be in the eyes of a psychologist.

'Gregory?' Still she waited, and expected. The rest of the room was hanging on by its fingernails, gripped by tension. 'Did you not realize what you were doing?' She saw the man in front of her visibly shrinking. He wouldn't look at her. She felt she had probably said enough, but she couldn't stop.

'I loved Giles.' She looked at Greg again, still bidding him to speak. She could hear her own tension, a howling tightness against her eardrums.

'Gregory…'

Simone wanted to reach over and commit murder.

'…I loved that man, and I lost him because of you.' She put her hand over her mouth. She had promised herself so hard that she wasn't going to cry but here deep within the moment she couldn't do it: she couldn't hold on.

Most of the room failed to hold on too. Leah's depiction of personal loss seared into Sarah Billings and right out the other side. Her red-raw emotion was also way too much for Tanya Howe even though they'd never met. Derek Hutchins reached for his pocket handkerchief. Andrea Potter-Symons, though mostly in the throes of disgust, had to wipe the corner of her eye with her hand. Giles McAndrew thanked God he was in a corner where hardly anyone could clearly see him. Iain Blame had seen too many emotionally destroyed people to be overly affected by the scene and Marcus simply watched the whole thing spellbound.

'So, Greg,' said Simone, 'I hope you can see now what the drawings have done. There's also the fact that after Leah, here, left Barton Townes, leaving her job and Giles McAndrew, the effect on him was so great that he lost his temper on air because of the stress, the result of which was the cancelling of his contract by Mrs Potter-Symons, here. Have you anything to say about that?'

Again the room dwelt in a booming silence. The subject looked down still.

'Let me go. Please. Let me go,' he said, almost inaudibly.

Andrea Potter-Symons spoke for the first time.

'Gregory,' she said. In one word she both expressed sympathy and asked him to resign. Simone heard the authority in her tone and couldn't help be impressed. She was no fool. Greg slowly looked over at her. 'Come on, now. I think you know what to do. Or do we have to go over the phone calls to the press and the fake fax as well?'

'Okay,' he said quietly, looking again at his knees. 'Okay, okay, okay, I'm guilty. Guilty as charged.'

'Come on,' said Iain Blame coming towards him from the door. Greg turned around.

'Are you arresting me?'

'Not as such. But I think you should come down to the station now with me so we can have a sensible conversation.' It was his turn to wait for a response. 'Come on, now,' he said, placing a firm hand under his elbow. Greg McKenzie nodded and got up from his chair. Someone opened the door and the two men left. Down the end of the corridor at the security door was a policeman in uniform. The door closed. The resulting break in the tension nearly blew the windows out.

Over the next five minutes, the room erupted into noise, much of it surrounding Simone, then began to empty, until there were just two bodies left.

'So...' said Simone Pound. What's it to be, she thought, but didn't say aloud? Do I win or do I lose?

Andrea Potter-Symons looked into her eyes, from the corner of which she noticed a hand coming steadily forward to touch, then rest, on her forearm.

'I don't know how you kept going through it all - and I think that just now you were unbelievable.'

'But you were right, using my husb – my ex-husband to trick Greg like that, it was completely unethical. Immoral.'

Andrea's eyes were suddenly darker, or her voice made it seem that way.

'Simone...' It was the first time she'd used her name all morning. She said it again after pausing to think, or choose her words more carefully.

'Simone, nothing much big gets done in this world without some sort of dirty or dodgy dealing going on. You had to do it, didn't you? Or something like that?'

Simone thought about the matter for just a second or two. 'Yes, I think so.' She was beginning to well up.

'You carry on. Carry on doing what you're doing.' She patted Simone's arm firmly, but still gently. 'You're doing a good job as far as I can see.'

I'm never going to call her 'Potty Training' again, she thought. But she just said,

'Thank you.'

'It's "Andrea."'

She laughed and dried her eyes with her right hand. Then her new friend was offering her a clean tissue.

'Thanks.'

'It's enough to make you think, "they're all bastards."' said Andrea.

'Yes, I suppose it is. But they're not, though.'

'No,' said the England boss, 'they're not. Just some of them.'

On the way out of the door to the car park, Andrea said,

'Where did you get the idea of filling the room with all those people?'

She looked serious and, Simone thought, genuinely interested.

'From a programme on TV called "Intervention."'

'I haven't seen it, but I've heard about it. I can see now how you adapted it. So clever.'

'No, it wasn't – but if it was, it wasn't down to me.'

'You must have been so worried that someone important might not turn up.'

'Just a bit,' she said, and her timing made Andrea laugh.

'But they all did, I take it.'

'Oh, yes - and I'm grateful beyond words to them.'

'You might like to think how you could adapt the idea for one of your shows.'

'Hmm, it's an idea.'

'Who might be the presenter to do it?'

'Oh, Giles McAndrew.'

'He's really good then, is he?'

'Well, you see, that's the point of the whole thing – he'd be terrific.'

'He can have his job back, you know.'

'Can I have that in writing?'

'Of course you can!'

Simone was not giving up hope yet of persuading Giles to stay.

'You know, I was terrified of meeting you...' she said to the boss of all England.

'Were you? You should have been.'

Simone laughed and was meant to.

'...but I'm so glad you came. I couldn't have done this without you.'

'I suppose you used me really, didn't you...'

'I built the morning around you, let's put it like that.'

458

'But it was amazing,' she said, and looked happily out into the very late morning. The sun had gone in, but it was still bright.

'Well, time for me to go. Whenever you need anything, give me a call, won't you...'

'Yes, I will.'

Simone walked back into reception.

'Why didn't you invite me to the intervention!'

'The room wasn't big enough, Jackie, I'm sorry.'

'Ooh, I do love you though!' said Jackie Husband and put her arms around her boss in a big embrace. 'The whole place is in uproar – good uproar! There's such a buzz. Noona's still on the air but she knows something's been going on – she's going mad.'

Simone just smiled and went back into the station saying nothing. She had no idea how big the smile on her face looked – pretty big, she imagined – but it was nothing beside the smile she felt inside. She felt it spreading out like a massive thing, like a giant dose of medicine. She felt her tiredness fall away and felt if she only had a pair of wings, she would fly above Barton Townes all afternoon long, screaming with delight.

28

Aftermath

Despite her euphoria, Simone received a shock when she walked into the newsroom: the place seemed to explode at her. The frantic noise of a dozen excited conversations changed to a sudden eruption of applause. It was something she had never imagined for herself, even in the idlest of daydreams. People began to surge round her. She hardly heard what they said. She caught just some of it.

'I've sent out for some wine, is that okay?'

'Incredible boss, incredible…'

'I never liked him,' she heard a voice say loudly half way across the room, even though someone was saying something nice right in her ear.

'He always gave me *the creeps*,' she heard Diana Clark shouting back. They could probably hear her in the high street.

'Brilliant,' someone else said. And someone else said,

'Were you in there? What was it *like*?'

At least two of her girl colleagues kissed her, but none of the men. She thought Big Dave Plymouth was going to give her a hug at one point but he seemed to chicken out. She didn't mind. She refused the demands to make a speech. High as she was, she didn't have the strength after the intervention. She shut her eyes and waved her hand to say 'no chance' several times until they stopped yelling at her. She went from group to group, thanking them for their support and asking them were they okay, telling them she was sorry for all the disruption of the past two weeks or so. Was it only that? It seemed to have gone on for a month; more, maybe.

She thanked the people who came from far away, especially Derek Hutchins, whom they'd hoodwinked.

'That's the great thing about being a headmaster,' he said, laughing, 'you can always make an excuse and get away for the day. But seriously, in the end I decided I had to come to do this. It's a form of closure for me.'

Simone nodded her understanding. 'Thanks so much for coming,' she said.

'It was a pleasure. Well, not exactly, but, y'know…you get my meaning.'

She nodded again. Her mind was phasing in and out, from absolute clarity to swimming in mud. Derek had found her in a clear moment.

'Then again, it was a pleasure in a way. That girl, what was her name – Leah?'

'Leah,' said Simone and Lucie in confirmation almost together. Lucie Bastable was in the group, looking so fabulous with an ecstatic face, Marcus couldn't take his eye off her for more than a few seconds at a time.

'I've heard a lot of speeches in my time, and people telling me their stories in my office, but that was something again. What a girl. Is she leaving you?'

'I'm working on it,' said Simone, 'don't worry.'

She turned around and there was Jackie Husband beaming radiantly at her.

'What are you doing here?' said Simone, but being playful.

'It's okay, Giles is manning the desk.'

'Giles?'

'Yes, Giles. You don't mind, do you?'

'No, of course not.'

Simone turned around and bumped into Sarah Billings, literally. Fortunately neither had a drink in their hand at the time.

'Sorry,' said Sarah.

'It's okay – I wanted to bump into you.'

'Oh, funny as well as extraordinary today, are we, hee-hee.'

'Listen, come over here, I want a word with you.'

They slipped over to the far end of the room where there was a bit of space.

'Yes?' asked Sarah.

'I want you to be my new number two.'

Sarah looked serious.

'Are you sure you're not rushing into a decision?'

'Are you calling me stupid?'

'No, ha-ha.'

'I need to get on with things. And you're my first decision.'

'Can you do it just like that?'

'Pretty much.' She thought of Mrs. Potty-Training and smiled.

'God, I'd love it.'

'It's a done deal.' She felt a sense of having more power than she ever had…

'Wow!' her body seemed to say…and liked the feeling a lot.

'What's the matter?' said Simone – Sarah looked worried. She was about to tell her she could do the job standing on her head and more than that, that she'd be great.

'Will we still have laughs?'

461

'You bet we will, girl.'

She went over to Leah who was talking to Daisy, Jane and Damien on the far side of the room. The wine had arrived – sparkling - and everyone was knocking it back with ice in. Someone had brought a huge bag up from the high street. After a few minutes, quite suddenly, she found herself alone with Leah. Simone laid her hand on her arm and looked at her.

'Don't say anything or I'll start crying again,' said Leah.

'Come to my office on your own when this dies down, will you?'

'Okay. Sure.'

'You haven't got to rush off…'

'No, no.'

'Good.'

'Simone, thanks so much for inviting me.'

'Thank me? You've got to be kidding! Without you, the whole thing might not have worked.'

'Naw,' said Leah, 'of course it would - you know it would. But it was easy, wasn't it? He crumpled up into a ball inside ten seconds, didn't he?'

'Did you think so?' said Simone, surprised. 'I didn't think it was in the bag until you got hold of him. You were…' She tried to make sure she had the correct word, looking at the grey tiled ceiling for inspiration. '…totally amazing, ha-ha.' She tried to keep it sunny in case Leah did cry. If she had, Simone would have followed suit and that she didn't want.

'Ha-ha – I wanted to say that stuff to him so badly.'

'What, about the drawings?'

'Yes. And about my regretting spending a second in his bed. I was being cruel though.'

'In what way?'

'It was my fault. I was absolutely smashed off my face that night.'

'Was it bad?'

'No – I didn't really remember anything about it the next day – but I woke up in this strange flat with that dreadful feeling, y'know - what the hell am I doing here?'

Simone wished she knew the feeling.

'And at work it was a bit awkward.'

'Greg, you mean?'

'Yes, but let's not go there – it's been such a good day so far.'

They had both become very serious all of a sudden. Simone decided she had something she had to confess.

'I was twenty-one when I lost my virginity – and I didn't know what I was doing. Neither did he, more to the point.'

'Oh, dear. Was it bad?'

'Painful.' Then she laughed. She took a glug of Prosecco. It was just cold enough with the ice. 'I was twenty-three when I slept with my second. He was my first husband. Barrie was my third. Not much of a racy youth, was it?'

'I was sixteen.'

'Well, your generation is in a different class, isn't it...'

'Ha-ha, I suppose. But I tell you what - I wouldn't like to be fifteen now.'

'It's all gone mad, hasn't it...'

'Mmm,' said Leah. 'I think it has...Can I ask you a personal question?' said Leah.

'Go on – but just one. I'd rather you and I went out and got pissed than got too serious.'

'And you can pick up a bloke while you're at it, ha-ha.'

'Good idea - I didn't think of that.'

'Oh!' Leah laughed, pretending to be shocked. 'You'd better watch it: the way you're going you'll end up at these Grab-a-Grannie nights at the Old Bull's Head.'

'Ha-ha, that's about all I'm good for.'

'You said it, not me, ha-ha.'

Simone took another slug of wine and watched Leah laughing for the first time for she didn't know when. She could have done with taking a whole bottle to her office.

'Leah. I want to ask you something; it might sound a bit strange...'

'Okay...'

'Have you got a friend over here who you've been sending to see Giles?'

'What? No, why?'

'No?'

'No! I'd tell you if I was. What do you mean – what are you talking about?'

'Oh. Well. It's just-'

But they were interrupted by Jackie.

'Derek wants to go, I think,' she said.

'Oh, right,' said Simone, 'I'd better see him off then. I'll see you in a bit, Leah.'

'Okay.' Leah sipped her wine and wondered what had been going on behind her back in BT while she'd been away.

'So,' said Jackie, 'Leah, it's great to see you back, love, are you staying?'

Simone said 'goodbye' to Derek Hutchins and sent him on his way south with heartfelt thanks. It had been a close thing with the headmaster. In getting him to come she'd had to own up to deceiving him terribly when she sent Tanya down to the school. It had taken ages to persuade him to come. She let the door swing closed and turned to see Giles smiling at her from Jackie's place behind the desk.

'Yes, madam, can I help you?' he said.

But his smile wasn't a happy one, she could see that. She looked behind her at the row of chairs to make sure they didn't have company.

'You're putting a brave face on,' she said.

'What do you expect?'

'You can come back now, you know.'

'Don't remind me. I'm tempted.'

'You'll be back behind the microphone in the morning though – to help me out – if nothing else…?'

'I want five thousand quid a show, in my hand. Not a penny less.' He smiled, but couldn't quite manage to cross over into laughter.

'You wouldn't let your old friend Simone down now would you?'

'No, I wouldn't. It'll be a pleasure. Until I can find what I want out there.'

'Thank you.' Where there's life there's hope, she thought.

'Have you talked to Leah, yet?'

'No.'

'You should.'

'What's she doing, do you know? Of course you know.' The last sentence was for himself.

'You mean, now?'

'Yeah. Work-wise.'

'Nothing yet. She's sort of resting. But why don't you go and ask her yourself? I'll look after the desk.'

The door opened and two people came through it, one a courier with a package and one a guest for the last half hour of Noona's show.

Just as Giles got back to his car where he'd left it in town, a familiar face appeared from a car two along.

'Fancy seeing you,' she said.

'Hello,' said Giles. It was the woman again. The messenger.

'So things went well this morning…'

464

'How do you know?'

She tapped one side of her neatly sculptured nose.

'I have connections to the inside of TCR.'

'Who?'

'Secret.'

'You're all secrets.'

'Am I?'

'Well, mystery.'

'Am I? Am I really?'

'Don't you think so?' This was the sharpest he had felt in his mind for weeks. Since... He was going to nail her this time.

'Just who are you?'

'Batwoman,' she said, and laughed. The sun caught her hair suddenly and Giles almost had to shield his eyes for a few moments.

'Very funny.'

'I was a help to you though, wasn't I?'

He thought about it for a moment, just so as not to be too easy.

'Yes, I suppose you were. Not that I asked for it.'

'Didn't you?'

She smiled.

'I don't remember asking for Batwoman to come down and help me.'

'No, that's true. Look, I have to go. Take care of yourself, Giles.'

'Hang on. Are you a friend of Leah Caighton?'

'Who?' said the girl, and turned to walk towards Barton Townes's long high street. Giles tried to study the look on her face but he was too late. The moment had gone. He was going to go after her, but, the same as that time on Tower Hill, something stopped him.

He smiled as he pulled out of the car park though. It was sunny now. He wound the window down and smelt the clean Bartonshire air. I wonder how I'll start the show tomorrow, he thought, and changed down to second for the right turn for home.

29

The Angel of Barton Townes

Tuesday May 23rd

A week or so after the intervention, a soft package arrived at the station for Simone. She opened it in her office shortly after nine. She removed a t-shirt from inside, a white one. It had writing on the front. *'The Angel of Barton Townes,'* it said. She went back to the padded envelope and looked carefully inside for a letter or a compliments slip, but there was nothing.

Simone called in her deputy-managing editor to see if together they could make sense of it.

'What do you think?' said Simone.

Sarah Billings opened the shirt out and held it out in front of her.

'Nice graphic,' she said.

'Mmm,' said Simone.

'Nice colour too.'

Sarah brought the fabric up to her face and smelt it.

'It's been worn,' she said as she took it away again.

'Oh, very nice.' Simone made a face.

'No, here,' she said, giving it back to Simone. 'It smells really lovely.'

'Is this for me or for you, do you think?' said Simone, inhaling the fabric perfume inquisitively, and then smiling.

'I've no idea,' said Sarah.

The two women looked at each other, then down at the t-shirt again and for a few moments, couldn't think of anything to say.

30

Wind Chimes

Friday June 21st

"Stay for breakfast – with Lucie Bastable – every weekday morning on Two Counties Radio."

'Oww-kay then, it's coming up to twenty-to eight. After all the trauma we've just been through with England's World Cup disaster, it's time we all moved our lives on a little bit. One thing we might do, especially now the summer's well and truly here, is go out on our bikes. Ken De Gaffner, a resident of Noreham, no less, has just had a book published on this very subject. It's called "Ken and the Art of Bicycle Maintenance" and he's right here in the studio with me...'

'Hi, Ken, welcome to Two Counties Radio.'

'Pleasure to be here, Lucie.'

'So, why should we be dusting off our Raleighs now that the weather's warmer and the evenings nice and long?'

'Well, of course, bicycling is fantastic for you aerobically, it gets you out into the fresh air, which at this time of year is full of the joys of Mother Nature and, if you use it to get from A to B, it's fantastic for the environment.'

'Ah, Marcus is here at last for Shout Him Down – where have you been? Not to the gents, I hope?'

'No, I was in the library doing some research into gearing systems.'

'I bet...'

'Hi, Ken – can I ask you something?'

'Of course; fire away.'

'You know there's been this surge in cyclists being pushed off their bikes by people in cars?'

'Yes, I do, as a matter of fact.'

'What's that?'

'You haven't heard about this, Lucie?'

'No.'

'Well, it's mostly in cities, but cars are slowing down to come alongside bikes so that the man on the passenger side-'

'It would be a man...'

'Don't start.'

'I'm just saying.'

'So the car comes alongside and the passenger deliberately pushes the cyclist over.'

'Oh, that's terrible! Don't you think, Ken?'

'Appalling.'

'Yes, dreadful. Isn't it, Marcus...'

'No, it's brilliant.'

'Oh, no, here we go...'

'Yes, I rather think your colleague is being playful.'

'No, I'm not – what this country needs is more cars on the road to liven our boring two counties up a bit and fewer dingbats in pink lycra.'

'What? You're mad. Do you agree with Marcus this morning? If you want to Shout Him Down, call us now on 0299 445445, Two Counties Radio...So Ken, how many gears do I actually need on my bike: is it 24 or 36?'

As Simone turned the volume down on her office sound system in Barton Townes, the county town of Bartonshire in the east plains of mid-England, two hundred and fifty miles to the south-west, a white taxi was just pulling up outside a house at the bottom of a long country lane. It was a old, neatly kept cottage, and it might have been a lonely one were it not for the sound of the Atlantic Ocean forever keeping it company.

'This is it,' said the woman.

'Funny,' said the driver, a man of more than sixty and looking it. 'I was here only the other day. Bloke had his car in for a service. Needed a ride into town.'

'Oh, yes?'

'Yeah. New round here, innee. Works at the radio station in St Ives. Is that right?'

'Yep, that would be right,' said the woman cheerfully, opening the door for herself and starting to get out.

'What's is name? It's something funny...'

'*Gilles* Wilkinson.'

'Yeah, that's it – is it foreign? Or is it made up? Do they still do that, them dee jays? They used to, did'nay?'

'No, it's his real name. His show's on right now if you want to hear it.'

'Oh, I don't listen to that local stuff.'

He opened the boot, from which he extracted slowly and with effort a substantial suitcase and a large shoulder bag.

'That's six-fifty, love.'

'Keep the change,' said the love, listening to the waves hitting the shore with the incoming tide.

'Thanks. You 'is girlfriend, then?'

'You could say that,' she said, putting her right arm through the bag straps and pulling up the handle of the wheelie-case.

'Just the weekend you're staying for, is it?'

'You're a nosy one, aren't you? Should I report you to the police, do you think?'

'No, not I,' he said. 'I just like to know who people are and what they're doing round 'ere so I can look after 'em. Trevor Newcombe's me name and I don't mind you knowin' it.'

'Well, Trevor Newcombe, no, it's not just for the weekend if you must know - the rest of my stuff is arriving later on – in a van, not a taxi, don't worry.'

'Oh. That's good, then. And your name is?'

'I've given you so much information already, I'm exhausted.' She gave him the full smile and he nearly melted on the spot. 'I'll tell you next time,' she said.

She was already at the garden gate. Trevor, not much given to the chuckle if truth be told, gave one up despite himself as he got back in at the driver's side, the radio already calling him towards another pick up.

As the girl bent down to remove the back door key from under the plant pot by the door, the wind chimes above her head sang a perfect chord of A major on the wind blowing in from the sea.

Author's Notes

The research for *The Angel* included several visits to 'BRBC' local radio stations in the midlands of England during the late winter and early spring of 2006. Thanks are due to a number of friendly, helpful, dedicated professionals there. Thanks are especially due to Andy Whittaker.

None of the characters in this novel bear the slightest resemblance to any real human beings in or out of local radio stations, alive or dead, or at least, if they do, this is entirely a matter of coincidence, chance or downright spookiness.

Thanks are also due to: Nastassja Thomas for her original cover art work; ALT, LPLT and JJCT, of course; to Ben Worthy and Amo for reading and support and finally to Bill Haddow-Allen for his entirely unsolicited review of the opening three chapters at YouWriteOn.com.

CWT, Derbyshire, 2008

Lightning Source UK Ltd.
Milton Keynes UK
25 September 2009

144153UK00001B/12/P

9 781849 237802